SECRET
SISTERS

ALSO BY JOY CALLAWAY

The Fifth Avenue Artists Society

SECRET SISTERS

A Novel

JOY CALLAWAY

HARPER

NEW YORK • LONDON • TORONTO • SYDNEY

SECRET SISTERS. Copyright © 2017 by Joy Callaway. All rights reserved. Printed in the United States of America. No part of this book may be used or reproduced in any manner whatsoever without written permission except in the case of brief quotations embodied in critical articles and reviews. For information, address HarperCollins Publishers, 195 Broadway, New York, NY 10007.

HarperCollins books may be purchased for educational, business, or sales promotional use. For information, please email the Special Markets Department at SP-sales@harpercollins.com.

FIRST EDITION PUBLISHED 2017.

Designed by Leydiana Rodriguez

Library of Congress Cataloging-in-Publication Data has been applied for.

ISBN 978-0-06-239164-3 (pbk.)

17 18 19 20 21   LSC   10 9 8 7 6 5 4 3 2 1

For my son, John

I solemnly pledge my loyalty to the sisterhood of Beta Xi Beta until the end of my days. I promise that above all else, my purpose will be to foster equality and intellect among women—for a chain of linked hands is mightier than the most menacing army.

—The Pledge of Beta Xi Beta

SECRET SISTERS

1

I HAD ALWAYS THOUGHT Christmas pudding a disappointing choice for a celebration. Most were either gummy or hard and our elderly neighbor's was the worst of all, yet Mother had always served it on Christmas Eve anyway. *"Here's to us. We may not be rich, but we're rich in what matters."* She'd said the same thing every year, whispering it in my ear as she handed me the white china saucer painted with holly leaves.

Realizing I was holding my train ticket in my hand—a train ticket I wouldn't get to use—I set it down on the window sill. I blinked back tears, grasping at unpleasant memories—the way the crunch of stale currants made my teeth hurt, the way my father had rolled his eyes the first time I'd cut a slice for my stepmother, Vera, and my stepbrother, Lucas, the year after Mother passed away. It didn't help. Nothing could change the fact that I couldn't get home, that a blizzard had taken the last trace of my mother at Christmastime.

Pulling the lace-edged cuff of my wool nightgown into my palm, I stretched my hands out to the steam heater. I could barely see out of the dormitory window. It was early yet and frost shuttered most of the pane except for a small edge at the bottom cleared by the steam. Normally, Lily and I had quite a view from our attic room—of Old Main's limestone tower down the hill, the south side of the old brick wall surrounding campus that Archibald Whitsitt had originally constructed as a settlement fence back in 1793, and the tiny line of buildings that comprised Whitsitt's Main Street in the distance. Today, I could only make out the snow gathering on the dormitory's roof and rising up the trunks of the ancient oak trees lining the drive down to campus. Even if the snow stopped, even if the trains were still running, I would never be able to procure a coach to the station in this weather.

I turned around, my gaze falling on the small leather trunk I'd packed the night before and then on the cherry armoire I shared with Lily. The door was open, displaying three of my ensembles and two of hers—all in drab winter shades of gray and brown. Lily's hunter green velvet costume was missing. I sighed and sank down on my single bed, fiddling with a fraying star patch on my quilt and leaning against one of the short carved posts at the foot. Lily's bed, identical to mine, was made up neatly, her grammar textbooks stacked on the table between us. Where had she gone? Surely not far. It would be impossible to venture out in this weather and she had planned to stay on campus for the holiday anyway. The New England Home for Little Wanderers wasn't exactly a home to return to and Vera had insinuated that she and my father and Lucas were quite cramped enough without a house guest.

"Come along, dear Beth, our Christmas tea awaits." Lily danced into the room, holding two sprigs of evergreen. She extended one of them out to me and inhaled the other and at once it occurred to me that perhaps missing my train was meant to be.

"What tea?" I asked. "And where have you been in this storm, I—"

"I know that you must be so disappointed, what with the blizzard and all, but Cook Evans kindly left a feast in the ice box and two baskets of pastries—same as last year—and we have the whole place to ourselves. It's like living in a mansion, really." I knew it wasn't true, that last year she'd been lonely and quite frightened in the dormitory all alone. Even our warden, Miss Zephaniah Stewart, departed north to visit distant relations in Michigan for the holiday. But this year was different. This year, we had each other, and since neither of us really had anyone else, I was glad for it. Lily breezed past me and extinguished the oil lamp on the table between our beds. She smelled like wood smoke and her dress was dotted with ash.

"Perhaps it is, though I doubt most mansion owners have to stoke their own fires," I said. Lily laughed behind me, a breathy whisper of merriment. Reaching into the armoire, I found a plain gray morning frock. Discarding my nightgown, I plucked my corset from the back of the wardrobe, fitted it around my middle, and sucked in as I did up the hooks in the front.

"I guarantee they do not," she said. I stepped into my skirt, pushed my arms into my sleeves, and turned to face her as I fastened the silk buttons at my wrists. She twirled the sprig of evergreen, the extinguished wick piping a trail of gray smoke up to the slanted roof behind her. "Several times each week in the winter, I'd walk into the Schraffts' house and hear Mrs. Schrafft mentioning that it was frigid, that the morning fires were already dwindling to embers, and would one of the maids be called to tend them," she continued. When Lily reached fourteen, the orphanage had allowed her indenture as a maid at the home of the Boston confectioner William Schrafft. Every cent she made went back to the school, so money was hardly Lily's motivation. She simply loved to be among the kind family and work in their grand library. The room was easily the most untidy one in the house, but she never minded cleaning and organizing there—she had always been fond of books—and it was through this familiarity with the Schraffts' library that she had decided to pursue library economics at Whitsitt.

"Tending hearths!" I scoffed, trying not to laugh. "I'd rather die than get soot on my Charles Worth ensemble." I tipped my chin up as I untangled my braid, held my hairdressing comb to the back of my head, and looped my locks through it.

Lily grinned.

"The peculiar thing is, they weren't like that at all. It seemed to me that they simply didn't know how and didn't find it necessary to learn."

"Of course they're lovely people. I'm only speaking in jest," I said. I glanced at my trunk, thinking I should unpack it, but then decided that I'd have plenty of time for that after Lily and I had had our tea. As we started to depart the room, Lily caught my arm.

"I'm sorry," she said. "Making you stay to rewrite the term paper was wrong. Professor Pearson should have to both apologize and find some way to get you home."

"He should," I said. I could feel disappointment bubbling up once more and forced it away. Professor Pearson had offered me either a failing grade or the option to stay a day after college dismissal to rewrite it. I had no choice, really. I couldn't fail. So I'd remained, writing frantically and watching from our attic window as other women stepped into waiting coaches that would take them home. I'd turned in the final paper yesterday evening, shoving it into Professor Pearson's already crammed mailbox in Old Main, not knowing that I should have hastened home to Chicago while I had the chance.

At once I thought of my father. Regardless of whether or not he cared about my presence at the family table at Christmas, he'd be wondering about me, worrying if something tragic happened when I hadn't been among the crush of people getting off the train. I'd yet to send a telegram, in part because I hadn't thought of a lie to explain my absence yet. Father didn't know he was to have a physician for a daughter, and I didn't feel I could tell him I was late because of a medical class. I had no doubt he'd be outraged, but he'd never taken the time to ask after my course of study. I figured he ignored the professors' periodic reports, simply paying the tuition and assuming my options were suitable for a young lady.

"Professor Pearson absolutely should apologize," I said again, figuring I'd come up with something and get a message to Father as soon as I could. "But you know he won't. It's only more of the same. If you'll remember, in my hygiene course, I was forced to sit at the front of the class beside Professor Young, in medical theory, Professor Blackwood continually referred to me as Nurse Carrington . . . and you've experienced much of the same."

Lily rolled her eyes.

"I'll never forget the scavenger hunt my cataloging classmates sent me on. I spent three hours searching Richardson Library for textbooks that didn't exist and missed the first class entirely."

I remembered the incident well. Lily had been marked as absent, though it was clear the male students had told her the wrong titles. We unfortunately had this sort of conversation more often than we should. Lily and I stepped out of the room and she paused to lock the door behind us, though the measure was entirely unnecessary.

"Sometimes I wonder if it's futile to study medicine or library science here. Why does Whitsitt even offer secular majors if they only want women to study divinity?" she asked, starting down the spiral staircase to the gathering hall. Everett Hall had looked the picture of holiday cheer only two days before from the evergreen and fruit wreath affixed to the entry, to the eleven-foot-tall tree in the gathering room adorned with candles that twinkled in the evening, to the garlands swirling the thick oak railing. Now, bits of garland and an unadorned tree were the only traces of festivity that remained. I ran my hand over a small strand of swag left dangling on the turn between the second and third floors, wishing the Women of Whitsitt—the divinity school's social club—had waited until after the holidays to take down their decorations. Then again, they had paid for the flourishes and spent hours festooning the place, so I suppose they were more than entitled to take pieces home to their families.

"It does seem that the divinity students are favored," I said as we reached the main floor. "I wonder if they experience anything unpleasant at all. They all seem quite jovial, flitting about to chapel or to weekly prayer meetings or to worship or to philanthropic work at the church."

Snow was still falling. The two expansive windows flanking the front door were frosted but clear, the wide front porch shielding the panes from the accumulation steadily climbing the steps. A trunk was propped beside the door on the antique oriental rug. Above it, a pin board featured Miss Zephaniah's conduct requirements—a ten o'clock curfew, no gentleman callers past eight, absolutely no spirits of any kind, no costumes of unfavorable length, no hats in the gathering room. Next to it, Whitsitt's student schedule was outlined—a six o'clock waking time, breakfast at the campus cafeteria, classes from eight until eleven-thirty, lunch, classes from twelve-thirty until five, followed by mandatory chapel at the Unitarian campus church followed by dinner at six and study hours from until nine.

"The divinity girls have each other," Lily said. "Thirty-three of them to our nine, and they're so often granted permission to alter their day in the name of philanthropy that they have a chance to know each other. Our schedules are so regimented and busy, I couldn't tell you anyone's name except yours and that peculiar girl from Chicago who—" Lily stopped short as the hallway of locked doors gave way to the twenty-five-foot ceiling of the great room and Miss Mary Adams, the subject of our conversation. She was reclining on the tufted floral longue in front of Lily's fire wearing her signature black frock, a half-devoured petit four clutched between her fingers. She looked startled at our entry before her face broke into a grin, and she stood, sweeping the white cake crumbs from her skirt onto the knotty pine floor.

"The rumor must be true," she said, her words echoing through the vacant expanse. She took another bite of Lily's petit four without apology. "You're the girls Miss Zephaniah's locked in the attic finally freed." Lily and I looked at each other and I laughed.

"Not quite. Lily Johnston and Beth Carrington," I said, gesturing to Lily and then to me. "I'm rather handy with a lock in any case."

"Mary Adams," she said, though of course we already knew her by her wardrobe, the same sort of funeral attire her famous suffragist mother, Judith Adams, donned in Chicago. She wore black every day as a symbol of mourning for the women trapped in meaningless, voiceless lives. Women like my mother. "You're rather handy with dead bodies, too, if the reports about you are accurate," she continued, withdrawing her black derby hat adorned with crow feathers. She didn't look away, but met my gaze straight-on, clearly curious herself.

My mouth went dry at the notion of a dead body, though I knew that next year in surgery I'd have to face a cadaver. No wonder the other girls seemed to balk whenever I approached. They likely thought I spent my evenings uprooting graves in the Green Oaks Unitarian cemetery.

"They're not . . . true, I mean," Lily said, sighing, as she glanced at the half-eaten tray of petit fours. "Beth can't even stomach mice. Her friend Will Buchannan was the pledge-appointed mouse catcher for Iota Gamma last year and she would—"

"Did you hear what happened?" Miss Adams interrupted, her black gloved hand catching Lily's arm. She leaned in as though telling a secret, as though there were a reason to be discreet in a vacant dormitory. "The board pardoned that imbecile, Mr. Simon. After four straight weeks of absences from class. Can you believe it? I don't know what power Grant Richardson and Iota Gamma have over the board, but to convince a group of able-minded alumni that somehow a month's absence should be excused? I can't imagine."

Lily and I sat down in twin yellow armchairs boasting a lovely carved rose motif along the rails. The fire was blazing, and I pushed away from the heat.

"I can believe it," I responded. Grant Richardson, president of Whitsitt's only permitted Greek organization, the son of a coal tycoon and the nephew of a congressman, was a powerful force. "It seems that Mr. Richardson does about anything he wants. Whitsitt instated the ban on Greek organizations and secret societies in 'Seventy-four, and yet, only four years later, Mr. Richardson arrived on campus and somehow convinced the board to allow Iota Gamma to come out of secrecy."

Miss Adams reached for another petit four—a chocolate one this time, neatly decorated with a pink rose. My stomach growled.

"The ban is quite silly anyway, if you ask me," she said between bites. "I know that nearly every school balked after that boy Mortimer Leggett died during the initiation ritual at Cornell, but the fact that colleges believe every fraternity is a devilish Masonic breeding ground only demonstrates their oblivion."

"Surely you're not saying that because you believe the Iota Gammas are angelic," Lily said, finally reaching for her tray of desserts. "Just because their practices were approved by the board doesn't mean they abide Christian principles when they aren't being watched."

I didn't much care personally what anyone thought of the Iota Gammas. They had little to do with my studies. True, they were a force on campus and my best friend from home, Will, was a brother, but that was about as close as I came to any sort of involvement with them. As far as I knew, their practices were innocent. I couldn't imagine Will participating otherwise—not that he was a saint by any stretch of the word, but he wasn't a heathen either.

I plucked a vanilla cake from the top of Lily's tray and took a bite. The butter cream was perfect, and it took everything in my power to chew politely instead of devour.

"No. Angelic isn't the word I'd use to describe those scoundrels. I'm only saying that banning these sorts of clubs only stifles the creativity of the students . . . in my opinion." Mary sighed and leaned back against the chaise longue. She looked as if she'd clearly intended to go somewhere, with a dainty sprig of holly berries pinned behind a large black jewel outlined in gold at her neck. One didn't dress with such care to sit alone in the Everett Hall gathering room.

"Why are you here?" I asked. "Rather than home, I mean." Miss Adams's hooded brown eyes snapped to mine, a smile on her lips.

"That imbecile Mr. Simon . . . and others, I suppose. They thought it would be humorous to tell me that female students were required to polish the instruments before dismissal. Since Professor Deal had departed for Milwaukee, I didn't have anyone to ask and didn't want to risk the marks for not doing it. Luckily, Professor Gram happened to walk by the music room last night and nearly had me written up for startling him." Miss Adams laughed, propping up her black kid leather boots on the stone hearth. "It was quite hilarious, actually. He was going round extinguishing the hall lamps when I called out. His eyes were round as saucers. But now I've missed my train and Mother will be alone this year. Of course she could impose at a friend's, she very well could, but she keeps to herself around Christmastime. My father died the day after, eighteen years ago, and it's still a day of mourning in our house."

The notion seemed strange, a woman like Judith Adams who did so much good for other women having nowhere to go.

"I wish there was a way to get both of you home," Lily said softly, her eyes cast toward the fire. I reached over and squeezed her hand.

"I'd rather be here with you," I said.

"Now that I know Miss Zephaniah hasn't had you locked in the attic all this time, why are you two still here?" Mary asked.

At once, I told her everything: about how hard I'd worked on my original midwifery term paper—spending long hours at Richardson Library, interviewing mothers from Whitsitt's head cook to the woman working the soda counter in town—and then how Professor Pearson had deemed it a failing study, giving me a chance to rewrite it with a "physician's eye less partial to the female condition."

"How terrible," Miss Adams said. "I'd like to throttle him. And Mr. Simon, too. I was rather hoping he'd be dismissed, but now, thanks to Iota Gamma, he'll be by my side for the remainder of our music courses. I can't fathom it anyway . . . Mr. Simon, a conductor?" Miss Adams tipped her chin up and at once I could see her, baton in hand, leading an orchestra.

"Is there nothing to be done?" Lily asked. She situated her velvet skirt and passed the tray of desserts back to Mary. "We have all been ostracized, penalized for our ambitions. It's not fair. Can you imagine the divinity girls being treated this way? There would be an uproar."

Her earlier words struck me. *They have each other.* And then I thought of Iota Gamma, of the presence they had on campus, of the respect they demanded.

"I know secret societies are forbidden, but . . . what if we were careful? What if we started a women's fraternity? For us, for the others, for the women after us?" I could hear the pitch in my voice rising, the excitement building. I could see it—the three of us united and then the nine of us. We wouldn't be mistreated then. We wouldn't allow it. "We . . . we need each other," I said, looking to Lily and then to Miss Adams for some sort of sign that they agreed, but both of their faces gave nothing away. "If nothing else, for the camaraderie."

"We need not start a fraternity to become friends," Lily said. She was hesitant for good reason, as she attended Whitsitt on a scholarship given by her orphanage. One misstep and her support could be revoked, her dream of becoming a librarian dashed.

"Could you endure it if it got worse?" Miss Adams asked, suddenly turning to Lily. "I suspect I'll be the subject of ridicule for the next two years unless something is done. I think it's a wonderful idea, Miss Carrington, a daring idea. My mother would be heartened to hear I was a part of something so important."

"We couldn't tell your mother, Miss Adams. I have no doubt Whitsitt would find it advantageous to have us removed from college for breaking our covenant," I said. "And please call me Beth."

Mary nodded. "Mary, please."

"If we don't plan to tell anyone about it, how do you suppose we'll ever be recognized? We don't have a Grant Richardson campaigning for our cause," Lily said.

I grinned, barely hearing the criticism in her question. She thought the initiative important enough to be a part of it.

"I don't know. But I'm confident we can find a way. Right now, we need each other, we need to begin. Determination and endurance are more powerful than any Grant Richardson."

2

M Y HEAVIEST GARMENTS were no match for an Illinois blizzard. I'd known that before I stepped outside, but now, standing shin-deep in snow, feeling the icy moisture taking hold of my wool skirt and then my stockings, the decision to follow Mary all the way across campus seemed entirely foolhardy.

"I thought you said it was unlocked, Mary," I said, watching as she twisted the old bronze doorknob for what seemed like the hundredth time. Lily's teeth chattered beside me, and she curled her shoulders inside a thin cloak she'd embroidered herself last semester. It was a beautiful garment, edged with silk roses and fringe, but a poor choice for the conditions.

"It *is* unlocked," she said. "I can feel the knob give. Something must be stuck." She jiggled the handle and struck the half-rotten door with the toe of her boot. I glanced around, sure that even though campus seemed to be abandoned, someone was watching this ridicu-lous display, but my view was obstructed by the gargantuan boxwoods behind us, the same sort that lined the whole of Old Main. We were standing on the far side of the building, at the basement door, a few

paces away from the stone archway leading out of campus to the Iota
Gamma house and the stables down Hideaway Hill below it. Though
I'd crossed campus more times than I could count, even standing next
to these very bushes waiting for my friend Will on the way to a cafeteria meal, I had never noticed another entrance to Old Main.

"I can't believe we left our chestnuts behind for this," Lily grum-
bled. After our introduction, Mary had gone up to change while Lily
and I decided to roast chestnuts. We'd just extracted them from the
fire when Mary had breezed into the gathering room looking like
she was going somewhere, wearing a long velveteen mourning cloak
trimmed with black Chantilly lace, and a cap made of beaver pelt,
shouting that we needed to get up at once and come with her, that
she had just thought of the perfect chapter room for our fraternity.
I had paused, quite content by the fire. I'd figured we would simply
meet in our rooms, but when the suggestion was presented, both
Lily and Mary crowed as if it were the silliest prospect they had
ever heard. "Miss Zephaniah snoops in everyone's rooms," Mary had
said. "She's right, Beth. We can't possibly keep a fraternity hidden in
the dormitory."

So, here we were, standing outside of Old Main's basement, listening to the chapel chimes singing a slow progression of the Westminster
Chime. The bells tolled two times after, the sound punctuated and
deafening in the winter silence.

"It seemed to open just fine when they brought me down here and
when I tested it a few hours ago. Perhaps the hinge has frozen," Mary
said. She kicked the door once again and stood back, appraising. Mary
had told us that she'd been lured to Old Main's basement the first week
of classes at Whitsitt under the guise that some of the orchestral music
was housed in an old desk there. While searching the hall crammed
full with discarded furniture, she suddenly heard the door shut and
realized she'd been locked in. After wandering for hours trying to find

a way out, she happened upon a small empty room, the doorway hidden by an old filing cabinet. Though it had been a dead-end, and she'd eventually found a staircase leading up to the main floor and pounded on the door until someone answered, she figured the room might serve us well now.

"Let me try," Lily said. She stepped around Mary, jostling her into one of the boxwoods that promptly deposited a dusting of snow on Mary's cap. "Apologies," she said, reaching out to steady Mary. Lily withdrew her brown velvet gloves, twisted the doorknob, and stepped back as the door creaked open. At once, the crisp scent of English boxwoods on the winter air gave way to the overwhelming stench of mildew.

"How did you—" I started, but Lily laughed.

"Mary has grown too accustomed to gloves," she said, gesturing for our new acquaintance to lead the way into the jumble of cobwebs, ruined furniture, and discarded draperies. "Back home . . . at the orphanage, I mean, we were required to prepare our own meals. Much of our food came from cans—preserves, beans, berries—and we learned rather quickly that a bare, dry hand was the swiftest way to supper."

"I'm so sorry to hear about your misfortune, dear," Mary said, turning in the doorway to grip Lily's hand.

Lily shrugged. "It wasn't so bad, really." She was used to people's pity. I had reacted similarly when I'd found out the lot she'd been cast, but she was always swift to say that she was lucky. She was here after all, the only woman from her orphanage awarded a collegiate scholarship for top marks in both her studies and her work.

"Are you sure we shouldn't meet in our room? There's no one at the dormitory and we could always find somewhere safe for future meetings," I said as I closed the door behind me. I scrunched my nose as we stepped into the musty hall. Water was dripping somewhere. I could hear the steady plop of it on the windowsills beneath the ceiling and looked down to see if it was pooling. "Oh! Oh my goodness!" I startled as I bumped into an old bookcase, nearly unsettling stacks of yellowed paper in an effort to avoid a group of scurrying cockroaches which quickly vanished beneath its bulky legs.

"What is it?" Mary called, swinging her arms above her head to dislodge a curtain of cobwebs. "And, of course we'll not meet in your room. We need a place to be a proper fraternity, to speak freely without the threat of Miss Zephaniah or one of the others overhearing us." The clutter suddenly cleared, giving way to a hall inhabited only by an old rotting music stand and a filing cabinet. Up ahead, the faint winter light streaming in from the windows shadowed the flight of stairs where I figured Mary had made her earlier escape.

Mary gripped the outer edge of the filing cabinet and pulled, and its legs screeched along the old brick floor. I stepped around to the other side and helped Mary lift it out of the way. Sure enough, just as she had mentioned, there was a door. I pushed it open and stepped into a narrow, windowless room. Water stains squiggled every wall except the one made of stone. It was a paltry excuse for a chapter room, but we would certainly be safe meeting here. I couldn't figure why anyone would purposely venture down.

"Oh! This is perfect." Lily clapped her hands together, but Mary had gone. "Some day we'll tell the others about this, about the place we began. How daring it will seem!"

"Can you imagine? Our sisters on this campus and others telling the tale of our meager beginnings?" I chose to invest in Lily's confidence instead of my doubts, though it took a good bit of imagination to believe that we would ever be anything more than a thought.

"How empowered they will be!" Lily continued. "I can see them now, meeting in grand drawing rooms in their own fraternity houses, chanting the name of—"

"Beta Xi Beta." Mary grunted, reappearing in the doorway carrying a small roll-top desk. She hoisted it into the room and set it down, then dusted her hands on her skirt.

"Beta Xi Beta?" I asked, not sure that I'd heard her correctly. We hadn't discussed names and the thought of using one letter twice seemed rather uninspired when we had the whole Greek alphabet at our disposal.

Mary lifted her index finger to me, waiting to catch her breath.

"Two and fourteen," she said. "My mother's lucky numbers. She always says two is a start and fourteen's a stand. Beta and Xi are two and fourteen, respectively, in the Greek alphabet, and I like using Beta at the end again to symbolize our intention to expand to other schools, that we'll only have to convince two girls on other campuses to join our cause before our dear fraternity is established there." She leaned on the desk and looked from Lily to me and back again.

"But we haven't—"

"We've haven't even officially begun here. How could we think of other chapters?" Lily and I spoke at once, her voice tapering as I asked the question.

"I suppose I just assumed," Mary said. "You agree that girls on other campuses might be in need of the same sort of camaraderie we are, don't you?"

I nodded, finding the notion that our fraternity would not only be established, but powerful enough to reach other colleges, nearly implausible at this stage.

"You're right," Lily said. "Though perhaps we should leave that sort of ambition for after we've made a name for ourselves here."

Mary shrugged.

"Fair enough. And, of course we don't have to use the name Beta Xi Beta, but Mother's promoted change her whole life and since we plan to offer bids to the other girls here as well, I—"

"I think it's a lovely name," I said. Mary was right. Judith Adams was versed at stoking people's passions and building them into movements that challenged the fabric of society.

"Aequabilitas Intellegentia," Lily said. "Fraternities have Latin mottos, you know, and I've been thinking that we stand for equality and intellect above all else."

"Beta Xi Beta, Aequabilitas Intellegentia." My words echoed over us. It sounded right.

Mary opened the desk and dug around for a moment before surfacing with blackboard chalk.

"I was hoping I would find some in here," she said. She paced over to the stone wall and began to write, her cursive perfectly slanted and looping. When she was finished, she stepped back and stood beside Lily and me. She reached for Lily's hand and Lily reached for mine. We stood there, connected, staring at the letters that I knew could be erased with the swish of a watery rag. Even so, it didn't matter. In that moment, standing in the shadow of our letters, we weren't just women. We were Beta Xi Beta, a women's fraternity.

3

ACCORDING TO OUR dormitory warden, Miss Zephania Stewart, there's only one acceptable reason for a young lady to be out of her room past ten o'clock: a fire. Otherwise, it'll be assumed that she's a drunkard or a fornicator—since those are apparently the only things to do in the evening hours.

I laughed to myself thinking of Miss Stewart hawk-eyeing each of us and what her reaction would be if she knew where I was sneaking off to at one in the morning. Hopefully she was as oblivious as all of the other girls tucked snugly in their beds until the morning bell began the school day. I glanced back at the expansive brick dormitory just in case my absence had triggered some type of combustion, but there weren't any flames lapping the dark windows, only the spidery veins of frost around the edges. And what would Lily and Mary think? Turning away, I tugged my wool cloak over my unruly mane and started down the hill, past the leafless, centuries-old oak trees lining the walk.

The lamps along the path had been put out for the night and moonlight cast eerie shadows from gnarled tree limbs in front of me, turning them into the pointing fingers of ancient witches. I shivered and looked around. As rebellious as I was in my mind, this venture was my first blatant act of defiance in a year and a half under Miss Stewart's thumb. Knowing my luck, one of the town vagrants would emerge from the darkness and kidnap me like they had Lynnette Downey, a Whitsitt student on her way home from a midnight tryst with her beau, some twenty years ago. Then again, we all wondered whether Lynnette's disappearance was just a myth created to scare us into submission.

Either way, I took a calming breath and kept my eyes straight ahead, noticing that the heavy scent of wood smoke spouting from our dormitory had lightened to a tinge on the crisp winter air. At the base of the hill, mist rose from the grass and patches of remaining snow, cloaking the brick entryway. I dipped through the arch and crossed the quad, feeling very much like Jane Eyre traipsing across the moors, though in this case, the moor was just a two-mile rectangle of flat Illinoisan plain. Everything was dark and still, a complete contrast to the daytime rush of life that had returned to campus this week. It had almost shocked me, the bustle of Everett Hall after a quiet break. The divinity girls had been rushing from the moment their trunks landed in the foyer, going from Green Oaks Unitarian's welcome supper to the women's chorale concert in the chapel to their monthly philanthropy reading to the children at the Whitsitt primary school, according to the schedule printed on Miss Zephaniah's pin board. Meanwhile, Mary, Lily, and I had been focused on our studies—and our fraternity.

I walked by Richardson Library, running my hands over the English boxwoods rigid with frost, and passed under the overhang of one of Old Main's ridiculous castle-like turrets.

Five more steps and I was out the back gate, frozen in the shadow of looming white pillars and tarnished Greek letters. I heard a faraway whinny from the horse stable down Hideaway Hill and paused for a moment.

What was I doing? Grant Richardson would think I was crazy—
the whole Iota Gamma fraternity would—and if I was caught, Miss
Zephaniah would have my head. Lily and Mary would wonder what
had come over me, too. Mr. Richardson wasn't anyone's favorite, and
for good reason. But that didn't matter. I wouldn't have to tell them
unless Mr. Richardson agreed to help us. I needed his help and this was
the only way I'd get him alone. Everyone from the faculty to the other
students fawned over him the moment he set foot on campus, and he
encouraged it. Trying to get his attention without others around was as
impossible as killing a fly in the dark. I'd tried both in the past week,
to no avail.

Snaking around the side of the massive three-story home, I gripped
the knob of the back door and pushed hard.

The place smelled musty, like cigars and dust. I entered into the
back foyer, running my hand across the gilded lion mural along the
wall, wondering how long it had taken for Grant and his brothers to
restore the old home after four years of abandonment. It was rumored
that the Iota Gammas had met in the basement of this house during
their banishment, even though they swore otherwise. My fingertips
brushed the silver rose in the lion's mouth with the words "*A Fortiori*"
etched in black cursive below it—"from the stronger." Arrogance at
its finest.

I heard a high-pitched whistling that unmistakably belonged to a
sleeping Will Buchannan. The first time I'd heard him snore was back
in Chicago, walking back to my family's home in Woodlawn from a
concert at the First Baptist Church of Hyde Park. I had taken the route
along the Midway Plaisance, past his family's luxurious brick apartment, and thought it was a child playing a swanee whistle until I heard
his neighbors commenting and gesturing toward his open window.

Following the sound of his snores, I started up the stairs of the Iota
Gamma house. I walked as close to the railing as possible, hoping the

wood wouldn't creak and give me away. On the second floor landing, I wrinkled my nose at the stench radiating from the bedrooms—of overflowing chamber pots and dirty laundry. I blinked, adjusting my eyes to the darkness, and crept down the hallway. Will's snoring was getting louder, ear-splitting in the otherwise silent space. *How in the world did anyone in the house sleep?*

Most of the doors were shut, but the third one on the left was flung open. I glanced in and clapped my hand over my mouth to stifle a laugh. Will's dark blond locks and white drawers were as bright as the moon against the dim of the room. His legs twitched with the intensity of another snore, disturbing the wayward sheet flung lazily across the base of his calves. Under normal circumstances, the sight of a half-naked man was a rare and potentially shocking display to a young lady such as myself, but Will was an exception. Since coming to Whitsitt, he'd become a bit of a playboy and had been involved in a few trysts, one of which I'd unfortunately stumbled upon. His skirt-chasing was ultimately why he couldn't help me. While most of his brothers had been taking the lead from their president, excelling in their studies while learning to maneuver around the important faculty, Will had gone another route—majoring in the architecture of ladies' undergarments. Considering I wore them daily, I certainly didn't need help with those.

I turned away from Will's room and stepped lightly toward the closed door at the end of the hall, my heart racing. Though I'd had one or two classes with him, I didn't know Grant Richardson well and doubted he'd take kindly to a relative stranger sneaking into his room in the middle of the night. *It doesn't matter,* I argued to myself, *I need to do this.*

Holding my breath, I pushed the door open before I could change my mind and stared at the form in the bed in front of me.

He was handsome, extraordinarily so, his face the perfect mix of masculinity and beauty—of chiseled bones and full lips and black curls. I hesitated for a moment, watching his chest rise and fall under his thin white nightshirt.

"Mr. Richardson?" My whisper was so soft I barely heard it myself. He didn't budge. "Mr. Richardson." I said it more loudly than I meant this time, and his lids fluttered open. He jerked at the sight of me, arm scattering his glasses and a pile of books on his nightstand as he stumbled and fell out of bed, hitting the floor with a thud.

"Wha-what? What is it?" Holding his hand out in front of him as if to protect himself from attack, his dark eyes were wide with disorientation. I took a step back. *Was I insane?* I suddenly couldn't recall why I'd thought sneaking into his room at night my only option for getting his support. "Who the hell are you? Why are you in my room?"

This had been a mistake, I realized. I had to run.

Gathering the length of my slate gray cloak in my hand, I whirled around to leave, but felt a hand clench down on my wrist, and was pulled back into the room.

"I asked you a question," he said, his voice low. A head taller than me, he glared down at me, not releasing his grip on my arm.

I opened my mouth, poised to apologize, praying he'd not turn me in to Miss Zephaniah, or worse, President Wilson, but no words came out.

He laughed, his narrowed eyes suddenly relaxing.

"Miss Carrington? Will's friend?" Mr. Richardson let go of my wrist, plopping down onto his bed with a sigh. "Forgive me. It's the middle of the night and . . . in any case, he's down the hall. Second room on the right."

My cheeks burned. "It's not—"

He shook his head. "I promise you it's of no consequence. It's happened before. It's dark; all of our doors look the same. And don't fret; I'll keep your visitation in confidence so long as you're discreet and don't implicate Iota Gamma if you're found out." He glanced down at his lap and slowly pulled his red jacquard coverlet over his legs. "You did scare me, though. With your cloak pulled over your head like that, I thought you were either the grim reaper or the ghost of Christmas past. I'm reading Dickens."

He gestured to the red book on the floor next to the scattered contents of his bedside table, and at once, I heard my mother's voice, saw the fire in the hearth reflecting in the window behind her as she began to read, "*Marley was dead: to begin with,*" but I forced the memory away.

"I . . . I didn't come here to see Will," I said, my voice wavering.

"You didn't?" Mr. Richardson's brow knit, but his lips turned up.

"I came to see you."

"Well, in that case, what can I help you with?" he asked, smoothing the coverlet. "And why on earth did you decide to sneak into my room in the middle of the night?"

"I knew that I couldn't get you alone otherwise," I said.

He looked down at the bed and then back at me.

"You're beautiful, truly, and I'm flattered, b—"

"No," I cut him off. "No. Of course it's not that. I needed to ask you a favor, and I'm not entirely sure that the faculty would be in agreement with it—or even the majority of the student population for that matter—so I couldn't afford anyone overhearing our conversation."

"I see." His gaze met mine and his lips pursed. "You do understand that just because I have influence, doesn't mean that I'll go along with what you want. There's a chance that I might not be able to help you. I may dislike your idea."

"I want to start a women's fraternity." The words came out of my mouth like a tidal wave—quick and fast and muddled.

His gaze didn't waver.

"Oh," he said, pushing back against his pillows. "Why?"

"Well, as you know, most of the women on campus are studying divinity and there are only a few of us concentrating on other things. Our schedules are so rigid we hardly know each other and there's certainly no camaraderie as it stands, so three of us decided to start meeting in secret a few weeks back to try to organize a—"

"No," he said, interrupting me. "I don't care about all that. Why *me*?"

I swallowed hard. "You're close to the faculty, for one, so you could help me convince them that it's needed, that we're not heathens, and two, your grandfather brought this fraternity to campus, and your father, an Iota Gamma as well, helped you revive it. I thought perhaps you'd know a thing or two about starting one."

"My grandfather died before I was born." Mr. Richardson yawned. "Miss Carrington, you seem like a lovely girl and I wish you luck in what you're doing—I even admire that you snuck in here to talk to me—but I'm not at all interested, nor do I understand the point in a women's fraternity. Men have no other option. They need to bond this way. We don't have the groups you all have—the supper club, the women's chorale—things like that."

I glared at him.

"We're not permitted to participate. The supper club and the women's chorale are divinity programs," I said.

He shrugged.

"Perhaps you should petition to join those," he said. "Or start a knitting club or a finishing group. I've heard both are quite well-received on other campuses. In fact, my cousins are involved in both at the Lewis Institute in Mississippi." He smiled at me and it took everything in my power to avoid throttling him.

"Perhaps you should dissolve your fraternity and start a chess club," I snapped, not bothering to take my case further. It was clear he couldn't be convinced. "It was a mistake to come here. Even though you find my proposal ridiculous, I'll ask that you keep it in confidence. Good day."

I pulled my hood over my hair and walked out of the room. His laughter echoed down the hallway.

"I think you mean 'good morning,' Miss Carrington," he called. "But, you have my word. Godspeed in getting back before Miss Stewart finds you."

4

THE SUN WAS out this morning, a yellow orb masked by the haze of a morning snow sky. It was a welcome sight on my birthday, a day that had seen blizzards the last two years. As beautiful as campus was when it was cloaked in white, I hoped that the sun would remain. Ice and snow made getting to class—or anywhere else—a challenge and I wanted to at least be able to get to the cafeteria for Cook's birthday dessert this year.

Campus was quiet, save the clacking of my boots on the brick walk. I quickened my pace and rounded the stone-pillared front of Old Main. Wind whipped over me as it fled between the buildings and the brick wall around campus, frosting the sweat on my face. I jerked the collar of my worn fox fur coat around my neck. In the distance, I heard the chapel clock chime. It was fifteen minutes off, and I was fifteen minutes late.

On a normal day, tardiness to Professor Fredericks's class would have made me quake. I didn't much enjoy being singled out more than I already was for being a woman in a classroom full of men, but this morning, I didn't care. Today, the cause of my discomfort was rage.

Ever since I'd left Mr. Richardson's bedroom, his sarcastic sideways grin kept popping into my head, the amusement in his voice jabbing at my wits like a hot poker. He'd treated me like a fool.

I drew my hand from my pocket, wiped my clammy palm on my coat, and yanked open the door to Old Main. Praying I wouldn't pass him on my way to the classroom, I hustled down the hallway, hearing the steam guzzling from the heaters along the floor. He'd made it perfectly clear, in our ten-minute conversation, where he stood on the topic of women's education and women in general. He must be one of the close-minded asses who still viewed us as accessories.

I knew that point of view well. My father had seen my mother that way. I'd recognized it plainly as she lay dying in a hospital bed at St. Luke's. She hadn't been conscious. I could still see her face now—rosebud lips ashen from lack of oxygen. Father had been holding her hand, muttering over and over to someone—I suppose it could have been God—that he needed her. I'd never seen him so much as kiss her cheek otherwise. In fact, the only times I recalled him speaking to her at all were in barking demands for dinner when he returned from work at night. Nevertheless, when the physician came in to tell us that she'd gone, my father broke down. At her funeral two days later, my father was still in quite a state, and when his cousin leaned in to embrace him, he whispered, "Don't worry, you'll find another one." Seven months later, he was remarried to a woman he barely knew. A woman whose presence bristled like his, chilling the warmth of my mother's memory. Mr. Richardson's wife—whomever he chose—would be like my mother. She'd long to be loved, but at the end of the day, she'd be about as important as a tarnished pair of cufflinks in a forgotten drawer.

I reached the end of the hallway and shrugged out of my coat. Through the classroom window, I could see Professor Fredericks pacing back and forth in front of an anatomical diagram of the human body and the same plaque of the Lord's Prayer that was displayed in every room. I eased the door open quietly, though it was as if I'd run into the room flapping my arms and yelling *fire*. A symphony of chairs screeched back from their desks and fifty-three pairs of eyes turned to face me as I slid into a seat at the back next to Will.

"Unlike you to be late, Beth," Will muttered. "But then again, I didn't expect to hear your voice coming from Grant Richardson's room this morning, either." He ran a hand over the blond stubble on his jaw and winked at me. "All I ask is that you're careful. You know how the school feels about women in men's quarters. If you were caught, I—"

"I needed a favor . . . for a friend," I said, cutting him off. Ignoring the questioning look that I'd see if I turned my head, I leaned down to fish a notebook and pencil from my brown leather briefcase. Looking up, I found Professor Fredericks and the rest of the class still staring at me.

"I'm sorry I'm late," I said loudly.

"Are you perspiring?" Will whispered. I ignored him and kept my eyes fixed on Professor Fredericks, wishing more than anything that I had an excuse. The truth was that I'd overslept. I'd made it back past Miss Stewart and into bed by two o'clock, but was apparently so tired that I'd fallen back asleep after Lily had woken me twice. "Are you ill? It's five degrees outside, and I can still see my breath in here. Look." I flicked my wrist at Will under my desk, annoyed that he kept trying to talk to me.

Professor Fredericks ran a hand down the expanse of his long white beard and drummed his fingertips across the top of the plain oak podium, still waiting for me to provide an excuse. I looked at the amused face of Will's fraternity brother, Sam Stephens, at the front of the room.

"Miss Carrington." My name came out with a boom. I dug my nails into the flesh of the pencil, as if the solid feel of the wood could steel me for the words to come. "Fifteen minutes late. Do you understand that, in the field, a matter of a minute—nay, less than half of a minute—could render a patient dead?" I heard laughter from the men around me and felt my forehead crease. "And, if your physician calls you and you're late, you, as the nurse, will be to blame. As skilled as the physician may be, he'll need more than two hands and—"

I slammed my pencil down and stood up.

"I'm studying to be a physician, Professor, not a nurse. That's why I'm in this class, and with all due respect . . ." I stopped myself before I went in to the exact number of times I'd had to remind him of that fact. I knew full-well he only pretended to forget—just like Professor Blackwood had last year.

He raised an eyebrow, daring me to continue.

"Never mind," I said, taking my seat again.

"Right, Miss Carrington," Fredericks said archly, prompting more snickering from the room. "Regardless, I trust you've gathered my point. If you can't manage to doll yourself up in time to make it to class, I doubt you'll be able to succeed in medicine."

I gripped the metal edge of my desk. Doll myself up? A hand materialized on my arm and squeezed.

"Don't let him see he's getting under your skin." Will's voice came low beside me.

I forced a nod at the professor, who was still regarding me with a smug grin.

"Now, let's get on with it," he said, turning to face the chalk-dusted board at his side. "As I was saying, you all know by now that anatomy is much more than just memorizing the parts of the body. The understanding of how they all work together—how the systems affect each other—will ultimately help you diagnose and treat patients." He tapped the brain, the heart, and the spinal cord, and then waved a hand at the organs in the lower cavity of the body. "Today we're going to review the cardiovascular system's great influence. Why, you ask, since we just went over it before Christmas? Well, because I deduce, by the number of you who appear somewhat gray and weak this morning, that you've done little to no studying over break." He whirled around and narrowed his eyes at us. "Don't think I don't recall the freedom of a break. I was young once and enjoyed many a drink and too many of my mother's meals. It left me drowsy. That's why I'm deciding to be generous and review this again, but keep in mind that you'll not have the luxury of a reminder when you're working as an apprentice. The physicians will expect you to know the body like the back of your own hand." He gestured down the length of the diagram behind him. "And as soon as Miss Sanderson appears with the copies of the practice exam, we'll be taking those."

Will huffed.

"I knew I should have skipped this class." I didn't know whether he was referring to the test or having to see Katherine Sanderson, Mary Adams's roommate, who always typed the examinations for Professor Fredericks as part of her secretarial coursework. I'd found them locked in an embrace in the ladies' powder room after the glee club's holiday performance, Will's hands inside her bodice. Though her highfalutin manner had always irked me—she was Southern and as traditional as they come—I began to dislike her in earnest after I stumbled upon her and Will. Will had been adamant that kissing her had been a mistake and that she'd been more interested in him than he was in her after their tryst, making any proximity or interaction uncomfortable.

"Beth—do you know the cardiovascular system?" he whispered. "I haven't been paying attention." I shook my head, keeping my eyes fixed on Professor Fredericks, who was pointing out the circulatory loops. "You don't?" he continued. "Haven't you been to every class?"

"Yes," I said, "but I can't remember all of it. And I won't know anything if you don't stop talking."

Edwin Putnam, a beast of a man in front of me, turned in his chair to stare at us. I forced my lips into a grin. He shook his head and shifted back to his notepad in front of him.

"I've been to most of them, too, but Miss Sanderson ogles me the whole time. It's distracting. Since she wasn't here when I walked in, I thought perhaps she'd taken this semester off from helping Fredericks, but I suppose I was wrong."

A man sitting next to Will slammed the cover of his notebook shut.

"For the love of Pete, be quiet," he said. "If you would have been paying attention, you would know that you could eliminate your attraction to Miss Sanderson by recognizing and eradicating the erotic mental impulses she's triggering in your brain."

"That, or kissing her at first urge instead of waiting three months," Will whispered. I made a face. He hadn't always been this vulgar and it didn't suit him.

"And, as you see, the systematic circulation loop carries oxygenated blood from the left side of the heart to the organs, all the while removing waste and ultimately returning deoxygenated blood to the right side," Fredericks continued.

"What, Beth? It's the truth," Will whispered. "Had I given in the first time, I would have realized that she's not the sort of woman I'd like for a wife." I could hear the smile in his voice. He knew how much his carelessness bothered me, the thoughtless manner in which he made advances. It wasn't really his true character. I knew he only did it to avoid facing the debilitating heartache of his breakup last year with then-senior Kate Cable. He confessed his love for her the morning of graduation, and she reacted with silence, leaving for a teaching post in Rhode Island the next day without a word. He'd found out she'd gone from her roommate. It hurt me to know that it still bothered him, but I knew nothing I could do would get him over it. I'd tried.

The door to the classroom creaked open, and Katherine Sanderson, all five feet of her, materialized at the back of the room. Her mass of blonde hair was fashioned in an elaborate plaited arrangement at the top of her head, and I couldn't tell if it was her attitude or her coiffure that prompted her chin to tip up. Despite my feelings toward her, I couldn't help but admire her costume. Though the color was a common russet, the ensemble was trimmed with brown and light blue faille and fringe. Mary had told me that their shared closet was brimming with lovely dresses, even a few Worth designs, and that Miss Sanderson's father—the owner of a large corn plantation in Morganfield, Kentucky—sent her a wardrobe of new costumes for each season. I couldn't fathom the fortune that must be spent on the collection every year.

Miss Sanderson marched toward Professor Fredericks, the stack of papers she held against her chest drawing attention to the cameo she always wore at her neck. He stopped lecturing and took the stack of papers from her hand. She turned to go, eyes searching the room—no doubt for Will—and the professor touched her arm.

"If you wouldn't mind staying for a moment, Miss Sanderson, we're reviewing the cardiovascular system and a real life example is in order. I need a woman's help." I glanced down at my skirts, wondering if perhaps he saw me as an equal after all.

"All right, students," he said, keeping an eye on Miss Sanderson, whose gaze had found Will. Will picked at his cuticles, likely avoiding her stare. "As today's time is dwindling and an opportunity for learning has just presented itself, we'll take today's examination next class. Now let me make my point. As you can see, Miss Sanderson is a perfectly healthy young woman." The professor's eyes settled on her bosom before addressing the rest of the classroom. "Her cardiovascular system is likely working as it does in most every woman, each month ridding her brain of a substantial amount of blood as she releases an egg and then menstruates. You do plan on having children, Miss Sanderson?"

My jaw clenched. He was teaching an unconfirmed hypothesis. He wasn't seeing me as an equal at all. I knew where this was going and prayed he'd stop for my sake.

"Of course," she drawled. "My goodness, what a question." She lifted her palm to her chest, round eyes going wide, as if even the thought that she wouldn't reproduce was offensive, though in my opinion, the world would benefit if she refrained.

"And your designated course of study is?"

"Secretarial science. You know that."

She smiled and Professor Fredericks nodded.

"Yes. A wonderful choice, my dear." He stepped toward the diagram of the body and pointed at the heart. "A woman's cardiovascular system is a bit unique. You see, the heart pumps blood to the uterus, and a large amount of that blood is expressed from the brain and other organs during the menstrual cycle, depriving the woman and allowing for healthy fertility. Now, if a woman routinely submits herself to mental fatigue, like, say, Miss Carrington, who has decided to ignore all medical evidence to pursue a career most unsuitable for a woman hoping to start a family, the body reacts differently." I looked away from the professor's sneering face to the diagram behind him. I fixated on the heart, feeling my own buzz with unquenchable rage. "Can someone tell me what the female body's natural reaction to mental fatigue is?" His question sounded distant.

I tried to calm myself. I couldn't let him unnerve me. It wasn't the first time I'd been singled out in a course, and it wouldn't be the last. I needed this class to move forward to other courses, to graduate, and I wouldn't let one old man stop me.

"The blood will reverse its natural course out of her uterus and travel upstream, clouding her good senses and putting strain on her already fragile brain," Edwin Putnam said. It was the first time I'd ever heard him actually answer a question.

"Oh my! Is that true?" Miss Sanderson exclaimed. Clearly she had no brain to strain in the first place.

"Yes. It's been scientifically proven, my dear," the professor said. I couldn't take it anymore. The pent-up fury of the morning overwhelmed me, and I rose to my feet.

"Of course it hasn't. There's still quite a bit of speculation. You would know, professor, if you'd read the piece in *The American Journal* last month."

"That was an editorial opinion piece by a very controversial female physician, a graduate of the Female Medical College of Pennsylvania," he said, drawing out the second *female* as though the fact of it discounted her findings altogether. "It's hardly legitimate. It's the same rubbish they published years ago claiming that the female brain is the same size as the male's."

His eyes slid from mine to rest on Will next to me. "In any case, the fact that you're in obvious mental distress right now proves my point. Mr. Buchannan?"

"Sir?" Will barked, a tone he only used in arguments.

"Considering Miss Sanderson here is perfectly healthy and Miss Carrington is not, what's the difference? And what would you suggest, as a physician, that Miss Carrington do to alleviate this unhealthy psychological strain? I expect your answer to be serious and well-reasoned, Mr. Buchannan, or I will be tempted to question my recommendation that you continue in this program next semester. We all know that I've been generous with regard to your lack of enthusiasm for this course."

Will cleared his throat. Though it was true that he was quite lazy when it came to his studies, he was more learned than our entire class about the actual application of medicine. He'd observed his grandfather, a family physician, since he was a child, but he'd also subscribed to every journal he could find for as long as I could remember, reading them over and over until the pages tattered or fell out. Only then had he loaned them to me.

I held my breath, waiting for the smart reply that I knew would make Professor Fredericks feel so foolish that he'd never call on Will again.

Instead he said, "I suppose most would advise a major more suitable to the fragile female condition."

I whirled toward Will, expecting to find him smirking, but he wasn't. Instead, he was staring straight ahead at the professor, refusing to meet my eyes.

"However," Will continued, in a tone I could barely hear, "I would—"

"Ratio!" I interrupted, slamming my hands on the top of the desk before the thought to stop the impulse passed through my mind. The room fell silent. "Haven't you heard of the elephant test, Professor?" I continued, my voice shaking. "Elephants have larger brain mass than human males, meaning that if the size of the brain were the factor signifying intelligence, elephants would be smarter than all of you. So, it was determined that the actual way to calculate intelligence is to figure brain weight relative to body weight, in which case, females have larger brains than both men and elephants." A murmur went across the room. I caught my breath, plucked my briefcase from the worn wood floor, and leaned toward Will.

"Here's a math problem for you," I whispered, noticing his eyes were fixed on the desktop. "If you've made overtures to nearly every woman on campus and never captured the heart of one, perhaps you should examine your own psychological strain before discussing mine."

Seething with anger, I didn't wait for his response and exited the room, satisfied by the slam of the door behind me.

5

THE DEPRESSED CROWN of my brown satin bonnet was collecting snow flurries by the time I reached the shelter of the turret protruding from Old Main. I was breathing hard, and tears pooled in my eyes, but I refused to let them fall. I edged the carved mahogany door open and removed my hat, realizing the black quills on the side of it had turned to ice.

I kept my head down, nodding once at the President's secretary sitting behind her desk in the foyer. Slipping into the hallway on my right, past vacant offices that smelled of old books and pencil shavings, I shivered, wondering if anyone had had the decency to start a fire. The place had fifteen fireplaces. On winter days, the building usually felt like an oven.

I walked toward a stream of gray daylight beaming across the end of the hallway. I could hear Professor Helms's gritty voice as I passed the open door of the lecture room, and wanted nothing more than to stop in the shadows and catch Lily's attention. As much as I needed her right now, Helms's grammar review was much more important. Lily had barely made the grades necessary to keep her scholarship last semester and had already been warned that one more slip in her marks would render it revoked. It wasn't that she wasn't intelligent enough—in fact, she was one of the brightest women I'd ever met. The problem was simply her lack of preparedness. Her tutor at the orphanage had taught her many things, but never an effective method of studying.

The distant wail of a cello playing a sad song momentarily mingled melancholy with my anger, reminding me of Will's betrayal. He and I had been friends for six years, ever since we'd been shoved into the last seats on a packed cable car coming from a matinee performance of *As You Like It* at McVicker's Theatre—an end-of-semester treat for good marks from our respective schools. As we discovered, his father was my father's boss at Western Wheel Works, and thus anything his father approved, mine did as well. Will was the reason I'd been allowed to attend Whitsitt in the first place. Initially, my father had been so appalled at the notion of his daughter living without a husband or father half a state away that he'd cursed at me in the middle of dinner. Will and I hadn't even been eligible to apply for three years, but in an attempt to make conversation, my father had asked Will about his plans to study. Unable to stop myself, I'd chimed in, mentioning that I knew Whitsitt was a co-educational college and that I'd like to study there as well. As horrified as my father had been, Will's father thought co-educational schooling beneficial, and had eventually convinced my father to send me to Whitsitt so long as Will promised to look out for me. He'd broken his promise.

I ran my hand along Patrick Everett IV's plaque on the Founders' Wall. A staunch Liberal Universalist and supporter of women's suffrage, Mr. Everett had refused to fund the college unless women would be allowed to study alongside males. Thanks to Mr. Everett, women had always been allowed to attend any of the colleges, though most besides the seminary had always been traditionally male. He'd passed away eight years ago, at the age of ninety-four. Since then, his principles had been begrudgingly followed—they were still admitting us, after all—but more or less forgotten in the classrooms where professors' views weren't so progressive.

Professors be damned, I thought as I slipped into the darkness of a short hallway, forced open the door to the stairwell, and descended the stairs into the basement.

Water was dripping somewhere. The drops slapped the brick floor as I felt my way down the hall, hands grazing the cold stones. My mother's voice rang in my head. *"At the end, your legacy will be a name on a forgotten slab and, if you're lucky, a story or two,"* she'd said, turning to clutch my hand as we'd passed a small plaque dedicated to Revolutionary War heroine Deborah Sampson Gannett. *"I beg you, Beth, do something worthy. You have the courage that I don't."*

I'd heard the echo of my mother's words for the first time when the coroner had come for her body. Everything about St. Luke's Hospital, from the physician's monotone to the barred windows to the sedated women on either side of her, had been cold and unfeeling, hopeless. In that moment, I knew I'd been called to medicine; specifically, to the battleground of a hospital. I not only felt my mother's urging to find an answer to death without definite cause, but to bring comfort to the families of the acutely and terminally ill, families away from their homes and physicians.

Feeling my way to the brass knob, I turned it and shrugged out of my coat, tossing it on the moth-eaten wingback in the corner. Over the last week, we had decorated the chapter room the best we could with the discarded contents from the basement. It didn't look half-bad. I closed the door. Opening the top drawer of the old secretary, I found the match book and struck one, lowering it to the first of three taper candles Mary had stolen from the chapel. The light cast a hazy glow on the pea green tufted couch below our letters on the back wall and the gray wingback chair.

I reached under the secretary, withdrawing the first of three navy blue hooded robes. Pulling it over my head, I inhaled. It smelled like starch, like home, like my mother ironing my father's shirts in the morning.

Lily had made the robes in haste last week, after Mary thought that we should wear a uniform of sorts, a visible measure of our unity, during meetings. Blue fabric was on discount at the Whitsitt Five and Dime—the only place to obtain supplies unless you had the time to secure a ride to Green Oaks—but we'd quickly decided to pretend we'd chosen the color to signify parity.

Fluffing the bangs along my forehead that had nearly fallen flat with the snow, I sank onto the couch, arranged the cloak over my gray velvet skirt, and wedged my fingers into the cushions to retrieve our braided silk wreath pins. We'd made them here a few nights ago with gold pieces from the Five and Dime's scrap basket while Mary and Lily bickered over the exact wording of the pledge that we'd asked Lily to write.

My fingers brushed something damp and I recoiled, edging to the center of the couch. Shutting my eyes, I imagined a house like Iota Gamma's to live and congregate in with my sisters instead of a dank basement. Each time that thought crossed my mind, though, I was reminded that I should be thankful for any space at all.

A long knock at the door startled me. I sat up in time to hear another long tap, followed by four short ones, and the roll of knuckles across the wood. The secret knock had been my idea. My girlhood friend and I had adopted the method for our club when we were children and would steal away to a small closet off her family's drawing room to play tea party. If a knock other than ours sounded on the door, we knew we'd been found out by one of her brothers.

"Who knocks on the door of Beta Xi Beta?"

"It's your sister, Mary, Queen of Debauchery," the voice said, followed by a waterfall of laughter. We'd made her claim the title after she'd admitted that she'd been the one to steal all of the liquor from the Iota Gamma house before their winter ball last year, a scandal that had enraged the Iota Gammas so much that it had made the front page of *The Whitsitt Cardinal*. Mary insisted she'd only done it for the good of their future wives—she was staunchly against male drinking, though somehow thought female imbibing more than appropriate. We'd given her the designation to shame her, but the moment we did, we realized Mary wasn't one to feel embarrassed about anything. Even if what she did seemed scandalous to the rest of us, Mary didn't see it that way.

"If it's truly Mary," I said, fixing my eyes on the orb of light around the candle, "please recite our pledge." A huff came from the other side of the door.

"Is that really necessary, Beth? You know my voice." I didn't say anything, but heard her clear her throat decorously. "I solemnly pledge my loyalty to the sisterhood of Beta Xi Beta until the end of my days. I promise that above all else, my purpose will be to foster equality and intellect among women—for a chain of linked hands is mightier than the most menacing army." She laughed. "My, that's ridiculous."

"What was that?" I asked. It was our pledge. It was to be taken seriously. The door flung open and smacked against the stone, echoing through the basement.

"The pledge is absurd, Beth, and you know it." She plucked her black trilby hat from her head, reached for her cloak, and stuffed an auburn curl back in its pin at the nape of her neck. "I know you won't admit that it's comical because Lily wrote it, Beth, but you should. Every time I say it, I imagine a Viking army with swords and clubs charging a line of women holding hands." Mary grinned and sat down at the desk, propping her kid leather boots on the top of it. Her pose reminded me of the only photo I'd ever seen of her mother on the cover

of a Chicago Suffrage pamphlet. Her legs had been propped on a large
table spilling with posters, a pencil clutched in her fingertips. Judith
had been heralded as heroine among many women in my school, but
was ostracized in the papers. The instigator of countless tavern protests
and rights marches, some of which had turned violent, Judith was one
of the *Tribune*'s favorite subjects. My father had always rolled his eyes
at the stories, muttering something about the "foolish black bat" after
he read them. I'd always quietly admired her.

"You have to agree that the pledge is a bit silly," Mary pressed again,
her green eyes squinting in the orb of the flame in front of her.

I sighed.

"It's not meant to be taken literally. It's just supposed to illustrate
the strength of sisterhood."

Mary rolled her eyes, yanked the cloak over her head, and swung
her legs down from the desktop.

"I know that." She crossed to the couch, withdrew the wreath pins
from the cushion, and leaned down to pin mine against my heart.
"I'm not an imbecile. I'm only saying that if she would have taken my
advice and changed the last line it would—"

Another knock sounded at the door.

"Who knocks on the door of Beta Xi Beta?" I asked.

"Lily," she said, and immediately recited the pledge without being
asked.

"Goodness, I thought I'd never make it." She burst into the doorway. "Professor Helms was rather long-winded today and . . . there's
only twenty minutes until lunch." Lily was covered in snow from her
hair to her black leather boots. Even in the dim light, I could see the
pink windburn across her cheeks. She took off her plain wool coat. "I
ran back to the room to get my notebook after class and found Miss
Zephaniah in our room."

"Why was she in there?" I asked, straightening my back against the couch. Surely Mr. Richardson wouldn't have turned me in, would he? Lily shrugged.

"Who knows, really. When I asked, she mumbled some nonsense about hearing a door open in the middle of the night and seeing a figure outside. She thought someone may have broken in to steal from us while we were asleep. Either that or she thinks she saw Lynnette Downey's apparition. I think she's just imagining things, the old loon. I swear our ninety-year-old warden at the orphanage was sharper. Even she didn't dream up such drivel."

I looked down at my shoes to keep from laughing, relieved that I hadn't been found out.

"Miss Zephaniah looked half-crazed when I saw her," Lily continued. "Her hair was down and scraggly and she was still wearing her nightshirt—you know, the one with the lace trim and scalloped edges—which makes her look ridiculous, like a gray-haired child. What is it?" Lily stopped, her expression quizzical.

"Nothing. I'm sure it was a ghost," I said, sobering up.

"I *knew* I heard the door open last night," Lily said, peeling her worn leather gloves from her hands without shifting her gaze from my face.

"Yes, where'd you go, Beth?" Mary asked.

"Never mind. You wouldn't dare," Lily said.

"Actually, I think she might." Mary's lips turned up and she plucked Lily's cloak from the desktop and handed it to her. "I was in the library studying for my classical history exam until a little after one this morning—Miss Zephaniah gave me permission. On my way out, I glanced out the window and could have sworn I saw Beth crossing the quad, but figured I was mistaken."

"Beth?" Lily's voice echoed against the stone. I could see her looking at me in my peripheral vision, her fingers working the pin into the fabric of the cloak.

"I went to see Mr. Richardson," I said. I tipped my head down in embarrassment, letting the hood fall over my eyes.

"What?" Lily and Mary said in unison.

"How did you know it was me anyway, Mary?"

"Your gait. You sort of bob when you walk." Her eyes tapered, as though I should have known the answer. I had no idea I did any such thing.

"Oh. Well. I suppose I should explain." I sank back against the velvet couch, feeling the cool patches where the fibers had been worn bare. "You might as well sit down." I pushed my hood back to my forehead and gestured to Lily. She was still staring, as though if she looked hard enough, the answer would come to her without me telling it. Mary stood up abruptly and pulled me into an embrace.

"I hope you're not in love with him," she said. "But, if you are, I'll stand by you. I'm your sister, first and foremost."

"Thank you, but he's the last person I'd entertain. You know that." She shrugged, and resumed her place at the desk. Mr. Richardson's merits and follies had been brought up several times since we'd formed Beta Xi Beta. He could hardly be avoided when discussing fraternities, after all. We'd settled upon the stance that we would tolerate sharing the same space as the man, even though both his father and uncle were staunchly against women's rights. I should have taken my sisters' views to heart before I'd gone.

"I went to ask him a favor," I said. "For us," I amended. "It was a mistake." I rubbed my palm against my arms, feeling the chill of the basement blocks seeping into my bones. "The other day, I crossed campus behind him. He was with one of the board members—Mr. Simon, I believe—and I couldn't help but overhear their conversation. It was something about the vote. Simon was saying that he thought it would be the downfall of our country, but Mr. Richardson disagreed with him. He said that there would be more votes to win, and that anytime there were more votes, parties could establish a new majority, which was a good thing. Simon came around to agreeing with him."

"And you took that to mean that Mr. Richardson was for us?" Lily asked.

"I suppose in part. But mostly, it made me think that he could help establish us. You know he has the influence over the board necessary to do so."

The popping of the burning wick was the only noise, until Lily spoke.

"You told him about us?" Lily's voice was low and breathy.

"So, what did you do?" Mary asked, "Sneak into the Iota house? Of course he has the power, but it's a given that he wouldn't help. If there's one thing I've learned from my mother it's that most men are unwilling and—"

"We swore we'd never tell anyone outside this room," Lily said, cutting Mary off. "You even forbid Mary to tell her mother."

"I already said it was a mistake," I started, "but if we want to extend a bid to the other girls on campus, if we want to secure a charter and offer a voice and camaraderie to other girls at other schools, we need to move forward somehow. If not, we'll be stuck meeting in this dungeon forever."

"That's better than being forced to disband before we've actually begun," Lily said, "or expelled for meeting at all. Does he know where we gather, who we are?"

I shook my head.

"I didn't get that far." I knew she was right. Even if Mr. Richardson didn't know the identities of the women involved, I'd told him that we'd organized. All it would take was his telling President Wilson and I'd be disciplined, if not dismissed from Whitsitt. And then I'd be forced to return to Chicago, to live in the shadow of my stepbrother, the boy my mother hadn't been able to provide my father, until I chose factory work, secretarial work, or marriage.

"You should have asked us first, before you decided to go off and talk to him without our knowing," Mary said. "That being said, was he as handsome in his nightclothes as he is in his suits?"

"What?"

"When you snuck up on him? Or, did he know you were coming?"

"No, he wasn't expecting me," I said, trying to hide my flushing. "And all I asked was that he help me petition the board to start a women's fraternity. I told him that there were already a few of us meeting, but I didn't mention any names or the location, of course."

"And he said what exactly? That he found the idea preposterous? We already knew that's what he would say." Lily stood and paced across the room. "Now we have to worry about whether or not he'll report us."

"I asked because I thought he could help us," I reiterated. "He has power, and his grandfather started Iota Gamma. When I heard that conversation, I thought he'd changed."

"People like that never do," Mary said. "Their ideology is so etched into their being that they can't escape it. It's as much a part of them as their heart." I thought perhaps she was thinking of her mother's beaus. The first day of classes, I'd noticed Mary wearing a black sapphire ring and she'd told me her mother had given it to her. It was one of the countless gifts from Judith's would-be suitors, gifts they'd hoped would change her sensibilities. But nothing ever could. Mary's father was the only man Judith had ever truly loved, a man who'd supported her mission.

"I suppose," I said. "He wasn't overly cruel though. He just said he didn't see the—"

A fist slammed into the door, paused, then knocked again, followed by four short knocks and the roll of knuckles. I looked around the room. We were all here. Lily's eyes widened, and she tugged her hood over her face. I had no doubt she and Mary jumped to the conclusion that I'd actually shared all of our secrets with Mr. Richardson—the location of our meeting room, our knock. All of us remained silent, barely breathing in case whoever was behind that door would sense our presence.

"Who knocks on the door of Beta Xi Beta?" I started at Mary's voice, wishing she would've remained silent. Whoever it was had likely been following one of us, and I doubted he or she was simply coming to say hello. I cursed under my breath. It was my fault. I shouldn't have approached Mr. Richardson.

"Katherine," a voice drawled from behind the wood. "Katherine Sanderson." I glanced at Mary, wondering if she'd let our secret slip to her roommate. She looked down and cleared her throat.

"It was me," she whispered. "She asked where I went every evening before turn in, and in the moment I couldn't think of an explanation. I didn't really think she'd come. I suppose since she's not a divinity girl we would've eventually gotten around to offering her a bid anyway. Regardless, I knew she wouldn't tell anyone. I've got a secret on her as well."

I rolled my eyes, recalling Miss Sanderson's proud face as Professor Fredericks touted her as the ideal woman. She was ill-mannered and shallow, not even close to admirable.

"Am I the only one to be trusted with our secret? I thought this fraternity was sacred," Lily hissed.

"I don't think she's right for us," I whispered, disregarding Lily's comment.

Mary snorted.

"Clearly, but is it because of Will Buchannan or something else?" Her eyes drilled into mine.

"You may enter," I said through my teeth. As much as Miss Sanderson's impropriety bothered me, Mary was right. Her casual involvement with Will irked me even more. The door screeched open, and she took a cautious step inside, finding me first.

"Miss Carrington?" she breathed as though my presence were a shock. Had Mary told her about us but not mentioned me? I nodded and forced my lips into a tight smile, supposing the cloaks weren't the effective disguises Mary assumed they'd be. "Earlier . . . I . . . I'm sorry for earlier. I had no idea why Professor Fredericks asked me that question. I shouldn't have let him treat you that way. He's so irritating. He thinks the sun comes up just to hear him crow."

I didn't respond, and silence eclipsed the room, leaving Miss Sanderson no other option but to continue. "I suppose I should explain. You see, I've found there's power in playing into who people think I am."

I could feel her eyes on me, waiting for some sign of approval to go on, but I didn't give it. I didn't want her here, and though I'd gone behind Mary and Lily's backs to ask Mr. Richardson for help, I hadn't gone so far as to invite another woman into our sisterhood without consulting them.

"We haven't quite set the rules for recruitment," I said, ignoring her attempt at enlightening me to her actual character. "So you'll understand if I ask you to leave and promise to keep this location and these members a secret until we can set things in stone."

Mary made a noise in the back of her throat and Lily shifted in her chair.

"I'm sure we can grant an exception this—" Mary started, but Miss Sanderson cut her off.

"You dislike me. It wasn't just this morning, was it? It's him, W-Mr. Buchannan, isn't it?" Her voice shook as she addressed me, but I kept my eyes fixed on the candle. "I-I know you two are close. I assure you,

Miss Carrington, I didn't break his heart. In fact . . . never mind. We had an agreement."

The vision of the two of them—her fingers woven through his hair, his mouth on hers, his hands on her skin—flashed in my mind, and I met her eyes. Her hands were balled in her gray silk taffeta skirt. I was rarely cruel to anyone, but today, the anger and irritation bubbled within me.

"I never considered his heart in danger," I said. "It's just that I find your actions rather crass." I stepped toward the desk and edged my way between Mary and the top drawer. The wood screeched as I forced it open and withdrew two rolled sheets, the bylaws we'd drafted only yesterday. "In any case Miss Sanderson, I have to remind my sisters of Rule Fourteen: change in, or addition to membership, or a campaign for formal recruitment must first be mentioned in closed chapter meeting, then voted upon, and finally assessed for a trial period. As you're probably aware, we haven't yet breached step one in regard to—"

Lily grasped my forearm and yanked me down to her level.

"Rule Twenty-Six," she said. "All actions designed to further or expand the presence of Beta Xi Beta will be discussed, voted on, and approved by the sisterhood before any action is taken. You're in violation, too."

"This fraternity was my idea." My words echoed against the stone, and I felt both supremely foolish and immensely annoyed at the same time. I didn't want Miss Sanderson here, but Mary's invitation couldn't be undone without damage. It reminded me of the dinner parties we'd have when my mother was alive, my father insisting we entertain the wives of the copper stamping supply chain managers above his station, women who oftentimes left their plates untouched, clearly disapproving of my mother's cooking and carefully crafted menus. In spite of my mother's dislike of them, she'd always been graceful and polite, an example I knew she was trying to set for me. She'd be ashamed of me right now.

"Don't worry, Beth, no one will mistake you for humble now," Mary laughed.

"Miss Sanderson, I apologize. Of course you can stay," I said. "I've been unnecessarily cruel, and I'm embarrassed. It's only . . . well . . . I've had a horrible day." Her face relaxed and she smiled, making me feel even worse than I already did.

"It's all right," she said. "And call me Katherine, please. I know how easily this school, these people, can work their way under your skin . . . which is why I so badly want to be a part of this." She turned to address the others. "It's hard to stay the course alone. I nearly dropped out last semester because of it. I couldn't stand the constant talk about me as though I hadn't a brain."

I nodded, choking back the compulsion to point out that her behavior suggested she rather liked the treatment, as did allowing men to treat her poorly.

"Well and good," Lily said. "Now that that's been settled, can we please get on with why we've come in the first place? Truth be told, Mary, I'm no good at coming up with lyrics to songs. I'm so terrible at music that I suppose it interferes with my ability to write. Perhaps you could dream it up along with the melody?"

Mary shrugged. She had wanted us to invent a song, an anthem, for our sisterhood together—the Iota Gammas had several—but neither Lily nor I were skilled at music.

"If we're not going to do that today, would it be all right if I excused myself to the library?" Lily asked. "There are additional books I've got to check out for the class debate on the Baconian method of classification compared to the Dewey system and I'd rather take my study hour in my room than in the library this evening."

She'd been studying the material for weeks, hoping her diligence would reward her with high marks in her Library Economy courses. Though I knew she was concerned about her grades, I'd never seen her so anxious. Something else was bothering her, something besides what was going on in the room. "Plus, I've been keen to sneak that copy of *The Canterbury Tales* off of the shelves for some time," she continued. "It'll be my reward when this debate is finished."

"Honestly, Lily, I'm in no mood to compose in a hurry. Perhaps we should postpone until next time," Mary said, passing her hand back and forth above the candle.

"How'd you find a copy of *The Canterbury Tales*? I thought they'd all been destroyed in '73, with the Comstock Law," Katherine said, disregarding Mary's comment about the song.

"Lily has a way of finding all of the most scandalous books. Last semester she found an unabridged copy of *The Arabian Nights*," I laughed.

"It's called an accident—or rather, fortune, I suppose," she said with a smile. "There's a shelf marked 'discard' at the very back of Richardson Library. No one ever goes back there, apparently even to empty it. I happened upon it after I'd scoured every other section of the library for a grammar book that I needed that strangely didn't exist."

Katherine huffed.

"Your classmates thought to trick you?"

"Of course. Three of them were speaking quite loudly outside the classroom the first day about Professor . . . Professor Helms's supposed required reading." Lily stumbled over the words and for a moment, her face paled. "When I heard it, I thought it'd be better for me to feign illness and skip class to find the book, rather than to show up unprepared and be chastised for it the rest of the year."

"We've all had to learn our lesson around here," Mary said. "Let's not ruin our evening by discussing the scum of the college."

"Agreed," I said.

"We better go on to lunch before the four of us make our entrance in the middle of Chaplain Blair's blessing," Lily said. I rolled my eyes. Miss Zephaniah was always carrying on about tardiness as though it was the gateway to hell.

* * *

As it turned out, I was the only one who was late. I'd stayed behind under the guise that I would straighten the room and put our things away. After the way I'd disappointed my sisters, and the way Will had disappointed me, I was in no mood for eating, and if Miss Zephaniah asked after me I'd simply say I'd felt a bit ill—which was the truth.

I closed our bylaws into the roll-top desk, reveling in the silence. I plucked my damp coat from the chair beside me, put it on, situated my hat, and blew out the candle. The smoke fled toward the ceiling for a moment and I inhaled, recalling the similar scent of birthday candles in years past. This year, no one had remembered my birthday—my father hadn't even sent a card—so I stood for a moment longer, closed my eyes, and conjured my mother's smiling face in my mind. *Happy Birthday to me.*

By the time I climbed the stairs and emerged on the first floor, the lanterns along the hall had been lit to offset the cloudy day. The flames danced against the medieval-looking iron sconces, sending thin shadows across the walls and on to the mob of silhouetted faces returning to their classes from lunch. I walked quickly toward the door to the courtyard at the end of the hall, hoping that a breath of cold air and a glimpse of new snow would refresh me for my chemistry course. I was exhausted, my wits frayed, and a nap in my modest twin bed seemed as luxurious as a canopy bed at the Palmer House Hotel.

"Beth." I heard my name shouted from behind me. *Will.* I didn't want to talk to him. Not after what he'd done. He called my name again, closer this time, and I ducked down the hallway leading to the

President's office, hoping to lose him. Footsteps came behind me and I quickened my pace. My breath hitched in my chest as I took in the mingled scent of mildew and crisp cold from an opened window.

"Beth," Will said again, and clamped his hand down on my fore-arm and pulled me to him. At once, I was face-first in the damp of his brown wool Norfolk jacket, breathing his sandalwood cologne.

"I don't want to talk to you," I said, jerking away, but Will's grip barely gave. "Let go." I refused to look at him, staring instead at the worn toes of his boots, currently exhibiting a slathering of mud and snow.

"We both know I won't until you hear me out, so you might as well listen," he said. He was telling the truth. While I preferred space and time to think, I'd had enough conflicts with Will to know that he'd badger me until I agreed to work it through. To be fair, most of our quarrels had been the result of my father's attempts to push me into the upper middle class world of the Buchannans, forcing invitations to socials and balls to which I hadn't been invited. It was awkward and clear from the start that I hadn't belonged—nor had I wanted to—but Will had always insisted I did, a measure that only reminded me of my father's prodding. It wasn't that I found the prospect of being attached to Will terrible, but he was my friend—one of my best friends, in fact—and I feared that a romance would only extinguish what we had. My father had only retired his hopes of my marrying Will and becom-ing a mediocre socialite when I'd convinced Will to invite Henrietta Anderson—a neighbor of his who was smitten with him—to a shared dinner last summer. Her interest and his false attentions had been so extreme that my father thought it clear they'd be engaged by fall, and he gave up his push. At that point, however, he seemed to have stopped caring. I'd already begun Whitsitt and his attentions had shifted to grooming Lucas for presumed greatness. I felt sorry for Lucas, too. It was clear that deep down Father had always desired acclaim and wealth, and since he hadn't been able to achieve it himself, he decided to project his dreams onto our generation.

"Fine," I said under my breath. I glanced up at him and his lips twitched as if he were about to smile, but he thought better of it.

"Good grief, are you really that angry?" I felt his fingers go slack on my arm and slung myself loose.

"Of course I am, you—you *ass*," I yelled.

Will's eyebrows rose as much at the cursing as the decibels and then he laughed. My hands opened and I felt one arm rise to slap him, but stopped myself, balling it into a fist instead.

"Is that the best you can do?" He grinned at me as though I'd just turned into a court jester.

"No," I spat, my fury returning. "You made me look like a fool. You're nothing but a disloyal, self-loathing boor. I can't believe I was so blind as to think you were my friend."

His dark blue eyes dulled. He looked down at the floor and shook his head. I instantly regretted the severity of what I'd said. "Will. I—"

He raised his palm.

"No need to act contrite, if that's what you really think," he said. "Regardless, I'm sorry. Truly. But if you hadn't interrupted me in the midst of my explanation, you would've heard me say that I would never recommend you do anything else, that you're as suited to be a physician as any of the rest of us."

He sighed before continuing. "I should have challenged Fredericks immediately rather than allowing him to believe I agreed with him at first. I should have told him that his viewpoints are archaic and offensive, but the truth is that he's right. I'm on the brink of failing his class. Father will kill me if I do. He's already threatened to withdraw me once, not to mention that the Iota house can't survive the slightest misstep from me without losing our charter. The dining hall fire last year isn't exactly something that can be forgotten."

I laughed before I could help myself. The edges of Will's coattails had been intentionally set on fire by one of his brothers at the annual veterans' memorial candlelight service, though the Iota Gammas all cried accident when the board inquired about it the next day—Grant had sworn that Iota Gamma wouldn't tolerate anything close to Masonic rituals, after all. The other five pledges had been hazed the same way, but the difference was that the rest of them had taken note of the heat radiating from their backsides before they'd walked all the way across campus and into the dining hall for dinner. No one had said a word to Will—until he leaned against a skillet of bacon grease left over from breakfast—a measure that started a small fire that the cook was unable to stifle before it made ash of half the kitchen.

I composed myself and touched his arm

"You know that's not really what I think of you," I said, conceding my anger mainly because I knew he was telling the truth. "Regardless, I wish you would've taken up for me without hesitation."

"I know, and I'm sorry. Oh, and Happy Birthday," he said. "I'm sorry it's been so tense. I'd planned to ask if you'd like to meet for dinner before, well, this morning."

"That would be lovely," I said. "Thank you for remembering."

"Of course I did," he said, offering me his arm as we walked back toward the main hall. "Where would you like to dine? There's the dining hall or . . . I suppose we could try to fetch a coach to Green Oaks if Miss Zephaniah would permit it on such short notice."

Downtown Whitsitt was only made up of three establishments— the Five and Dime, the post office, and the soda counter. To dine out, one had to go to the slightly larger Green Oaks ten miles away, which only had two choices—Smith's or Russell's, both expensive steakhouses.

"The dining hall it is," I said, knowing there was no way Miss Zephaniah would agree to my traipsing all the way to Green Oaks in a coach with a man who wasn't my father or brother. The only reason she allowed women to ride unchaperoned to the Iota Gamma winter ball was because the ball itself was attended by faculty. "I heard they're serving turkey pie this evening."

We turned into the crowded hallway and Will squeezed my shoulder.

"Nearly as delicious as filet mignon." He winked at me, then ducked under a sconce as we wove through the stream of students heading to their final classes.

"Thank you for arranging such a classy feast in celebration of the start of my twenties," I said with a smile as we joined the crowd.

"Can I ask you a question?" he said suddenly.

I nodded.

"What was so important that you felt the need to sneak into the house in the middle of the night? Why didn't you come to me for help?"

I couldn't tell him, not now. My sisters were already angry with me, and Will wasn't exactly the most discreet.

"It was nothing you could help me with," I said quietly, and Will stopped in his tracks.

"Wait, Beth. It just occurred to me. You wouldn't—I mean—he surely didn't ask you to . . . in exchange for a favor," he sputtered, eyes boring into mine. I stared at him, open-mouthed, having no idea whether to laugh or find offense in the fact that he'd think I'd stoop that low. "I'd kill him, you know."

His eyes broke from mine, scanning the students around us as though Mr. Richardson would suddenly materialize.

"No, Will." I grabbed his forearm. "I mean, no, nothing happened. I only needed his connections for something. I'll leave the other . . . um . . . things to you."

"I appreciate it, though know this: I'm always honorable. I would never engage a woman in exchange for anything. That kind of behavior is repulsive and—"

"Hello Miss Carrington, Buchannan," said a voice behind us. I whirled around to find Mr. Richardson there.

"Richardson," Will said, extending his hand. Mr. Richardson took it without a glance his way, choosing instead to maintain his gaze at me. I opened my mouth, but no words came out. Mr. Richardson smirked, but he didn't look away, causing a mix of embarrassment and irritation to burn my cheeks. We stared at each other for what seemed like minutes before he blinked and turned toward Will.

"Did you get a chance to follow the freshmen I asked you to examine?" He removed his black felt derby and waited for Will's response. Will shook his head. What a strange question, I thought.

"Regrettably, no," Will said. "It's snowing. The last thing I want to do is scour the entirety of campus in the freezing cold to find five men who are likely just doing what we all do with our limited leisure time."

"What you do and what the rest of us do are very different, Buchannan," Grant replied. Even the way the man spoke to his friends came off as smug.

"Is that so?" Will asked. "I meant studying." His gaze wandered over my head, and suddenly a short man with a thin moustache tapped him on the arm.

"Mr. Buchannan, Miss Anne Cole would like a word with you." He gestured down the hall.

"Certainly," he said to the man. "Excuse me." Slapping Mr. Richardson on the shoulder, he started to walk away, before hesitating and turning back. "You enjoy your studies," he said, "and I'll be sure to enjoy enough of my leisure for the both of us, Richardson. See you tonight, Beth." Will winked at me, then flicked a lackluster wave at Mr. Richardson.

Suddenly I couldn't stomach my proximity to the man who had so callously disregarded me, and found my voice.

"So you don't trouble yourself with it later, I wasn't asking him to help me."

"Ah, I sense that our earlier conversation struck a nerve." He turned to face me and pushed an ebony curl back from his face. "Please let me explain my behavior, Miss Carrington, when I've not been confronted dead asleep and half-exposed."

"I'm listening," I said, wondering why in the world he'd wait for an invitation to continue.

"Right. Well, it boils down to the fact that—as you may know—my uncle is a congressman and quite traditional when it comes to his stance on suffrage," he said matter-of-factly, and then shoved his hands in the pockets of his gray tweed sack coat as though that were the end of the story.

"Do you share the same brain as your uncle, Mr. Richardson, or do you possess one of your own?" I didn't mean to, but the question came out in a hiss.

"Touché, Miss Carrington," Grant chuckled. "However, you have to understand that, regardless of my stance, which is honestly just shy of his very traditional view, I couldn't help you even if it did align with my beliefs. The college has always supported his political career, you see, and therefore sees me as a sort of representative of him because—"

I held up my hand to stop him.

"You're not being sincere," I said. "Your uncle is really quite ir-relevant, isn't he? The truth is that you don't want to risk losing what you have on campus. It's clear that you're rather fond of your pompous reputation and the spoon-feeding by everyone around you."

Grant shook his head. I knew I should walk away, that the only response I'd get from him now would be curt at best, but something inside wanted to hear Mr. Richardson's honesty.

"I'll tell you what," he said. "As insufferable as you are, you've caught my attention, so I'll do you a favor. You can accompany me to the annual Iota Gamma winter ball."

I blinked at him. Surely his invitation was in jest. I'd rather spend an evening emptying chamber pots.

He grinned. "What is it? You don't suppose this is the first time I've heard unfavorable things about myself, do you? Far from it, though you are the first woman bold enough to tell me so. I quite respect you for it, though I still, regretfully, don't agree. So, what do you say? Will you agree to go along with me?"

"Have you lost your mind?" I managed to say. "Why would I ever accept any sort of proposition from—"

"I suppose I forgot to remind you that it's a faculty-attended function," he interrupted. "If you're so determined to start your beloved women's fraternity, petition President Wilson yourself. He'll be in attendance."

6

IT WAS AS if my mind hadn't had a chance to process the question in time to stop my head from nodding. Finding myself just down the hill from Everett Hall, I'd endured an entire lecture and crossed campus in a daze, unable to explain how or why I'd agreed to be Grant Richardson's prize pony for the winter ball—though I somehow doubted that's exactly what I was. I glanced up at my attic window to find candlelight beaming through the glittering coat of ice. Lily was home. I'd have to explain to her that I'd agreed to the ball before word got around.

"Miss Carrington," a high-pitched voice croaked behind me.

"Yes?" I spun around, shocked out of my thoughts by the sight of Miss Zephaniah coming up the walk after me, with wisps of gray hair sticking haphazardly out of her old war-era spoon bonnet.

"You needn't startle. I simply saw you and thought I'd say how-de-do. I didn't see you at lunch." Her lips pursed for a moment and then she strode past me, huddling her thin neck in the folds of her weathered mink coat.

"I thought I had a touch of a cold. I didn't feel well, but I suppose I was mistaken because I've recovered," I said, half-running to catch up. "How are you today?" I attempted again. Under the sanctuary of the porch, she dusted the powder from her shoulders.

"To be quite frank, Miss Carrington, I'm a bit frightened," she said, stomping her black boots and sending packed snow sliding across the wood. I could see a throng of divinity girls through the windows. They were laughing and talking as they tied bonnet strings around their necks, readying for their weekly philanthropy. I couldn't wait until Beta Xi Beta grew in size. How lovely it would be to be among a large, like-minded group of women.

"I'm sure your roommate has informed you of my visit this morning," she said.

I shook my head. I wanted to hear it from her, to tell if a summoning from the president's office for my sneaking out was imminent. Miss Zephaniah never handled matters herself. Instead, she took her grievances directly to President Wilson, usually without mentioning it to the offender. I suppose she figured it would catch us off-guard that way, allowing no time for an excuse. I had to give her credit for the effectiveness of her method, though. Last year, she'd had a girl expelled for repeatedly sneaking a man into Everett Hall after hours.

"I have reason to believe that someone may have compromised our safety," she said. Her neck crooked my way and her eyes sliced through mine in the flicker of the gas light, as though if she stared hard enough she could worm her way into my brain. "You're not missing anything, are you?"

"We're not. At least that I'm aware of." A gust of wind blew through the narrow passage, and I glanced at the double doors, wishing she'd step inside so that I could follow. "What did you see last night?"

"I can't be certain. A hooded figure just over the hill. I was jarred awake by footsteps half an hour before, and made a round through the halls, but found nothing amiss," she said with a sigh. "I opened every door, checked every room. I know it wasn't the doing of one of you. At least I hope it wasn't. Expulsion does not please me." I couldn't tell if she sincerely believed that we were all innocent, or if she suspected me and wanted to gauge my reaction. She twisted the doorknob, but her palm slipped and the latch slung back into place.

"I'm certain it wasn't," I said. "We're all too serious about our studies to jeopardize our future." I hoped she would believe me. As much as I thought our fraternity important, as much as I wanted to make a difference at Whitsitt, I also needed to become a doctor. If I was expelled, my dream would be nullified. There weren't many traditional medical schools keen to admit women and even the few schools exclusively for women would doubtless balk at an application from a student who'd been driven out of her previous college due to poor conduct.

Withdrawing my ungloved hand from my coat, I edged the door open and followed Miss Zephaniah into the open foyer, past the horde of women. I smiled as I passed a group of girls sitting on matching damask longues, but my attempt at friendliness went undetected. They were so absorbed in each other that they didn't notice me—they never noticed any of us. Some of them were singing *Christ the Lord is Risen Today* and I couldn't help but hum along. The hymn was an Easter favorite, sung every year before the benediction at our church, First Unitarian of Chicago.

"The coaches have arrived!" someone shouted, and at once the girls were gone, leaving the foyer suddenly so quiet that I could hear the ticking of the old grandfather clock. Passing the floor vents steaming with heat, I started up the stairs, edging out of my coat. I was halfway to the second-floor landing when I heard a throat clear below me.

"There's one more thing, Miss Carrington." I stopped in my tracks and my heart began pounding. I clutched the cool iron banister and looked down to meet Miss Zephaniah's stare, praying she hadn't decided to accuse me. "Let me be blunt. I was coming from reporting an unseemly incident to the president this morning, when I happened upon you having a private conversation with that rabble-rouser, William Buchannan." She looked away from me for a moment as she removed her gloves. "It goes without saying that I disapprove of your association with such a man. His influence could have the power to ruin an intelligent woman such as yourself and—"

"He's an old friend," I said before I could stop myself. It was instinctual for me to defend him. I only wished he had had the same reaction this morning in class.

"I wasn't finished," she snapped, starting toward me but stopping short of the steps. "Did he mention anything that would suggest that the break-in was the doing of Iota Gamma? Everyone knows that they have little to no regard for the college. After last year's fire—started by your *friend*, I might add—I'm surprised they weren't shut down again. The board would have never stood for that kind of behavior if it weren't for their pet, Mr. Richardson, who is a heathen in the flesh, if you ask me. At the start of my tenure, the college and the church wouldn't have compromised their morals for anything." She wagged her finger at me as though I were contesting her. "Especially to defend an organization with the devil at its core. I told President Wilson he would live to regret allowing it, that he was only encouraging Whitsitt to fall prey to the same sort of scandal brought about by that young man's death at Cornell. The Bible says, 'thou shall not kill.'"

"No, he didn't mention anything of the sort," I said evenly. Her fear was the same sort of ridiculous panic that had ruffled the feathers of our normally reasonable denomination—most of the others, too—encouraging criticism of hundreds of perfectly devout men involved in fraternities across the nation.

"According to the president's secretary, Miss Bradley, your Mr. Buchannan is in charge of the pledges this year," she said. "Rumor has it that they've begun recruitment. If I find that he's put the freshman men up to this, I will go to President Wilson straightaway."

I took a breath and met her eyes.

"I didn't want to say anything for fear of startling you," I said, biting the inside of my mouth to keep from smiling.

Her eyebrows rose.

"I'm sure it's nothing," I continued. "Then again, remind me of the date today?"

"January fifteenth."

"Isn't it . . . well, never mind . . ." I trailed off. "Intelligent women don't abide such nonsense."

"What nonsense?"

"Lynette Downey. We all know that she disappeared on March 12, 1862, but during orientation last year, one of the girls I was touring with seemed to know more about her. She mentioned that her birthday was in January, January fifteenth to be exact. That date has haunted me since."

I shook as though the thought terrified me.

Miss Zephaniah's wrinkled cheeks seemed to go taut with panic.

"If you're suggesting that I saw an apparition, that's ridiculous," she crowed.

"I'm not suggesting anything of the sort," I said. "But it is rather coincidental, is it not?"

* * *

I laughed silently as I reached the second floor landing, glancing down once to find Miss Zephaniah in the exact place I'd left her, fingering the brim of her bonnet. I felt a slight bit guilty that I'd frightened her, but then again, I'd diverted her suspicion away from supposing the hooded figure could be me. The thought of my disobedience reminded me of Mr. Richardson, of my agreeing to attend the ball. I didn't want to tell Lily about it after I'd already betrayed our sisterhood to him, but I couldn't avoid her. Eventually, I'd have to return to my room.

"Miss Carrington." Miss Zephaniah's shrill voice rang up the stairwell one more time. "I forgot to mention that a letter's come for you. I'll go fetch it if you'll be so kind as to come back down."

I leaned over the railing to tell her that I'd get it later, but she'd already gone to retrieve it. Taking a deep breath of the air tinged with the overbearing scent of nearly two hundred women wearing rosewater perfume and the undercurrent of what I'd come to recognize as the gummy aroma of an old, drafty house, I headed back down the steps. Recently, the only letters I'd received were rejections for apprenticeship requests and a short one from Vera telling me she'd taken the liberty of giving my small attic bedroom in our townhome to Lucas, and asking where the key was.

"Here you are," Miss Zephaniah said, breezing out of her room with a letter.

"Thank you," I said, taking it from her. I tipped my head at her and started back toward the stairs. The left-hand corner of the letter held the stamped block insignia of the Cook County Hospital. I stared at it, waiting to feel the anticipation that came with a possible yes, but optimism was difficult after many dismissals. I ran my index finger under the seal, feeling the sharp edge of the paper slice across my skin.

"January seventeenth, Miss Carrington," Miss Zephaniah called out. I glanced back over the railing. "I took a quick look at the dormitory residents' log. Lynette's birthday was the seventeenth."

"Is that so?" I said. "If I believed in apparitions, I suppose that would confirm she's haunting us. You know the old saying—three days from birth, three days from death, the spirit roams the earth, longing for its last breath." I pulled the letter from the envelope and turned away from Miss Zephaniah, but not before I saw her face pale.

Dear Miss Carrington,

Regrettably, our apprenticeships have already been filled.

Sincerely,
Henrietta Rogers, Administrator

I shoved the letter into the envelope and tossed it into a small trash bin. I'd written to request a summer apprenticeship from every major hospital in Illinois, and thus far been turned down by Katherine Shaw Beathea, Swedish Convenant, and Mercy. I was beginning to wonder if I'd graduate with any clinical experience at all. At least Cook County had been polite. Mercy had responded with the sentiments that they found female physicians to be unnatural to the order of creation, and hadn't I heard the theories of Harvard professor Edward Clarke that women in strenuous courses of study would develop monstrous brains, puny bodies, and weak digestion? I ran my hand along the polished wood railing as I climbed the remaining steps to the fourth floor, to the only room occupying the rafters, refusing to give into the thought that I wouldn't be accepted anywhere.

I stared at the tarnished numbers on the mahogany door, *401*, before deciding that my best course of action would be to fling it open and come out with my news about the ball as quickly as possible. I clutched the doorknob and paused. I couldn't bear to look upon Lily's face shrouded in disappointment again.

I pushed the door open, the wood meeting plaster as the door slammed into the wall. Lily was reclining on her bed, her face eclipsed by a grammar book.

"Mr. Richardson cornered me in Old Main and asked me to be his date for the Iota's winter ball. I said yes because the president will be there, and I'd like a chance to speak with him about the possibility of a charter." The words came out in a quick cascade.

"And you couldn't schedule an appointment to speak with the president on your own?" Lily's voice was icy. Clearly angry with me, she didn't even bother to set down her book.

"You're right," I said, crossing to the armoire to hang my cloak. "But you know it would take months to get in to see the man by himself. Not to mention that he'd want to know the reason for my visit. Even if I lied to him initially, the minute I started speaking of the fraternity, he'd have me removed." The president wasn't known for his kind demeanor. "If I'm Mr. Richardson's date, perhaps he'll think—at least until Mr. Richardson tells him otherwise—that he agrees with the idea. He'd at least hear me out."

"Perhaps," Lily said. "You're going to have to tell the others though. Be prepared for more questions. You're making it hard for me to believe that you don't secretly admire him."

I removed my hat and placed it on the hook. I didn't know if I'd ever pined after anyone. I'd found men handsome of course, and had certainly felt a flutter of nerves when I'd had occasion to dance at balls, but admiration was a strong word, a word far removed from my feelings toward Mr. Richardson.

"Don't be ridiculous," I scoffed, unlacing my boots and then plodding toward Lily's bed, determined to convince her that I was sincere. "Mr. Richardson is so far outside my realm of interest that I—"

I stopped cold when I pulled the book from Lily's hands to see her face and eyes swollen from crying. In the year and a half that we'd occupied the same quarters, I'd never seen her this upset.

"Lily. What's happened?"

She refused to look at me. Her thumb ran back and forth over the edge of her quilt, which was tucked and folded in neat precision beneath her, eyes trained on the grammar book in my hand.

"Lily." I set the book down on the nightstand between our beds. Her tears glistened in the light from a lone oil lamp. "Please tell me." She remained silent, her head bowed. "Whatever it is, we'll get through it." I clutched her hand, knowing her problem had to be severe. She'd endured more than I could imagine in her life and when she spoke of her past, she was matter-of-fact. Her mother had abandoned her and her father when Lily was still a baby. Until she was four, her aunt took care of her while her father and uncle worked the lines in the Domino Sugar factory. But then her uncle and his family had moved west, and Lily's father was faced with a choice—cease work and move to the slums or give her a chance in an orphanage. She told me once that he'd visited daily at first, but that the visits quickly dwindled to weekly and then monthly ones. At the start, Lily would often fantasize about her mother returning, reuniting with her father who would immediately come for her, but she knew, the last time he visited, that that possibility was gone. He'd given himself over to the bottle by then and had barely been able to speak, but told her that her mother had run off with one of his friends and that she'd never loved either of them. The following week, she'd received a notice that he'd been found lying outside the door of their old apartment, having died from cirrhosis.

"Lily. Please." She met my eyes and began to sob, and she suddenly reached out and pulled me to her. Her arms constricted across my back as she buried her head in my shoulder.

"It's horrible, Beth," she went on. "I'm such a fool."

She broke our embrace and looked down again, fingers smoothing the dark blue stars on her quilt. She always tidied when she was out of sorts, a compulsion from her days as a maid at the Schrafft mansion.

"You're the farthest from a fool, Lily," I said. "But what is it?"

Lily took a deep breath, then wiped her face and looked at me. "Professor Helms." Her mouth remained open as if she'd meant to say more, but didn't have the strength.

"What about him? What did he do?" If he'd failed her, I'd take the case to President Wilson. I'd make him retract his marks . . . somehow.

"Beth, I . . . I think I'm with child."

I froze. Confusion overtook me.

"How? I mean, what do you mean? Who?" I stumbled over the words. Lily had always been firm in her belief that romantic gestures were reserved for marriage, a view I agreed with, and she hadn't told me of any feelings for anyone, let alone a connection so strong it had the power to render her with child.

"My cycle is late," she said dully, "going on a week. Beth, do you know how to tell for sure? You must have gone over it in your courses."

I heard the hum of her words, but couldn't believe them. How could it be?

"Surely it's nothing but a fluke, Lily. You've barely eaten as of late. Perhaps you've lost weight and your cycle is adjusting." I spoke quickly, sure that she was mistaken.

"I pray that that's the reason Beth, but I—"

"In any case, you've yet to tell me about the man you love, though I'll admit I'm not fond already given the knowledge he's compromised you."

Her face paled.

"I've told you already, Beth," she said, her voice barely audible. "Professor Helms."

Shock struck me through, and I stood gaping at her before anger took over.

"What? How . . . how did this happen?" It couldn't have been voluntary. He was at least thirty years her senior.

"It was right before break. He took me aside to tell me that he knew I was failing and could help." Lily pulled her knees into her chest. "He asked me to meet him after class. I-I thought he was going to tutor me."

"He's going to answer for this," I said. Without thinking, I stepped forward and slammed my fist into the bedside table. The small purple vase I'd bought her for her birthday last year swayed and she reached out and steadied it.

The disgusting vision of his advances crept into my imagination and I nearly gagged. I wanted her to tell me exactly how he'd ruined her so that I could have him fired or locked up, but Lily burst into tears before I could get more from her. I couldn't bear the thought that Helms was free, unscathed by the atrocity of what he'd done.

"It was my decision." Her voice was soft.

"Look at me and tell me that." I forced calm, knowing my outrage was only making matters worse. I scooted a pile of books toward the foot of her bed, and sat down to listen.

She sighed.

"It was my decision."

"Are you in love with him?" I asked. As much as I couldn't fathom it, perhaps she'd fallen for him. She'd never had a beau and I knew she was fairly shy when it came to men. Perhaps Professor Helms had wooed her and she been so taken aback by the attention that she'd agreed.

"Are you insane?" She half-laughed, half-barked the question. "Have you spoken to the man? He's about as dull as an ox and equally as attractive. When I met him that day, he told me that he was going to fail me. He said that I wasn't making the grades to pass grammar, that he had no other choice but to fail me and recommend my removal from the college . . . unless I would allow him to . . ." Her face burned, lips pinching shut as though she couldn't bear to complete the sentence. "I agreed. I . . . I didn't see another choice. But, in the end, he didn't . . . we didn't . . . he was pressed against me when . . . when he heard someone coming to the door. It was a classmate, Mitchell King, and . . . and he asked so many questions that I was able to leave before . . ."

Fury sparked within me.

"He blackmailed you. And you didn't think it wise to tell me, tell anyone else, what he'd offered before you decided to do it?" I snapped. The moment I said it, I regretted my tone and knelt down beside her. Why hadn't I recognized her fear or anger before this? I'd seen her that evening. Had I been so absorbed in myself that I'd overlooked her despair? "I'm sorry, Lily, and I really doubt you're with child if he didn't . . ."

"He was turning in the marks that night," she said. "My final exam wasn't good enough to bring my grade higher. I didn't have time to consider it; I just did it. I thought I was saving my future, not jeopardizing it. Right before Mr. King came in, he made me swear I'd never tell anyone and that if I did, he'd deny it and fail me anyway. He said no one would believe me regardless . . . save my handful of friends, and that they didn't matter. I hadn't any father or relatives to threaten him." She began to cry again—silent tears that trickled down her cheeks. "I know you say I can't be expecting, but . . . but he was so close. Surely things like this have happened before."

"Lily," I said. "Unless he reached a certain advanced state in the act . . . a state he clearly couldn't have achieved without . . . without actually engaging you, there's no way you could've fallen pregnant."

I was basing this on what I'd read in my midwifery textbook. The only things I knew about reproduction came from that course. My mother had only briefly mentioned it and Father had certainly never enlightened me on the subject. "It must be your worry muddling your cycle. And he's absolutely wrong. You have me; you have my family. I could tell my father. I could have him report Helms to the board."

I started toward the dressing table, toward the drawer full of paper. I would send my father a telegram. As distant as we were from each other, he'd be disgusted by what Helms had done to Lily. He'd have to help her.

"No. It would still be my word against his."

I paused. She was right.

"Then I'll tell Will," I said, the answer suddenly dawning on me. "I'll have him find Helms. He'll make him regret what he's done."

Will wasn't opposed to solving problems with fists, in fact I thought he likely enjoyed them. He'd been involved in several fights back home in Chicago, most a result of his quick temper, and had always left the offender worse for the wear.

"No," she said evenly. "You won't do that either. You won't tell anyone." I started toward the door, thinking I'd disregard her, but she lunged for my wrist. "Beth, I said no."

"Then what will you have me do? Sit by while he goes along with his life?"

"Yes. And you may as well know that if I find that I'm with child, I'm planning to raise the child myself."

"Don't be ridiculous. I already told you that that possibility is highly unlikely," I said, but I worried that despite what I'd read in my textbook, I was wrong. None of us knew much about the ins and outs of having children. Most of us had only been provided with the understanding that a proper woman practiced self-reverence, modesty, and self-control.

At once a solution dawned on me. I'd heard whispers of women taking a mixture of herbs to restore the menses. The actual dosages hadn't been published anywhere, of course, but I recalled overhearing my mother speaking to a neighbor about her daughter's recent rebellion and the abortifacient solution that cured her "situation."

"Lily, I'd have to do a bit of research, and like I said, I doubt you'll need it, but I believe that with a mixture of ergot of rye, pennyroyal, slippery elm, and rue, you could—"

"No. I know you're going to be a physician and I know that until quickening life isn't present, but if I find out for sure that I'm in a way,

I'll not do that." She glared at me. "Have you ever been witness to a termination? I have. My roommate when I was fourteen fell pregnant by her employer's son. Our headmaster forced her to take a solution of pennyroyal, tansy, and cotton root bark. She came in the middle of the night for my roommate. Held her down with leather straps while a nurse pried her mouth open and forced in the solution. For a week and a half she remained in bed vomiting and soiling herself and fainting. She cried through it all, begging me to help her, begging anyone to ease the pain. She was never the same after that."

As horrible as it all sounded, I wasn't sure which was worse—to raise a child out of wedlock or undergo the temporary pain.

Lily plucked her book from the bedside table as though she meant the conversation to cease. "If it comes to it, I'm going to raise the child, Beth. I've made up my mind. I don't have a family and I've searched my whole life looking for an anchor that isn't there. As much as I loathe my mother at times, I know that if she returned, I'd accept her. I love her even though I don't know her. I could never abandon any child of mine, even if that meant I'd be ostracized by everyone else." She ran her hand down her braid, fingers tangling in the loose bit at the end.

"All right," I said. I was angry, so angry at Professor Helms. I couldn't understand why she'd not want to punish him, but there was nothing I could do. "We'll wait and see, but come what may, we'll do this together. I'll help you."

"I know." She opened her book and began to read as though the issue had been resolved. "Would you do me a favor?"

"Of course," I whispered. All of my strength seemed to flee from my body in the course of those two words, and I felt my shoulders slump.

"When you go out for dinner, request that the campus courier bring me a meal. I'm not feeling up for going down." I nodded and opened my armoire, surveying my two evening dresses before selecting the one I'd worn the least—a brown wool costume with a bit of Chantilly lace on the hem.

"Beth. I was serious," she continued. "Don't tell Will. Leave it alone. This is the only way I can bear to continue here, do you understand? I will have my diploma."

Her jaw locked for a moment and the resolute, strong woman I knew came back into view. I wanted to argue for vengeance, but stopped my thoughts knowing she'd already decided, and began to undress.

"Fine," I said, smoothing my corset cover and fashioning my skirt around my waist. "But the moment he threatens you again . . ." I trailed off and the edges of her lips turned up.

"That's fair. But he won't. Come May I'll be finished with his class. I'll never speak to him again."

I did up my bodice quickly, hurriedly doing up the buttons down the middle.

"I wish I could have him fired or strung up and beaten."

"I know. I do too." She rubbed the skin at the corner of her left eye, burned pink from crying. "But if you wouldn't mind, I'd like to be left alone."

I crossed to the door, having no idea how to contain the rage and melancholy and revulsion I felt.

"Would you do me one more favor before dinner?" she asked. "Find Mary. Katherine too. Call a meeting for this evening directly after dinner. I think I'd like to tell them what's happened to me. To be entirely honest, I was managing quite well until I realized I could be with child. I need you—all of you—especially until I know for certain." She mustered a smile.

"And if one of them slips and tells someone? You said that if Helms finds out you told, he'll fail you."

"No. They won't. They're my sisters and I trust them." Snapping the book shut, she pivoted off the bed and opened the top drawer of our night stand. Withdrawing a bottle of clear liquid, she uncorked it and took a long draw, nose wrinkling as she swallowed the fizz. "It's sparkling water. Mary had them fill a bottle at the soda counter in town. It's supposed to settle the stomach," she explained, holding the bottle toward me.

"No, thank you." I'd had a carbonated water only once, with my friend Sarah before a meeting of her mother's suffrage group. The bubbles had itched my nostrils so intensely that I'd sneezed for the next thirty minutes.

"In the meantime, have you learned of any tests in your classes, any way to tell pregnancy for certain?" Lily asked.

"No. I'm sorry. Well, actually," I said, recalling an article I'd read in the *Boston Medical and Surgical Journal*, "there's one strange test that they say is fairly accurate."

"Good. What is it?"

"You have to urinate on wheat and barley seeds over the course of a few days. If the wheat sprouts, it's a girl, if the barley sprouts, it's a boy, and if neither of them sprout, you're not expecting."

Lily huffed.

"That's ridiculous."

"But it might work. If you want to try it, I can sneak around in the kitchen tonight. The dining hall will probably have both and—"

"Absolutely not," she said, interrupting me. "I've already lost enough dignity. I'll not subject myself to some nonsensical experiment, expressing myself on crops."

"I understand," I said, stepping into the hallway, and away from the pain etched on her face. "I'll go speak to the girls and I'll see you tonight."

7

WILL HAD BEEN waiting for nearly half an hour by the time
I'd tracked down Katherine and Mary and made my way to
meet him. I took a deep breath as I passed under the arch, wishing
I hadn't made plans for dinner. I wasn't in the mood, even if it was
my birthday. I glanced across the circular quad to the whitewashed
wooden dining hall—the original building first used for instruction at
the college's inception in 1853. It now looked terribly out of place in
the midst of the newer red brick and limestone buildings. Even though
one of the lanterns on either side of the door had been extinguished,
I spotted Will immediately. He was a head taller than the other three
unfortunate men waiting outside for a lady. He was also the only one
who'd deemed a meal at the dining hall a formal enough occasion to
wear a top hat. Leaning against the iron railing along the stone steps,
he fiddled with his overcoat and then looked toward Everett Hall on
the hill, no doubt wondering if I'd show up.

A rotund man standing beside Will began to shift his feet from
side to side, blowing breath into his gloved hands. His discomfort
made me want to tell him to get inside, but I knew that even if I did,

none of them would listen. It was a known fact that the founding men of Whitsitt had always lingered outside of the dining hall, waiting to open the door for the ladies they were meeting. The tradition had stuck. The gesture was nice, but absurd in this frigid January.

Will removed his hat and smoothed his blond hair. An unremarkable man on the other side of the doorway scuffed the toe of his boot against the rail, clearly irritated by the wait. As I approached, I heard Will attempt to engage the man in some light conversation.

"First time courting a lady?"

The man glared, but Will smiled, not bothering to straighten from his position against the rail. "They're not always the most punctual and—"

"No," the man snapped. "It's not my first time." He kicked at a bit of ice on the edge of the step. "And I'm not courting her. I simply asked her to dinner. She's a friend. There's a difference, you know."

"I'm aware," Will said. "I hope she comes." Will knew full well why the man was being so short with him. He was worried he'd been forgotten. But Will enjoyed getting under people's skin. He found it entertaining. "Ah, here's mine now." He swung down from the steps to take my arm. "Miss Carrington, good evening."

"What're you doing?" I said under my breath. I wasn't in the frame of mind to play along tonight. Will didn't answer, but escorted me past the man to open the door and practically shoved me inside. I jerked away from him. "Stop it."

"I apologize, m'lady," he said with a smirk. "I suppose I was overzealous in my desire to get away from him as quickly as possible. That was one of the gentlemen I'm to shadow for Iota Gamma. Don't mention it to anyone. I'm not supposed to tip anyone off as to who the prospective pledges are, but I'm sorry to say that that one isn't going to work."

"How do you know?" I asked as we made our way down the narrow hallway, past several framed maps of Illinois on the wall. "You don't even know him." I knew I was projecting my anger on Will and took a breath, trying to contain it. The building smelled of buttery pastry and roast turkey, and though I wasn't hungry in the least, my stomach rumbled.

"He's too smug." Will stopped at the cloak closet, edging out of his overcoat before reaching to my shoulders to help me out of mine. "And pompous," he whispered behind me, leaning into my ear as the man in question suddenly appeared without his date. Will tipped his hat at him before handing our coats to the attendant. I gave Lily's dinner order to the maître d', and started toward the dining room at the end of the building, not bothering to wait for Will. He'd hardly given the man a chance. He'd made a snap judgment. The same treatment Mr. Richardson had bestowed upon me. The manner was all too familiar, reminding me of my father, and I didn't wish to associate with men like him.

"Wait, Beth, I—"

"That makes sense," I snapped when he caught up, "because none of you are either smug or pompous."

Will's eyes narrowed.

"I didn't say that we didn't already have brothers with those unfortunate qualities," he said, lingering on "unfortunate." "Sometimes people deceive you at the beginning, you know. It's just that we'd prefer to keep the pretentious out, if we can help it."

"And these guidelines come from the most imperious of them all, I'm sure. The pot calling the kettle black, is it not?"

Will let a ragged sigh escape his lungs. He turned into the dining room, glanced across the heads of at least one hundred others eating and talking, and pointed to a small table in the corner beneath a window.

"Sit there while I fetch your pie," he said. "And then you're going to tell me exactly what it is that's ruined your birthday this time."

I did as he said and started toward the table, wracking my brain for a reason other than Lily's calamity to excuse my mood. Lost in thought, I struck the edge of a chair at the end of one of two long banquet tables with my leg. I winced.

"Are you all right, miss?" A thin man with flaxen hair and doe eyes looked up at me from his chair among a group of what appeared to be freshmen men. He looked strangely familiar, though I couldn't place him.

"Yes. Thank you. I apologize for the interruption," I said.

"It's not a problem. Enjoy your meal." I tipped my head at him and settled into my chair a few feet away. Stretching my hands toward the fireplace, I glanced out of the window at the ice and snow piled up on the sill.

"Here." Will plopped down in his chair and set the steaming pastry in front of me with a clatter. The scent of rosemary and thyme seeped into my nostrils and I plucked my fork from the tablecloth in front of me and grinned.

"A smile. Did you have a change of heart in the two minutes it took me to retrieve your dinner from the kitchen?" he said before shoveling a substantial bite of his own pie into his mouth.

"Not quite."

"All right. Then, out with it. What happened?" He balled his napkin and set it on the table next to his pie, as though he wouldn't take another bite until I told him. I'd seen his father make the same gesture; he had done it the night he'd convinced my father to allow me to attend Whitsitt. He'd asked my father if he didn't think me important and then he'd ceased eating until my father found the silence too uncomfortable and mumbled that of course he did.

I stared at Will, wracking my brain for a response, but none came, so I was silent.

"Is it me?" he asked. "Are you still angry with me for this morning? I'm sorry, Beth. I truly am."

"It's not you," I began, then stopped abruptly as the one excuse I could use dawned on me. "I was denied an apprenticeship with Cook County Hospital, my fourth rejection."

"I'm sorry, Beth, but you'll find a position. You're smarter than all of us, not to mention more ambitious. I haven't even written a request letter yet." He smiled and reached out to pat my hand. Will was planning to be a family physician like his grandfather—a man who, despite his age, was still caring for nearly two hundred households in Newark. With his connections, it would be easy for Will to secure an apprenticeship. "I know it's frustrating, but don't let it ruin your birthday."

I nodded, but stabbed my fork into my pie a bit too forcefully.

"That's not it, though," he said. "Tell me the truth." I swallowed, the lumpy peas squeezing past the knot in my throat. I'd run out of anything I could tell him—and then, I remembered the ball.

"When you left me with Mr. Richardson earlier, he asked me to the ball, and I—"

"I shouldn't have done that. Did he force you to accept his proposition because of what you shared with him this morning?" Will's eyes flashed. "Beth, if he did, tell me now."

The thought of force made my skin crawl. My face must've paled because Will rose from his seat, sending its wooden legs tipping back to land with a clack on the floor.

"No," I said quickly, my words stopping him. Will took a moment, but he sat down. "You keep saying that about him. Is he in the habit of compelling women to do things for him?" I continued.

He scratched at a sideburn and shook his head.

"Well, no. Not directly at least. He's got money, and with it comes power, but no." He dug into his pie again. "He must be rather fond of you." Will shot me a humorless smile. I figured he was wondering about Mr. Richardson and me, about what I'd shared with him that I hadn't told Will. Surely Will wasn't jealous.

"I assure you, he's not," I said, turning the ring on my right pinkie. My mind wandered back to Lily and her tear-streaked face, and I swirled my fork in the creamy center of the pie, watching the carrots rise to the top and then sink to the bottom. "I think he feels bad for the way he treated me earlier. I can't figure why he'd ask otherwise . . . then again, I can't figure how or why I accepted either."

Will dabbed the napkin to his lips.

"Perhaps, as much as you want to act as though you despise him, there's an attraction."

"No," I said. I loathed that anyone, especially Will, could assume I'd melted in Mr. Richardson's gaze.

"Or perhaps the reason you refuse to tell me the reason for your midnight visit is because the two of you are having a secret affair," he laughed. His words felt like worms twisting in my gut. All I could see, though my eyes were directed at Will's face, was Professor Helms pinning Lily to his desk. My palms started to tingle and I clenched the stem of my fork.

"I've-I've got to go," I said under my breath. I had to get back to Lily. I shouldn't have left her alone in the first place.

"No," Will declared. He stood, grasped my shoulders, and gently guided me back into the chair. He held me there for a moment, his gaze boring into mine. "You're going to tell me if he's harmed you, do you understand me? Otherwise, I'll have no other choice but to hurt him. I live under the same roof as the man. He can't hide from me."

"I'm telling you the truth. I have no idea why he'd ask me. We're not having an affair." My voice was shaking and I tripped over the last word. I'd never even kissed a man. I could feel the heat of my anger rising in a warm blush from the base of my neck. "Please sit down."

Will did as I asked and glanced at my fingers clutched hard around the silver. He reached over and forced my hand open, plucking the fork from my grasp.

"You're not all right, and I need to know why. I promised I'd be there for you from the start, and I meant it."

"I suppose it's not anything in particular," I said slowly. "It's everything today—Professor Pearson's comments, your response, my apprenticeship rejection, the whole thing with Mr. Richardson. It's just been difficult, that's all." Sitting back in my chair, I stared at the fire, knowing if I looked at him long enough he'd still see through me.

Will adjusted his white bow tie that had somehow become lopsided. "I'm so sorry for my contribution and I wish I could make it better."

"Tomorrow is another day," I said. I sighed, hoping to dispel a bit of the tension across my chest.

"That it is," he said. "And if it would help to settle a bit of your troubles, I'll say that being invited to the Iota Gamma winter ball isn't the worst fortune you could have. It's quite an affair." He took a sip of his water, and his brow furrowed for a moment. He'd taken Miss Cable last year and I knew that the memory of such a happy time with her had to be an unwelcome intrusion.

"Perhaps. Though I would rather go with you," I said. "I'm afraid I'll be rather lonely with Mr. Richardson. We have nothing in common and it's almost certain that I won't know any of the other girls."

"Strawberries and cream? I heard it was your birthday." The cook, Mrs. Perry, appeared at my side holding a small bowl.

"I would love some. Thank you," I smiled at her before she quickly set the bowl in front of me and disappeared.

I pushed the bowl into the middle of the table and gestured to Will to share, but he was toying with one of his cufflinks—an Iota Gamma rose.

"What would you think about me asking your roommate Miss Johnston to the ball? I'll do it gladly if it would make the evening more enjoyable for you."

"I would love that. But isn't there another girl you're thinking of asking?" I thought of Lily's distress. Attending a ball wouldn't award her the calm she needed right now, but I knew she'd feel pressured to accept Will's invitation for my sake. Not to mention, Lily and Will were only mildly acquainted and they weren't a match by any means. While Will was light-hearted and carefree, Lily was serious most of the time and as straight as a nail when it came to her ambitions.

He took a bite of the strawberries and cleared his throat.

"There was, in fact, a girl I thought to ask, but she's already committed." He winked at me and settled back in his chair. "I'd be honored to take Miss Johnston if you think she'd accept my invitation."

"I suppose there would be no harm in asking," I said. After all, her attendance would mean we'd be at the ball together when I approached President Wilson about Beta Xi Beta.

"I'll write her a letter first thing tomorrow." He stood and held his hand out to me. "Feign surprise when it arrives."

* * *

I waited for a few minutes until I knew he'd disappeared through the wall on the other side of campus before I set out across the quad myself. I couldn't afford to risk him seeing me walking toward our chapter room. My eyes trailed the path to Everett Hall, wondering if I'd see any of the girls making their way toward Old Main, but I didn't. Pulling my hood over my hair, I balled my freezing fingers into the warmth of my palms. Even the heavy wool pockets couldn't keep the cold out.

The lanterns on either side of the chapel door flicked light on the clock just below the steeple. I gasped. Seven-thirty-five. No wonder I hadn't seen anyone coming down from the hill. Once again, I'd lost track of time and was late. I snaked diagonally across the quad toward Old Main. I glanced under the arch leading out of campus to the Iota Gamma house, finding the entire place dark. *Where were they?* I knew Will had mentioned that they were starting recruitment, but as they hadn't chosen anyone yet, it was too early for their initiation traditions . . . whatever they were. What was it then that would merit the entire chapter's absence? My eyes scanned the brick base of the white house, stopping when I spotted a bit of light coming from a tiny window in the cellar. But as interested as I was, I couldn't delay tonight's meeting any longer.

I looked behind me, found no one following, and edged into the door at the back of Old Main. Immediately wishing I'd remembered to bring a candle, I stumbled blindly through the rubble.

The basement was freezing in the chill of night. I heard scurrying all around me. I made it to the closed door, guided by the little strip of light escaping from the seam. Raising my fist, I struck the door once and lingered, then tapped four times, and rolled my knuckles across the wood.

"Who knocks on the door of Beta Xi Beta?" Lily's voice filtered through the door, barely loud enough to be heard.

"It's your sister, Beth," I said. The door creaked open and Katherine's gaze met mine, her tears catching the candlelight. Lily had already told them. Without preamble, Katherine embraced me, the intense scent of rosewater perfume engulfing me as she did. Slightly shocked by this immediate display of affection, I clutched the bunch of ivory lace along the back of her bodice and glanced over her shoulder at Mary's cloaked figure draped protectively around my roommate. They both smiled at me, though Lily's face looked gaunt, as though she was in danger of collapsing at any moment, and Mary's eyes were fully hidden by the cloak's hood and a black blusher veil, making her look as though she'd just come from a funeral. In part, I suppose she had—the death of Lily's innocence.

"She's decided to keep the child . . . if she's with child, that is," Mary said, as though I hadn't been privy to any prior conversation. "I told her that I doubt she's fallen pregnant. I overheard Mother speaking to one of her friends once, and it's apparently quite difficult to do even if a woman is trying for a child. And since she and . . . and since they were not made one, it would be highly unlikely. I know you said the same." I nodded. "I also said that if by chance you and I are wrong, Mother would know of several reputable practitioners—despite the procedure being contrary to the law—if she'd like to resume her cycle, but she'd have nothing of it."

I didn't reply, knowing Lily desired no further discussion on that matter.

"If I do have a child, the child and I will be just like you and Judith," Lily said to Mary, mustering a bleak smile.

"Yes. Always the best of friends," Mary said with a wink at me, knowing I knew the truth. The evening after Christmas, after Lily had retired, Mary and I had begun a conversation about parents. In reality, Judith and Mary hadn't always been close. After Mary's father's death, she had been raised in part by an elderly neighbor, Miss Verona, who'd cared for her while Judith fought for the cause. For years, Mary didn't understand her mother's absence and snubbed the movement because of it—it had only made her a subject of ridicule at school. But then, on her seventeenth birthday, Judith decided to take the day off. She'd worn a floral costume instead of her token black and they'd gone to high tea at the Palmer House Hotel. She hadn't even corrected the waiter when he'd mistakenly called her "Mrs." On the way home, however, the coach passed by a middle-aged woman crumpled next to a brownstone and Judith had immediately ordered the driver to stop.

The woman was one of Judith's organizers, and she'd been beaten by her husband so severely that her nose had been broken and her cheek crushed. Together Mary and Judith ushered her to the hospital, and for the next month, the woman lived with them. That day, Mary came to understand her mother's passion for women's rights, and began to wear black in kind.

"Well, now that Beth's here . . ." Mary trailed off and left Lily's side to pluck the candlestick from the desktop. "Gather 'round," she said, gesturing to Katherine and pushing my cloak into my hand. I ducked into the garment, realizing Mary had already fastened my wreath pin to the fabric at my chest, and reached to clutch Lily's hand.

"Right before my mother's friends decided on a mission for the cause, they'd stand in a circle in our living room and pass a candle," Mary continued. "At times, they'd sing a song as they went, but the meaning was always the same—whatever the secret they shared, whatever danger the mission entailed, it would be kept in solemn confidence between them. I propose that we adopt this ritual as our own . . . if that would be all right with the rest of you."

"I think that would be lovely," Katherine said.

Mary started to hum the beginning notes, but Lily stopped her.

"A moment first?" Lily bit her lip, looking over the three of us. "Thank you, all of you, for loving me. For responding in love to my news instead of judging what I'd done. I've always wanted a family more than anything, and I've found it in you."

"That's what sisters are for," Katherine said quietly. "Any of us could have found ourselves in a similar fix."

My thoughts immediately flashed to Will, and I wondered, given Katherine's lenient morality, if she'd ever fallen pregnant. Then again, I had no idea if she'd ever actually been intimate with a man, and she didn't seem like she'd be ashamed to say if she had, given Lily's circumstance.

"And I'm thankful you're mine." Lily grinned at her. "I'll make a cloak for you as soon as I can procure the fabric, and a wreath, too."

Katherine blinked back tears and smiled back.

"Now," Lily went on, "I told all of you that I didn't want any of this mentioned to Professor Helms or anyone else, but I didn't say that I didn't want the score settled."

"Thank goodness," Mary breathed. "I would have gone along with your wishes, but I want, more than anything, to send him straight to hell. How shall we do it?"

"We're not going to kill him literally," Lily responded. "Only in a roundabout way." Her hazel eyes met mine straight-on. "Beth, I want Beta Xi Beta to take on new members. I want this fraternity to grow in numbers and resilience until we are so powerful that the board will be forced to listen to us, grant us a charter."

I opened my mouth to agree with her, but she held her hand up and continued. "And when that time comes, when our voices are officially worth the weight they're due on this campus, I'll be long finished with Professor Helms's course. Our influence will be like the Iotas, too great to ignore, and then we'll find a way to ruin him." The last words came out in a sharp whisper.

"Then let's begin," Katherine said. "In the meantime, I'll pray for nothing more than his calamity."

All three of them looked my way.

"What is it?" I asked.

"You're our president," Mary said, the edges of her lips turning up in a grin. "Perhaps you were right to seek Mr. Richardson's help after all. What was it about Iota Gamma that convinced the board to approve them? How did they recruit new members when they were meeting in secret? We've never done it of course, and will need a process."

I had no answer to either question.

"We can't just take anyone that'll have us yet, Beth, seeing as we'll still have to be covert. We're not exactly supposed to be meeting," Lily said.

"That's true, but there are only five other women in non-traditional concentrations. We only have five prospective pledges to begin with right now. I say we consider all of them," I said. "And I'm not quite sure how they did it. Mr. Richardson would never tell me anything about their procedures, even if I asked. He doesn't qualify as a friend and it's clear that he holds Iota's secrets close to his chest."

"If we could somehow figure their methods, their rituals, how their relationship works with the college, we could copy it," Katherine said. "Industry does this all of the time with great success. My father's fortune was won by following the example of another grower and—"

"Why would we want to do that?" Mary asked, though my mind was in a different place for a moment. How would Katherine know about industry? Though she'd said her traditional reputation was a ruse, the use of the power she said it wielded wasn't immediately clear.

"Beta Xi Beta should be entirely unique, set aside from the Iota Gammas, a true sisterhood built for camaraderie, betterment, education," Mary continued. "The only reason I suggested looking to their strategy for engaging new members is because they're quite good at hiding their interest until they're certain. In any case, their process isn't the cause of their clout. Mr. Richardson is."

"I disagree. True, the Richardson family has always elevated Iota Gamma's influence, but Iota Gamma has been a force on this campus since its inception. It only requires a look through the *Cardinal's* archives to see that," I said. We'd been required to learn the history of the school's medical program through the paper's records, and I'd ended up fascinated, perusing the papers from before the war. "The first mention of Iota Gamma was in 1854. They won a case against the school insisting that Hawthorne's *The Scarlet Letter* be permitted for study—an important victory because one of the founding Iotas had been caught with a copy."

"Very well. They've always been influential; but I still don't understand why we'd want to imitate them," Mary said.

Suddenly I recalled a bit of information from the introductory pamphlet we'd been sent upon acceptance.

"Because, beyond the fact of tried organizational success, if we modeled our fraternity after the Iota Gammas, there'd be no difference between our fraternity and theirs . . . other than the sex of our members. Their practices have been examined by the board and found satisfactory. If we mimic them, it would give the board almost no room to deny us," I said. "As it is, our social experience as women outside of the divinity course of study is nonexistent. If I fail in convincing President Wilson otherwise, I say that we—"

"During your romantic appointment with Mr. Richardson?" Mary snickered. Lily had apparently told the girls about my agreeing to accompany him to the ball.

"Hardly. But, for some reason he asked, and seeing as how it will award me an opportunity to speak to the president about our establishment . . ." I paused, smiling to myself. Regardless of secret societies being forbidden, it gave me great joy to know that we'd begun our fraternity before any sort of approval. "I thought that I should agree to it. With your blessings, of course."

"As long as President Wilson isn't made privy to the knowledge that we've already begun," Lily said. "I would rather loathe getting expelled after what I've done to stay."

I squeezed her hand.

"Of course I'll keep our secret in confidence. In any case, I'm hoping that the president is a reasonable man and hears our plea, but if, as I'm expecting, he doesn't, we'll have to find another way. If we recruit the right women, mass expulsion won't be an option, and modeling our fraternity's bylaws and actions after Iota Gamma certainly won't hurt. It may give us enough strength in both establishment and numbers that we could petition the college with the argument that not allowing us to organize would be in violation of Mr. Everett's intent to integrate the sexes. Is that what you meant earlier, Katherine?"

"Yes. And if I'd been able to get a word in edgewise, I would have explained myself," she said, glancing at Mary, who didn't seem to notice.

"Why couldn't we go to the board with that argument now?" Lily asked, her face suddenly lightening with the possibility.

"Right now there are several things against us," I started. "All they would see when they examined us—if we weren't exiled from Whitsitt on the spot for organizing in secret—would be a glaring suffragist agenda, four women out of nearly forty on campus, a damp basement room, homemade cloaks and membership pins, and a measly two-sentence pledge—"

"That we should discard immediately," Mary said, avoiding Lily's gaze by adjusting the positioning of her blusher.

"Why?" Lily's eyes narrowed at Mary and I coughed, hoping Mary would drop it. This was not an argument we needed to have. Not now.

"Never mind me." Mary slapped on a counterfeit grin and laughed. "Everyone knows I love the pledge. I was just making sure you were still with us, old girl." She elbowed Lily in the ribs and swiveled her head to face me. "So, to begin, what have you picked up from the King of Flirtations, Beth?" The abrupt subject change worked. Lily's focus snapped to me and I laughed under my breath at Will's title, wondering what Katherine thought of it.

"Not much, unfortunately. All I know is that Mr. Richardson has asked him to follow five select freshmen around campus to see if they're worthy of the Iota Gamma letters. I'm not sure how they decide on the men, but I did witness him screening one tonight. He gave the gentleman the benefit of one interaction." I shook my head. Given how utterly disgusted I'd been by Katherine until just this morning, I was aware that our perceptions were often tied into our prejudices. "I'd like to think we'd give our potential members more than one opportunity."

"Are you sure that's Mr. Richardson's method of doing things or Mr. Buchannan's?" Lily asked. Will did have a reputation for being impulsive and a bit slapdash.

"Likely Will's," I conceded. "But anyway, we need to find a directory. I'll wager that's how Mr. Richardson finds them, likely choosing those with important last names first."

"Or it could be by impression," Katherine ventured with a smile. "Perhaps the brothers are asked to be mindful of recruitment during fall semester, looking for any freshmen that affect them. Then, the prospective selections are discussed in chapter meetings and the few that all of the brothers agree on are secretly observed during the spring semester."

Mary cleared her throat.

"You aren't speaking from conjecture," she said. "How do you know?"

Katherine let go of my hand and twisted the wispy blonde curl at the side of her head.

"It might be because my younger brother made an impression on Mr. Samuel Stephens last semester and Mr. Stephens warned him to be on his best behavior come January."

"Mr. Stephens? Will's friend?" I asked. I couldn't believe that one of the brothers would so readily share the fraternity's schemes.

"Of course. Don't seem so surprised, Beth," Mary answered for her. "It's widely known that if you'd like a secret to be known all over campus, tell Mr. Stephens." She twirled the candle in her hand, making me wonder if she'd been in Mr. Stephens's confidence before. But why would she? As far as I knew, she hadn't done anything remotely scandalous except spend an evening in New York City with Roger McDonnell, a fellow student keen to become a conductor, to watch Theodore Thomas lead the Philharmonic—but they'd been chaperoned by one of Miss Zephaniah's friends in the city, hardly a romantic rendezvous.

"It's true," Katherine said. "Mr. Stephens told my brother, James, everything—prefacing all of it with an oath not to snitch, of course. The problem, though, is that James isn't the least bit interested in joining, so he had no qualms telling me about it."

"Iota's recruitment strategy seems fair," Lily said. "Perhaps we should adopt it for our own and spend the next week observing the other girls. Each of us could take one of the others—"

"James could probably be convinced to play along with the Iotas if we wanted him to. He could let us in on their secrets. He owes me a favor," Katherine interrupted. She smoothed the lace at her bodice and waited for us to consider the idea.

"You really suppose he'd do that for us? What if he changes his mind?" I asked, finding the prospect of a secret informer in the Iota Gamma house a risky one. Mr. Richardson was too charismatic. He won everyone over eventually.

Katherine shook her head.

"You don't know James. He's much too intelligent to succumb. He had a rather strange experience with the Masons when he was younger and walked out on initiation. He found it too hedonistic and cult-like. He assumes that the fraternity is the same and stands with Whitsitt on the ban."

"And you don't?" Mary asked, gesturing around the circle.

"Of course not," Katherine said, wrinkling her forehead as though it was the most ridiculous question she'd ever heard. She lifted my hand and Mary's. "I've joined a family. Unless I'm sorely mistaken, you aren't going to ask me to pledge my soul to the devil or pay nearly one hundred a semester to wear your letters."

"One hundred? Each semester?" Lily spat.

Katherine nodded.

"That's the rumor," she said. I watched this exchange with a bit of trepidation. Eventually, we'd have to collect dues as well. That's how houses were bought and bills paid. But there were more immediate hurdles to overcome right now. "Plus, James and I are so different you'd wonder if we were actually related. You'll see when you meet him."

"Do you think this is the wisest plan?" Lily asked, lips pressing together for a moment as though she wasn't sure. "If he gets caught and tells anyone about us . . ."

"We're not going to force him to help," I said. "And we may not need him if the president agrees to hear our proposal. But if I fail with President Wilson and Mr. Sanderson agrees, it'll give us another chance to establish Beta Xi Beta as a real fraternity."

"He'd have to swear secrecy," Lily said.

"That goes without saying," Katherine said.

A bit of hot wax dripped onto Mary's hand and she winced, shifting the candle to the other. "So, we'll wait to hear back from Beth following the ball next Friday, and if she fails, we'll approach Katherine's brother."

"That's right," I said, and Mary sighed.

"Now that that's settled, we'll pass the candle. It will forever be our symbol of trust and honor," she said, staring down at the flame. "I'll begin to sing a little song I wrote in music theory earlier and we'll pass it. When I stop, Lily will blow out the candle and her confidence will never be broken."

We were silent for a moment as she passed the candle to Katherine.

"After the flame is extinguished, after the secret is kept," Mary sang in her smooth soprano. Katherine handed the candle to me and I held it for a moment, feeling the contrast of the cool wax and the slight bit of warmth from the flame. "After we've left the chapter room, after our hands have unclasped." I handed the candle to Lily and watched her stare at the light. Her mouth pursed for just a moment and then she smiled to herself. "Four hearts are opened, if you knew them all—you would know our sisterhood is stronger than them all."

The last note echoed in the room and a hush fell over us.

"Thank you," Lily whispered, her eyes glistening. She inhaled and then let out a breath. The flame flickered once and then died, leaving the four of us with our hands gripped together, watching the thin trail of smoke dissolve with the words we'd said.

8

I HEARD THE DISTANT hum of a pitch pipe from where I sat by the fire in the dormitory's gathering room and glanced up from a diagram of the organ systems in my physiology textbook. The old cherry grandfather clock next to the fire began to toll seven, and I hoped it was running fast. As grateful as I was to have the opportunity to speak with President Wilson in a few short hours, I was still not looking forward to being on the arm of Mr. Richardson. I hadn't seen him since he'd asked me to be his date to the ball two weeks ago, and I had a feeling our interaction would be uncomfortable at best.

Lily absentmindedly tucked a stray tendril back into the mass of hair gathered in a loose bun at the top of her head as though she hadn't heard the pitch pipe. Perhaps I hadn't either, though the sudden squealing coming from the eight divinity girls gathered across from us told me otherwise. The loudest girl, who had a beautiful face and a ready smile, was Luetta Grace. I'd never spoken to her, but I'd heard her name so often in passing that I'd eventually figured out who she was. I eyed the group, confused at their willingness to involve themselves with fraternity men. *Whitsitt had examined Iota Gamma and found them satisfactory to the Christian lifestyle*, I reminded myself, but even so it seemed peculiar when the college and the church seemed to abhor fraternities as a whole. Then again, at least one of the Iota Gamma brothers was studying divinity. I vaguely recalled him offering the dinner prayer in place of Chaplain Blair one time last semester.

The breathy whistle came again and I pressed my elbow into Lily's ivory kid leather gloves. I knew what was coming next, and the prospect of being serenaded by a man I didn't even like made me wish I could disappear. Lily, who had clearly thought my nudging an accident, kept her eyes on the fire in the floral tile-lined hearth as she smoothed her gold silk dress across her stomach. As Mary and I had predicted, she'd resumed her menses last week, and every time she'd tried on the dress—an old costume of Katherine's she'd had sent from Kentucky for Lily—I noticed her running her hand along her torso. She was overjoyed that she would remain free for a while longer, a schoolgirl without the complication of motherhood and the reminder of the despicable Professor Helms.

Lily shook the skirt, which she'd carefully embellished with *mousseline de soie* ruching, over her crossed legs. Footsteps echoed from the hall to our left and I took a deep inhale of the cedar smoke.

"Lily," I whispered. "They're coming."

"I'm so excited," she said. "I've never been to a ball besides the all-women cotillion that the orphanage held. I know the steps to most of the dances, but I've never had a proper partner before. What if I—"

Her words were suddenly eclipsed by the baritone of four male voices.

"Iota Gamma Sweetheart, you are the silver rose that grows in winter."

Will wasn't singing, I could tell, because the song was beautiful, without a trace of his monotone. I closed my eyes for a moment, enjoying the smooth, deep harmonies, trying to pretend that I was enjoying a simple choral performance.

The floorboards creaked beneath the Iotas' procession as they made their way down the hall. I tried to ignore the nervous fluttering in the pit of my stomach and forced my body to relax, slouching against the old leather couch. I'd been to plenty of balls, but none with an escort. Will and I had attended a few together, but his sister had always been with us and it had hardly been a romantic pairing anyway. Perhaps I'd never been asked because men thought me dull or plain. The constriction of the dress I'd asked Vera to send from home protested my slumping, black silk bodice bunching the glass straws and pearls embroidered in a leaf motif. I forced the insecure thoughts from my mind, wondering why I'd decided to think them in the first place, and straightened my posture. It didn't matter what Mr. Richardson thought of me. He would never be my beau.

I opened my eyes and looked up at the bare wooden beams along the ceiling forty feet above me. The room was the original structure, part of a former lecture hall they'd converted to a dormitory thirty-two years ago, when the number of female students studying at Whitsitt outnumbered the Green Oaks Unitarian families willing to house them.

"The loveliest blossom in a world that's cold and dim." The song went on, voices growing louder as they neared. A blotch of black appeared in my peripheral vision and I turned toward the frosted windows. I didn't want to watch the men enter the room and be forced into the uncomfortable predicament of how long I should gaze upon Mr. Richardson before he stood in front of me. I let my eyes rest on Lily instead, and was shocked at what I saw. Her face was flushed, lips turned up in a grin. Nearly turning to follow her stare, I stopped myself. I didn't have to. She was looking at Will. I'd seen him have that effect on a young woman many times, but never on her.

When she'd received his letter, she'd been as perplexed as I thought she'd be at the prospect of attending a ball on the arm of Will

Buchannan—they were only acquaintances, after all. She told me as much, worrying that she feared she wouldn't be up to conversing if she found she was with child. The only thing that had made her change her mind was the reminder that she'd be there with me when I spoke with President Wilson. The thought that she was actually looking forward to it now hadn't crossed my mind.

Mr. Richardson's stare burned my face, and I looked away from Will and Lily to meet his gaze. He was dressed in a black tuxedo with silk lapels and a silver bow tie like the rest, but somehow he was more striking than all of them. I wished he'd break eye contact, but instead he smoothed his dark curls, smiled, and knelt in front of me. I heard a snicker and looked up to see Will laughing. In contrast to Mr. Richardson's elegance, Will hadn't bothered to shave and looked as though he'd pulled his tuxedo from a heap of soiled laundry.

"Miss Carrington." My eyes snapped back to Mr. Richardson in front of me as he slowly reached for my hand.

"Miss Carrington," he started again, "may I have the honor of—" Unable to meet his stare for a moment longer, I stood up, interrupting the formality. I'd already accepted; of course I was going.

"Yes," I said abruptly. "Now, let's get on with it." I started toward the foyer, not bothering to turn around to make sure he was behind me. Will hooted. I'd lived up to the warning he'd doubtless issued Mr. Richardson.

"Am I that intolerable?" Mr. Richardson's voice came from behind me. A few girls coming in from dinner stopped at the base of the stairs to stare. Unable to tell if he was embarrassed or angry, I shook my head, but didn't turn to face him. I stepped into the cloak closet to retrieve my mother's old fox fur, but he circled my wrist and pulled me back. "Really, Miss Carrington. Am I?"

I studied his face for a moment. His eyes glistened as though what I'd done had amused him.

"I'd prefer you call me Beth, and no," I said, though I was a horrible liar. "I mean, I suppose not."

Mr. Richardson plucked the coat from my grasp and stepped behind me, fitting it over my shoulders.

"Oh. So you're not sure," he said softly. "Well then. Why ever did you agree to accompany me?" Mr. Richardson laughed as he pulled his jacket down over his broad shoulders and strode past me toward the door, where he fitted his top hat on his head, and flicked his wrist at Miss Zephaniah, who stood at the entryway. "Miss Zephaniah," he acknowledged without respect or formality.

"Mr. Richardson."

"Ten o'clock," he said. "And no inappropriate conversation or contact while in the coaches unsupervised or we will be strictly repri manded. Yes, I know."

Miss Zephaniah nodded and then slunk back against the wall. As irritating as I often found her, I doubted she merited Mr. Richardson's contempt.

"I'll see you then," I said to her. Her eyes were narrowed to a hawk's glare in the shadows. "She didn't deserve that," I whispered to him as he opened the door and a frigid gust of wind whipped over us, catching the large ostrich feather in my cap, nearly sending it flying from my head.

"Yes, she did. She had a sister of my best friend from home expelled two years back for trespassing in her room," he said as he reached over and situated my hat. "For the record, she wasn't. She was on her way to ask Zephaniah a question, found her door open, and stepped in to see if she was available to talk. In any case."

"You didn't try to stop her expulsion? Surely you could have." Perhaps he hadn't wanted to, I thought. Perhaps she'd been a former sweetheart and he didn't truly mind her absence.

"I didn't know about it. Neither did she, before she was called to the president's office and swiftly escorted back to Milwaukee. By that time, the paperwork had already been submitted and there was no undoing it." He flexed his open hand and I took it, glancing out at the lawn. It looked just like a Currier and Ives print. Five covered sleighs lined the drive and bells jingled on the horses' reins as they pranced beneath the lantern-light in the snow, waiting to take us to the abandoned colonial gathering hall—a venue between Whitsitt and Green Oaks that the college used for nearly all of its formal functions. Stunned by the sight, I barely registered that Mr. Richardson was leading me forward.

"It's beautiful," I said, before I had a chance to stop myself. I didn't want him to think that I was enjoying myself at all. I cleared my throat, remembering his question I'd left unanswered. "Because you promised me a favor."

Mr. Richardson's breath billowed out in a cloud in front of us, and he tucked my hand into the crook of his arm.

"What?"

"You asked why I agreed to accompany you. It's because you're doing me a favor. You know I need to speak with President Wilson."

The driver climbed down from his perch at the front of the sleigh and let us into the coach. I reveled in the warmth of the cab, stealing a glance at Mr. Richardson as I did. He looked at me as though I'd recited a joke. I didn't understand his merriment. I hadn't been the least bit pleasant; in fact, I'd been altogether rude.

"The better question is, why? You won't help me yourself, so why would you do me a favor?" I asked as he climbed in. Leaning out of the open door for a moment, he dusted the flakes from the top of his black hat before taking the tufted leather seat across from me.

"Perhaps it's because I find you captivating, Beth Carrington," he said with a raised eyebrow, then looked down to adjust his bow tie, which was already perfectly arranged.

I laughed.

"No you don't. You don't know me."

"I know you well enough," he said. "You're honest. To a man like me, that's more enchanting than the loveliest face . . . not that yours isn't lovely, too, of course."

"Honesty isn't exactly a rare quality. I can't help expressing my thoughts around you anyway," I said. "You're infuriating, Mr. Richardson."

He chuckled.

"Thank you, but please call me Grant. And, actually it is. Quite a rare quality, I mean. At least for me." The sleigh began to move and the bells jingled steadily with the horse's swift trot. He lifted his index finger to the window beside him and began to draw on the frozen pane. "You know who I am."

I didn't conceal my annoyance.

"Because everyone should?"

Grant drew his finger upward, rounding out what looked like a pillar with a large base and quickly added a cross on top.

"No," he said, his voice nearly a whisper. "Because it seems that everyone I've met on this campus already does."

"It seems that in your case, it's an advantage, not a problem. But perhaps I'm mistaken." I looked down at the white chiffon lining my bodice. His sudden melancholy confused me. It was unnerving and completely contradictory to the overconfidence I was used to from him.

"It's not," he said. "Not an advantage, I mean." He paused as though he wanted me to ask him to elaborate, but I didn't.

I couldn't understand why he'd sought me out, why he wanted my company in the first place, but the thought that he found me enchanting was obviously not the reason. "Do you know what that is, Beth?" He gestured to the window pane.

"No," I said.

"It's a chess piece, the king. That's what I am."

"Of course you think of yourself that way—the most desirable, valuable player on the board. It's quite humorous that I thought you were actually attempting a conversation involving the slightest bit of humility. You're nothing but a—"

"Please stop." His hand found my knee and before I could move it he leaned forward. We were so close I could smell the coconut and palm oil in his hair. "That's . . . that's not what I meant. You're right. It's the most desirable piece on the board, but why? Not because it's intelligent, witty, or honorable, but because it has power, and the players will stop at nothing to capture it."

I didn't know what to say.

Grant sighed. "My apologies. I didn't mean to fill your evening with my problems, but you wanted to know why I asked and, in a way, this is it." He prodded the drawing with his finger. "For three and a half years, I've been the recipient of flattery and bribery from everyone I've met. At times it's cloaked in friendship, at times respect, but never honesty."

Suddenly, the carriage was uncomfortably quiet save the dull skidding of the blades and the distant jingle of bells.

"I needed something from you too. I still do." I suddenly felt strangely ashamed that I'd taken advantage of him, even though I knew that given the opportunity I'd do it again.

"I know," Grant said. "But you asked me straight away and when I chose not to give it to you, you didn't succumb to groveling or worse, enticement . . . Though you did nearly cause me to piss myself when you snuck in that night."

I looked away, the image of Grant in his nightshirt materializing in my mind. And when that faded, the memory of his haughty response punctured the warmth that had overcome me.

"I didn't know how else I could get you alone," I said evenly, unwilling to pretend that I remembered our introduction fondly. I stared out of the window, though I couldn't see anything through the frost beyond the intermittent glow of street lamps. The drive seemed to take much longer than it should have. A train whistle blew in the distance, signaling the eastbound train that would make its way to Chicago in a matter of six hours.

"I knew then that you were different," Grant said.

"You made me feel like a fool that night."

"I apologize for that. You have to understand though, Beth. I'm trying to explain. When everyone wants something from you, you come to expect it, and sometimes you simply wish it would stop. I didn't intend to offend you. I was being honest when I told you that I didn't agree with your cause and therefore wouldn't help you myself, but *would* assist you in finding a way to speak with the president alone. Regardless of my beliefs, I think that everyone should have the opportunity to voice their ideas and—"

"I don't understand. You say you disagree because of your uncle's stance on suffrage, and to an extent, I follow your mentality, but what's your position? Is it that you believe women aren't intelligent enough to need an outlet like a fraternity? Or perhaps you don't think that we should be educated at all?" I realized my voice was rising, and stopped there. As angry as he was making me, I knew that my rage was in part because his calm disapproval reminded me very much of my father's— though even he'd been influenced into allowing my education.

"On the contrary," Grant sighed, running his thumb along the scrolled copper lining the carriage door. "Everyone knows about my father, our company, and my uncle. Somehow, my mother's influence seems to have slipped by without a thought. My mother is of Spanish nobility, second cousin to King Alfonso. When she married my father, it was fairly well known that she was a fortune hunter. Her family had a title, but no money left, so . . ." Grant trailed off and for a moment the cords of his neck tensed. "Nevertheless, after some time, I believe she truly did fall in love with my father, but that was after he gave her the reins to his company."

"He did?" Grant's father was widely regarded as one of the most successful business tycoons of his time. An innovator in coal harvesting, he'd bought up nearly all of the coalfields in Virginia—and now West Virginia—and worked with the Carnegies and Fricks to power the country from his lush mansion on New York City's famous Fifth Avenue.

"A little known fact. My father doesn't like to admit that he's been emasculated by both love and my mother's intelligence. No one knows that he's not the one in control. My mother is a genius." He smiled, though his eyes were void of any of the light I'd seen earlier. "And I don't really know her. You see, my father handed her the power six months after the birth of my sister, Clara. I was two at the time and mostly raised by our *au pair*, as we all are, but my mother supposedly made regular visits throughout the day, as did my father. When he gave her the company, she left. She's lived in Richmond since. She's come home thirteen times in my life. My father, as you can imagine, is lonely and regularly takes mistresses." He said the last bit matter-of-factly, as though nothing of this confession was strange in the slightest. "Since then . . . well, I'll never succumb to cowardice like my father, and I'll never agree that women keen to have a family should pursue a career."

I shook my head, shoving the litany of offenses I felt at his assumptions to the back of my mind.

"I'm sorry for your loss, Grant. I truly am. But campaigning for our stupidity as a sacrifice to our future husbands and children is the most narrow-minded, idiotic thing I've ever heard."

"That's not what I meant!" He jerked forward, raising his voice. "There's value in educating women—personal wellbeing, first and foremost. I'm not saying that women should sit idly like brainless peons. What I *am* saying is that, whatever they do, the family should remain first priority. If women are tempted to relinquish that responsibility, who will pick it up? Certainly not men. And I know I'm not the only one of this opinion. Some of the girls studying divinity aren't intent on a degree, but a husband. They know that understanding is important in a marriage and that mothers equipped with learning are their children's best teachers."

Despite the cold, I felt heat prickling my skin.

"Your mother is just one person, one case, Mr. Richardson," I said, ignoring his praise of the divinity girls. "Plenty of modern women balance both."

"Is that so?" He shifted his weight, causing the cab to rock slightly. "Name one."

"Elizabeth Blackwell," I said, choosing not to elaborate that the first female doctor in America was a spinster.

He took a moment to respond. Perhaps he'd never heard of her.

"The good doctor has never married, Miss Carrington," he said with a tight smile.

"Even so, there are plenty of women who work in the factories or in seamstress shops every day, lest they be forced to live on the streets," I argued. "And I'm certain that at least a sizeable majority of them are good mothers."

"That's different. They *have* to work. They're not seeking it out because they want to. When they go home to their children, they pay attention to them, they nurture them. The women I'm speaking of are upper-class women who choose to work because it's their lifeblood. Look at Elizabeth Cady Stanton or Matilda Gage. Surely they're out of the home at speaking engagements much more than they're there."

"You're only speculating about their schedules, and, in any case, they're fighting for change for their daughters, for all of us. Not to mention, I've heard both are wonderful mothers."

I looked at Grant and knew the argument was falling on deaf ears, but I didn't need him to agree with me. He was nothing to me, to any of my sisters, and beyond the favor he was doing for me, he had no place in my life. Regardless of men like him, we would persevere. We would become more than the repressed women of our mothers' era, locked in our homes without a voice besides our husbands'.

The sleigh stopped moving and the bells tinkled at random as they settled. Grant cleared his throat and forced a smile at me. The carriage door opened and a footman in a maroon suit stretched out his hand. I took it and stepped out of the cab, Grant on my heels.

"Don't misunderstand me. I want to believe you're right," he whispered, "but I don't think it can be done without a price." His eyes searched my own for something—perhaps for a way to reconcile his beliefs. "You've somehow compelled me to help you anyway, regardless of the fact that the thought makes my heart wither." He sighed. "Even so, because I don't want you to meet the fate of those before you, because I don't want you to sacrifice future happiness for the hollowness of a profession, I don't wish you to succeed tonight, Beth. I hope you fail."

9

Of course he'd wanted me to fail. The statement didn't shock me, but the way he'd said it so bluntly made anger rise anew. Regardless of our argument, he'd wanted to escort me into the hall as a proper man should, but I'd gone ahead of him. I knew I'd have to concede at some point—I was his date, after all—but I could barely stomach him right now.

"Beth." Will materialized beside me as I crossed over the hall's foyer, Lily's arm in his.

"Are you—"

"You're upset," she whispered, interrupting Will. I knew Grant was mere paces behind me, so I shook my head in case he was close enough to hear this exchange. There was no point in causing a scene. He'd simply confirmed he was the person I'd thought he was.

"What'd he do?" I could feel Will's eyes on my face, waiting for an excuse to confront him.

"Nothing. I was cold. He was walking too slowly."

"I don't believe you." I glanced over at Lily and narrowed my eyes, hoping she'd let the issue drop. Lily loosened the collar of the Russian fur coat she'd borrowed from Mary with her free hand and pursed her lips as though she'd forgotten how adamantly Grant opposed us. Recanting our conversation in front of Will meant having to tell him why it mattered, letting him in on our secret. Will leaned in to me.

"I don't believe you either. The look on your face . . . you look as though you want to kill him. If he's insulted you in some way, I—"

"He hasn't. I told you. I was cold." I turned away from Lily and Will to join a throng of strangers flooding through the open double doors to the main hall. The venue looked lovely—obviously not the doing of the brothers. Silver candelabra were set atop lace tablecloths, the tables situated in a semi-circle around an open wood floor. Enormous bouquets of baby's breath and lily of the valley were placed randomly around the room on windowsills—beneath colossal silver Iota Gamma letters situated on a bare wall, and atop the closed lid of the grand piano in the corner of the room. I lingered on the woman at the piano bench, expecting to see Miss Rigby, who always played and sang for these sorts of functions, and instead spying a woman dressed in black. I squinted, trying to make out her face, when the musician's gaze lifted from the music to scan the room. I lurched from my position against the wall.

"Mary," I said when I reached her. Her lips lifted as she swayed to the melody of Brahms' *Rhapsody in B Minor Op. 79 No.1*, her fingers tripping over the notes. She hadn't come to Whitsitt to study performance, and I knew that the only piano instruction she'd ever had had been from her elderly neighbor and sometimes nanny when she was young. "What are you doing here?"

She didn't look at me, but laughed under her breath. Her shoulders rustled the black mass of feathers pluming from her demure trilby.

"Is that a *D*?" she asked me, nodding toward the music. "Thirty-first measure, second beat?" The candle next to her stand was dwindling, but I didn't bother to look—not that I'd know how to read the music anyway.

"You don't trust me, do you? I promised I wouldn't mention that we'd organized," I whispered.

"On the contrary," she said, leaning toward the stand. "Both you and Lily were attending tonight. I didn't want to be the only founding member absent when President Wilson agrees to charter us."

Mary flipped the page and stole a glance at me. "Go on then," she said. "Retrieve a drink or walk around a bit until you are calm. You reek of anger."

"I'm sorry." I fingered the black lace at the edge of my puffed sleeve. "Grant has—"

"Insulted you? Attempted to douse your enthusiasm?" Mary grinned. "You know what he is and somehow expected him to change his mind?" I watched her fingers clumsily search the keys as she began the lovely fluid notes of Mozart's *Piano Concerto No. 23*. I suppose, deep down, I'd thought there was a chance Grant could come to his senses. There had been a moment in the sleigh where he'd let the mask of arrogance and strength drop away in front of me, and for that moment, I'd let myself believe that he wasn't the man I thought he was.

"You're right," I said, my anger cooling. I looked over the sea of black tuxedos and fine silk dresses spilling through the doors toward their seats, and spotted Lily and Will at a table beneath the Iota Gamma letters. She was laughing hard, hand covering her nose and mouth before Will grasped it, stared at her for a moment, and kissed her gloved palm. A stab of jealousy startled me. Had he been lying to me about his feelings toward her? But why would he? Surely he knew I'd be supportive of his pursuit of Lily.

"How'd you convince Miss Rigby to let you play?" I asked, still scanning the room for Grant.

"I didn't have to," Mary said, her eyes glistening with mischief. "She was tied up . . . or rather all of the violin strings were. Someone had gone in and tangled them. There's a concert tomorrow, so it was imperative that she sort them tonight."

I laughed.

"How did you think to—"

"President Wilson. At the table to the right of Mr. Buchannan and Lily," she interrupted, jerking her head. Sure enough, I spotted his head of thick white hair, as fluffy and stark as a cotton blossom against the low light, as he helped his wife to the table, situating her indigo skirt in front of the chair legs.

"Won't you come sit next to me, my dear?" Grant's voice startled me. I conceded because I couldn't see an alternative, taking his outstretched hand. "Excuse us, ma'am," he said, tipping his head at Mary, who didn't bother to look up from her music.

I steeled myself for a verbal lashing for the way I'd stormed away from him, and prepared to tell him that his ignorance negated my respect. Instead, he remained silent as he led me across the room. I felt stares, likely those accidentally sliding from my date to myself, and stole a glance at Grant before turning away just as quickly. I didn't want to look at him, didn't want to appreciate the way his smile was returned by everyone it fell upon.

"Mr. Richardson, lovely to see you." The Vice President of Admissions, Mr. Stout, rose from his chair at a table in the middle of the semi-circle. "I see that we have the honor of your company this evening," he continued, gesturing to Grant's name in perfect calligraphy on a name plate next to mine.

"That you do," he said, clapping the man on the back of his brown jacket. I glanced across the room, disappointed to see that we were seated as far from possible from Will and Lily and President Wilson. "If you'll excuse us for a moment," Grant continued, turning from

Mr. Stout and those at the rest of the table and leading me a few paces farther to an unoccupied space against the wall.

"What are you doing?" I tried to pry my fingers out of his grip, but he tightened it.

"I'm doing you a favor that you've gladly accepted, so you'll listen for a moment," he said, his voice edged with fury. "And when we return to the table, we'll not argue in front of my guests."

I stared over his shoulder at the wait staff filing out of the kitchen instead. His free hand materialized on my chin and tipped my face to his. I jerked it away, veins coursing with fire, but held his gaze. Grant was smiling—likely to keep up the appearance that he was having a civil conversation—but his dark eyes were tapered and nearly black with anger.

"You came here tonight knowing how I felt about your . . . your fraternity." He whispered the last words. At least he had the decency to be discreet. Mary's words echoed in my head. I knew she was right about the kind of man he was. So was he. "And yet you somehow seemed offended, or rather, shocked, when I mentioned it. I told you about my family to explain my stance and you—"

"You told me that you hoped I'd fail." I slung my hand from his grasp as small group of divinity girls started to sing *The Doxology* behind me.

"Of course I do," he said, his tone suddenly warmer. "You're a smart woman. Surely you could deduce that I meant it as a compliment."

"What?"

"I don't need to repeat myself," he said. "If you don't remember what preceded that statement, which was my reason for saying it in the first place, then I suppose you'll never know."

I stared at him, vaguely recalling some mention of his desire for my happiness, but none of the rest.

"Very well. All I ask is that you remain somewhat civil to me for the remainder of the evening. After that, we'll not speak again," he concluded, holding out his hand to lead me back to our table. When I didn't take it, he took my wrist and enveloped my limp palm in his. "I'd hoped that if I was honest with you, you'd understand my point of view. It was my wish that we could at least coexist. The Republicans and Democrats do it often . . . though not very well, I'll admit."

"The fraternity is my passion. Your views are insulting," I said in a low voice, smiling at Will's friend, Mr. Stephens, who'd looked up from his seat at the table next to us. Across the vacant dance floor, I could see Will laughing, gesturing toward someone out of my view with his fork. I glimpsed President Wilson and then my eyes caught thinning salt and pepper hair and my breath hinged in my throat. Professor Helms. He was here. I'd thought the ball would only be attended by administrative faculty, the board, and a few select professors invited as special guests by fraternity officers. I never figured someone as unimportant as Professor Helms would make the cut. I looked back at Lily, but her back was toward him as she talked to an older woman I didn't recognize. I'd have to distract her. I couldn't let him speak to her. It would ruin her evening.

"And yet, I'm still willing to help you. Perhaps I've lost my mind." Grant's voice startled me back to the moment as he pulled my chair out for me. "Don't fret about the situation of our seats. You're looking at President Wilson. I've already spoken to him and the two of you will have a dance. I always cut in and take a turn with his wife, Merrilee, anyway."

"Good of you to finally join us," Mr. Stout said. He wiped a bit of chowder from his long brown beard and chuckled, setting his round belly to shaking. "I quite thought you were going to miss the first course. Chowder's wonderful."

"I'm glad to hear it," Grant said. "Apologies for our tardiness. Miss Carrington and I had some details to discuss." He shook his linen napkin and set it gently over his lap. I took a spoonful of the chowder and lifted it to my lips, savoring the sweetness of the corn and the salty bite of the ham. Seated as we were at the end of the table, our appearance had been ignored by the rest of the guests, who seemed to be absorbed in conversation headed up by a brother I recognized but didn't know. The man took off his glasses and gestured to one of the divinity girls sitting beside him, but I couldn't hear him over the hum of voices and music.

"So. Miss . . . Carrington, is it?" Mr. Stout started. I nodded and lifted another spoonful to my mouth, realizing as I did that the corn bore an uncanny resemblance to Mr. Stout's teeth, both in color and size. "What are you studying? And how did you manage to catch the eye of Mr. Richardson here?"

Grant choked on his soup.

"She quite startled me, Mr. Stout," he said quickly, nudging me under the table, as though he was worried that I'd recount the real story. Despite my feelings about Grant, I narrowly kept from laughing. "The woman has as much gumption as she does beauty. When I happened upon her, I was appalled that I hadn't noticed her before."

"I'm studying medicine," I added, watching Mr. Stout's face. I played a game with myself from time to time, betting how long it would take for a man's expression to go from jovial to stern at the discovery of my major. In this instance, it took five seconds, and then Mr. Stout's gaze settled on Grant.

"Is that so?" Mr. Stout asked as Grant concentrated quite hard on buttering a sweet roll. "And you're not worried that that line of work will, you know, interfere with her . . . abilities, if the two of you were to progress in your affection?"

Grant's face burned deep auburn, which surprised me. I hadn't assumed he could blush. Mr. Stout seemed to be waiting for an explanation as to why he'd waste his time on a woman whose delicate brain couldn't handle the mental stress of a medical degree. My fingers closed around the roll on my plate, and I wished, more than anything, I could bean Mr. Stout in the forehead with it.

Instead, I spoke up.

"That's actually a misconception—"

"I'm not concerned, actually," Grant interrupted.

"That's strange for a man who's clearly on the traditional side of suffrage," Mr. Stout said as a waiter deposited the main course in front of him. He inhaled the aroma of the roast pork and potatoes and licked his lips before turning to me. "Your beau may not have mentioned that I'm quite progressive in my views—one of the only faculty at Whitsitt to wear the badge—but it serves the college well. As I'm sure you're aware, we've got to take so many female students per Patrick Everett's arrangement."

"He's not my beau," I said. "We're only . . . friends, I suppose." The qualification was a stretch.

"Well, that's just marvelous. Broadening your horizons, are you, Mr. Richardson? I'm impressed." Mr. Stout, I noticed, spoke with his mouth open, the mix of potatoes and meat now a disgusting brown puree that sprayed from his mouth. My mother would have made him sit with his nose in a corner for at least half an hour for such poor table manners.

"I've always been an advocate of listening to other views beyond my own. You know that," Grant said, cutting a piece from his roast. His complexion had returned to his normal olive tone.

"How is it that you came to study medicine, Miss Carrington?" Mr. Stout asked. "I so often hear that our female students choose a conventional course—divinity, secretarial science, nursing, and the like."

"My mother died from a sudden and undiagnosable illness," I said, amazed that the sentence had come out without my voice shaking. "It hardened her heart, then her lungs. When she finally passed on, she was blue from oxygen loss. The physicians had no other choice but to stand by and watch her die." I paused to take a sip of wine, unable to look at either Grant or Mr. Stout, though I knew both of them were watching me, likely waiting for me to burst into tears. "Nothing they tried could stop its progression. I want to find a cure for illnesses like hers, or at the very least find a name for them."

As I spoke, I saw my mother's face, smiling at me as they'd wheeled her away to the hospital room, gray eyes like mine alight with the promise that they'd be able to cure her. She'd been having trouble breathing for several weeks before that, and our physician, Doctor Pines, had run out of treatment options at home. He'd recommended that she be admitted to St. Luke's Hospital, and she never came out.

Grant's hand gripped mine. His eyes were warm with a sadness I'd never seen. I blinked back the tears stinging my lids.

"I'm sorry for your loss, my dear. I'm sure your mother would have been proud of you," Mr. Stout said.

"It's all right. She died four years ago. Her only request was that I make something of myself, that I strive to be more . . . more than she was." I could barely articulate the last words, and by the time I said them, Mr. Stout had swiveled to engage in conversation with someone on his other side.

"'All that I am or hope to be, I owe to my angel mother,'" Grant said, squeezing my hand and then letting it go. "Though I doubt angel is accurate for mine, it seems that Abraham Lincoln's sentiments are perfectly fitting for yours."

* * *

The rest of the dinner passed in relative calm—at least when it came to our end of the table. Grant listened and chimed in on topics ranging from the tenderness of the meat to the speculation that a Chicago tailor was thinking of occupying a storefront in Green Oaks to the regimented schedule of the average Whitsitt student, but we didn't speak directly to each other. After our earlier words and the emotional exchange about my mother, there was little left to say. I licked the remaining cream cheese icing from my fork and took a sip of coffee as I eyed Will and Lily still smiling and laughing with the other guests at their table. Will's arm was casually draped across Lily's shoulders as if he did it often. Perhaps something had sparked, or perhaps despite their differences they were getting along much better than I'd thought.

I finished my coffee and noticed Grant looking at me. His gaze jerked away as I met it and he reached for his wine, finding just a thimble's share of purple liquid in the bottom of his crystal goblet.

"There's nothing—"

"You're out." We spoke at the same time, and he laughed.

"Isn't it a cardinal rule? That a glass should never be empty?" I asked.

"You're right. Sam," he muttered, leaning into the gap between our tables. Mr. Stephens bent his long neck toward him.

"Chief?"

"Where in the world did you acquire these waiters? They've left my glass dry." Grant laughed and Mr. Stephens chuckled, gesturing to the woman next to him.

"Meet Miss Anne Rilk," he said, letting the front two legs of his chair clatter back to the floor. "They've been graciously poached from her father's and grandfather's estates in Green Oaks."

Miss Rilk was quite pretty, with hair nearly as black as mine and a petite, plump frame. I'd heard her name, but couldn't quite place her. It was almost a given that I would have seen her before, but she didn't look familiar either. Perhaps she lived at home with her family.

"That's not all true," Miss Rilk piped in. "Some of them were re-cruited from other area estates by our employees. I obviously can't vouch for them, but I assure you that ours are the best in Illinois. I should know. I trained them."

Suddenly, it dawned on me. She was one of our potential pledges. Katherine had invited herself to dine with a table of freshman women one afternoon, and had mentioned she'd been impressed with a woman who had enrolled in business administration, but been forced to resign her place and enlist in secretarial science at the insistence of her father.

"Very well. I'll take your word for it," Grant said. "Any way you could beckon one my way for a splash?"

"Certainly, Mr. Richardson," she said and raised her hand to a young man balancing several discarded plates.

Grant turned back to our table. "Will you dance with me? I mean, once the instruments have a chance to set up." He nodded toward the door, where I saw a line of musicians in black filing toward Mary. "If you can bear it."

The waiter Miss Rilk summoned appeared at once, pouring Grant a sizable glass all the way to the rim. Grant held his hand up. "Thank you, sir. I doubt I'll be in need of more all night."

"Of course," I said. "How else will we cut in on the Wilsons?"

He nodded and leaned toward me with a half-grin.

"We have nothing in common and the lion's share of what we've said to each other has been shrouded in argument. I doubt you'll find the need to seek me out after tonight, so if we never speak again, Miss Carrington, know this: for as strange as knowing you has been, I've actually had quite a time."

The small orchestra struck an opening note and he stood quickly, extending his hand. "I'm the president. I'm required to dance first," he said as I stood, nodding at those seated at the tables around us as we crossed to the dance floor.

"And if I'd said no?" I asked, but my question was lost to the music.

"A grand Iota Gamma welcome from Mr. Grant Richardson and

Miss Elizabeth Carrington," an old man holding a horn in one hand boomed. I caught Mary's smirk as Grant spun me around, and nearly did a double take. Her expression was almost identical to the one Grant had given me before he'd led me out to dance.

"My name is Beth," I stuttered. I hadn't danced with a man alone—save being matched in a quadrille—since I'd taken a turn with Will at one of his friend's balls in Chicago two years ago.

"I apologize. I just assumed it was short for Elizabeth," he said, extending his hand out to where President Wilson sat with his wife. "President and Mrs. Gregory Wilson," Grant shouted, and the room erupted in applause. Professor Helms was turned the opposite direction from the rest of the guests, staring at Lily, whose face had drained of color. She started to stand, but Will caught her arm. He leaned over to whisper something to her. The roar of cheering and clapping died down as Mary started to trill on the keys.

"Thank you! Thank you all for coming," Grant bellowed, bowing over his one free arm. "It goes without saying that the brothers of Iota Gamma are forever indebted to every one of you for your sacrificial commitment to our future excellence. Now, let the true celebration begin! May your glasses remain full and your feet never stop."

He turned from the guests to face me.

"Grant, I-I don't think I can do this," I whispered. I could feel the whole room looking at us. I wasn't even sure of the steps. I started to pull away, but Grant held me tighter.

"It'll only be a moment," he said, his breath warm on my ear. "Once the song begins, others will join us." He pressed me closer to his chest. At once, I was acutely aware of the weight of his palm on the small of my back.

"Tell me the tales that to me were so dear," a baritone voice sang. "Long, long ago, long, long ago."

"Sing me the songs I delighted to hear, long, long ago, long ago,"

Grant sang along, drawing his cheek next to mine. Like he'd predicted, others slowly filed away from their tables towards the dance floor, but in the moment, I was barely aware of anyone else.

"Who taught you to waltz like that, Carrington?" Will's voice behind me drew my cheek from Grant's.

"Let me guess. You?" Lily asked, swatting Will on the arm. Will didn't respond, staring at me as if my eyes could tell him if my association with Grant had gone beyond whatever transaction we'd arranged. In fact, I was wondering the same.

"I'm sure she's rather enjoying the improvement in partners then, Buchannan," Grant said, not bothering to adjust our steps to meet theirs. Will laughed, drawing Lily's golden waist closer to him before dipping her dramatically. I remembered how it felt to dance with him—his sure steps leading me around his parents' sitting room to the scratch of a gramophone record playing Bach's *Waltz from Swan Lake*. His younger sister had been somehow bribed to operate the hand crank, but had given up after nearly an hour of my missteps.

"I've no doubt she's in the arms of a superior dancer," Will said, turning around us. "However, her enjoyment of it is yet to be seen."

Grant chuckled under his breath, pulled back and looked at me, as though to make sure I hadn't taken to crying or scowling in disgust.

"I'm having a fine time," I said, meriting a triumphant smile from Grant.

"I thought we'd be seated next to each other. I feel as though I haven't seen you all night," Lily said to me.

"I thought so too. We were, however, seated next to Mr. Stephens. I was introduced to his date, Anne Rilk. She's quite lovely," I said, meeting Lily's eyes. She grinned, catching my meaning. She danced on her tiptoes for a moment, scanning the room for Mr. Stephens and our potential pledge.

"We aren't allowed to be placed with our Iota Gamma families.

It's in the bylaws so that we're given the opportunity to converse with brothers whom we don't see as often," Grant said, interrupting my thoughts. My face must've exhibited my confusion because he chuckled. "Buchannan's my little brother. You see, each year, an older brother has the option to adopt a pledge, to help bring him up in the Iota Gamma way. Guide him."

I looked from Grant to Will and back again, wondering how in the world Grant had decided on Will. They were completely different.

"Grant was paired with me quite by default," Will said, grunting as he dipped Lily again and then drew her upright. "His first choice, Cyrus McCormick of the International Harvester McCormicks, withdrew to take over his father's company."

"Don't be ridiculous," he said, glaring at Will. "I chose you. I was impressed by your—"

"Ability with the ladies?" Will's eyebrows rose and Lily snorted. "We both know I wasn't chosen by the others and so, when Cyrus withdrew, you were forced to adopt me. You are the president, after all. Your role requires the noble task of clutching the hand of the outcast."

"I'm sorry," Grant whispered, as though Will's boldness was new to me. It was clear that he wasn't a man who spoke of things that shouldn't be mentioned, things intended to remain as quiet as issues dealt a real family. I respected that and hoped my sisters and I would follow suit. We were all searching for a family—each one of us hoping to remedy the absence or disappointment of our kin with Beta Xi Beta.

Grant spun us toward the Iota Gamma letters, in the direction of the president and his wife, who were dancing in relatively the same place they'd dined. Will and Lily followed closely, and then the crowd parted to allow us through, forcing us to pass Professor Helms sitting at a table alone. He looked up from his empty dessert plate as we went by and lifted a glass filled with what looked like bourbon to his lips. I glared at him, but he didn't notice, choosing to stare instead at Lily.

"Are you all right?" Grant asked me.

"Of course. I just saw—" Before I could get the last words out, I heard a crash behind me and turned to find Will on the floor behind Professor Helms's chair. The instruments kept on, thankfully, but the people around us fell silent.

I looked around for Lily, but couldn't find her anywhere. Will stood up, dusted himself off, and thumped Professor Helms hard on the back. The old man choked on his drink. His eyes watered as he coughed and he lifted his hand to draw what remained of his scraggly gray-brown hair back across the top of his head.

"Watch where you place your chair," Will barked, and started into the crowd of dancers. I began to walk after Will, but Grant caught my arm, seeming not to have registered the confrontation.

"It's almost time for the next dance."

I looked at him blankly and his brow furrowed.

"With President Wilson?"

"Oh. Oh, yes," I said, attempting to compose myself.

"Your friend will be all right," he said. "She just jerked Buchannan the wrong way and tripped him. I'm sure she's simply embarrassed." I forced my mind to focus on my impending conversation with President Wilson rather than satisfy the impulse to run after Lily. She wouldn't want me to miss this opportunity.

Suddenly, the horns and the violins stopped as Mary's fingers began to trip up and down the keys to a *mazurka* I recognized instantly as Chopin's *E Flat Minor*. The piece wasn't long. I'd only have six minutes at most to convince President Wilson to accept my proposal. Grant spun me out to face Professor Wilson and his wife. I glanced toward the dance floor, hoping to catch the steps. I couldn't remember past the first glide.

"Mrs. Wilson, may I have the honor?" Grant's hand clamped down on my arm. "You're losing time," he muttered to me before leading Mrs. Wilson away.

"Thank you for agreeing to dance with this elderly man, Miss . . ."

"Carrington," I said, taking President Wilson's outstretched hand. His eyes crinkled as he smiled at me, reminding me of my paternal grandfather—a soft-spoken man who was nothing like his son.

"Wonderful to make your acquaintance, Miss Carrington." At once I was filled with warmth, as though his resemblance to a man I found most dear was an omen that he'd grant my request. I heard Mary's fingers slip on the piano keys and knew she was watching me instead of the music.

"What are you studying?" President Wilson asked, hopping lightly on his left foot.

"Medicine," I said, echoing his step on the incorrect foot. "I'm sorry. I must admit that I'm not well versed in the *mazurka*."

"I don't mind. I remember your application." His kindness seemed to dissipate in that moment. "Beth Carrington from Chicago. The board decided to honor your request seventeen to fifteen. I was on the losing side. I didn't find the major fitting for a young woman, but the progressives won out in your case."

I wanted to explain, to argue as I did with every other person who questioned my aspirations, but I'd already done it once and didn't have the strength to do it again in the span of one night, especially with a man who had the power to breathe life into Beta Xi Beta. "Regardless of my opinion on the matter, are you finding your studies fulfilling?" he continued.

Lily and Will danced by and her eyes widened as they passed. I shook my head at her and President Wilson laughed.

"You're always able to change your concentration, you know," he said, mistaking my gesture as an answer to his question. "In fact, in your case, I would celebrate it."

"Oh, no. I'm quite happy with my studies," I said. "It's . . . something else."

"Please. Tell me," he said, crossing his left foot behind his right.

"The women here—how do I put it—find themselves feeling quite alone at times." My stays felt like they were suffocating me, but I had to do this.

He grunted.

"And how is that? There's an entire dormitory filled with forty-three women just up the hill."

"Living together is one thing, but we don't know each other. Thirty-three of the girls are studying divinity and the rest of us have such rigid schedules that there's no room for camaraderie, or even a conversation," I said. "I only know three other girls, one of whom is my roommate. It's a shame that those of us outside of the seminary aren't peers. Quite honestly, we need the support. It can be quite challenging to be the only girl in a classroom full of men. Even the professors make it clear they think us jokes."

He snorted as if I'd said something humorous.

"Some of our professors are traditionalists, Miss Carrington. I'll give you that. But, they don't play games with their students."

Either he was naïve to the matter or had decided to ignore it. I was guessing the latter.

"In any case," I started again. "I have a proposition that I think you'll be interested in hearing. It's a—"

"I don't intend to be rude," he said, staring over my head, "but I'm a guest. I've come here to enjoy myself. And, as a policy, I don't hear presentations from students outside my office or in the absence of the board. I'm certain you understand."

"I do," I said, narrowly stopping myself from begging for an exception.

"But if you'd like to bring your idea to the board next Tuesday at eleven-thirty in the morning, we'll hear it . . . we have to hear every student case." He pressed his lips together in a forced smile. "I happen to know that we've just had a cancellation in that time slot. You'll need to confirm with Miss Bradley, but as far as I know, it's still available. The one after that is sometime in June."

"Thank you," I said, feeling my desperation ease.

"You're welcome," he said, pulling away as the music concluded. "Now, if you'll excuse me, I'm going to retrieve my wife from that dashing date of yours."

President Wilson turned and disappeared into the mass of black jackets and pluming hats either idling on the dance floor waiting for the next dance or making their way back to their seats. I searched the room for Grant, eyes pausing on every small gathering of guests, figuring that wherever he was, he'd drawn a crowd.

I slogged back toward my table, half glad for his absence as I knew he'd ask how my conversation had gone and I couldn't bear to see his satisfaction when I told him that I'd been put off. Will stood next to it, talking to Mr. Stephens and Miss Rilk. He clapped Mr. Stephens on the back, and his eyes lifted to the dance floor, likely looking for Lily. I waved, but he didn't see me. He took two steps away from Mr. Stephens and then started to run toward the door, disappearing into the hallway next to it.

Without thinking, I took off after him. Will hadn't dawdled. He'd run toward whatever he'd seen, and if his reaction was any indication, he was about to do something he'd regret, something that could jeopardize his future at Whitsitt.

He was nearly down to the end of the hall by the time I spotted him.

"Will," I called, but he didn't stop. I ran faster, gathering my skirt in my hands.

"Get . . . off of her." Will's growl echoed down the hall and I heard the hiccup of a woman's sob before something heavy crashed into a wall. My heart was drumming quickly by the time I reached the last room. I glanced into the vacant office. Inside, I saw Will, his back to me, leaning over a limp figure on the floor. I froze. With one swift movement, he slung his fist down. I heard the dull crack of knuckles meeting cartilage, followed by a guttural yell from the man on the ground.

"One more noise and you'll regret what you've done for the rest of your life," Will hissed. I wanted to interrupt, to stop Will from doing any more harm, but was too frightened to move. A gurgling sound that I took to be laughter came from the floor. "All right. I warned you—"

"Will, stop!" I yelled, finally finding my voice. I clutched his arm, but he jerked away from me, swearing under his breath.

"Leave me be, Beth. Turn around." Will jabbed his hand into his pocket and I saw a flash of silver. He'd always carried his grandfather's knife, an accessory he'd said was handy in the case he needed to open a package or filet a fish. Of course, he'd been joking, but I'd never thought he would actually use it on someone.

"You . . . wouldn't . . . dare." The voice was breathy. I tried to look over Will's shoulder, but he elbowed me back. Will turned the knife over in his hand and laughed.

"Oh, but I will. And I'll enjoy it." I watched his hand close into a fist around the blade's handle. "I saw the way you grabbed her, the way you forced her off the dance floor against her will thinking no one was watching. And then to see you about to—"

"Stop! Will, I beg you. You'll regret this," I said.

"Turn around!" he shouted at me. I swiveled and gasped. Lily was quivering in the corner of the room.

I ran to her and hugged her, but she didn't return the embrace, only folded limply over me.

"He . . . he tried to . . . to force me," she stuttered.

I spun back around to find Will clutching Professor Helms by his vest, his stout figure splayed across the ornate mahogany desk.

Thankfully, he'd put the knife away, but blood spewed from Helms's nose down the side of his face.

"Are you all right?" I breathed to Lily. As worried as I was for her, I wanted to stop Will.

"Yes," Lily said, her tone soft but direct. "Not like this, Will. I'll not have you ruin your life and make him a hero in the process. He'll pay for what he's done. But it'll be my doing."

Professor Helms's attention drifted from Will to Lily.

"I knew . . . you . . . wanted . . . me."

His sentiments made my skin crawl. Will jerked Professor Helms toward him and then slammed him into the desktop once again.

"You're a disgusting imp!" Will's yell silenced the room.

"What in heaven's name is happening in here?" Grant's voice came from behind me. He entered holding a candelabrum, his glare piercing.

Professor Helms laughed and wiped at his broken nose, which was already starting to swell into his cheeks.

"It seems that Mr. Buchannan thought I deserved a beating for dancing with his lovely date."

"Is that so?" Grant said, setting the candelabrum on the desk. He looked down at his polished black boots and cracked his knuckles. No one spoke. I could tell by Lily's silence that as much as she wanted Professor Helms confronted, she also wished to retain her dignity. "Buchannan's had his fair share of mishaps, that's for certain, but Iota Gamma men rarely throw a punch unless it's merited."

Grant's gaze met mine and I knew what he was after—he wanted me to enlighten him if Will had been uncouth in dealing with Professor Helms.

The professor took advantage of the silence. "The entire faculty knows that Mr. Buchannan should have been expelled last year when he started that fire at the dining hall and—"

"That's what I thought," Grant said. "You have a reputation yourself, you know," he continued, more loudly. He circled in front of Will and Helms, scuffing the floor as he went as though the professor wasn't worthy of his attention.

"That's correct. A reputation of honor for the work I've done here."

"No," Grant contradicted. "I'll not humor you with the details. I'm sure you know what I mean. Miss Carrington, will you close the door?"

I complied and Professor Helms shrugged free of Will's grip.

Will snatched the back of his vest and yanked him backward. "You're not going anywhere."

"Stop," Lily said. "I've tired of this. I'd like to move forward with my evening. Just let him go."

"No. What are you saying?" I knew she'd always been one to deal with things on her own, to brush them under the rug. Perhaps it was only that she was used to defending herself because she hadn't had a family to count on. But she had me now, and I wouldn't permit Professor Helms to go free. Not after what he'd done.

"I'll not." Will's blood-streaked fingers tightened around the professor's vest.

"Miss Lilian Johnston, is it?" Grant asked.

Lily bobbed her head.

"Good evening, Mr. Richardson. It was lovely of you to come to my defense, but truly I'm all right. Now please, let's enjoy the ball." She started to walk past him out of the room, but Grant interrupted.

"Miss Johnston, I can't let you go until you tell me what's happened. I swear to you, whatever it is will remain in confidence, but I cannot let that man roam free if he's done something . . ."

"Tell him, Lily," Will said. "Tell Richardson. Regardless of your opinion of him, his word is as good as mine."

"He found me on the dance floor looking for Will and dragged me in here, where he . . . where he—" Lily stopped short.

"He tried to ruin her," Will spat.

"I did no such thing," Professor Helms said calmly.

"He said that if I told anyone about it, he'd fail me," Lily responded just as evenly.

"Is that so, Professor?" Grant stepped forward to occupy the space next to Will.

"Either hurt me or let me go," Professor Helms muttered. "Get on with it."

Grant laughed and backed away from him.

"I think we'll do neither. Instead, we'll be reporting your unfavorable perversion to the board."

Professor Helms scoffed, wincing as he did.

"And you think they'll believe you? I've worked here for nearly twenty years. The word of four children has hardly a chance," he wheezed, drawing out the word *children*. "I'll simply say that you decided to blackmail me in order to spare Miss Johnston's enrollment. She *is* failing my course."

Grant bent down to Professor Helms.

"You may have tenure, professor, but they'll do as I say."

Helms turned his head away from Grant, and Lily and I both gasped. The light flooded Helms's face, and it was clear that his septal cartilage had been severed. Not that he was a sight to behold to begin with, but the man would certainly never look the same.

"You're giving yourself an incredible amount of credit, Mr. Richardson," Professor Helms said finally. "You truly believe that thirty-two of our most prominent alumni are going to forget they have a brain and side with you, a student?"

Grant paced the room, running his hands along the thick molding inlaid with an ivy pattern in the middle of the wall.

"You seem perplexed, Helms. Let me enlighten you." Grant turned back to face him. "Right now, Whitsitt receives the crumbs that fall from the gold-plated tables of both my uncle and my father, totaling, I don't know . . . fifty thousand per year?" He flicked his right hand in a sweeping motion to illustrate his point. "But this year, on my twenty-first birthday, June twelfth to be exact, I'll receive my trust fund—a collective contribution from both men. On that day, my uncle and father will cease funding to Whitsitt, leaving the decision to continue the contribution to me. It all depends on if I feel that Whitsitt is still worthy. So, you see, your measly reputation is of no consequence . . . that is, unless they'd like to release, um, let's see"—he brought his thumb to each of his fingers as he counted—"three-fourths of the staff?"

Will laughed under his breath and I watched Helms's face pale.

"Is that a satisfactory explanation for you?" Will asked. Helms rose to his feet, though Will's hands were still gripping his vest.

"You'll have me removed, then?" His voice was hoarse in defeat.

"I'm a kind man," Grant said. "And as much as I think you deserve the wrath of hell, something tells me there's another way to get what I want without your departure leaving a smudge on my conscience." Grant walked to the desk behind me and picked up the candelabrum. The candles had dwindled to nubs. A few of the flames glowed blue above the silver bases, threatening to extinguish at any moment. "You can either pack your things tonight and resign quietly, leaving no later than noon tomorrow, or we can go through the mess of your good name being smeared—no, submerged—in the muck of what you've done."

Professor Helms stood there for a moment and then started to walk out of the room.

"Good riddance," Lily said, her voice like ice, as he staggered into the hallway.

"I'll send a coach around to dispose of him," Will said to Grant.

Grant shook his head.

"Absolutely not. You'll escort him discreetly out of the front entrance so that none of the guests are alarmed by the state of his face. Last I checked, you hadn't broken his legs. He can walk. I'll call a sleigh for the ladies, however. They've had quite a night."

"I was wrong . . . about Grant and Will," Lily whispered, as we followed the men down the hallway.

Grant opened the front door, and a gust of frigid wind chilled me through. Will led Professor Helms through it, not bothering to bid farewell as the man teetered slowly down the frozen drive. I watched him go, round figure slumped forward as he stumbled into the black night, barely hearing Will's shout for a driver and the jingle of sleigh bells as one complied. I couldn't understand what had driven Professor Helms to darkness, to the acceptance of a mentality that the harm he dealt others was somehow merited.

Will went ahead of us, helping Lily across the icy drive to the sleigh. I turned to face Grant, supremely handsome in the lantern light.

"Thank you," I said, and he blinked at me.

"For what?" He extended his arm and I took it. "For doing the right thing? Please don't." His hand found the top of mine, shielding it from the chill as he led me around the back of the sleigh. Grant reached to open the door, but I stopped his hand. The outline of the king, the chess piece he'd drawn, was still visible on the window.

"What is it, Beth?" I could feel the heat of his body, smell the coconut and palm in his hair. I opened my mouth to say something and tried to tear my eyes away from his face, but could do neither. "Thank you for accompanying me this evening," he said.

"Perhaps you were right," I said. "Perhaps the only thing you are to most people is a chess piece, the king, something to be won." Grant started to distance himself, but I gripped his hand. "Even if that's what you are, you used it for good tonight. I was wrong about you." Grant's hand rose to my neck, fingers tangling in the hair at my nape. I knew

I should pull away, but I couldn't. The wind started to blow, sending the bells on the sleigh jingling and the dry trees groaning, and Grant shifted our locked hands behind my back and drew me to him.

"And I was right about you," he whispered. His lips drifted across my cheek, and then they found mine. My body tensed. I couldn't kiss him. It wasn't right or proper and I didn't know how. He stepped forward, pushing me against the cool window, and at once I couldn't remember my reservations as my mouth opened to the warmth of his. He tasted sweet and bitter at the same time, the wine still on his tongue. His lips broke from mine, but he didn't back away.

"I'm truly nothing but a chess piece," he said. He let me go and opened the carriage door. "But perhaps you're not playing."

10

LILY HADN'T SAID a word to me in the coach on the way home. I'd mentioned that we'd received an appointment with the board, but she hadn't responded. Instead, she'd smiled and taken my hand, turning away from me to gaze out of the window, fully content to listen to the soft sound of the blades cutting through ice and the rhythmic tinkling of the bells. I didn't know if she'd seen Grant kiss me or not, but if she had, she hadn't let on.

In the silence, my mind raced with the implication of that kiss—the kiss I could still feel on my mouth hours later. I was no better than Katherine, no better than Will. I shouldn't have let Grant kiss me. We weren't a good match, that much was obvious, and I knew that most of my affection toward him was simply a result of my relief in his disposing of Professor Helms. Even if I was wrong, even if my sentiments ran deeper, it didn't matter. Grant would never believe in the things I found most important regardless of his feelings for me. That was one of the rules my mother had taught me early on—never be so arrogant as to think you can change someone.

I sat up in bed and glanced over at Lily's sleeping silhouette in the dark, her fingers clutched to her quilt. I shivered and mimicked her, pulling my quilt up in turn, but it didn't encourage sleep. I plucked a book of matches from the top of the dressing table, struck one, and lowered it to the oil lamp. If I couldn't rest, I might as well be productive. I leaned down to pick up my anatomy book and the latest *American Journal of the Medical Sciences,* and Lily stirred.

"What are you doing?" she asked, rubbing her eyes.

"I can't sleep, so I thought I might as well study."

"If I wasn't so exhausted, I'd be as restless as you are." Her brown hair had come loose of her braid, and golden strands gathered in wisps around her face. She patted the spot of mattress next to her, and I wrapped my quilt around me and shuffled over.

"I feel so wonderfully free," she whispered, tired eyes alight. "And it's all because of Will and Mr. Richardson. I'm sorry, Beth. I should have trusted your judgment on enlisting Mr. Richardson's help." I forced a smile and she patted my arm. "It was such a wonderful, romantic evening, wasn't it? Well, besides the latter part of it, of course. Thank God the men came to the rescue." She smoothed a hand over her plain cotton nightshirt. "I know that this was only my first ball, but you've been to others. This one was one of the grandest, wasn't it?"

I nodded, thinking back to the few balls I'd attended in Chicago. They'd all been beautiful, in their own way, but nowhere near as elaborate as this one. I could understand why Lily was so enchanted. "Will was so handsome in his tuxedo. I couldn't stop looking at him. And Mr. Richardson . . . was his kiss as sweet as he is?" In the lamplight, I could see the joy in her eyes. I wanted to tell her about the strength of his arm around my back, and the way his lips seemed to dance against mine as though he'd known exactly how I liked to be kissed, but I didn't. Our flirtation couldn't go further. We were too different.

"Are you all right? Surely you knew that I saw," she said. "You were right outside of the coach and . . . did you not want him to kiss you?"

I shook my head.

"No. I mean, I suppose I did in the moment. It just . . . it wasn't proper and I—"

"Oh, Beth. Don't fret so much. I'm sure most girls on campus have kissed a man," she said. "And I know that he says he's against us, but I doubt that he actually is. Mr. Richardson seems like a perfect gentleman otherwise. He helped us get in front of President Wilson, after all." Her cheeks flushed with the excitement of recent memories. Suddenly, she sobered.

"Beth, I . . . I was wondering," she continued, looking away from me. "I want to tell Will that . . . that this wasn't the first time that Professor Helms . . . I owe him honesty, don't you think?" She ran her palm across the embroidery of the quilt, picking at a pink thread that had come loose of a bloom. "That is, if we're to continue courting."

Under normal circumstances, I would have gone along with her assumption that an invitation to a ball indicated serious affection, but I couldn't let her hopes hinge on Will. He wasn't the courting sort, at least not right now, with his heart still reeling from Miss Cable and flirtations cast far and wide.

"Are you sure Will would consider the two of you courting?" The words were out of my mouth in an instant, and I immediately wished I could take them back.

"What do you mean?" Lily pushed back against the headboard. "He asked me to the ball. We had a wonderful time. He saved me from Professor Helms." She glared at me. "Do you not think me good enough for *your* Will? Do you suppose I'm too ordinary, too poor, too dull?"

Her face burned. A million responses flooded my mind, but none were satisfactory. I'd insulted my best friend when she needed love and assurance more than anything. Was I jealous of their attachment?

"I'm sorry, Lily," I said softly. "Of course you're good enough for him; you're the best match he could hope for. You're kind, beautiful, smart." She wouldn't look at me. "My words were misplaced. It's only that he's such a flirt right now, and I . . ." I trailed off, knowing stating his reputation would only make this moment worse.

The truth was that, despite the way they'd been drawn to each other at the ball, Will's attention rarely lingered, and though I hoped she would be the one to sweep him out of his heartache, I also didn't want her to be left broken if she wasn't. She didn't deserve it. Not after everything with Professor Helms. But, I didn't want to be wrong about Will's affections and rob them of happiness. I recalled the way he'd held her while they danced, the easy way they'd interacted. "Lily, please forgive me," I went on. "You should have seen the way he looked at you tonight . . . I know he feels for you."

"No," she said softly. "He only asked me in the first place because he knew you wanted me there. He'd do anything for you. He's in love with you."

"Don't be ridiculous, Lily. We both know that's not true. We've only ever been friends and—"

"Maybe you've never felt anything for him, but I doubt it given how defensive you are about him. And looking back on tonight, the only thing he wanted to do was poke fun at Mr. Richardson and dance next to you," Lily said, blowing out the oil lamp and getting back into bed. She was being absurd. If he had any regard for me beyond friendship, he'd never shown it.

"I understand you're upset, but that doesn't mean that he loves me, Lily. Will has never liked Grant. And perhaps he thought that he should dance next to us for our sake, so that we could talk."

I let out a long breath and sat down on the end of my bed. I could see her silhouette in the dark, her body turned away from me.

"He does. The way his face looked . . ." She stopped. "He begged me to tell him why you'd gone to see Mr. Richardson that night and I did . . . right before you stepped out for the first dance. I thought that if you had the right to tell our secret, so did I."

I froze, unable to believe her. She was only saying it to hurt me, to teach me a lesson.

"You didn't . . . wouldn't do that."

"He couldn't understand why you didn't tell him. He said that he knew he didn't have the influence Mr. Richardson did, but that he has always supported you, that he would have tried to help us. He swore he'd take our secret seriously. He knows what the repercussions are if he doesn't."

I curled my legs against my chest, as though I could somehow shield my crushed heart.

"I was going to tell him. I was going to ask if I could at our meeting tomorrow. After our appointment with the board, everyone will know about it anyway," I said, stumbling over the words.

"I suppose it's too late," Lily said. "I'm sure you're proud of yourself. In the course of an evening, you've shown your two best friends such kindness."

Somehow I had to make it right. I absolutely couldn't lose them. I wouldn't be able to bear it. The echo of the crushing pain that came with the end of a friendship struck me. I'd fallen out with my friend Sarah the month before I left for Whitsitt. Her family was progressive, her mother the leader of our suffrage group, and I'd thought she should go to school with me. Instead, she kept trying to talk me into staying, a measure I adamantly refused and couldn't understand. As time passed, I came to realize that it wasn't really about me remaining in Chicago, it was about her wanting my approval. She'd wanted me to tell her that I'd stand by her if she chose to marry her long-time beau and forgo college, but I hadn't been able to fathom that life—for her or me—and so I'd refused to let the subject drop. I'd wanted her to have everything, to have both, and I'd been too insistent, too callous.

Eventually, love won and I lost. I couldn't lose again. Not with Will and Lily at stake.

Tears dripped down my face.

"Please, Lily. I love you. I'm so sorry."

"As you should be," she said. I heard the rustle of her mattress as she lay down. "Perhaps you should go sleep with Mary and Katherine tonight. I don't want to talk to you now and I need distance before our chapter meeting in the morning."

* * *

I searched the grass for a stone or a stick, something to throw at Will's window. It was a little past seven, and I knew he was still asleep. Contrary to Everett Hall's liveliness at this hour—Miss Zephaniah had made it known that we were all to be up by six-thirty—the Iota Gamma house was still silent save a few men intermittently emerging from the front door to sleepily trek across the quad for breakfast. Unlike Miss Zephaniah, Grant didn't much care if his brothers missed their morning meal, so long as they were on time to classes, but today was Saturday, and the only requirements were study hours and chapel.

The morning sun washed the white clapboard in soft yellow and pink—the beautiful promise of a new day—but I wasn't optimistic. My best friends were angry with me. The same sentiments had played over and over in my mind all night. Instead of going to Mary and Katherine, I'd gone down to the gathering room and tried to read my textbook, and later, to sleep, but it was impossible. The moment the first group of girls departed for breakfast, I practically ran down the hill and across campus. I needed to right my wrongs.

The chatter of a few men broke through the quiet of the morning as they stepped down from the front porch and walked toward the arch. I paused in my pursuit of a rock, sure they'd notice me idling, but they didn't.

Huddling into my cloak, I wandered closer to the side of the house and found a few acorns buried in the frosty grass below an old leafless oak. I could hear Will snoring and tossed the first acorn at his window. It pinged off the pane and I waited. Nothing. I was rewarded by a loud snore, and threw another and another and another. It would take more than one little noise to wake him.

As the seventh acorn hit the pane, the drapes were drawn away and he appeared in the window. He yawned, rubbed his eyes, and looked down, his brows knitting at the sight of me. Holding up his index finger, he mouthed, "Wait," and disappeared. I swallowed, finding the cords of my neck strained, and paced back and forth below his window. Even though I'd rehearsed my apology all night, it wasn't satisfactory. I didn't know what I'd say

"Beth, what're you doing here?" Will said, coming down the back steps, his hair wild from sleep, his nightshirt tucked into a pair of gray trousers. "You do realize it's Saturday and that study hours don't begin until nine. It's absolutely frigid. Whatever business you're on better be important."

He paced over to my place beneath the oak and saw my quivering lip. "Has something happened?"

"My melancholy is my own doing," I said, blinking back tears. "Please forgive me."

Will stared at me blankly.

"You know about our fraternity."

He nodded.

"I'm sorry," I said. "I should have told you. I didn't because if anyone finds out we've organized, we'll doubtless be expelled."

"I know."

"Will, if I hurt you, I . . ." I trailed off, not sure what else to say.

He laughed quietly.

"It's of no matter. I obviously haven't lost any sleep over it. You know that I would've kept your confidence if you would've told me, though. I would never do anything to jeopardize what you've worked so hard for. Grant . . . well, I can't necessarily say as much for him."

Will's mouth was turned up in a grin, but his eyes were dull as they met mine. He was trying to act as though what I'd done hadn't mattered, but it had.

"I can. He won't hurt me," I said, stunned that I believed it. "Regardless, I should have told you. I only mentioned it to Grant because I thought he had the influence to help us."

"That, and you didn't think you could trust me," Will said. "Judging by my misstep in Professor Pearson's lecture, I suppose you were right. I'm not the most reliable."

"I was wrong," I told him, as a few brothers filtered out of the house and cast an interested gaze in our direction. "You're the best friend I've ever had. Reliability is your strength. You're the most loyal man I've ever known and, beyond delaying coming to my defense in class, you've always stood by me."

I stepped closer and his hand met my shoulder.

"Thank you for that," he said. "And I hope you're right about Grant."

"Do you really question that he's good? What he did for Lily last night . . . I have to believe that underneath the arrogance, he's honorable."

Will chuckled.

"It didn't cross your mind that perhaps he only did it to win you over, so that you'll trust him? Don't tell me that something as meaningless as a kiss has transformed him into your champion."

"You . . . you saw that?" I stuttered, not knowing what else to say. I hoped no one had overheard—the last thing I wanted was to be the talk of Whitsitt—but thankfully we were alone.

"I was on the other side of the glass, Beth. Of course I did." Will bit his bottom lip and crossed his arms, likely to keep from shivering. "It didn't seem as though it would have been all that enjoyable. For you, I mean," he amended. "Then again, I suppose I have quite a bit more practice than he does."

"Would you get dressed and accompany me to breakfast?" I asked, choosing not to address his evaluation of Grant's kissing. I wanted more time to apologize as many times as it would take to go back to the way we were. "I'm already late, and I'd love to—"

"I'm quite tired," Will said abruptly, turning toward the house. "And I'm not too keen on Cook's boiled eggs. But surely your friends will still be eating. If you hurry, you'll be able to join them."

My neck was tight with tension as he disappeared into the house. Regardless of what he'd said, I'd hurt him. He was angry with me. I walked around the side of the house, my feet crunching the frozen grass, blinking back tears. As well-intentioned as I'd been in both situations, I knew that I should have taken more care in thinking them through. Neither slip, telling Grant or kissing him, had been worth the price of my friendships.

The chapel clock tolled eight and I began to make my way down the brick path from the arch to the Iota Gamma house. There would be no point in going to the dining hall now. Breakfast was almost over and I wasn't hungry in the first place. I heard footsteps coming behind me and slowed, waiting for whoever it was to pass. Misery was best experienced in complete solitude. As I passed under the arch, I felt a hand touch my arm.

"What are you doing here?" Grant materialized behind me holding a briefcase. He situated his gray wool trilby and pushed his hand back into the pocket of his smart black overcoat.

"Oh. Hello," I said, forcing a smile. "I came to . . . Mary Putnam Jacobi." The name shot to the forefront of my mind. *Why hadn't I been able to think of her in the coach?* "She's a successful physician with a husband and a dau—"

"Did you come for me?" he interrupted, not acknowledging my victorious revelation.

"No," I said.

"Have you been crying?" He caught my hand and stopped me in the shadow of the arch. I shook my head, but he withdrew his handkerchief anyway and gently dabbed my cheek. "Please tell me how I can help."

As he folded the linen, I noticed the initials stitched on the bottom. "A.R. Did you borrow someone's handkerchief?"

"Alexander." He laughed. "I'm a second. I go by my middle name. If you didn't come for me, then why are you here?"

"I had to speak to Will."

"This early in the morning? Surely he wasn't awake."

"He wasn't, but I threw acorns at his window until he stirred." Grant looked skeptical. "I had an argument with Lily and she mentioned that she'd told Will about the fraternity. I'd kept it from him. I had to apologize. I didn't tell him about it in case . . . in case he slipped and mentioned it to someone. I couldn't risk it."

"Is that why you're so upset?"

I swallowed. I couldn't cry again. Not in front of Grant. "To make matters worse, I insulted Lily last night. I've been terribly unkind to my dearest friends and I won't be able to bear it if they'll not forgive me."

"If they're truly your friends, you haven't. I can't imagine Buchannan being that sore over you coming to me instead of him for something he obviously couldn't have helped you with." He tilted his head at Old Main beside us. "Come with me, will you? I was heading to my office. We'll discuss this business with Buchannan and you'll see that everything will be all right."

"You have an office?" I practically laughed the words. He was only a student, but then again, if what he'd said last night was true, and his family truly kept Whitsitt afloat, maybe it wasn't that odd.

"It's not much," he said as we climbed the steps to the entrance of Old Main. The iron rail felt freezing even through my thick wool gloves. "Just a closet, really, but I store all of the fraternity records there for safekeeping."

Grant withdrew his hat and overcoat and settled them both on the hook beside Miss Bradley's vacant desk. He turned to me and drew me toward him, undoing the button at the neck of my cloak and slipping it over my shoulders before his fingers threaded through the hair at my nape. My heart pounded. It wasn't right, but I wanted him to pull me closer. Instead, I felt something give and his touch dissipated as he dropped my hatpins on Miss Bradley's desk and lifted my wool cap, hanging it next to his on the rack. He dug in his pocket for a set of keys and unlocked a door I'd never noticed before, directly adjacent to President Wilson's unoccupied office.

At once I realized how quiet it was, how alone we were. The rest of the students would be setting up at Richardson Library by now, or back at their dormitories readying their textbooks for study hours. I glanced at the carved mahogany grandfather clock occupying the wall beside President Wilson's office door. Eight-twenty. Forty more minutes and Miss Zephaniah would be making the rounds and I absolutely couldn't be absent.

"Won't you come in?" Grant smiled at me, and held the door open.

"I—"

"I'll only be a moment and then I'll see you back to Everett Hall . . . that is, if you wouldn't mind my company?" He rounded a plain oak desk and set his briefcase on the top of it. His eyes met mine and remained. Suddenly, the memory of last night's embrace seemed to settle on both of us, and he looked away, unsnapping his bag. I felt my face flush and turned to the opposite wall, pretending to appraise an old rendering of the town of Whitsitt before the college's founding, before the Unitarians built the small row of brick buildings that encompassed

Main Street. The town had only been an ordinary piece of flat Illinoisan land before they'd given it a name.

"Ah, an excuse to see Miss Zephaniah again?" I asked. The response was delayed, but it broke the awkwardness that had befallen us moments before.

Grant laughed.

"Oh, but of course. How perceptive you are. My talk of her abhorrent behavior must have only been a consequence of a lovers' quarrel."

Abhorrent behavior. I sat down in a sizeable striped armchair in the corner of the room, my thoughts drawn back to Will, to Lily, and to the pain I'd caused.

"Something I said reminded you . . . I'm sorry," he said, sober now. "Do you truly suppose Buchannan won't recover from your coming to me first? He and I are different, of course, but I can't imagine he'd be so sore that he'd sacrifice your friendship."

"He didn't act as though he cared, but I know he did. I'm sure he took it to mean that I didn't trust him."

"You trusted me?" Grant's gaze met mine.

"Of course not. I didn't know you."

"Do you trust me now?"

"You haven't given me a reason not to," I said.

He cocked his head.

"But you're not convinced that I won't."

"I don't trust anyone completely. Not even myself," I said. "My mother was a saint, but she . . ." I trailed off. I hadn't intended to bring her up right now and didn't want to be reminded of the way I'd begged her to leave my father in the years before her death. Despite how scandalous divorce was, how it would affect my reputation and hers, we needed to go. My father had begun to accuse her of infidelity, likely to mask his own guilt, though he'd never actually been found out, and it infuriated me. After one particularly bad row they'd had over my father's delusions,

I'd asked if we could leave him and she'd said we could. I'd waited. Weeks turned into months, and when I asked if she'd changed her mind, she said she hadn't, but we never left. Somehow he'd kept her tethered.

"Perhaps you're right, but I trust you—even though that might mean I'm a fool." Grant rose from his chair and rounded the desk. He leaned down in front of me, steadying himself on a small tea table boasting a half-smoked cigar. It reclined in an ashtray, the head of it wedged in the belly of a cherub. I studied it with great interest, knowing I wouldn't be able to resist if he'd come to kiss me.

"I don't think you're a fool," I said.

Grant took my hand and pulled me to my feet. His arm encircled my waist, drawing me closer, his fingers drifting over my cheek. "I'm yours, Beth. You can trust me."

The warmth of his touch spread through me, and when his mouth dropped to mine, I kissed him back, knowing a proper lady wouldn't. I still had so many doubts about him, but the feel of his hands on my body was nearly intoxicating.

"I want to," I whispered when we broke our embrace, but Will's warning still rang in my mind. *It didn't cross your mind that perhaps he only did it to win you over, so that you'll trust him?* I backed away from Grant, the pad of my thumb gliding across my lips in an effort to both remember and erase his embrace. He smiled and squeezed my hand before he withdrew to his briefcase, extracting three files and placing them in the bottom of the desk.

"What are they?" I asked, sitting back down.

"Roll sheets from the past forty years," he said. "One of our brothers has made it his mission to update our library and found them among the books last week."

I wasn't excited in the least. I was hoping they were notes from the fraternity's Historian, something useful to Beta Xi Beta, something I could casually ask Grant to peruse while he tied up the rest of his business.

"I meant to ask you," Grant continued. "What did President Wilson have to say yesterday evening?"

"Nothing really." I looked at him, waiting to see a glimmer of victory in his face, but it never appeared. "He gave me an appointment with the board this Tuesday."

"I suppose that's a start," he said matter-of-factly, with a smile I read as pitying.

"It is. It's promising. I'm planning to tell the others when we meet later today." I stared at him, daring him to condescend to me.

"Oh good," he said. "I'm happy for you." We fell silent for a moment, both knowing he was lying, and then Grant reached into his briefcase and extracted a thin book. "At least two nights each week, I can't sleep. Last night was one of them, so I went down to our library and found one of Margaret Fuller's essays. I don't know how it found its way into our house, but it's here nonetheless. *Women in the Nineteenth Century*. I'm trying to understand, Beth."

"Thank you," I said, unsure what else I should say. I'd read Fuller's essay some time before, but couldn't quite remember if it lined up with my thoughts, but I knew she'd been a pioneer and a known feminist. "What do you think of it?"

"I agree with her, actually. On most points. The main theme . . . at least that I've gathered thus far, is that elevating the education and enlightenment of women will, in turn, elevate that of men. I told you already that I see a need for females to seek higher education."

I nodded, forcing myself to hear him without offense.

"Does her essay speak to professions?" I asked, knowing full well that I was plunging head-first into a territory that could swiftly end our conversation.

Grant shrugged.

"Not specifically. At least I haven't gotten there yet." He placed the book back in the briefcase and snapped the clasp. "Fuller did write something interesting, something I hadn't thought of before. She basically says—and I'm paraphrasing here—that the only thing anyone wants is freedom. And that if a man exercises superiority over his wife, he is in essence, stealing her freedom, robbing her of her self-worth, encouraging a struggle for power in his marriage."

"I can understand that point," I said.

He looked down at his hands and then at me, brown eyes soft. "Perhaps I haven't come across it yet," he continued, "but how is a marriage supposed to work if the man gives his wife reign of everything, and instead of coexisting harmoniously, she takes the power for herself?"

"There's always the risk, I suppose," I said, trying to understand his point, but all I saw in my mind was my mother on her hands and knees scrubbing the floor—my father couldn't stand a dirty home— while he repeatedly called for a beer from his worn leather chair in front of the fire. What would she have done if she'd had the freedom to choose?

"Don't you think that your mother would have turned the tables on your father if she'd had the freedom to do so? That she would have disappeared from your life as my mother has?" Grant asked, as though he'd somehow read my mind.

I looked at him, expecting smugness, but instead, I saw confusion. He was trying to reconcile his hurt, trying to fit his family into a formula that didn't exist.

"No. She wouldn't have ever left me," I said. "Above all else, she loved me. Her heart wouldn't have allowed her to leave." I blinked to stop the burning behind my eyes, startled by my grief.

Grant was silent, his head bowed.

"I'm sorry."

I'd only been honest, but in the course of it, I'd just reminded him that his mother hadn't loved him—at least enough. I reached for his hand and his fingers curled around mine, but otherwise, he didn't move. Unable to stand the silence, I spoke. "My parents didn't know each other before they married. They were from neighboring towns. My father was selling firewood door to door and when my grandfather answered his knock, he saw my mother sitting next to the hearth. He asked after her immediately and my grandfather essentially agreed to their marriage on the spot. She was the youngest of five and they were poor, so my grandfather needed someone else to take care of her. They married two weeks later."

My mother had told me the story on Saint Valentine's Day when I was young. I'd asked how they'd met and she'd recounted the story without a hint of a smile. She'd been an arrangement. From that point on, I'd looked at my parents differently, doubting my mother had ever been happy.

"Sounds a bit like mine," Grant said. "My grandmother was determined to strike a deal with a business tycoon in America—a match promising a connection to the peerage for a son and money for her daughter. My grandfather was the only man in New York greedy enough to take the bait. By the end of the week, my father was engaged to my mother." His hand broke from mine and rose to my cheek.

"Both arrangements sound terrible," I said.

"Beth . . . I . . . I've never felt comfortable speaking this candidly to anyone." Warmth pooled in the pit of my stomach as I took him in— the strong jaw, the full lips, the eyes that suddenly seemed to blaze.

"I'm so glad you confided in me," I said.

"I know we haven't spent much time together, but for the first time in years, I've felt like myself," he said. "And I can't help but think it's because of you." He stood and leaned into me, and I could feel the whisper of his lips on my ear. "Our parents didn't have a chance. They didn't know each other. Perhaps, somehow, there's a way for us if we take our time, if we do."

His lips met my forehead, but I was only vaguely aware of it. In a matter of a day, he'd begun to look ahead, to see his future changed. And, he'd thought about it with me.

11

A FEW HOURS LATER, I descended the library steps on the heels of a group of men talking about a girl named Julianne Peterson. Richardson Library had been a popular choice for study hours—I'd barely been able to find a seat—and shortly after I'd located the college's copy of Carl Ernst Bock's *Atlas of Human Anatomy*, I knew why. A group of divinity girls keen to be pastors had planned to practice their sermons to a crowd of senior men, and nearly the entire library was filled for the occasion. Only a few of us hadn't realized our mistake by the time the attendance logs had been passed around for signatures and study hours officially started. The first two girls were somewhat bearable, their voices almost droning and easy to tune out, but the third, Miss Peterson, was both passionate and striking, her sermon on Romans 8 a compelling, well-thought lesson on the scripture. Though I'd never heard of her before this morning, I wasn't likely to forget her.

I glanced across the frozen quad to the hill, wishing I could see Everett Hall through the old oak trees' gnarled arms, but could only make out the wash of yellow sun on the horizon. I wondered if Lily had slept, if she'd been able to forget about our argument.

I'd withdrawn from Grant after his revelation. I couldn't help it. He'd been searching for a sign that I felt the same, but I refused to answer him, finally saying that it had been quite a morning and that I was exhausted. Thankfully, he'd believed me, but had still wanted to walk me home, an occasion I knew would encourage more questions I wasn't prepared to answer. The riddle of his feelings and mine, Lily's anger, and Will's hurt were all too much to process. So I'd told him that I'd decided I was going to study at the library—only a building over—and that there was no need to accompany me.

As I left the library, campus was still quiet as it always was on Saturday mornings. The majority of our classmates would remain tucked away in their dormitories until the Unitarian service at eleven-thirty. The clock on the chapel read five until ten. An hour until our meeting. I shivered, bunching my cloak's overhanging sleeves around the cuffs of my dress.

I paced back toward Old Main, figuring I'd wait for the girls there instead of making the trek back up to the dormitory only to turn around and come back. Getting to the chapter room early would give me time to think anyway, to figure out a way to make things right with Lily.

I slipped into the dark damp of the basement, reaching the room in a few strides. I turned the knob, but it didn't budge. I tried again, pushing my hip into the wood, but the bolt simply jostled in place. It was locked. I backed away and slumped against the stone wall. The chill seeped through the heavy fabric at my back as I stared at the patches of waterlogged rot along the bottom of the door. They'd locked me out. Suddenly it made sense. Lily had asked me to leave so that she could call a meeting without me, a meeting to vote me out without giving me a chance to apologize, to explain myself. I knew my logic was ridiculous, that our friendship, our sisterhood, was stronger than a quarrel, but I worried the worst all the same. I placed my palm on the door, unexpectedly homesick for the tiny room and the handwritten letters that I'd found so temporary and unsatisfactory before. It was a glint of gold in a pan of pebbles, the start of a dream, and I'd taken it for granted.

Something clattered on the other side of the door, followed by the soft padding of footsteps. I rapped my hand against the wood, did it again, knocked four times, and rolled my knuckles. Perhaps they'd show me grace. The jangling stopped abruptly and I heard a cough.

"Who knocks on the door of Beta Xi Beta?" Katherine. Before I could answer, the door opened.

"Beth," she breathed, but I barely noticed. The floor was blanketed with crates, some in stacks four or five high.

"What . . . what's this?" I edged past her, barely able to fit through the doorway. Katherine fiddled with the brass buttons lining the front of her white shirtwaist, fingers pausing on the cameo she always wore in the middle of her bodice. Instead of explaining how and why the chapter room had been turned into a storehouse, she just looked at me as though I was carrying a secret. Perhaps I was. I'd kissed Grant twice, after all.

She reached to straighten my cap and snorted.

"I knew it. He kissed you, didn't he? Already this morning, too."

"I—" I started to explain myself, but she cut me off.

"Your lips are a touch swollen, your cap is cockeyed, and though you're trying your hardest, you can't help grinning."

"It's not what you think," I said, knowing she was likely thinking I was as carefree as she was, that I'd had a romantic night with Grant and couldn't resist falling into his arms again this morning despite my reservations. In a way, she'd be right. "I got into an argument with Lily and . . . and Will as well. I spent the night trying to study in the gathering hall because I couldn't sleep and then as soon as the first girls went out to breakfast, I went out to speak with Will."

"And then Mr. Richardson stole you away for a morning tryst." Her lips pulled up at the corners.

My cheeks were hot and I shook my head.

"It wasn't like—"

"Don't be so embarrassed. Being close to a man you enjoy isn't a crime."

"Perhaps you don't see it that way, but I wasn't, Katherine. I only—"

She waved her leather-gloved hand at me.

"Protesting only ruins the story, dear. If it makes you feel more comfortable, I first kissed a boy the day after my sixteenth birthday, and every week after for nearly a year until one evening it became something more. After, I knew I should be ashamed, frightened about what should happen if he should leave me with child, but I kept doing it. We were careful, of course." I nodded, holding my tongue from commenting something disapproving. "At first it was because I thought he loved me and I felt whole in his arms, and then, after I found out he didn't, I did it to win his heart . . . until I realized that I didn't care anymore, that I was only offering myself because I wanted to. I miss it. I've yet to entertain another man in that way, and I doubt I will again unless I get married, lest I turn away all prospects with my reputation. It's silly, really, the stigma that comes with intimacy. I don't see what all the fuss is about."

Pregnancy, an undesirable reputation, disease—the arguments for abiding morality's rules struck my mind, but I didn't bother voicing them. She wasn't a dolt and something about the way she acted as though the man hadn't mattered made me altogether sad for her. He'd clearly mattered a great deal.

"Tell me what this is," I said, casting my hand over the sea of crates, and Katherine smiled.

"You're being entirely unfair, you know, withholding a delightful story from me. I was the only sister absent from the ball. I think I deserve at least a bit of gossip as a consolation."

I kept my gaze fixed on the boxes. Katherine hadn't been asked because she was Southern. She knew it as well as I did, even though no one really talked about it. I'd seen the way men looked at her. She was alluring, beautiful, and wealthy, easily the most eligible woman on campus if she hadn't had the misfortune of hailing from Confederate stock. But her heritage prevented interest from any well-to-do Northerner. Families still recalled the war, remembered the sting of loved ones lost to the rebels. Both of my uncles had died fighting for the Union.

Katherine sighed at my silence. "I suppose I'll concede a subject change this once. You're looking at two hundred gallons of Kentucky's finest rye. I'll have it out of here tonight . . . at least I hope."

"What?" I ran a hand across my face, wondering if my exhaustion was causing me to hallucinate. "Why would you have two hundred gallons of whiskey?"

"To most, Daddy's a corn grower. To some, Daddy's a distiller," she said. "And not quite of the legal variety."

I felt my mouth drop open. I suppose I hadn't asked about her family, but she didn't seem like the type. When I thought of illegal distillers, my mind didn't exactly conjure a woman as elegant as Katherine. "I suppose I should have asked y'all before I volunteered the chapter room, but I found out last night that Daddy's man in Green Oaks was arrested by the revenue agents the other week, so naturally his barn's out of use."

I had no words. Was she out of her mind?

"Are you upset with me?" She looked shocked at my stony countenance. "Like I said, I would have asked, but seeing as how all of you were at the ball without me, I—"

"Are you truly wondering if I'm angry at you for storing your *illegal* liquor in our chapter room?" I could feel my wits snapping like tiny explosions in my chest. I knew that my reaction was in part due to the fact that I'd felt altogether undone since my conversation with Lily last night, but it didn't matter. Mary had been wrong to let her into the sisterhood so quickly. I'd been right to keep my distance.

"Yes."

"Of course I'm mad. I'm livid. It's obvious that you didn't think. Did it even cross your mind that we'd all be expelled if you were found out? And even if you could somehow convince President Wilson that all of this was your doing alone, they'd find our things, they'd know we'd been meeting here." I inhaled the mildew-tinged air, trying to calm down.

She opened her palm, and it was then I noticed she'd been holding a wreath pin. Lily must've made one for her. I narrowly refrained from snatching it from her hand.

"Of course I thought about it," she said. "But, Beth, no one comes down here. Otherwise, y'all wouldn't meet here, and you have to understand. James and I . . . we didn't know what else to do—"

"You told your brother about us? You took him here?"

"No," Katherine said, grabbing my wrists. "I would never. I just told him to tell Daddy's driver to deliver to the back of Old Main and that I'd be waiting. Our driver loaded it in here himself. He's from Kentucky. He didn't pay one bit of mind to the letters on the wall or ask any questions." She paused for a moment and let my hands drop. "I would have left them in the hall, but I worried that someone might come down here and see the crates. I thought that they'd be safer behind a locked door."

"Who's coming to get it?"

"Another one of Daddy's drivers. He'll be here at eight. He's carrying them up to Chicago in a livestock wagon." She smiled, as though she thought disguising liquor as livestock was genius. "And before you ask, we'll make sure no one is about while he's loading the wagon. He won't think twice about the letters on the wall either. In our business, this isn't even close to the strangest thing he's seen."

I fingered the black braided stitching along the cuff of my cloak. My anger couldn't change the fact that our chapter room had become a distillery's storehouse.

"Is breaking the rules worth this much hassle?" I asked, scanning the piles of beaten crates. Some were splintered, exposing the necks of dark brown bottles. "Why don't you do it the legal way?"

"We turn a thirteen dollar a gallon profit while the legal distillers are lucky to turn five. So, yes it's worth it," she said. "And it's what we're due for the work. Mama was a terror to be around after she settled the books each month back when we were simple corn growers. We were always on the brink of losing granddaddy's farm until Daddy's friend in Ohio, a distiller himself, came calling. I remember listening outside of the drawing room door with his son, George." Katherine's cheeks flushed, and I wondered if he was the man she'd referenced earlier. "That was the first time he held my hand. I shouldn't have let him. In any case, Mr. Foster told him that the administration's only taxing hard-working people like Daddy so that they can pay off the cost of a war they started. Daddy's never been one to sit on a profitable idea, so he began forming the distillery the following week. Since he didn't want to be a part of this country anyway, Daddy doesn't see why he should pay for it to be rebuilt."

I flinched, thinking of my uncles.

"If you're so loyal to the Southern cause, why aren't you still there?" I was losing my composure, but could hardly help it. Each time I began to calm, she riled me anew.

"I said that that was my daddy's view," she said. "Not mine." She sat down on a crate, causing the glass necks to clang underneath her.

She situated her red velvet skirt over her legs and attached the wreath pin above her heart. I couldn't believe she had the gumption to believe she'd still be accepted as part of Beta Xi Beta after all of this.

"And you aren't worried about getting caught yourself? Shouldn't your father be worried about you?" My mind swum with the contradiction of who she'd convinced me she was and the person sitting in front of me.

"No," she said, pursing her lips. "I've never really been Daddy's focus. See, first it was my sister, trying to tame her rebellion, but then she died and he turned to grooming James." I expected her to elaborate on her sister's death, but she kept on. "I suppose he and Mama assumed I'd turn out fine. The only time he really paid me any mind was when he thought I'd be Mrs. George Foster and would need to know the business like Mama does."

She peeled the gloves from her hands and set them on her lap. "And as far as worrying about being found out? I'm not. I've been caught before, see." She grinned. "It's like I told you, Beth. There's power in playing into who men think you should be."

"So you're saying you talked yourself out of being arrested? Katherine, you really should have been honest with us about the nature of . . . of your dealings." I took in the sea of crates once more, stunned that we'd chosen to absorb a bootlegger into our fraternity.

"I *was* honest," she spat. "No one asked about my family. I would have gladly volunteered the information. I trust all of you. And, I didn't say I had to talk myself out of anything. Each time I've been caught, I've been in the possession of at least twenty gallons of rye. All I have to do is bat my eyes, get real close to them, and say that I hadn't any idea of the contents, that my husband forced me to deliver the packages and doesn't take well to my asking questions. They assume that I'm beautiful but dense and let me go—after asking who my husband is, of course, but I refuse to say."

"I'm sorry. You're right. We didn't ask," I sighed, choosing not to point out that her playing into stereotypes wouldn't do much to change them or that most of the suffrage movement agreed that liquor was inadvertently the cause of many wives' oppression and abuse. I didn't feel up to arguing. "Is there anything else we should know?"

"All right, Beth—I suppose I'll just tell you everything." She shivered as a cool draft wavered over us. "Chicago is our most profitable market, and because the cities are rampant with agents, we needed someone on the outskirts to run the distribution, to make sure it gets to our buyers. James was supposed to be the one to do it, but at the last minute, he decided that he didn't want to be a part of the family business—at least not right now. He wants to be a lawyer instead."

I stifled a laugh. An illegal bootlegger turned servant of the law.

"Daddy wasn't too happy about it, so I offered to help so that James could concentrate on his studies. I figured I could enroll and learn a thing or two about bookkeeping while I was here. Mama was scandalized when Daddy agreed, but she couldn't really do anything about it," she said, shrugging. "That's why James will pursue Iota Gamma if I ask him. He owes me."

"Hopefully he won't have to. I've got an appointment with the board this Tuesday," I said. "But, what about you? You aren't interested in an education, in a career at all besides keeping your father's books?" Her whole situation confounded me. Katherine laughed.

"Of course I am. That's why I'm doing this. I'd like Daddy to realize that he doesn't need James. I could run the distillery. The only problem is that he's determined to ship me off to Virginia to marry a widower, Rob Lee Junior—son of the general, you know?"

"Really?"

My face must've shown my alarm because Katherine shook her head.

"I'm sure you've heard a lot about him, but the general was a wonderful man." She drew a deep breath. "I don't love Rob, and last I heard, he was sweet on a girl from Louisiana, some relation of John Burnside, the sugar tycoon. But if Daddy agrees to give him my hand, that won't matter. His wife, Charlotte, passed on eight years ago, and his sisters are keen to see him settled with an appropriate wife." The inner workings of the upper class were altogether foreign to me. Her story brought to mind that of Grant's parents. I couldn't imagine a marriage arranged for advantage, though I suppose that had been my father's goal in pushing me toward the Buchannans' circle. "I spent so much of my time as a young debutante with George, that many of the men I could have loved had married by the time I found that George had become involved with another woman back home."

"I'm sorry he hurt you," I said.

She shrugged again.

"He told me that he was getting married directly after we'd been intimate. I was still dressing when he told me. I cried for an entire afternoon and then swore I'd never let him ruin another hour of my life. All that to say that marrying Rob wouldn't be such a horrible fate. I'd have the means to do whatever I wanted."

"Except to pursue a career. I doubt that this Rob fellow would think too highly of a business woman."

"Oh to be sure. He'd not have it, but if I can't run Daddy's operations, I don't think I'd care to run another. I wouldn't have the passion for it. I could still continue my education—read, travel, employ instructors on whatever subject I chose." She stood and cleared her throat. "So, I suppose if this doesn't work out, I'd like to marry rich, at least. But enough of that."

I tried to wrap my mind around a single-focused ambition, but couldn't. If she really did have the drive to run her father's company, then she'd surely have trouble sitting idly in a mansion somewhere. I couldn't picture her lounging on the white-pillared porch of one of those Southern plantation homes I'd heard so much about. As much as she thought she'd be able to do whatever she wanted, I doubted her optimism.

I heard footsteps echoing in the hallway. Katherine swung herself into the hallway as though she could somehow stop Mary or Lily from coming in and seeing that our chapter room had been transformed into a warehouse.

"Oh. Glad to see you, Katherine," I heard Mary say before she appeared in the doorway. "The strangest thing just happened. I was crossing campus and a young man came running through the arch. He was handsome, blond, with the most captivating eyes. Anyway, he asked me if I knew you and gave me this letter."

"My brother," Katherine muttered, scanning the letter as she spoke.

"What in the world does it mean?" Mary asked, a smile in her voice as she read over Katherine's shoulder. "'*The cart's been overturned and needs repairs. It's in the care of Stephen Marshall and will be finished at 1:30 in the morning*'?"

Suddenly, a gust of wind smacked the door against a box, clanking the bottles. Mary gasped.

"What it means is that my daddy's driver has been arrested and a new one, by the name of Stephen Marshall, will be here to pick up the rye at 1:30 tomorrow morning," Katherine said matter-of-factly. "My family deals in Kentucky rye."

Mary started laughing and lifted the black blusher over her brimless cap to survey the room as she squeezed herself in.

"My goodness. Can we have some?"

"What in heaven's name is going on?" I heard Lily's voice come from behind Mary and Katherine and felt my heart skip. Mary may have accepted Katherine's scandalous dealings without issue, but Lily absolutely would not.

"Katherine's a bootlegger," Mary said without turning to face her. "How many gallons do we have here, Katherine?"

"Two hundred," Katherine said, swiveling to face Lily, whose hazel eyes were narrowed, the dark bags beneath them making her irises look almost luminous.

"A bootlegger?"

Pushing past Katherine and Mary, she took her hand to her chest, fingers nervously prodding the maroon stitching lining her gray wool jacket as she took in the sea of boxes. Her arm dropped suddenly, hand smacking against mine, but she didn't bother to acknowledge me. "Beth was right to question our letting you in," she said, as if speaking of me in absence. "You'll get rid of these immediately."

Katherine looked at me as though my word was the deciding one.

"It'll draw more attention to have them removed now than to wait until Katherine's driver arrives," I said, knowing how little my opinion currently meant. I felt Lily's eyes on my face, but didn't look up to meet them. "Look at all of these crates. It would be noticeable."

"It would," Katherine said.

A faraway drip from a leak in the stones echoed over us as we waited for Lily to speak, but she didn't. Instead she pushed past Katherine and Mary and stood in the hallway with her arms clasped across her chest.

"Speaking of drawing attention," Mary said to me, nudging my arm. "The prevailing Beta Xi Beta rumor is that you kissed Mr. Richardson."

"I suppose I did, but—" I tried to say that I'd tell her about it later, but Mary laughed, interrupting.

"How scandalous," she said. "Good for you. He's beautiful . . . even if his views are inexcusable."

"And she's been in his company again this morning," Katherine pointed out.

"Not intentionally," I said quickly. "I was up early and had gone to speak to Will about—"

"I'm sorry." Lily's voice startled me, cutting through mine. "You didn't deserve my anger. I wanted to hear that Will was different with me, that you could see the man he'd been before Miss Cable broke his heart when we were together. The whole night, I thought he was interested in me, but he wasn't. I felt like a fool."

"You don't know that." I squeezed past Mary and stood in front of her. Lily looked like she hadn't slept either. Her pale skin was nearly gray with fatigue and her typically tidy hair was pulled into a cockeyed bun at the top of her head. "I told you. It was his idea. He wanted to ask you."

"He had to save me from the advances of an old man," she whispered. "I can't believe I thought he'd want anything to do with me."

I clutched both of her shoulders.

"Look at me," I said. She complied, lips pressing together as though nothing I could say would change her mind on the matter. "Professor Helms's perversion is not your fault. Will would never think less of you for it . . . no decent man would."

"I appreciate it, Beth, but I meant what I said last night. He loves you," she whispered, before stepping around me. "But this isn't what we came here to discuss. Gather around. I'll retrieve the robes."

Katherine plucked a box from the floor and set it on top of another and Mary did the same, giving us little more than a ten-foot square to congregate. Lily stretched across the crates, attempting to reach our robes beneath the desk, but couldn't. "We'll have to conduct this meeting without proper dress, I suppose. We have a few things to celebrate thanks to our president." Lily winked at me. "First of all, after last night, Professor Helms will no longer be a problem. It seems that Beth's new beau has a valiant side . . . as does Will."

"He's not my—"

"How pleasantly surprising to find men of honor," Katherine chimed in, cutting off my protest. "I'll agree that Mr. Buchannan is kind."

Mary coughed. Katherine hardly knew Will. Their connection had only been physical. At once I felt the burn of Will's hand on my shoulder, resenting the way Lily's insistence that he loved me kept worming its way into my mind.

"President Wilson was kind enough to grant me an appointment with the board on Tuesday," I said, diverting the subject.

"I knew it. I kept watching the two of you and he smiled quite a bit for a man who'd declined," Mary said.

I snorted.

"His smiling was an act. He didn't let me propose the idea and he's not in favor of anything remotely progressive. He made that clear when he mentioned he'd voted against admitting me because of my major. In any case, we have the appointment."

"What does that mean for the rest of us?" Katherine asked. "How can we help?"

"It's up to you, really," I said, sinking down onto a crate. "We can go together, but as you know, the idea will be immediately shut down if they think we've already organized. Not to mention, there could be repercussions."

"I think you're right," Mary said. "You should go alone. It was your idea to start Beta Xi Beta anyway."

Katherine nodded and I glanced around Mary to find Lily.

"I agree with Mary," she said.

"All right then. I suppose I've only got a few days to prepare, and I'll—"

"Wait," Lily said. She drummed her fingers along her knee. "The board room is an open forum. If there are enough people, we'd have no problem blending in without seeming as though we're there for a reason."

"Have you ever gone?" Mary asked. "I have. There's always a lot of debate about the music curriculum, students vying for and against the instruction of contemporary pieces, so the professors force us to go. There are never more than three people there unless they have to be—"

"Even so, at least one of us should go in support of Beth," Katherine interrupted. "Why don't you plan to attend, Lily? Mary and I could wait outside for your word. We'll come if there are enough people for us to blend in."

"There will be," Mary said suddenly. "I have an idea. If the male students think that a proposal is going up to make the campus dry, they'll revolt, they'll be there. There's nothing our classmates are more passionate about." She turned to Katherine. "Thanks for the inspiration, my dear."

"And how will you arrange it? With a rumor like that flying around, someone will inevitably ask President Wilson and he'll dispute it," Lily said.

"Not if there isn't time," Mary said, grinning. "Plan to tell everyone you know beginning Monday at five o'clock. The minute President Wilson retires, I'll find the King of Gossips, Mr. Samuel Stephens, and let the rumor slip. The board room will be packed."

My stomach flipped at the notion of presenting to a room crowded full of students who'd find the idea of a women's fraternity disreputable.

"Do we want that?" I said, swallowing to relieve the dryness in my throat. "All of campus will know about our proposal to start a women's fraternity. We'll be asking for ridicule. Though, I suppose it will really only be me."

"If there's one thing I've learned from my mother, harassment is a complement to change," Mary said.

"It's not as though any of us are avoiding it now," Katherine said.

"If we fail, I think we should be ready to ask James to help us," I said.

"We won't need to ask him," Katherine said. "He'll do as I say."

"That's all well and good," Lily said. "But we won't fail. Beth won't let that happen, will you?" Her eyes met mine, and as I shook my head, I wished I was as convinced as she was.

12

I COULD HEAR THEM before I could see them. I stepped through the
front doors of Old Main and paused for a moment in the sunlight
beaming through the windows. It was a beautiful day, warm for late
January, and the distant chatter of a large crowd made it all the better.
Even so, I was nervous. Though my efforts could better the lives of
Whitsitt girls forever, they could dissolve Beta Xi Beta just as easily.

"Are you certain you want to go down there? There's a mob this
morning . . . for some reason," Miss Bradley said, looking over her
wire-rimmed glasses at me as I walked down the corridor toward the
board room.

"Thank you for the warning," I stuttered.

"I can't figure it for the life of me," she called. "It's only you and
Professor Helms's student assistant on the docket today—though he
says he can't locate the professor anywhere."

I couldn't help but smile. Apparently Professor Helms had decided
to disappear rather than tell President Wilson he was leaving.

"There's a rumor going around that someone is going to propose the campus go dry," I said, finally finding my voice. "Perhaps that's the reason for the crowd this morning."

"Oh goodness, no," Miss Bradley said. Her hand flew to her neck, palm flattening on her out-of-fashion vulcanite brooch. "How long has this rumor been circulating? The men will revolt without their glass of brandy during study hours. And what about our dinnertime wine? Do I need to send for Mr. Stanley?" Mr. Stanley was the janitor. Standing well over seven feet tall, he'd been a champion boxer in Cuba before making his way to the United States—or so it was said. His mere presence had the power to scatter a fight. I'd seen it happen.

"Only since yesterday," I called to her as I turned into the main hallway, and nearly fainted on the spot. The hall was jammed with students, encouraging the pungent odor of body sweat to prevail over the ordinary scent of cleaning vinegar and wood smoke. I pushed my way through the heavy swarm of wool morning coats and pulled the high neck of my velvet dress, hoping to relieve some of the heat. I didn't see Mary, Lily, or Katherine, who'd gone down to the dining hall to eat breakfast without me since I couldn't bear the thought of food, but I hoped they were somewhere in the throng.

"Beth." A hand brushed my shoulder and I turned to find Grant. I hadn't seen him since Saturday morning after the ball. The memory of what he'd said about us, about a future together, filtered through my mind, but I forced myself to forget it. I couldn't think about it. Not now.

"How are you?" I asked, avoiding his eyes by scanning the crowd over his shoulder.

"Absolutely terrible," he said, and I looked at him, wondering what had happened. He smiled. "It seems like I haven't seen you for a week." His lips kept moving, but I couldn't hear him over the boom of a chant coming from behind me.

"I can't hear you," I yelled.

"We are the majority! We will prevail! It is our right!" Grant rolled his eyes and the crowd parted for President Wilson as he made his way down the hallway. The swarm pushed forward suddenly, sending me careening into Grant. He caught me, holding me for a moment longer than was necessary as students funneled into the small board room.

"Has something changed?" he asked. I barely heard him over the roar of voices and the whirring of my heart in my temples. Perhaps our idea had been a stupid one. There were now too many people. My hand lifted to the wreath pin against my heart. *I promise that above all else, my purpose will be to foster equality and intellect among women.* The words of our pledge rang in my mind. I had to do this. I owed it to the women who would come after me, the women whose intellectual pursuits dared to deviate from the divinity school.

"Beth?" Grant's hand caught mine and I startled.

"I'm sorry," I said. "No. I'm just . . . I'm nervous."

"Don't be. You can look at me if you start to feel tense. I'll be in the front." I looked through the door at the mob of students already jostling for the space at the front of the gallery. The room was set up like a courtroom—mahogany railings separating the students from a semicircular grouping of chairs on a small riser. I still didn't see my sisters and hoped they were only hidden by the height of the men. "They'll move for me," Grant said, following my eyes.

"Did you come to stop the alcohol proposal? I thought you wanted me to fail," I blurted.

"My brothers came for that," he said, gesturing to a grouping of Iota Gammas occupying the entire left-hand side of the room. I caught a glimpse of Will at the front of the crowd as he turned, finding me immediately, as though I'd called his name. He smiled, and then Mr. Stephens circled an arm around his neck and pulled him to an area directly across from the President's bench.

"I came for you," Grant said. He ran a hand through his hair. "I may not agree with you, Beth, but I do care for you. I want you to—"

"Order!" someone called, followed by the banging of a gavel. Most of the voices stopped at once and the roar of the room lowered to a murmur. "Sit down," President Wilson boomed. "All of you." Chair legs screeched as everyone found a seat. Grant squeezed my hand and let go, snaking through the crowd to the front. I watched him walk away, studying his tailored black jacket in an attempt to forget that I'd be presenting my proposal in front of what appeared to be the entire student body, though I knew that the room couldn't actually hold three hundred and thirty students.

When Grant reached the front of the room, a brother stood and immediately relocated. I scanned one more time, finally spotting the crow's feathers in Mary's hat, and then I saw Lily leaning against the wall, arms crossed against her chest. Katherine had taken a chair directly across the aisle from the Iota Gammas. She looked less nervous than smug, no doubt pleased with the turnout. I hadn't figured they'd separate given the crowd. Then again, it was probably smart to do so. There were only two other women in the room—at least that I could see.

President Wilson sat behind his desk at the end of the row and rapped his gavel again.

"Board members, please enter."

The door behind me opened and a line of gray-headed men followed by one hunched-over, elderly woman filed down the center aisle. As the board settled into their chairs, President Wilson shuffled some papers on the front of his desk and cleared his throat.

"The board calls Miss Beth Carrington," he said.

I felt paralyzed, remaining in the shadows at the back of the room watching the morning sun filtering through two stained glass windows behind him. "Miss Carrington?" he said again, sounding as though he were speaking through a funnel. Finally, I forced myself forward.

"Now, before we go on," he said, "I should let all of you know that Miss Carrington's proposal has nothing to do with banning alcohol from this campus. At least that's my understanding."

The students began to stir behind me.

"You're correct, it doesn't," I said as loudly as I could, and the room silenced once more.

"Miss Carrington is the only student on the docket today, everyone," President Wilson said, rising from his chair. "If you're here to show distain for a proposal to proscribe liquor from this campus, I'm sorry to say that your presence isn't needed. It seems that you've all been baited by a rumor."

I heard a chair screech across the floor, followed by another, and suddenly the room was alive with the sound of students filing out.

"Best of luck." Will's voice cut through the noise behind me.

"Thank you."

"Professor Michaels posted a notice allowing us to be tardy to his Sociology examination if we were attending the proposal to ban liquor. 'Participate, observe the behavior,' it read," Will said, rolling his eyes. "But now that the liquor ban isn't in question, I suppose we'll have to take our exam straightaway. Of course I'm not exactly prepared. I should probably skim the textbook on my way over there."

"That would be a good idea," I said, my chest tightening with nerves.

"I wish I could stay and support you, but I doubt you need it," he said cheerily, though he knew that his presence would help settle me.

"Good luck on the exam," I said, casting an eye at the board. They were all looking at me. Will reached over and squeezed my arm. In the next instant, he was gone.

"Now that the mob has dispersed," President Wilson boomed. Everyone was gone, save Lily, Katherine, and Mary scattered intermittently about the room, Grant in the front, and five other men who'd likely remained out of boredom.

"Let us join together in prayer." Everyone's heads bowed.

"Father, today as we gather, give us wisdom. In your name."

I opened my eyes and found President Wilson staring at me. "Now to the matter of our student proposal," he said. "Miss Carrington, I dismissed the others as a favor, to save you some embarrassment."

"Why would I have been embarrassed? I'm here to propose an idea," I said, refusing to let fury rise.

President Wilson set his fingers in a bridge beneath his chin.

"Is that so?"

"As I mentioned at the ball, women outside of the seminary often feel lonely, as though they don't have a place to belong," I said. "When Patrick Everett helped found this college, he fought to integrate the sexes. I can't help but think that when he did, he did it intending for all females to be treated fairly. Whether or not you're aware of it, we're often mocked in our classes by professors as well as fellow students, and unlike the divinity girls, who have several outlets to know each other socially, we don't. We need support from each other, we need camaraderie, and right now we absolutely do not have it."

"Is that all?" The old woman's voice cut me off. Her jowls shook as she spoke. "You're allowed to attend this college, dear. Isn't that enough? In my day, we weren't permitted to occupy the same building as the men, let alone learn beside them."

I wanted to argue that although society had certainly progressed since her time, it wasn't nearly enough. Instead, I nodded.

"I'm not here to suggest anything new for the classroom . . . although reform would be nice," I said, forcing my voice to be steady. "I'm simply asking permission to start a women's fraternity. And . . . and I'd eventually like to gain a charter to encourage women on other campuses to—"

"No. You're not asking permission," Wilson said, setting his glare on me. "You're asking us to allow you to continue it."

I felt heat wash my face.

"I'm afraid I don't follow your meaning." I shifted my eyes, just slightly, to free myself of the President's stare and found Grant instead. He was looking down at his hands, and at once it was clear. He'd told President Wilson about Beta Xi Beta. This time, he hadn't just hoped I'd fail; he'd made sure of it. I wanted to wring his neck. Lily stood and began to walk out of the room. I couldn't blame her. She shouldn't have to risk expulsion along with me. My thoughts raced, trying to come up with a way to explain, to free myself of whatever consequence was to come, but I knew nothing would work. I was stuck.

"Your beau won't be able to help you this time," President Wilson said. "Miss Carrington, one of the professors' aides made a trip down to the basement of Old Main yesterday to find a place to deposit a few old desks. Do you know what he came across?"

I shook my head, having no idea if he'd unearthed the fraternity creeds and bylaws and the four bottles of Kentucky rye that Mary had insisted we keep for our contribution to Katherine's cause. I closed my eyes, trying to call up the image of the papers we'd drawn up. I saw my name clearly on the top of the second page, officially identifying me as president. No one else held an office yet, I realized, relieved that they wouldn't be able to prove that any of my sisters had anything to do with it.

President Wilson reached into his desk and extracted our creeds and bylaws.

"Beta Xi Beta. Clever," he said. He leaned down and righted with the four bottles of rye, setting them on the desk in front of the papers one by one.

I could feel eyes on the back of my head and knew Mary and Katherine were trying to decide their next move, whether they should remain in their seats and risk being called out for involvement or disappear as Lily had. Without a word, President Wilson flattened the paper on his desktop.

"Beth Carrington, President," he read, tapping his index finger on my name. "I'd say that it's clear you've already begun your fraternity. Who are the others? Them?"

He tipped his head toward the chairs behind me, but I looked straight ahead.

I shook my head.

"No, sir. I hadn't sought membership yet."

He laughed.

"You mean to tell me that you decided to create what appears to be a fraternity chapter room and procure four gallons of illegal rye for yourself?"

I nodded, and he stopped laughing. His nostrils flared, and he lifted his hand, smacking it hard on the top of the desk. "Who are the others?" Each word came out in a low staccato.

"I told you, sir. It's only me." My stays felt as though they'd turned to iron.

"Secret societies are forbidden," he barked. "Do you know why?"

I remained silent, gritting my teeth in concentration, as though I could make myself disappear. Of course I knew that after Mortimer Leggett's hazing death at Cornell in '73, Whitsitt, like nearly every other faith-based institution, banned Greek fraternities on the grounds that their practices were seething with the plots of Lucifer. Stating that fact would only make my idea seem purposefully disobedient, which I suppose when it came down to it, it was.

"Of course, the whole country knows what set the ban in motion— the treacherous death of that boy at Cornell who fell into a gorge while on a midnight initiation walk in the woods—but almost no one knows that Mr. Leggett's death was only the final straw, that another incident

preceded Whitsitt's decision," he said. "In 'Fifty-five, a new, secret fraternity almost ruined this college."

"The Saviors," the old man next to Wilson warbled. "Or at least
that's what they were called when the scandal broke."

"They were a fraternity founded on the idea that excessive wealth
was despicable, so they'd do things like steal livestock from well-
known farmers who'd lived peacefully in Illinois since the beginning
of the century, sell them, and give the money to various almshouses,"
President Wilson continued.

I'd never heard of this. In fact, it sounded a bit too much like the
legend of Robin Hood to be real.

"Whitsitt was quite unaware that these robberies were initiated by
gentlemen on our campus until one of the brothers was shot in the
side breaking into a barn in Green Oaks. He recovered, and while he
was away, told his father that he had only been compelled to steal onto
the property in order to prove his worth to a group he was keen to
join. His father reported the incident to Governor Bond, who nearly
shut Whitsitt down." He cleared his throat. "Greek fraternities—save
Iota Gamma, which I assure you has gone through a vigorous screening process complete with random visits from our board—seem to be
drawn to darkness, to the allure of Masonic hazing. Quite frankly,
Miss Carrington, groups like that are contrary to our faith. We cannot
risk life lost to demonic ritual."

"We absolutely cannot," the old man said, chiming in again. "We
were only saved then by proving that we had no knowledge of the
group."

"As terrible as that sounds, sir, it's clear that I wasn't planning on
doing anything of the sort," I said.

"The Saviors were begun on a simple contrary idea—the same
sort of idea you're proposing. Would any of you oppose me on this

point?" President Wilson asked, glancing down the line of board members.

Every head shook except one—a slight man who appeared to be his early forties, nodding enthusiastically.

"A woman's place is in the home," Wilson continued.

"You're acting like a blasted fool, Wilson," the man said. "Have you gotten into the liquor again? You're a traditionalist, sure, but you're usually reasonable. This woman wants some company, some friendships. She's not trying to stage a revolution."

Before I could stop myself, I laughed out loud.

"That's enough, Miss Carrington," the president said. "And, Torrey, regardless of her intent—innocent or not—a women's fraternity would be a revolution. There hasn't been one permitted in the entire state of Illinois and I don't intend on leading the way. Whitsitt will not be a beacon for frustrated suffragettes."

Torrey must be the slight man, I realized. I recognized the name, but couldn't place it. Regardless, I loved him in that moment.

"You say that, and yet you don't vote to repeal Everett's mandate when it's addressed," Torrey said, glaring across the semicircle. "Which is at least once a semester."

"We're not here to argue about my voting habits, Torrey," President Wilson said. "For what it's worth, I don't vote for it because I don't figure it would make a difference. It'll never be repealed. We need his money. Anyway," he said, pinging his index finger across the necks of the rye bottles. "Miss Carrington, it really doesn't matter whether you've organized or not. Your guilt or innocence in arranging a secret society has been negated by the fact that you've vandalized our property and have obviously been in contact with a bootlegger. I have no choice but to expel you."

"No."

"It was me." Two voices rang out in tandem and I whirled around before I could fully process what he'd said.

Katherine and Mary were both on their feet. Mary yanked her black hat from her head and crushed it against her chest as though she were about to beg President Wilson for my life.

"The writing on the wall was my doing, sir, as was the—"

"The liquor is mine," Katherine said. "My father is a—"

"Corn grower," I said quickly. "Thank you both. You're my friends, but you can't take the blame for the things I've done."

The fraternity had been my idea. I'd brought them into it, and couldn't have them expelled. I felt sure of this, but as the realization of my fate dawned on me, my vision blurred and I reached out to clutch the railing behind me. What would I do now? No college would admit a woman who'd been dismissed. My father would be furious, our family name tarnished with my scandal. I'd have to move home and either find a position doing something menial or a husband with both liberal views and pockets deep enough to send me back to school—about as likely as finding a hen with teeth.

"Don't you think that expulsion is a bit extreme, President Wilson?" Grant asked as he rose from his seat.

"I'm afraid I do not," Wilson said.

"I'm a traditionalist like you, sir, but as much as I agree that Miss Carrington's actions deserve some type of repercussion, I have to point out that she's one of our brightest female students and the only one studying medicine."

President Wilson didn't respond, so Grant went on. "You can't expel her. Must I spell it out for you?"

"I suppose," Wilson said. I didn't understand where he was going with his argument either.

"When you review applications in the spring, how many females must you admit to retain Everett's funding?" Grant asked, his tone suggesting that the president was his fraternity brother instead of the man who occupied the highest position on Whitsitt's campus.

"Five percent of each class must be female," the old woman answered for President Wilson.

"That's right, Mrs. Smithfield, five percent of each class, freshman to senior. And what else does his trust mandate?" Grant asked.

He was met with silence.

An exasperated sigh escaped from his lips before he continued. "That of that five percent, there must be at least one female per class enrolled in each non-traditional major. You know that, Wilson."

This was news to me. I'd had no idea, though it did explain why I was the only woman in my classes.

"Of course I don't," President Wilson said. "Mr. Stout is in charge of applications. It's his job to know the particulars. I'm simply charged with voting on them." He balled his hands into fists on the desk top. "And you'll address me properly, Mr. Richardson."

"Apologies," Grant said, the corners of his lips rising. "Miss Carrington is the only female student studying medicine."

President Wilson shrugged.

"So we'll obtain another woman to take her place."

"Ask Mr. Stout how many applications Whitsitt receives from women desiring a sophomore medical placement," Grant said. "Actually, don't bother. The answer is zero."

"Then what'll you have me do, Mr. Richardson?" President Wilson sounded annoyed at being treated like a fool. I didn't blame him. Perhaps he should remember the feeling.

"You're the president. Find another way for Miss Carrington to pay for her sins and let her get on to class," Grant concluded. Reaching into his pocket he withdrew a silver watch and opened the clasp. "I have several brothers in her physics course. It begins in eight minutes."

Behind me, I heard Mary snicker, no doubt amused by the exchange.

"I apologize to all of you for drawing you from your homes unnecessarily," President Wilson said to the board.

"Don't bother," Torrey said, smiling. "The only appointment I had today was lunch with my wife's childhood friend and her husband. The man is a bore. This has been much more entertaining."

"Very well," President Wilson said. "Miss Carrington, you'll report to your course, but immediately following, you'll go directly to Miss Zephaniah. She'll be instructed to monitor you closely."

I nodded, relieved, the notion of being trailed by Miss Zephaniah a much more appealing option than expulsion.

"And in the meantime," he went on, "I'll be on the lookout for a suitable student to take your place if you decide to disregard our rules again."

I exhaled, waiting for the repercussions of breaking two of Whitsitt's rules.

President Wilson's brows rose.

"Would you like me to reconsider? Get to class, Miss Carrington."

"Thank . . . thank you, sir," I stuttered. I started unsteadily toward the door, not gambling another millisecond by waiting for Mary, Katherine, or Grant to catch up with me. As angry as President Wilson had been, it seemed quite strange that he hadn't given me some sort of punishment beyond a metaphorical smack on the wrist, but I wasn't complaining. I found my way out of the door, and paced down the empty hallway, realizing only after I'd made my way to the stairwell that I was shaking.

13

THE HALLS WERE vacant as I climbed to the general science hall on the third floor. The flood of students transitioning to their next classes had dispersed with the clock's shift to eleven-thirty. My chest still ached with the echo of my heart thumping. I'd almost lost everything. We'd been too hasty in approaching the board, our passion for immediate recognition fueled by Professor Helms's disgusting overtures and the atrocities dealt us in the classroom. But now that we'd been found out, it could happen again, and I doubted President Wilson would be as quick to dismiss it the next time.

The heady stink of formaldehyde forced its way into my nostrils as I reached the third floor landing. I coughed, my mind conjuring its source—the dozens of bloated frog corpses floating in jars at the front of the biology laboratory—and felt thankful that I wouldn't have to participate in another dissection course until next year. Last semester, I'd gone to the laboratory every evening and each time I'd been confronted with the lifeless forms, I'd been reminded of the vision of my mother's body, swollen and pale in our living room. The lid of the oak coffin had been propped open, sprays of flowers arranged around her soulless shell like the brightly colored lanterns in front of a freak show—attracting people to a sight so sadly unfair it would stay with them for years to come.

As my mother came into mind, I realized what I had to do. I had to dissolve Beta Xi Beta. It wasn't worth the risk. We'd given it a valiant effort, but we'd failed. I couldn't let the fraternity ruin my future or my friends'. If I was expelled, my life could mimic my mother's, and that kind of legacy wouldn't honor her. President Wilson was right: a women's fraternity would be a revolution, and I hadn't come to Whitsitt to start one. I'd come here to become a physician.

I took a breath through my mouth and made my way toward the physics classroom at the end of the hall. I spotted Will shuffling lackadaisically down the corridor in front of me in an indigo wool coat, as though he wanted to be later to his test than he already was.

"Will," I whispered. He stopped and turned to face me. "We were found out. One of the aides found out about . . . about us. President Wilson excused the offense this time, but—"

"What?"

I reached him in a few strides, realizing that in the seconds it had taken me to get to him, his attention had been drawn over my head. I could smell ginger candy on his breath. It was the only way he could make it through a test without vomiting, an antidote he'd discovered last year after he'd regurgitated his breakfast during the freshman seminar final. Examinations had always unnerved him, and though he insisted his lack of preparation had nothing to do with it, I begged to differ.

"Did you hear me?" I asked, but he didn't. His face paled. I heard a door slam, watched Will's shoulders twitch, and turned to find Kate Cable, the only woman Will had ever loved, standing alone in the middle of the hall. She was looking the other way, toying with a stray auburn strand that had come free of her loose bun as though she hadn't any idea which way to go. Miss Cable revolved toward us, and before I could comprehend what her presence meant, a strong arm swept across my back, jerking me into an embrace, and a hand wrapped around the nape of my neck. His lips fell on my forehead before I could stop him, and then in an instant, he released me. Neither of us moved, as though if we did, the crack that Will had just scored down the glass castle of our friendship would shatter.

"Yes," he whispered, answering a question I'd forgotten I'd asked. "Are you all right? I'm sorry. I should've been there."

"Mr. Buchannan. How nice to see you," Miss Cable said beside us. I stepped farther from Will, thinking that if I walked away now, while they were still staring at each other, I could spare myself the possibility that Miss Cable would bring up the embrace she'd just witnessed.

"And . . . and you, Kate . . . Miss Cable," he said. She'd flustered him—as she always had. I could still recall the blush on his face the night he met her. He'd been coming back to Whitsitt after Christmas, and had stopped his coach upon noticing hers had careened off the snowy road to campus. They'd got on instantly, and were barely separated after—until her departure. I'd asked him if he'd had any clue of why she hadn't responded to the confession that he loved her, why she hadn't said goodbye after graduation, but he'd had none. He still didn't. He thought they'd been in love.

"Miss Carrington," she said, tipping her head at me. I nodded, surprised she recalled my name. I wasn't going to act as though I liked her. She'd broken my best friend's heart. "I just knew the two of you would eventually find each other." Neither of us said anything. Will was still staring at her. I wished he would snap out of his shock and return to normal. Miss Cable pursed her rosebud lips.

"Well then. I suppose I'll be going. I've just come to retrieve something I left behind last year." She lifted her gloved hand to clutch Will's arm.

"What? What did you leave?" His question came out in a hoarse whisper, no doubt thinking what I was: that she'd come back for him. Miss Cable threw her head back and laughed. She'd known exactly what she was doing baiting him that way, knowing that he'd think she was referring to him, that he was what she'd left behind. I wanted to speak up, to tell her how little I thought of her, but that would only humiliate Will.

"My briefcase of course, I—"

"Apologize." Grant's voice boomed down the hall and my heart lurched in my chest. "I said, apologize to her, Buchannan. I thought my eyes were deceiving me. They weren't." I didn't turn around. I couldn't face him. How long had he been standing behind me? Apparently long enough to see Will pull me against him. Will blinked, gaze blank over my shoulder.

"I should go," Miss Cable said, but I barely heard her.

"You'll apologize to Beth," Grant said. Grant pushed a hand through his black hair and waited for Will to say something, but was met with silence. Suddenly, Grant lurched forward, snatching Will's lapels.

"You'll do as I say." Grant snarled the words, but Will didn't seem to register, eyes still focused on the empty space where Miss Cable had stood moments earlier. "Apologize," Grant said again, jerking Will toward him. At once, the haze cleared from Will's eyes and he laughed.

"Unhand me, Richardson," he said, attempting in vain to back away from Grant. "I wasn't trying to steal your sweetheart. I was trying to show a certain woman what she'd lost."

"You're a cad," Grant said. "It wouldn't matter if you *were* trying to entice Beth. She wouldn't choose you."

He let Will go, and I backed away from them.

"Are you all right?" Grant asked. His eyes creased with worry. I nodded. I didn't know why Grant seemed so concerned, unless he was more perceptive than I thought.

"It was just an embrace." Will said, shrugging as though his kissing my forehead were a habit, as though he hadn't altered our friendship with one gesture. He rolled his eyes at Grant and then looked at me. "I'm sorry, Beth."

"It's fine," I said. "Good luck on your test."

"I'll need it." He walked away. I watched him go, running his fingers down the wall as he went. He was selfish. He wasn't my friend. He'd used me and sacrificed the purity of our relationship in turn.

Grant clutched my arm.

"I'm sorry that I didn't get here in time to stop him. I followed you up here to make sure you were all right after what happened with the board. I came up the stairs at the far end of the hall," he said, tipping his head to a spot over my shoulder. "I saw a man grab someone, but I couldn't tell it was you and Buchannan until I got closer. I'm near-sighted, but I rarely wear glasses. Even given his . . . his tendency for escapades, I didn't think he'd be so crass."

I couldn't read his face, whether it betrayed either jealousy or anger. Whatever it was, he was trying hard to disguise it.

"Will loved her . . . Miss Cable," I said, stunned that even in my anger I'd defend him. "He didn't think before he did it. He panicked. When he let me go, he looked as though he'd seen a ghost. In any case, I was much more disturbed by my near expulsion, but your reasoning with President Wilson saved me."

Grant nodded and then he smiled. I leaned toward him and took his hand, remaining close as I took in the notes of coconut and palm oil in his hair.

"Without you, I'd be on a train back to Chicago by sundown."

"Thank goodness I could think of a way to help. I couldn't bear the thought of you gone," he said. "And I'm sorry about the fraternity. Even though I was never for it, I know how passionately you loved it."

"It's all right," I said. "It meant a lot to me, but my studies mean more." I studied the detail on the row of brass buttons along his wool coat in an attempt to distract myself from the sadness I felt at the loss of our sisterhood. "And as much as I want to, I can't risk trying to convince him again. Perhaps someday, after I've graduated, I could petition the board to start one for the women after me . . . if there are any left."

Grant laughed.

"The women will still be here," he said. "Patrick Everett made sure of that, and Whitsitt can't survive without his money . . . well, without his money and mine."

The church tower rang in the distance, signaling half past twelve.

"I've got to get to class," I said, feeling suddenly exhausted.

Grant lifted my hand to his mouth, kissed it, and let it go.

"I'll see you later, Miss Carrington," he said. "And, perhaps you're right. Perhaps, when you come back to this school as a regarded female physician, they'll actually listen."

* * *

Professor Stallings barely acknowledged me when I walked into my physics class. The room was windowless, lit only by four oil lamps spread along a desk at the front. He squinted at the door, gestured for me to sit with the small rod he always carried, as if it didn't bother him that I was late, and turned back to a representation of waves on one side of the board and tiny dots on the other. I sank into a chair at the back, thankful that the rest of the students were mostly gathered in the front half of the room. As hard as I tried to concentrate, Professor Stallings's voice was only a hum somewhere on the periphery of my thoughts.

"Mr. Goldin, tell me about A.J. Fresnel's Wave Theory."

"I . . . I'm not sure sir."

My attention snapped back to the lecture. He never called on anyone. If he called on me next, I was unprepared to respond.

The classroom erupted in laughter as Professor Stallings attempted a joke about a particle traveling light, but despite my effort, I could barely remain present. Instead, I felt the echo of tension in my chest as President Wilson had extracted our bylaws from his desk, felt Will's lips on my forehead, and saw the genuine concern on Grant's face when he'd asked if I was all right.

Grant had saved me yet again, calmed my heart for the third time. I was thankful for his momentary stability because as angry as I was at Will, I was also concerned for him. From the moment Miss Cable had broken his heart last year, I'd worried about him—and rightly so. He'd careened into debauchery with such ease, acting as though nothing had the capacity to hurt him, but it was easy to see that that was only an act. His heart had been severed anew when he'd seen Miss Cable today. Unlike Grant, who masked his pain in an arrogant façade so practiced that the only way you'd get through was if he chose to let you, Will's wounds were always visible. They were so easily detected that Miss Cable had known exactly the right place to prod her knife to see if she still had an effect on him. Her callousness made me sick.

"Augustin-Jean Fresnel was so confident in his findings that it's said he found greater pleasure in being right than he did in receiving compliments from his critics," Professor Stallings said before pausing to examine the room. He leaned toward us. "You must understand. When you're long graduated and finished with studying physics or anatomy or biology, you must find pride in yourself, you must believe that you possess the power to restore health. Your patients will feel your confidence, and they'll be at ease in your presence."

Professor Stallings turned back to the board to continue his lecture. He drew his rod along the waves, emitting a terrible screeching noise that made the hair on my arms stand on end.

"With all due respect, Professor, what does any of this have to do with diagnosing and treating patients?" The question came from someone behind me, interrupting Professor Stallings's lecture. Professor Stallings laughed.

"Believe it or not, Mr. Alcott, you're not the first student to ask. But, the truth is that the study of physics is the basis of everything you'll do. It's the study of matter, the very particles of the body. If you don't understand the way matter reacts, you'll never understand how the body works. I'll give you an example," Professor Stallings said, tapping the top of his desk. "I trust you've secured your summer apprenticeship, Mr. Alcott. What will you be doing?"

My heart sank at the mention of an apprenticeship. Will had said only a few weeks before that I was ahead of everyone else in my search. Perhaps I'd only been more aggressive than him.

"My father specializes in optics," the student responded with a sigh.

"Ha!" Professor Stallings responded, thrusting his finger toward Mr. Alcott. "Fresnel's Wave Theory will have a direct impact on your practice. You see, his hypothesis was a breakthrough in magnification. As of now, it's only being used in lighthouses, but it's rumored that with a bit of time, the same technique can be utilized in eyeglasses."

The professor paused, clearly expecting some type of wonderment from Mr. Alcott.

"Oh," he said.

Stallings shook his head and glanced around the room.

"This is a deviation from the syllabus, but . . . if you've secured an apprenticeship, please raise your hand."

Papers shuffled as nearly every student abandoned their notes to raise their hands. Urgency raced through my veins, and I tried to quash the notion that if I hadn't found a position yet, I never would.

"Thank you," Professor Stallings said, and the hands lowered. "Mr. Washburn. Your apprenticeship will be?"

"I'll be working with my family's physician in Connecticut, sir."

I stared at Mr. Washburn's back, at his red curly hair and stick-straight posture, wondering if his bedside manner would be as rigid as he was.

"You'll be responsible for quite a lot," Professor Stallings said. "I imagine you'll do a fair amount of hernia repairs. In 1646, a man named Blaise Pascal inserted a tube into a barrel filled with water. He then poured water into the tube and the barrel burst."

The professor stopped for a moment and drew a rudimentary depiction of the experiment on the blackboard. "The notion that the change in pressure at any point in an enclosed fluid at rest is transmitted undiminished to all points in the fluid will be important to remember because it'll help you reduce cut-through. The thickness of the suture will determine the tissue reaction."

Stallings dusted the chalk from his hands as his eyes settled on me.

"Miss Carrington, what will you be working on this summer?"

My mouth opened, but nothing came out. Surely he'd noticed that I hadn't raised my hand.

"Miss Carrington?" I waited for him to go on, to make an example of the only female medical student, a student without an apprenticeship, but he didn't.

"I'm . . . I'm afraid I don't know yet," I said. "But I've applied to several hospitals. I'd like to work with acute and terminal cases."

"Interesting," he said, his tone even. "I imagine most hospitals are still living under an archaic system. It will be rather difficult to secure an apprenticeship as a female, I fear."

Voices and laughter rose in response to his words and my jaw pinched shut.

"Silence!" he shouted. I'd had no idea that Professor Stallings was so progressive. "If you can't secure a vocation close to home, I recommend you try the New England Hospital for Women and Children, if you haven't already, or any of the larger institutions in New York City. They seem to be a bit more enlightened."

"Thank you, sir," I said.

"In any case, you'll see mostly diseased organs and tissue as a hospital physician dealing with acute illnesses. That line of work will demand that you have a solid understanding of the body at an atomic level, because that's where disease begins and spreads. Most of the time, patients requiring acute care will need to be dealt with swiftly—if they are to live at all. Are you certain that you want to subject yourself to the heartache, Miss Carrington?"

I nodded, hearing the faraway sound of my mother's screams as they'd cut into her chest.

I'd been on the other side of the wall, in reception, when they'd decided to see if her lungs had been restricted by mucus. They'd given her ether, but not enough. They said she'd gone into shock after, that her lungs hadn't been able to keep up with her hysteria. Whatever the actual reason, she'd died three days later.

"Very well, my dear," Professor Stallings said. His voice sounded tunneled and hollow to me, far away from the memories at the forefront of my mind. "You're much stronger than I." He glanced at his watch. "It seems that we're out of time, class. We'll continue with the wave theory first thing next week."

I departed the room and found Mary waiting in the hallway. She ran her fingers along the spine of the crow's feather shooting from the hat in her hand.

"What're you doing here?" I said. "Aren't you going to be late for your organ course?" Every student of the conservatory of music had to have at least a rudimentary knowledge of organ, and the only organ on campus was in the chapel, at least a ten-minute walk away.

She shrugged.

"Probably so, but Professor Martin is only having us listen to some organist from Maryland play in the chapel today, so I signed the attendance log early and came here. I'll sneak into the chapel after I tell you what I came to say. Professor Martin won't be the wiser."

"We could have spoken afterward," I said. "There was no need for you to risk trouble."

"Yes there was. This matter is of utmost importance after what transpired in the board room," she said, walking with me as I made my way down the hall. "I think I've found a new place to meet. It'll require us to be incredibly careful, but—"

"We'll not keep it up," I whispered. "I'm dissolving Beta Xi Beta. We tried, but we failed. You heard President Wilson. If we continue, we'll be expelled. I'm not willing to risk everything on an idea." I felt Mary twitch away from me, but I couldn't look at her. I knew what I'd see—almond eyes tapered like a hawk, mouth pinched in a manner that would force me to reconsider, and I couldn't. She'd grown up with a woman whose demonstrations and work for women's rights put both herself and Mary in peril daily. For Mary's mother, Judith, it was worth it. She was fighting to reform the way generations of women were treated. We were campaigning for a group that, even if we did succeed, might not last another class, let alone to our daughters' possible attendance.

"Stop being such a coward. You know how important this is for the future of Whitsitt women. We cannot continue to allow them to treat us as though we're lesser. We have a plan. James will come through for us and we'll start recruitment, we'll—"

"When I graduate and become a physician, it won't matter," I interrupted, stopping in the middle of the hallway. I felt cold and selfish, as though I'd traded my future for the happiness of my friends. "All of us will earn our diplomas. I'll not let the fraternity stand in the way of that. I'll not have us forced into menial lives because we chose to defy the board. It was a lovely idea, but it's over."

"You don't have to participate," she said quietly, "but you're not going to be the one to make that decision. It's been my dream as much as yours and I'll see it through. We will continue." She spun away from me, paced to the stairwell, and disappeared. I bit my bottom lip to keep it from trembling and reminded myself that I was doing the right thing.

14

JANUARY 23, 1892

Lily grasped a clump of my hair, forced a pin around it, and thrust it across my scalp. The silver point prodded into my skin and I winced, looking up from the new *Boston Medical and Surgical Journal*.

"Stay still," she said. "Unless you want to be late." She appraised the mass of hair swirled loosely at the top of my head in a style identical to hers.

"No, I don't. Of course I don't," I said, roused from my thoughts. I'd been scanning a new article on the dangers of overlooking lead poisoning as a factor in nerve disease, while really thinking of Will and Grant. I hadn't seen either of them in several days and couldn't help but wonder if what had transpired between Will and me had altered Grant's affection. I knew I shouldn't care, but my feelings for Grant had deepened regardless of my intentions. I'd been fretting about my relationship with Will, too. Thinking of him at all made me feel uncomfortable and I doubted he'd avoided the feeling—which would explain his distance. He'd come to Professor Fredericks's class late and quickly departed at the conclusion, before I could make my way to the back of the room.

I'd told Lily about Will's embrace straightaway, that he'd only done it in an attempt to make Miss Cable jealous. I couldn't keep hiding things from her hoping that I could somehow revert back to the past and change them. She'd laughed, saying she'd known she was right about Will loving me—even though his gesture hadn't at all been about us—but I could tell in her expression that she was disappointed. Even so, she'd received a note from Will yesterday asking her to accompany him to Iota Gamma's Saint Valentine's Bird Party. Traditionally, it was a romantic event meant to symbolize a bird's everlasting commitment to his mate, although in true Iota fashion, it was taken much less seriously, mostly used as an excuse to embarrass the pledges. Lily hadn't answered his note straight away, insisting that he was only asking because I was taken. But I wasn't. Grant hadn't asked me yet, and I wasn't convinced he was going to.

"He's been busy, Beth. He'll ask. The law students have had exams this week. The library was teeming with them last night after I met with Mary and Katherine," Lily said, as though she'd read my mind. Her blue eyes squinted as she took a final section of hair from the nape of my neck and pinned it up. "Are you sure you'll not consider rejoining the fraternity you started?"

I shook my head. She hadn't argued with me when I'd told her that I wasn't planning to continue on, but she'd met the news with silence, before diverting her attention to the composition book in her hand. I'd been confused by her reaction. I'd assumed that she'd left the board room during the hearing because she was afraid of getting caught—a sign that she'd agree with my abandoning the fraternity—but she later mentioned that she'd only stepped out because she didn't want to risk being late for class.

"Very well. I'm finished," Lily said as she stepped away from me, head cocked to the side as she looked at our reflections in the mirror. She was beautiful. Her pale skin had always been flawless, but tonight it looked as though her cheeks had been brushed with crushed rose petals.

"Thank you for going with me tonight. It's not exactly your field of study, I know," I told her.

Elizabeth Blackwell was making a presentation to a group of Eastern Star suffragists in Green Oaks. Mary's mother had organized it and Mary had invited me, knowing how enthralled I was with the famous doctor.

"Of course," Lily said. "You'll likely be the only other physician there anyway. Everyone else wants to hear her because she's a pioneer." She glanced at herself in the mirror. "Do I look all right?"

She was wearing a new dress she'd been working on for a month, made of pieces of chine silk of variegated colors. It was her best work by far, constructed from nearly a dozen old costumes.

"You're stunning," I told her sincerely.

She shook her head.

"What did I do to deserve a friend who will resort to lying when I need reassurance?"

I laughed, pointing to the mirror.

"You know I'm not exaggerating. Look at yourself."

"I can't with you standing beside me. You're only the most gorgeous, sought after woman at Whitsitt," she said, smiling. "I do believe you've stolen the title from that divinity girl, Luetta Grace."

I doubted that. Perhaps I'd won the title of the most gossiped-about girl on campus. It had only taken a few hours before it seemed that every student knew about my proposal—not that anyone had actually said anything to my face, but the looks had told me all I needed to know.

"And I know you haven't asked, but I can tell you're wondering," Lily continued. "I haven't decided whether I'm going to accept Will's offer or not. I find it quite valiant of him, but I know he's only asking because he supposes you'll be there with Grant and you'd like my company." She lifted her arm to silence me before I could argue. "I wasn't fishing for a response. I was merely thinking out loud."

"I think you should go," I said.

She leaned down and untucked a wayward seam of the ivory lace yoke attached to my bodice. My father had sent the costume from Chicago a week ago. "For as slippery a man as you make him out to be, your father has fine taste in fashion." I shook my head.

"It's not him. It's Vera . . . his wife," I said. From the moment she'd married my father, at least half of his pay had been invested in fashions—never mind the fact that we lived in a modest middle-class neighborhood where the average woman likely acquired no more than a single new dress each season. That's why I hadn't worn it yet. Each time I saw the box at the bottom of my armoire, I saw her face scowling at me from flouncy collars of pleated chiffon.

"Either way, it makes you look as beautiful as a painting," Lily said. She grasped a bit of my skirt—light green-blue silk decorated with olive green velvet flowers. "The color brings out your eyes."

I snorted.

"My eyes are gray," I said. "About as beautiful as flint. Let's hope they don't cross. I might start a fire."

* * *

By the time I checked in with Miss Zephaniah—something I was required to do three times each day since the board meeting—and we made our way to the foyer, it was pouring. Lily edged the door open, squinting past the porch in the darkness to see if the coach had arrived. The cold crept in, smacking my cheeks, and I huddled into my coat, wondering how it wasn't snowing.

"Not here yet," she announced loudly, though I could barely hear her over the downpour. It sounded like the dormitory had been swept beneath a waterfall. A group of four girls, completely drenched, suddenly burst through the door, all of them laughing.

One of them smiled at me and then turned back to her friends.

"I haven't been this soaked since the coach's wheel went flat after our first welcome dinner at the church. We had to get out and wait in the rain while it was repaired. Remember?"

They kept on down the hall, laughing and reminiscing as they made their way to the gathering room. Their closeness stung so soon after I'd decided to withdraw from my sisters. I forced the thought of the fraternity out of my mind. I'd still have Mary and Lily and Katherine regardless. Just because I wasn't a part of Beta Xi Beta didn't mean they'd abandon me. *But they'd have new memories.* Memories I wouldn't share.

"Perhaps they're just delayed on account of the weather," I said, hoping conversation would distract me from my melancholy.

"Or maybe Mary forgot to call a driver for us." Lily sighed. "We should have requested a coach from the school instead."

"It'll be here," I promised her, glancing at the grandfather clock. Seven-fifty. The talk began at eight and it would take us at least ten minutes to get out of Whitsitt and into Green Oaks.

"Come on," Lily said, yanking my arm. "He's here."

I pulled the collar of my coat over my head in an attempt to shield my face from the rain. The last snow had mostly melted, only present in some spots where the sun never hit. The excess water made the ground spongy, absorbing the heels of my kid leather boots with each step.

"I hope Doctor Blackwell doesn't mind that I look like I've come from a swim," I said, depositing myself in the coach. My cloak would have to be cleaned. Sediment lined the hem and rose upward, clinging to the damp in haphazard waves that lightened at my shins.

"She's a doctor, not a fashion designer," said Lily, whose dress was still immaculate, but hair was drenched. Long drips of water trickled down her face, and she pushed the saturated tendrils back with her palm.

"Have you thought of what you'll say to her?" Lily asked. "You've wanted to meet her for years."

"I don't know," I said. The rain beat hard on the top of the coach. "I suppose I never thought I'd have the chance."

I tucked my legs against the bench seat, feeling the chill of the wet fabric on my skin. At once, nerves eclipsed my excitement. I couldn't face her. I was going to be late and I looked like a mop in a dirty bucket. She deserved better than my worst.

"I can't do it," I said. "Signal him to turn around, will you?"

Lily laughed as the coach careened right.

"Don't be silly. We're almost there."

I looked out the window, but couldn't see a thing through the curtain of rain. It had been at least five minutes, more than enough time for us to reach the row of three street lights along Whitsitt's Main Street, but I hadn't caught a glimmer. The coach slowed and I edged closer to the window, where I could see that we were passing under a stone arch.

"This isn't the way to Green Oaks," I said, unease prickling my skin. "We're going the wrong direction. We're going to be late."

"No we're not," she said, blue eyes glistening with mischief. "Doctor Blackwell has been . . . delayed."

Before I could ask what she meant, the coach shook to a halt.

"Are we stuck?"

"No," Lily said. "Come on." I remained seated as she opened the door and reached back for me. An enormous white clapboard house stood next to us, seeming to materialize like an apparition in the dim.

"Where are we?"

"Patrick Everett's old estate."

All of the windows were dark and the white paint was peeling. The house looked haunted. The wind howled through the open door of the coach, blowing stray droplets of rain inside. I didn't move.

"Why are we here? I don't want to miss hearing Doctor Blackwell."

"Doctor Blackwell isn't coming," she said. "She never was. Now, come with me."

She walked out into the rain, but I remained, refusing to budge until she told me the reason she'd brought me here. As she turned back and called my name, something altered my stubbornness. I'd have to trust her. It was always my inclination to refuse to cooperate unless the idea was mine. As much as I tried to fight it, at times, I failed, and my friendships suffered.

"Wait," I called to her, not bothering to shield my head this time as I exited the coach. Wind ripped through my hair, tearing it from the pins as drops pelted my face. I lifted my skirts to my ankles as we hastened around the side of the house, which had a sagging wide front porch. Upon closer inspection, I noticed that some of the windows were broken. I stopped.

"What're you doing?" Lily yelled over the roar of the wind and the scrape of dry tree branches against the slate roof. There was no moon tonight. The clouds had covered it, and I could only make out Lily's silhouette in front of me.

"Am I going to die?" I asked her, only half-joking. Lily huffed and yanked me forward, finally leading me around that back of the house and up the steps of a small porch looking out on a crumbling brick carriage house and a vacant field. I wiped the water from my face and hazarded a glance through the windows, noticing a tiny flicker of light coming from a center room. Lily stopped in front of the door, knocked twice, tapped four times, and rolled her knuckles.

"No." I whirled around, anger racing through my veins. "I can't believe you tricked me into attending a meeting. I'm going back to Everett Hall. I told you that I was finished with Beta Xi Beta and I meant it."

"Beth, wait," Lily said, but I didn't stop as I made my way down the porch steps. Rain poured over me, and I squinted down at my boots. My chest smashed into something, and I stumbled back, meeting the face of a man who laughed and lifted a hand to shield his doe-like eyes from the rain.

"Apologies," he said. He looked familiar.

"Where do you think you're going, Beth?" Mary's voice rang out and I turned around looking for her.

"I told you that I didn't want any part of this," I said as she emerged from behind the man I'd just collided with. If Miss Zephaniah had had me followed—something she'd threatened to do after President Wilson had demanded that she keep a closer eye on me—they'd know that we weren't attending a talk but were sneaking away to an illicit fraternity meeting . . . and utilizing the private property of one of our school's founders to do it.

"Yes, you do. You fought for his fraternity to the point of expulsion," Mary declared. Water drizzled over her brimless black hat, plastering her short bangs to her forehead. Her eyelashes gleamed in the starlight, frozen in the chill. "I know this is still your dream. You're just scared. I won't let you give it up."

She was right. I wanted more than anything to fight harder, to show President Wilson that he couldn't stifle us, but I couldn't risk it again.

"You'll have to," I said. "You don't have a choice."

"No. If we're found out, I'll say that we forced your involvement," she said with a shrug. "It's the truth."

"They wouldn't believe it. And what are we doing here anyway? Who's that?" I asked as I gestured to the man behind her. He was staring at the sky, top hat clenched in one hand while the rain drenched him.

"Katherine's brother, Mr. Sanderson," she said, leaning in close to my ear. "He's as handsome as a dream, isn't he? And, if you come in, I'll tell you why we're here." Her breath reeked of alcohol, a cocktail of sweet-sour and oak.

I shook my head, glancing from Mr. Sanderson to Mary and back again, wondering how much rye they'd consumed between them.

"Do reconsider, Beth. You're already here. You'll have to walk otherwise. The coaches aren't due back until nine-thirty," she told me, nodding toward the drive, which was vacant.

I sighed.

"Very well. I'll come in. But I'm not going to change my mind."

Mary smiled and whirled on her heel, only to stumble over her brocaded black skirt. I lunged for her, righting her just in time to keep her from plunging into the mud.

"Thank you, Beth. Come along, Mr. Sanderson," she called.

"How much rye did you and Mr. Sanderson have before you got here?" I asked, not bothering to lower my voice. I couldn't hear her laugh over the rain, but watched her smile as Mr. Sanderson sprinted up to the porch, taking the stairs two at a time.

"Half a bottle . . . maybe a little more," she admitted, barely meeting my eyes before turning her focus to Mr. Sanderson, who stood with his hat flattened over the breast of his soggy brown jacket. "His coach got stuck in the mud, see? So I volunteered to go retrieve him. We had to wait on another, so to pass the time—"

"M'lady," Mr. Sanderson drawled, extending his hand to help

Mary up the stairs. She giggled as he swept her up the last step and pulled her under his arm.

I watched the interaction with interest, never having had occasion to see Mary flirt with a man.

"No," Mary edged in front of Mr. Sanderson, who had started to turn the knob, and pushed his arm away sloppily. "You must knock first."

"All right then, ma'am. Go on," he said, scuffing his boot on the bowing wood. "I didn't mean offense, but seeing as nobody's told me why I'm sneaking around dead people's homes, I didn't know better."

Mary ignored him and knocked.

"Your sister didn't tell you?" I asked. His gaze met mine and he shook his head, closed lips quirking up at the edges. As I registered that expression, I remembered. He was the boy I'd run into in the dining hall the night I'd found out about Lily's entanglements with Professor Helms. I'd thought he'd looked familiar then, and now I knew why. He and Katherine may as well have been twins.

"She did not," he said steadily. "Just told me to be ready at seven and that the coach would know where to take me."

"Who knocks on the door of Beta Xi Beta?" Lily's voice sounded faint.

"I'm indebted to my sister," he continued to me, as though he hadn't heard Lily's reply. "Quite severely, in fact, so when she told me that I'd find out when I arrived, I didn't ask."

"It's Mary, Queen of . . . the Universe," she said, and turned to me. "Since Beth is no longer President, I shan't accept the throne of debauchery."

"Neither of you can be president," Mr. Sanderson said, swaying in place. "Chester Arthur is Commander-in-Chief." I laughed, highly confused, but also amused. He was so intoxicated.

The door opened and Lily looked past Mary and Mr. Sanderson to me. She fingered the brim of the blue hood and her eyes pooled with tears.

"Thank goodness. I knew you'd change your mind," she whispered.

As though her words reignited a flame, I glared at her.

"I'm not returning to the fraternity," I said. "There wasn't a coach and it's pouring or I would have walked back. If all of you would like to risk your diplomas, so be it. But I will not."

Lily blinked at me.

"Very well," she said. The old wood floor screeched beneath our feet as she led us down the dark hallway, echoing the dusty, fallow smell of the place. Voices hummed somewhere, but I couldn't tell where they were coming from or where we were going. I reached out to run my hands along the wall for balance. Instead of plaster, my fingers grazed splintered wood and I winced.

"The plaster's all but come off of the walls," Lily said. "There are leaks all over this place and the termites seem to have made their home in the beams."

A hinge creaked ahead of me and a bit of light spilled into the hallway, brightening an expansive foyer. A chandelier of cobwebs swung from the pitched ceiling.

"Come on." Lily grabbed my wrist and dragged me away from my appraisal of the once-grand home.

"We're going to have to swim back to campus," Mr. Sanderson said as we entered the sitting room. He walked over to one of two windows flanking the wide plaster arch of a colonial fireplace.

Katherine laughed. She was tucked into Lily's homemade cloak, sitting on a threadbare oriental rug next to Mary who was propped in a wooden chair, watching her rain-soaked sleeves lighten the finish. Katherine nodded at me, and handed Mary a cloak.

"You should pray you don't have to," Katherine said. Her brother swayed and reached to steady himself on the windowsill. "You'd drown. You're a terrible swimmer when you're sober, let alone positively bashed."

Lily disappeared from my side, skirting a lighted candelabrum on a mahogany table in the middle of the room to settle on a green leather settee. She was stony-faced as she appraised Mr. Sanderson and Mary. I knew she was thinking of her father, of the way he'd been wasted by drink at the end. She'd told me that she tried to erase the memory of his miserable later years, of his slurred words and stumbling gait, but that at times, the vision materialized anyway.

"I am not," Mr. Sanderson said. He whirled toward his sister, nearly dislodging a portrait of a woman's naked backside over the mantle. "A terrible swimmer, I mean."

Mary snickered.

"Don't fear, darling," she said. "My mother insisted that I don a bathing costume every week when it was warm enough and plunge into the Long Island Sound. I could save you . . . though, swimming in the company of these skirts might make it difficult." She pinched the cloak covering the black satin fabric across her knees.

"Are y'all going to tell me why I'm here?" Mr. Sanderson paced back and forth in front of the fireplace. "I don't much like this place. I can feel ghosts." I could tell that he was trying to enunciate his words, but the rye overrode his effort, sliding one syllable into the next.

"I do too," Mary said. "Every time I'm here, I can feel his spirit, as though he's saying, 'I'm with you, Mary.' It's quite comforting."

Lily coughed.

"Every time you're here?" I asked. *How often did she break into Patrick Everett's home?*

"I have to let the Illinois chapter of Women for Women in from time to time," she said, referencing her mother's organization. "We're almost exactly halfway between Springfield and Chicago, so they meet here instead of having to travel back and forth to each city."

"You've decided to make a habit of breaking in to the home of one of our founders? Aren't you worried you'll be expelled?" I asked.

Mary shook her head, running her fingers along the ruined black crow feather attached to the side of her hat.

"A few weeks ago, Mother ran into Mr. Everett's daughter riding her wheel back home on the Midway Plaisance. She stopped her and asked for permission. Of course she didn't mind, seeing as they've no use for the place and are staunch suffragists themselves."

"This is fascinating, truly, but if y'all have ripped me from my studies for the sole purpose of my company and my handsome face, I'm afraid I'm going to have to retire," Mr. Sanderson said, leaning against the mantle and staring at Mary until she looked up at him.

"Considering no one else is speaking up, I will," Lily said. "As you may know, Mr. Sanderson, Miss Carrington recently spoke to the board about starting a women's fraternity."

He laughed.

"Oh yes. And was almost dismissed from Whitsitt. Well, for that and possession of four bottles of rye."

"Yes," I said, cutting him off. "And that's why I've resigned my membership in this fraternity."

"I should have known you'd tangle yourself in something of this nature, Katherine," Mr. Sanderson said. "But what does it have to do with me?"

"You're going to accept Mr. Stephens's bid to join Iota Gamma," Katherine said. "And then, you're going to tell us their secrets, their procedures, all of it."

"Why?" he said, his forehead crinkling. "You know how I feel about societies, Kat. I can guarantee they've simply copied the Masonic rituals. They take you in, make you swear your life and soul to their cause, and force you to attend meetings discussing forbidden topics and conspiracy—"

"I highly doubt they have any similarities to the Masons given their scrutiny by the board," Katherine said, cutting him off. "But if we can figure their secrets, if we can organize exactly as they are, then we can petition the board based on Mr. Everett's stipulation that women be allowed equal rights."

"That, or blackmail Mr. Richardson to force the board's hand if we find something unfavorable," Mary said.

Her words took me by surprise. They couldn't blackmail Grant. Not after what he'd done for me, for us.

"You can't do that," I said. "He's kept our secret. He saved me from expulsion."

"Don't mind her," Mary said. "Mr. Richardson fancies her and she him."

"I'll not allow you to do that," I said again. "And I wouldn't say that I—" I started to argue that I didn't have any feelings for him, but Mary cut me off, saving me from my lie.

"He's done some honorable things as of late, but I can't help but think that it's all tied to his feelings for you." She stared at me, eyes flushed from the rye. "And you won't be involved anyway. You're not a part of this sisterhood, remember?"

"Even if you replicated Iota Gamma perfectly, it wouldn't matter. You'd all be expelled for organizing a secret society," Mr. Sanderson said, preventing further discussion of Grant, to my relief. "I don't see how that would work."

"We'll be starting recruitment soon," Lily said. "We're hoping to initiate at least one woman from each traditionally male field of study. We discovered at the board meeting that Whitsitt has to maintain at least one female in each."

"And you're counting on the hope that they'll not simply expel all of you and find replacements?" Mr. Sanderson asked. He smoothed the corners of his blond moustache.

"It worked in Beth's case," Katherine said.

Mr. Sanderson took a step and stumbled unsteadily into the mantle.

"You realize that it's a gamble at best. I hate to bring him up again, but part of Miss Carrington's luck was Mr. Richardson," he said.

"You owe me anything I ask," Katherine said.

"You're asking me to ruin my potential legal career for this scheme," he snapped. "You understand that, don't you? It's already difficult to get enough studying in without the distraction of a fraternity."

"And the only reason you're here in the first place is because I agreed to pick up the slack for you," Katherine said, betraying no acknowledgment that taking over his responsibility was exactly what she'd wanted. "This fraternity is important to me. You know . . . you know I've already lost our sister, James. I miss her. And as wonderful as you are, it's not the same. I need these girls and this group."

"You won't regret it, Mr. Sanderson," Lily said. "I promise. Anything you tell us will stay in this circle."

Mr. Sanderson grunted.

"I suppose I don't have much of a choice." He glared at Katherine. "I'd already declined, but I'll write back to Sam telling him that I'll accept the bid after all."

Mary clapped and jumped up, barely stopping herself from throwing her arms around Mr. Sanderson's neck.

"We'll swear to it . . . on our sisterhood," she said to him. "Gather around, ladies."

Lily stood to join Mary and Katherine, but I remained seated. I was only a spectator to this disaster. I clasped my hands in front of me and stared at my mother's plain silver wedding ring to avoid the others.

"This pledge is our promise to Mr. Sanderson, to each other, that we'll keep all of this in confidence," Lily said. She reached for Mary's hand, then Katherine's. She squeezed their hands and their voices joined.

"I solemnly pledge my loyalty to the sisterhood of Beta Xi Beta until the end of my days." Goosebumps prickled my arms. I'd never heard our pledge recited without my own voice in the chorus. I looked at the circle of women, my best friends willing to sacrifice their futures for the sake of women to come, and suddenly felt selfish. Redeeming my mother's meaningless life was about something greater than me, about something greater than my success. I couldn't alter the way women were treated on my own—neither could Susan B. Anthony or Doctor Blackwell or Elizabeth Cady Stanton. They needed each other and the thousands of women fighting for change, for understanding.

"I promise above all else, my purpose will be to foster equality and intellect among women." I found myself mouthing the words, and broke into the circle between Mary and Lily. "For a chain of linked hands is mightier than the most menacing army," I said, and as my voice joined with theirs, as my sisters' fingers clutched mine, I knew I'd found my way back home.

15

A S WE WALKED to the Iota Gamma house together, valentines clutched in our fists, masses of feathers fluttering from our dresses, the sun was sinking over Old Main, washing the campus in coral. In front of me, Mary laughed at something Katherine said, startling me from my dwelling on an apprenticeship rejection I'd received from a hospital run out of a private home in Elgin. I watched as Mary straightened the orange paper machete beak against her forehead—the only part of her that wasn't covered in black feathers. She and Mr. Sanderson had been assigned to dress as blackbirds, a convenient species for a woman who believed in a monochrome color scheme regardless.

"Have y'all ever heard that a canary is meant to represent a gossip?" Katherine asked.

"No," I said. "I've always heard that they're a symbol of freedom, or perhaps intellect."

"I've never heard that. At bird parties back home, the canary was always designated to the nosy parker, someone always in another's business," she said, lifting her chin. Regardless of the significance, the costume was perfect for Katherine, the yellow feathers at the crown of her head nearly blending into her blonde hair. "So, I've been wondering all this time if the Iotas intended to humiliate me or if they were thinking of my date . . . what's his name again?"

She'd been set up with a pledge brother of Mr. Sanderson's, a man she'd only met once in passing.

Mary shrugged.

"Oh, I remember, Peter. Mr. Peter Morgan," Katherine said with a smile. "He doesn't seem as though he speaks much at all, let alone takes to gossiping."

"Sometimes the subdued are the most trouble," I said. The worst behaved boy in my grammar school had been a mousy twig who sat in the corner pretending to read. Every time the teacher turned her back, he'd shoot spitballs at her.

"I suppose it doesn't really matter," she said. "The only important thing is that I'm coming. I wouldn't miss the chance to see my brother in a bird costume for the world."

We passed the dining hall, meriting strange looks from a group of freshman men congregating on the steps. Our costumes didn't faze the other students, who knew quite well where we were headed. The Iota Gammas held the same party every year.

The tiny bells attached to the edges of my lace-trimmed paper heart jingled and I grinned at the thought of Grant gluing the lace in precise strips down the edges. When I'd received it, I'd doubted that he'd actually made it. I still did, but the nearly illegible scrawling along the front was definitely his doing—a short but beautiful poem. "*You caught my interest from the start, as though from the crows there descended a dove. Since, you have captured my heart, and in turn, I give you all my love.*" His earnestness had at first caught me off guard, though it shouldn't have. In the month and a half since I'd met him, he'd always been quite frank with me about everything, but I hadn't expected that he'd fallen in love with me. I suppose I thought loving someone required knowing them for longer than we'd known each other, but perhaps I was wrong.

I sighed and tucked the valentine under my arm. My fingers grazed the décolleté lace across my chest, embroidered with red and brown thread and glass rubies. Grant and I were cardinals. A sign of nobility, passion, and beauty, it was a fitting symbol for him, but I would have preferred something more daring myself, like a wild duck. I clutched a handful of scarlet feathers at my skirt as I followed Mary and Katherine across a puddle of mud pooling along the walk. A bright blue feather floated on the puddle, and I wondered if Luetta Grace and the divinity girls had already arrived. We hadn't seen anyone else with appropriate bird party attire in Everett Hall, and though I knew not all of the Iota Gammas invited Whitsitt girls, I had a feeling the same girls from our dormitory who'd attended the winter ball would be here.

Mary leaned in to Katherine's ear and whispered something. They started giggling like little girls and I wondered if perhaps Mary was reminding her of the manner in which Mr. Sanderson and Mr. Morgan had come calling. It had been their first task as a pledges before their official naming tonight. The brothers had given them Shakespearean costumes of puffed short pants atop long stockings, and had forced them to recite the soiree invitation to Mary and Katherine in Old English. The four of us had gone down to the foyer to watch the spectacle. Mr. Sanderson had embraced the role, dramatically clasping his hand to his heart while kneeling in front of Mary, while the other man trembled and mumbled the words. I'd laughed until I couldn't breathe myself and had noticed that Miss Zephaniah had almost laughed as well.

"I shouldn't have accepted." Lily's voice startled me out of my thoughts. She held Will's valentine out in front of her. It was a mess, in typical Will fashion. The heart was misshapen, one side of it larger than the other, and he'd decorated it with a menagerie of mismatching tassels and lace.

"Why would you say that?" I asked.

"He doesn't feel for me," she whispered. "He's only ever called to ask me to accompany him to events, never to take a walk or escort me to class or on a whim. And yet, I'm gallivanting around Iota Gamma parties on the arm of a man who has clearly humored me thus far only because he remembers what happened with Professor Helms and feels sorry for me."

"That's not—"

"You're my best friend," she said, cutting me off, "and I know you're going to try to make me feel better, but he told me so himself several weeks ago when he brought the invitation by. I asked him why he asked me and he said that he thought we'd had a grand time at the ball and that we'd make good friends." She rolled her eyes.

A sharp wind whipped over us, teetering the red bird wings atop my head. I took a breath of the crisp winter air tinged with wood smoke and sighed.

"Saying that he enjoys your company doesn't sound like he's feeling sorry for you," I said. In truth, I wouldn't know how he felt. He'd been friendly but distant since the day of the board meeting, the day we'd embraced in the hall.

"I know," she said. "I suppose I was just hoping that I'd find something more . . . not necessarily with Will. I'm not even sure that I fancy him at all beyond friendship." She shrugged. "At the ball . . . well, I'd never been asked to accompany a man to anything, and so I suppose I was enraptured with the possibility. I've made him into something he's not. His sporadic, reckless manner would drive me insane. Though I could see it working for the two of you."

"Please stop saying that," I said, slinging my arm through hers.

"Will and I are friends, and I quite enjoy Grant's company, though I know he's not everyone's favorite."

"Everyone or Mary? She's the only one who disapproves, but even she doesn't object entirely. I've never said I dislike Mr. Richardson. In fact, he's done some very valiant things on our behalf, and if anyone has the power to influence him to alter his views, it's you."

I knew I was holding him at a bit of a distance for that reason. Even though he was trying to understand my beliefs, I doubted that he'd ever accept them as his own, and I didn't know if I could attach myself to a man who didn't agree with my ambitions—even if he wouldn't try to stop them.

"I'm not sure that I'll ever be able to convince him to our side," I said. "But I'm sure you'll find someone perfect, my dear."

"Or, I'll simply do without. I already have a family now," she said, gesturing to Mary and Katherine and lightly knocking into me, "and that's all I've ever wanted." She flattened a few wayward black feathers across her stomach. "Do I look like an imbecile or what?"

I surveyed her bald eagle costume, from the pluming white feathers on her head to the dark tufts along her skirt.

"No. Quite the opposite. You look lovely."

As we passed under the arch, I noticed that Mary and Katherine had disappeared in front of us, likely already dissolved into the madness of the Iota house. "And the eagle quite suits you both. You're both spirited and horribly infuriating when it comes to your pursuit of personal freedom," I continued.

Lily laughed and squeezed my hand.

"Don't act as though stubbornness is such a foreign trait, my dear," she said. "Lean over here. Your wings are lopsided."

* * *

Two things were clear from the moment the door opened: that this wasn't a faculty-attended party and that the Iota Gammas had spent a pretty penny on a decorator.

"How are we supposed to find them?" Lily yelled. I could barely hear her over the roar of voices and the blast of horns coming from somewhere close by, though there was no way to tell what the band was actually playing over the noise. The great room was lined with human-sized nests of all shapes and sizes, all of them equipped to hold seats for a brother and his date. Partygoers were jammed into the middle of the room under several silk garlands hanging from the ceiling. Each strand held a massive bouquet of red roses in the center, permeating the air with a sweet fragrance that masked the familiar stench of old tobacco and manly sweat.

"Let's start looking," I said, taking Lily's hand and pulling her into the mass of pluming hats and feathered dresses, scanning the men for a streak of red. All of the brothers wore full masks with beaks—a potential problem if you weren't familiar with other distinct qualities of your escort, since there were several varieties of each color.

"Remove your hands from me this instant!" A woman's voice cut through the racket as we passed a shallow straw nest with two armchairs perched atop it. I looked toward it in time to see Anne Rilk smack the brown mask from Mr. Stephens's face. His eyes were glazed, and he was clearly intoxicated. I thought back to Mr. Sanderson at Mr. Everett's house, the way he'd allowed liquor to compromise his behavior. Mary had done the same. Why did they assume that the rules of etiquette didn't apply to them? Excess drink only led to foolishness.

"You're embarrassing yourself. You've had too much punch. I told you that I wouldn't allow you to touch me that way until we're at the very least engaged, and I meant it," Anne went on, not bothering to lower her voice.

"Would you like a chocolate—" A waiter in a plain black beak and tails started to ask, before a large man careened into him. He slammed into us, silver tray soaring out of his hands. Lily caught the waiter by the arm. "Thank you," he muttered. Lifting his beak from his face, he stared at Lily for a moment before he composed himself. "I beg your pardon. Miss Johnston, correct?"

I nudged Lily.

"Oh. Yes. That's me," she said.

"You're in Professor Helms's grammar class with me. Or, I suppose you were until he disappeared," the man said, plucking the coated chocolate eggs from the floor and situating them back on the tray as though he still planned to serve them.

Lily only nodded, doubtless unnerved at the mention of the professor's sudden departure.

The desserts mostly revived to their earlier placement, the waiter stilled and leaned toward my friend. "Miss Johnston, I've had just enough of the Iota's famous hummingbird punch to tell you that I find you breathtaking . . . both in beauty and resilience. It cannot be easy enduring the jeering of fifty-three men."

"I remember you," she said. "The day that they told me I couldn't take the test . . . that I'd missed it when I was ill. You told me that they were only joking and that I hadn't missed a thing."

He smiled, two dimples appearing at the sides of his mouth.

"David Langley," he said, extending his hand.

At that moment, I glimpsed a streak of red out of the corner of my eye and grabbed the red-jacketed arm.

"Grant!" I shouted.

The owner of the red jacket swiveled toward me.

"I wish I was," an unfamiliar voice called back. "I'd love to have a girl like you on my arm." Two beady orbs peered down my low round neckline from the eyeholes in his mask, and I clasped my hands across my chest. "He's back there," the man said, flinging a limp hand behind himself. "In the most extravagant nest, of course, right next to the fireplace. You can't miss him."

I glanced around, found Lily still speaking to Mr. Langley, and pushed my way through the crowd.

I passed the band, which had been set up behind the open pocket doors in the sitting room. The brass instruments blared four short notes, followed in quick succession by the deep tones of a cello. A short middle-aged man with a silver beak and an extraordinary moustache bellowed the first words to "Golden Slippers."

"*Oh, my golden slippers am laid away, 'cause I don't 'spect to wear them 'til my wedding day,*" he sang, as lively as if he were in a tavern. I suppose it was close enough.

"*And my long tailed coat, that I love so well, I will wear up in the chariot in the morn.*" I hummed along until the singer's voice faded, absorbed by the shouts and laughter coming from the rest of the room. I snaked around a small nest made to look like it was being held up by a green stem, and stopped in my tracks.

The man was right. I couldn't miss Grant's nest. He'd had the deep straw structure painted gold, and the flames from the adjacent fireplace reflected along the bottom of it and danced upward, like a beacon to the high rim where Grant was leaning. He grinned when he saw me and lifted the vibrant red beak from his face. He spread his arms out, no doubt asking what I thought of the nest, and then his gaze trailed down my dress. I could feel my body tense. He was extraordinarily handsome. This wasn't a new revelation to me, but tonight the candlelight made him look as though he'd been painted, the red feathers sewn to his suit brought out the tan olive of his skin, and the glittering gleam from the nest below his hands flashed light into his dark eyes.

"Oyster, miss?" A waiter tapped me on the shoulder, shaking my focus from Grant's gaze.

"Oh . . . um . . . no thank you," I said, thoroughly discombobulated.

"You're here . . . finally," Grant said, stepping into an opening where a small stool waited. I eyed the wooden legs at the base of the nest, wondering if it was sturdy enough to hold both of us. "Come on." Grant's voice was soft, but I somehow heard him over a chant being yelled.

"*Brothers eternal, kings of the world! Proud and valiant, honorable and free. Iota Gamma forever to thee!*"

"This is incredible. I'm so glad to be here," I said.

"Join me," Grant said. "Take my hand. I've been waiting all night to look at you." My fingers found his and his arm constricted, practically pulling me up the step and into his chest. I breathed him in, smelling the coconut and palm in his hair over the bouquets of roses and the heady stench of someone smoking a cigar nearby. "Your wings are as sharp as daggers," Grant said, laughing. He pulled away a few inches to rub at a small abrasion beneath his chin left by my wings.

"If we're to walk home in the dark, at least I'll have a weapon to guard us," I said with a smile.

Before I could stop him, his hands lifted to my hair and he unpinned the wings, tossing them across the nest, onto a far corner of the red velvet lining.

"Those were—" I started to say expensive, but stopped myself. I'd ordered the headpiece from a store in Chicago last week for five dollars—more than I'd spent on the entire dress.

"I'm sorry. If I've ruined it, I'll buy you another," he said. His thumb swept my cheek and then he pulled away abruptly. "Sir!" he shouted, flagging down a waiter balancing a tray of champagne flutes. The waiter hurried over, and while Grant retrieved two glasses, I looked around the room for my sisters. Instead, my eyes landed on Will's across the room. He turned away quickly, but before he did, I saw his expression—brows pinched together, eyes narrowed. *Why had he been glaring at me?*

"Thank you," I said as Grant handed me the glass.

"Hummingbird punch," he said. "Champagne and strawberry juice."

I hesitated, wondering if I should refuse the drink, but I was thirsty, and I was only going to have one. He took my hand again and as we sat down, he pulled me to his side. At once, we were alone, shielded from sight by the nest's high sides. The roar of the room subsided in the cocoon of twigs, straw, and velvet. He took a sip from his glass and set it down to take my other hand.

I suddenly remembered the words he'd written on my valentine and my chest constricted. Despite my attraction, my admiration, I didn't know if I loved him back. I was wholly confused and flustered. I wanted to be certain about my feelings, but I wasn't, and the last thing I wanted to do was lead him on.

"Beth, I—"

"Did Rumpelstiltskin build this nest?" I interjected quickly, referring to the gold-painted straw, hoping to stop him from any sort of declaration. If I knew there was a chance that his opinions couldn't be changed, what was I doing with him? I suppose I was having fun, giving in to my feelings. But perhaps I wasn't being fair to either of us if our end could only be heartbreak.

"No. It's a little-known fact, but cardinals are the original spinners of gold." Grant winked at me and his thumb grazed over my knuckles. I pushed my reservations to the back of my mind. I could face them later when he wasn't touching me, making my heart beat fast. "I know this isn't you," he said, gesturing at the extravagance around us, "and I knew before I did it that you were going to poke fun at me for it, but I wanted you to have the loveliest nest of all." He looked down at our hands, and I watched him flush. He was going to say it, to tell me he loved me.

Before I could think of another way to stall, he leaned over and kissed me. His mouth moved slowly on mine, the sweet taste of strawberry on our tongues. I gripped his lapel and pulled him closer, immediately surprised at the way I'd responded, feeling the light pricks of the feather tips along his jacket in sharp contrast to his soft kiss. The thought that someone could come up the steps and find us flitted through my mind, but as his touch blazed through me, I prayed they wouldn't.

"It's time!" A trumpet rang out and Grant leaned away from our embrace.

"Damn," he said. "Beth, I-I'm sorry." He grinned, licked his fingertips, and ran a hand through his hair before leaning down to kiss me again. "It's the pledge announcement."

"I'm pleased to introduce our fearless leader, President Grant Richardson." Grant clutched the rim of the nest and hoisted himself up, waving to the room. I pinned an unruly strand of hair back to the top of my head, wondering what had come over me. I thought of the way I'd judged Katherine for her passionate kissing with Will. I shouldn't have. I'd never known how difficult it would be to push a man away while your heart was pounding and everything inside wanted him to keep kissing you. Grant leaned down, plucked my hand from my side, and squeezed it.

"This will only take a few moments." He disappeared down the steps and I stood on my tiptoes to look over the edge of the nest, watching his broad frame edge though the crowd to where the band stood on a short stage in the drawing room. The singer extended his hand and Grant took it, materializing over the rest of the partygoers. The room slowly quieted.

"Thank you all for coming," he yelled. Someone whooped somewhere, a noise that sounded half-owl, half-lion, prompting a spattering of the same sound from at least a dozen others. Grant lifted his hands to his mouth and answered, calling out the same way.

"I call to order an open meeting of Iota Gamma," he shouted, after the clapping and whooping died down. He pinched a red feather that had come loose from his jacket and tossed it to the ground before turning his attention back to the room. "As most of you know, it's an Iota tradition to introduce our new pledges in a public forum. That way, if anyone—a brother or otherwise—observes them acting in a manner uncharacteristic of the Iota way, he or she can report the prospective brother to me."

Grant leaned back and said something to the singer behind him. He smiled at the crowd, and I wished he'd get on with it and come back to me. I felt the burn of eyes on my face. Will was standing by himself, staring at me. He shifted his mask to the top of his forehead, and I started to wave, but his gaze shifted back to Grant and he spun his thumb around the rim of his empty champagne flute. Where was Lily? I looked over the crowd in front of me and spotted her in the exact place I'd left her, still talking to Mr. Langley. I hadn't seen Mary or Katherine since we'd arrived and hoped they weren't getting into trouble, though I doubted it.

"The ten men I'm about to announce have been noticed for their gentlemanly manner, their intelligence, and their natural charisma—the three common characteristics found in every leader of this great nation and every brother in this fraternity. When I call your name, please join me in the front." Grant withdrew a sheet of paper from his pocket and announced, "Mr. James Sanderson."

There was a small ado from the other side of the room and an orange beak appeared, followed immediately by another. Mr. Sanderson straightened his beak and yanked his black feather-lined tuxedo jacket down as he snaked through the crowd. "Mr. Sanderson is a freshman, a legal studies major hailing from Kentucky. We've decided to overlook the fact that he's a rebel by blood, so long as he promises that he's for the right side should a fight break out again."

"Hear, hear!" someone yelled. Mr. Sanderson's lips pursed and his eyes began to roll as he accepted Grant's hand up to the stage, before he remembered that he had to appear amiable.

"As you can see, I assigned Mr. Sanderson the blackbird, a symbol of a higher way of living—of enlightened ideas and thoughts. He was nominated by my grand-little brother, Mr. Samuel Stephens, because of his quick wit and intellect in the classroom, though there's more to Mr. Sanderson than intelligence. He carries himself with a sense of mystery, as though what's seen is not nearly all that there is to this man. I look forward to finding out what that is." Grant thumped Katherine's brother a little too hard on the back. Through his smile, I could tell that something had made him suspicious. Mr. Sanderson nodded at Grant, but as he pivoted toward the crowd, his eyes fixed on a spot between Will's nest and mine. I turned to follow his gaze, finding Katherine standing alone, her face pale. Mr. Sanderson didn't like the insinuation that Grant would be studying him closely, and Katherine didn't either.

The introduction of the pledges lasted for nearly an hour, much longer than Grant had promised, and by the end, my feet were pinched in my boots from standing on the uneven nest for that long. After going through the same process with each of the Iota Gamma men, Grant walked down the line of pledges, whispering something to each of them. The strings began to play a lovely meandering introduction and then, in one collective breath, the brothers started to sing.

"*Fierce and brave, mighty and strong, we'll lead like lions into the throng.*" A hush fell over the festivities, the united baritone voices filled the room. "*Tender and loyal, honest and right, we'll carry the silver rose into the light. A Fortiori, from the stronger we've come, to pass the Iota Gamma sword to our sons.*" The final note rang out over the silence, and then a brother whooped once again.

"I am pleased to announce the 'Eighty-one Iota Gamma pledge

class," Grant yelled. The pledges shook each other's hands and walked off of the stage. The crowd began to roar once more, but a shrill whistle silenced it.

"There's one more thing I'd like to do," he said with a glance at me. "You see, when a cardinal decides that he's found his mate, he feeds her. I've already done that tonight, thanks to the spectacular catering, but that's not my point."

His eyes didn't break from mine. I couldn't look away, but my head began to spin. *What was he doing?* Surely he wasn't going to propose right here, in front of everyone. Someone clapped nearby, but the sound was muted in my ears. My face felt hot and I lifted my hand to my flushed cheeks.

"Similarly, when an Iota Gamma finds a woman he loves, he asks her to wear his letters," Grant continued, reaching into his jacket and removing a gold necklace that he dangled between his fingers. Simultaneously relieved and nervous, I knew what accepting his lavalier meant: that I was serious about him, that I was serious about us.

"It has been rather irritating to my brothers, I'm sure, to hear my constant talk of the woman that has stolen my heart. Miss Beth Carrington, will you come up here and join me? Will you accept my letters as a token of my love?"

A sigh of adoration passed through the women in the crowd. Grant's declaration was nearly every Whitsitt girl's dream. He was handsome, wealthy, powerful, and bright; the perfect man. I nodded mechanically as I stepped to the edge of the nest and down the stairs. I paused in the shadows between our nest and the fireplace for a moment, trying to compose myself. Just a look at him made me both weak and furious with want, but did I love him?

"Beth?" Grant's voice rang out again and I pushed through the crowd, which parted like the Red Sea as I made my way toward the stage. My eyes met Grant's and a smile came across his lips. My heartbeat quickened. I watched his broad shoulders rise and then fall with a breath, as though he'd thought there was a chance I wouldn't accept. He extended his hand and I took it, reveling in the warmth of his palm around mine as he helped me onto the stage.

"I love you," he whispered, as he spun me around and looped the chain around my neck. "I've wanted to tell you for a week now, but I . . ." As soon as I felt the clasp catch, I turned to face him, unable to shoulder the collective gaze of the partygoers watching to see how I'd react. Someone whooped and then the rest of the crowd began to cheer as Grant lifted my hand to his lips. He leaned back to look at me, no doubt waiting for me to whisper the confession he'd just made in turn.

"I—"

"Richardson," a short young man with a disheveled mane of carrot-orange interrupted my reply. Only then did I realize that I had no clue what I'd been about to say. "We forgot a pledge," he said, and gestured toward a tall man in a blue feathered suit at the edge of the stage. "George Holmes. He was late on the train from Chicago."

"I'm sorry," Grant whispered. "We've got to introduce one more." He lifted his hand to my cheek. The simple gesture made my heart flutter. "I want nothing more than to kiss you properly. Wait for me in the nest?"

"Of course." He kissed my hand once again and released me. I made my way back toward the nest, nervous and confused, as my fingers clutched the letters around my neck.

"Brothers, it seems that we have one more pledge." Grant's voice hummed behind the symphony of excited congratulations as I crossed the room. I wished he would have told me for the first time in private, in a place where I could have explained both my affection and reservations. He would tell me that he loved me again later, I felt sure. At least now I had a solitary moment to compose myself, to figure out my reply. I broke free of the crowd and paused in front of the fireplace, staring at the flames.

"Come with me." A deep voice startled me and a calloused hand materialized on my arm. I caught a glimpse of a white beak and moved away.

"No. Will, I—"

"If you'd like to keep his lavalier after what I have to tell you, I'll take you back to him myself." His voice was edged with fury and without another thought I followed him.

Will didn't speak as he led me out of the back door of the house into the wintry darkness. I shivered and he edged out of his black feather coat and flung it around my shoulders, engulfing me in a cloud of sandalwood cologne. The moonlight danced across his blond hair, lighting his jaw, which was gripped with rage.

"Tell me now," I said, and I stopped, but he shook his head and beckoned me forward. He glanced back at the door, making sure no one was following us, and then led me down Hideaway Hill, into the thin woods between the house and the stable.

"Walk faster," he whispered as our silhouettes disappeared into the shadows of leafless oaks and long-needled evergreens. "He'll be looking for you."

A strange feeling tingled at the base of my spine, as though we were fleeing from a murderer.

"Is he going to hurt me?" I asked as I ran to keep up with Will's long stride. He laughed softly, breath puffing outward in a cloud before dissolving.

"Of course not. Not like that," he said.

Relieved, I took a deep breath of air tinged with the crisp scent of pine needles and the tang of horse manure. Will opened the lid of a small box tacked to the side of the stable door, then struck a match and lowered it to a tiny nub of a candle.

"Come in here. It's warmer," Will said, pushing the heavy wooden door open with a creak. His hand drifted to the beak at his forehead and he tossed it into the dirt aisle ahead of us. A horse snorted somewhere and I heard the muted stomp of another's hooves on the hay.

"This way," he whispered, as though the loud whine of the door hadn't already woken the horses. He turned into a tack room and I followed. Saddles lined the walls, engulfing me in the scent of polished leather.

"Please sit down," he said, gesturing to a bench in the corner.

I sank onto it and tried to steel myself for whatever he was about to say.

"Get on with it," I said.

Will cleared his throat and ran a hand through his hair, avoiding my eyes.

"I know that . . . I know that you keep some things from me because you think it best I don't know. I thought at first that I was doing the same by keeping his secret, but I can't any longer." He lifted his head. "He made me swear on our brotherhood, as if it meant more to me than you."

"Will, I wish you would just—"

"Richardson," Will said, his voice strained and low, "tried to pay the board to deny your fraternity."

I froze. Will was mistaken. He had to be lying.

"At first, President Wilson refused. He said he couldn't accept a bribe, and when Richardson realized that Wilson wouldn't budge, he followed you. He found your chapter room and sent the president to see for himself."

I couldn't move, couldn't even blink. I could barely force the words from my lips.

"Why? I don't believe you." Surely Will was only speculating. After all Grant had done for me, it couldn't have been for nothing.

Will's eyebrows rose.

"All right then," he said, and began to walk away. "At least it's off my conscience. I've warned you, Beth."

My heart churned, feeling as though at any moment the velocity of it would send it shooting from my chest.

"Wait," I called. "Please. My words were misplaced; I apologize."

Will stopped at the doorframe and turned back around.

"He loves you, that's why," he said, answering my question. "At least that's what he said when I questioned him about it. It's clear that he wants you to fit in his future."

"And *I've* made it clear that my views and ambitions won't change," I said, feeling tension clutch my chest.

"I told him as much . . . I know you, Beth. But he heard nothing of it. He thinks that without your fraternity, he has two more years to convince you that you belong with him in his mansion on Fifth Avenue instead of by the bedsides of patients. Without the other 'bleeding suffragists,' as he calls them, he's certain you'll come around to seeing that your real purpose is family life . . . with him."

"That's ridiculous." I stood from the bench, nearly knocking it over. "Grant's tattling to President Wilson almost had me expelled."

"No. You would've never been dismissed. That was all part of the charade, don't you see? He wanted to come off as the hero."

I raised my hand to my mouth, remembering that just an hour before Grant had been kissing me and I'd been happy. Now, everything was tainted.

"How did you find out? When?"

"Yesterday. President Wilson paid him a visit in the library downstairs and they didn't bother to close the door. I suppose he thought they were alone, and they were, until I decided to write a letter to my parents in the great room." Will stopped and shook his head. "President Wilson kept going on and on about how Richardson was right, how he should have taken his money and trusted that he was doing the right thing. I knew that he'd decided to guilt Richardson into giving him the money anyway, because when Richardson didn't say anything, he started in on the fact that he really should have expelled you."

"How dare they," I said.

My mouth was dry. Will paced toward me and took my hand.

"I'm sorry, Beth. I know how upsetting this must be."

"Did he give it to him?" I whispered, disregarding Will's attempt to comfort me.

"I don't think so," he said. "At least I didn't hear him say he would."

"Why would you ever question whether or not you'd tell me this?"

Will's face was suddenly stony.

"Don't act as though I owe you honesty after the way you've treated me," he said.

I'd never seen him this angry, heard him speak this frankly. Even in our early rows, he'd never fully lost his composure.

"I told you I was sorry for everything and I meant it," I said. "I'm not going to say it again."

Will sucked his bottom lip into his mouth and let it out, his anger suddenly gone.

"When President Wilson departed, Richardson followed him out and saw me sitting there," Will said, letting go of my hand and moving his palm to my cheek. "Beth, he said that you loved him and that he loved you . . . that he was only doing what was best for you, for your heart. I have an interest in that too, you know, and I—"

"Damn him." I pulled away from Will, infuriated at the insinuation that Grant thought I loved him without my saying so, that he thought ruining my dreams was best for me. The vision of him standing on the stage proclaiming his love for me burned in my mind. If he loved me, he would have supported what I loved, or at the very least stood aside while I tried, like he'd been pretending to do all along.

I left Will standing in the shadows and ran out of the barn. The barn door crashed behind me, echoing in my ears as I pitched my skirt and started up Hideaway Hill toward the house. The sharp quills prodded my palm and I relished their feel, clenching my fists harder.

I paused at the back door of the house. Light spilled from every window and I could hear the hum of voices and music. A familiar cascading laugh startled me and I looked toward it to see Katherine embracing her date in the shadows. I cleared my throat loudly and he jerked away from her. Katherine smoothed her skirt and straightened her back.

"Where have you been, Beth?" she asked, as though I hadn't found her in any sort of compromising position.

"Everyone's been looking for you," her date chimed in, his voice nasal. "You should be ashamed—disappearing on Richardson after he declared his love. On Saint Valentine's Day, no less."

"Have either of you seen him?" I asked.

"I suppose he might be in the library, the only quiet place in the house," the man said, pursing his lips at me. "After it was determined that you'd left him, he was rather grieved—"

"I doubt that," I said. Even if he had been upset, Grant wasn't the type to cower and lick his wounds, in fact, he'd be much more likely to act as though it didn't bother him. I started to turn away, but saw Katherine's date lean in to kiss her.

"Don't." Even though Katherine liked to pretend otherwise, I knew her promiscuity wasn't only a result of her enjoyment. I'd seen heart-ache masquerading as carelessness for far too long in Will. It would only lead to emptiness and regret.

"Come along now," she said to her date. "I'd like to dance."

I followed them through the back door and paused in the solitude. Absent the fragrance of roses, the back hallway smelled rank like it always did. Laughter and the trill of a piano drifted across my ears and light beamed from the great room, the reflection of it illuminating the mural along the wall.

I turned and walked through the dining room. My fury seemed to cool with each step, leaving only sadness by the time I reached the closed library doors. Perhaps I did love him, and that was why I was so melancholy. Because, I couldn't allow myself to continue seeing him. Not after what he'd done. I would never be able to trust him again.

I rapped my fingers on the door of the library.

"Who is it?" Grant's voice came from the other side. Rather than answer, I opened the door to find him sitting on a leather settee holding a horrid-smelling cigar in one hand with a red-covered book in the other. He looked up from the book and his eyes widened when he saw me.

Grant set his cigar down in a bronze ashtray detailed with a lion, pulled his glasses off, and stood.

"Beth, I wondered where you . . . what's the matter?"

I stared at him, at the full lips that had been on mine, at the forehead crinkled in concern—concern that I knew now stemmed only from selfishness.

He reached for me, but I put a hand on his chest, stopping him.

"I need to ask you something."

"Anything."

"Is it true?"

He squinted at me.

"What do you mean?"

"Did you sabotage my fraternity?" I said, and waited, feeling the fury rise anew. He didn't speak. "Answer my question."

"Beth, you know I wouldn't do anything to hurt you," he said. "I love you." His hand swept mine, but I backed away.

"You bribed President Wilson and had me followed so that he'd deny me. You knew you were hurting me and did it anyway," I said, my voice shaking. "Don't deny it. Will told me that—"

"Damn him!" he shouted. He sat down, gripping his head in his hands as though it were the only thing stopping him from overturning the table in front of him. "He swore on our brotherhood. I'll have him voted out."

"No, you won't," I said. "If you do, I'll tell the rest of the house what you've done."

"Don't act as though Buchannan's your defender," Grant said. "He's a jealous fool. He's so envious of what we have that he'll go to any length to ruin it."

I laughed.

"You've already done that yourself. He'd never do this to me."

Grant's jaw relaxed, and his rage was suddenly replaced by desperation.

"Please, Beth," he implored. He stood and reached for me, gripping my hand so hard that his fingers went white at the joints. "Beth," he repeated, searching my eyes as though, in doing so, he could make me speak, could make me understand. "I only did it because I love you. I've been waiting my whole life to find someone who understands me, that I could spend the rest of my life loving, and when I met you, the very first time you stole in here that night, I knew."

My eyes began to burn and I worked my hand free to unclasp the lavalier.

"I thought that you knew me too, that even though you didn't agree with me, you respected me. You acted as though you were so sorry I'd been denied," I said. "But it's clear that that wasn't the case. I was right about you from the start, but after I got to know you, I didn't want to believe it. I thought that I'd had a glimpse of who you really were, that deep down, you were someone better."

I stole a glance at his face and was surprised to find his eyes pooling with tears as I went on. "How could you know me well enough to love me? You were too busy trying to find a way to change me."

My voice was hoarse and I looked away from him to the window. It wasn't as though I didn't understand. I'd wished that he'd come to see how important my ambitions were and agree with them, too, but I hadn't bribed the school's president hoping I could dash his dreams and transform his future. The lantern light washed over the front lawn and a group of partygoers sauntering back toward campus arm-in-arm, feathers rustling in the wind.

"That's not true," Grant said, touching my chin and tilting his face to his. "God knows I love you so much it pains me. I was only trying to make you see that what really matters is us. Not degrees or professions or fraternities, just us, together. Beth, we can be happy."

I closed my eyes, unable to look at him. I couldn't stay with a man who'd never support the things that meant the most to me. I knew he believed he was doing the right thing for us, that my ambitions were the only thing standing in the way of a joyful future together, but that didn't change what I had to do.

I plucked his hand from his side and dropped the lavalier into his palm. "I told you about my mother, about why I wanted to be a physician, about why I wanted to make a difference in the lives of women who didn't have a voice, but you disregarded all of it." My voice came out in barely a whisper.

"Please," he said. "I'll spend the rest of my life making it up to you if you'll forgive me this one time, if you can reconcile the fact that the only reason I did it is because you hold my heart in your hand and I would give everything to know that you trust me with yours. Buchannan was right to tell you. I made a mistake, Beth. I'm sorry."

"I have an interest in that too." Grant's mention of Will conjured Will's words in the stable, silencing Grant's plea. Will had been telling me he loved me and I hadn't even heard him.

16

WILL WAS GONE. Even though I'd returned immediately after speaking with Grant, the stable was dark and completely silent. I stumbled down the aisle feeling weak. It had been immediately clear, in the seconds after I'd remembered what Will had begun to say, that I needed to come back and find him. I'd never been willing to admit it, but I'd always felt for Will. For years, we'd built a wall around our feelings to protect our greatest friendship, but his words had dissolved it.

I hadn't thought of it in a long while, but could still recall the way I'd felt when I first saw him emerging from the opposite side of the crowd gathered on the train platform after the matinee at McVicker's, his teacher frantically clutching his linen suit jacket in the same manner as mine was grasping the sleeve of my new white polka-dot frock. The instructors had been keen to get the students in the trains as swiftly as possible. Will had been joking with his teacher, who pulled him forward with stern gusto, and I'd been unable to keep from staring. His smile was put on with ease, an inviting feature that drew the eye and held it there. I'd thought him exceptionally handsome. So handsome, in fact, that the moment he was close enough to notice me, I'd looked away for fear I'd blush, even when we'd been situated knee to knee on the train, sharing the last seat, even when he'd asked my name. Will had stood the moment he'd realized we'd both been intended as the last passenger, that there wouldn't be another seat to be had. He'd had to bend over me, his lanky frame blocking the window, his arm balanced on my seat back.

"Amen!" he'd shouted, after long minutes of awkward silence, startling me to the point that I'd looked at him. "I'm only saying a quick prayer for you," he'd said, "that I won't crush you. You see, the last time I was on a train, I overturned the refreshment trolley and . . . there were casualties."

"I'm sure the teacups had a pleasant life," I'd replied, having taken his smile to mean he was speaking in jest, but I was met with silence.

"Lacy and Rachel . . . their limbs crushed," he'd said, and turned his face away.

"I . . . I apologize," I'd stuttered, horrified that I'd made light of a fatal accident.

"As you should," he'd said, his countenance slowly brightening. "They were my sister's favorite china dolls, brought all the way from New Jersey, and their demise has beholden me to her every whim for at least the next six months."

We'd both laughed, and in that moment, the handsome stranger disappeared, replaced with my new friend, my Will.

A horse snorted, bringing me back to the empty stable, and I walked toward the tack room, thinking I'd sit alone and think.

I turned into the doorway and my heart stopped. Will sat on the wooden bench twirling the extinguished candle nub in his fingers. He didn't lift his head.

"So, what'd he say?" Will asked. He didn't look at me, fingers turning the candle around and around. I opened my mouth to speak, but couldn't. I wanted to come out with it straight away, to ask him to tell me what he meant by saying he was interested in the matters of my heart, but my voice refused to come. *What if I'd misunderstood? What if he'd meant that he just cared for me as a sister or a friend?*

"Did he apologize at least?"

Even in the darkness, I could see his eyes soften when they found mine.

"Yes," I whispered.

"Oh. Good," he said as he rose. "I assume the two of you worked things out then."

I shook my head, but he didn't see me as he smoothed the black feathers along his jacket and continued, "Congratulations on becoming an Iota sweetheart, I hope—"

"I'm not. I gave the lavalier back."

His brows pinched. I reached for his hand and his fingers closed around my palm. "There's something I need to know, Will," I went on. He tipped his head just slightly.

"What is it?" he asked.

I closed my eyes, reveling in the touch of his hand, praying I'd not regret what I was about to say.

"Right before I left . . . you said you had an interest in . . ." I stopped and tilted my head up to look at him and spoke before I could stop myself. "Do you love me?"

He drew a breath and his hand tightened on mine. I stared at his mouth, willing him to answer, but he didn't.

"Beth, I—" Without a thought, I stood on my tiptoes and leaned in to his mouth. My lips brushed the rasp of his cheek, and I opened my eyes to find his closed, face turned toward the saddles along the wall. He gently pushed me away. I'd been wrong. The air suddenly felt thick, suffocating. I let my fingers go limp around his, but he didn't let go.

"I do love you," he whispered. The hair along my arms rose, and I looked up at him. He smiled. "I always have. Even back home, when our fathers wanted so desperately to make us a pair. I would have agreed from the start. But I never wanted to tell you for fear that you didn't feel the same. And then, when I embraced you in the hall that day . . . I did it at first out of spite, to show Miss Cable that she didn't affect me." I looked away from him, the knowledge of his love for me chilled by the remembrance that he'd so recently been devoted to someone else, that the only reason he'd kissed me was to get back at her. "But the moment I did it, I knew I'd made a mistake. I forgot she was standing there, Beth. When she spoke to us, I could barely respond I was so stunned at myself, so angry that I'd kissed you that way. You deserved better. And since, I haven't been able to stop thinking about you, wishing you loved me. It's been horrible, watching you with Grant. Kissing you gave you my whole heart . . . a heart that I didn't know I'd ever get back. "

"I feel for you, too, you know," I said, and realizing it sounded as though I still only regarded him as a friend added, "deeply."

He laughed under his breath.

"Perhaps," he said, "but I tried to tell you earlier and you didn't hear me. You were too stunned by Grant's betrayal to comprehend anything else."

"He ruined our chance with the board. He nearly got me expelled. I was furious, Will. I didn't—"

Will's shook his head.

"I know. And I'm sorry for it. But anger wasn't the only reason you went to him so quickly. I saw your eyes when I told you. You were hurt. You felt . . . you feel enough for him that you couldn't wait another moment before you asked him yourself."

I started to argue, but Will put a finger to my lips. "It's all right, Beth. I want nothing more than to kiss you until my lips burn with the touch of yours, but I can't," he whispered. "I want your heart . . . all of it, and I can't bear to think that he still holds a part of it."

Grant's face materialized in my mind—how his eyes had pooled with anguish as I'd turned and walked away. The remembrance made me feel hollow.

I clutched a handful of feathers at the back of Will's jacket and pulled him closer to extinguish the sensation.

"I do care for you . . . and love you," I said, knowing that regardless of the way I felt about Grant, I meant it. I'd always loved Will. He'd been there for me since the moment we met, and regardless of my insistence otherwise, there had always been an attraction.

"I'll never tire of hearing you say that," he said, letting me go. "And when your heart is whole again, when it's fully yours to give, I'll be waiting."

17

I T WAS SNOWING—A rather mild March storm, but snowing just the
same—an unfortunate turn of weather since I was huddled behind
the arms of an old holly bush without a cloak. I'd forgotten it at the
dormitory this morning and there had been no time to retrieve it without being tardy to class. A frigid wind whipped over me and the sharp
leaves bristled across my thin green silk faille sleeves and my cheeks.
The sensation reminded me of Will's rough face against mine. We
hadn't spoken in two weeks, besides a friendly hello in class, and it was
killing me. I hadn't seen Grant at all. The thought of either conversation from that night made me sick with sadness and regret.

The door to Richardson Library slammed and I hunched down
further, rising back up as a man sauntered down the steps with his
nose in a book. My knees burned, protesting the strain from sitting on
my haunches, and I leaned back against the brick, extracting my cuffs
from the holly snares while cursing Mary's genius idea to spy on our
prospective pledges. Though the Iota Gammas did the same thing, we
had two reasons for doing it. Not only were we following these young
women to verify their character, we were doing it to find their most

guarded confidence, something that they wouldn't want Whitsitt, or their peers, to know about. At first I thought the idea cruel, against the very fabric of sisterhood, but Mary insisted. Without some sort of private information, we wouldn't be able to guarantee the silence of any women who refused our bid, and we certainly couldn't afford to expand at the expense of expulsion.

So far, we'd found that Margaret Yance habitually stole paints from the art department in order to produce free-form modern art—a forbidden style; that Sarah Van Meier was at times seen promenading a little too closely with a much older physician in Green Oaks; that Collette Burns sneaked into the dormitory past curfew every Tuesday night after providing legal counsel to the incarcerated females of Green Oaks; and that Victoria Simkins skipped lunch to visit a tiny apartment on the edge of Whitsitt every other day to learn Greek from a tutor. We hadn't been able to find a thing on Anne Rilk, though it hadn't been for lack of trying. We'd taken turns following her everywhere—to and from classes, to an appointment with Mr. Stephens, to her father's estate in Green Oaks, and we had come up blank, which was why I was hiding in the bushes. If we couldn't find anything in the next five hours before we'd whisk our potential pledges to Mr. Everett's estate, we'd have to leave her out.

I wiped a few snowflakes from my lashes and started to stand when the door hinge creaked and Miss Rilk emerged. A gust of wind coiled around the building, and I opened my mouth to catch my breath. I watched her do the same before she fluffed her black bangs, situated her red felt hat, and walked down the steps. I shuffled out from the row of shrubbery, legs burning, and stumbled after her, keeping a moderate distance.

Campus was mostly quiet. Classes had let out for the day and, in the white-gray of an impending snowstorm, it seemed that everyone had retreated directly into the warmth of the dormitories or the library. I pushed my hands into the folds of my black damask skirt and watched the whisper of gray smoke rise beyond the tree branches that concealed Everett Hall's chimney, wishing I was cocooned in warmth instead of following a classmate.

Miss Rilk passed under the stone arch. I lifted my hands to my mouth and breathed into my leather gloves, wondering if I'd ever regain feeling in my fingers. My calves burned as I scaled the hill. I wanted nothing more than to lie down the moment I reached the dormitory, but knew I'd first have to hunt down Miss Zephaniah to check in for the second time today. I was looking forward to the semester being over and along with it, this tiresome practice of informing Miss Zephaniah of my every move.

Miss Rilk was gone. The realization struck me too late, as I made my way under the final stretch of oaks along the walk. I turned around, but didn't see her behind me, and I knew that there was no way she'd made it all the way inside. I shuffled back down the hill, looking through the mass of skeleton branches and gnarled tree trunks for a splash of red, though the only shade of the color I could see was the enormous ribbon affixed to the wreath left over from Christmas still hanging on the front of the Whitsitt Five and Dime in the distance.

I was almost back to the arch when I spotted her. She was down the hill from me, talking to an older woman in a plain brown dress. I picked up my pace and made my way down the campus side of the wall until it curved. I leaned against the limestone, hoping I'd be able to hear her voice through it. I couldn't get closer and risk her seeing me.

"It was certainly an experience, ma'am. And quite enjoyable, if I'm honest," a husky female voice said. Miss Rilk laughed, and I waited for the woman to elaborate.

"I certainly hope Papa wasn't too harsh. He nearly struck the last one."

Wind whipped across the courtyard, and I pressed harder against the stone, hoping I wouldn't lose her voice.

"He wasn't. Only swore a few times and asked how it could be that I'd hired help so incompetent that in a matter of a day, they'd broken five place settings of china and left the stable doors open. Then he told me to get out."

"Well, good," Miss Rilk said. I couldn't quite understand what she was up to, though I figured it had something to do with her father's farm and the way it was run—or rather, who it was run by. "Here are your wages as promised. You can count it if you want."

"No. I trust you," the woman said. "You know, it's none of my business, Miss Rilk, but how many of us have there been? Actors, I mean."

I gasped, hoping she couldn't hear me.

"Oh. You're the thirteenth. That's my lucky number, see, so I'm thinking you'll be the last. He'll come to his senses eventually and let me run the place like I was born to."

The moment she said it, I saw the determination in her face when she'd mentioned training her father's employees the night of the winter ball. It was the same sort of resolve that Katherine had.

"I hope you're right, my dear," the woman said. "Though you may have to end your relationship with Mr. Stephens first. Your father goes on and on about the intelligence and competency of your beau, saying what a wonderful successor he'd be."

"Sam is a nit when it comes to business."

"I didn't mean to rile you," the woman said. "I was only telling you what I'd heard. What would be the harm in letting your father *think* Mr. Stephens was running the place anyway? He could be the figurehead, you could be the brains and hands and feet."

"No," she said, her voice icy. "That's not good enough. It will be me. Good day, and thank you." I waited for a reply, but heard none.

"Are you being punished?" Will's voice startled me and I whirled toward him. "If you are, you're free to lift your nose from the corner. Whoever's supposed to be keeping watch is gone. The walk to Everett Hall is clear."

He stood on the snow-covered pathway laughing at my position pressed against the wall and gestured toward the arch with the black bowler he'd taken off. I wanted to say something smart, but the sight of him stole my wit. He stared at me, doubtless awaiting my response. I walked toward Will, wondering what I should say. He'd begun our conversation as though nothing had changed, as though he hadn't been keeping his distance, as though he'd never told me he loved me. His indigo eyes looked lighter in the pink and gold of sundown, gray jacket hanging neatly over his tall frame. I noticed that it hadn't a wrinkle.

"Meeting President Arthur today?" I asked, deciding to match his tone. I cast my eyes down and toyed with my mother's ring in an attempt to stop thinking of the way he'd looked at me the last time we'd stood this close.

"No." His eyes wandered over my shoulder to the arch behind me, and suddenly, I knew. He was meeting a woman; he had to be.

"You're waiting for someone, aren't you?"

Before he could answer, I turned to walk away. I couldn't bear to watch him struggle to come up with an explanation, to hear the excuse that the appointment and the woman meant nothing. He didn't really love me. How could he? He'd only waited two weeks before deciding to move on.

"Beth, stop." Will clutched my wrist. "You couldn't possibly think that I . . . I told you I love you. I meant it. You misunderstood." He ran a hand over his face. "I applied for an apprenticeship with Dr. Dillenger, Meredith Dillenger's father, just to see if I should branch out from under my grandfather's wings, but I didn't get it. He hinted that it was because she spoke poorly of me and so I wrote to Miss Dillenger to see if she'd meet me. I wanted to know why."

"Oh," I said. "I thought that you . . that you were meeting another woman for . . . for—"

Will shook his head and took my hand. "I'd be offended at your assumption if it wasn't so characteristic." He pushed a stray tendril back from my face. "I've finished with that, Beth."

I leaned into him, craving his touch after weeks of distance.

"Dr. Dillenger is a fool for passing you up," I said. "It's true that you're no star in the classroom, but I'd wager you know more about the practical application of medicine than almost anyone else."

Will shrugged.

"Perhaps. Have you heard any news from the hospitals?"

"Yes. A rejection last week from Kankakee State."

"For the insane?" He furrowed his brow.

"They have an acute care hall. Regardless, the letter did mention that since I was a female, they'd be happy to consider my application for their school for nurses." I exhaled, feeling the weight of disappointment at my shoulders. "I applied to some others though—The New England Hospital for Women and Children, Bellevue in New York—"

"I'm sorry," Will said. "I'm sorry that you're having such a time with this and I'm sorry that I've been distant." He lifted my hand and kissed it. "I don't want you to have any question of the way I feel for you. So, I'll tell you again—I'll wait. For as long as it takes. I know you need time, Beth."

I wanted to tell him that I didn't, that I was his right now. I knew how much I loved him. But, as I started to say it, I remembered the way I'd felt standing in Grant's room, the way he'd looked at me when

I pressed his letters into his palm, and a tiny bit of my heart throbbed. As subtle as the pain was, it still bore Grant's name.

* * *

Miss Zephaniah stopped me the moment I walked through the door of the dormitory and escorted me into the great room. It was sweltering, the fire of hell radiating from the hearth. I wanted to ask her what I'd done—it wasn't even past curfew—but I held my tongue.

"This . . . man is here to see you," she said, her voice echoing through the mostly vacant room, reverberating off the soaring wooden beams. She narrowed her eyes at Mr. Sanderson, who was standing by the mantle surveying his gold pocket watch, pretending not to notice. The room was startlingly silent otherwise. Most of the women had likely retreated to their rooms to dress for dinner.

"I appreciate it, Miss Zephaniah," I said.

"He asked for the woman in black first, and then for Miss Sanderson, but neither seem to be available," she said. Miss Zephaniah always referred to Mary by that term, making it clear that she found her choice of costume unsuitable. She glared at me as though she knew their absence meant we were up to no good.

Mr. Sanderson cleared his throat.

"I do appreciate your locating Miss Carrington for me."

Miss Zephaniah didn't answer him, and instead leaned close to my ear.

"As much as I abhor everything about Mr. Richardson, I must advise you to remain loyal to him. It is unseemly to take a solitary appointment with a man while intimately connected to another . . . and this man is a rebel, no less." Her breath smelled of green onions and garlic, and I backed away from her, as much to distance myself from the mention of an intimate relationship with Grant as to flee from the reek of her dinner.

Mr. Sanderson coughed, clearly trying to keep from laughing, wearing an expression nearly identical to his sister's.

"Mr. Richardson understands the relationship I have with Mr. Sanderson. He's my friend's beau and another friend's brother. My reputation is safe in his hands," I said, not bothering to dispel her belief that Grant and I were still courting. The vision of Grant in the library struck my mind again, weighing on my heart as though our end was my doing. It wasn't. *He'd* lied to me. *He'd* ruined us. "And I should also mention that the war has been over for seventeen years, Miss Zephaniah. Mr. Sanderson is not a rebel. He's simply Southern."

"I would never compromise a woman's virtue," Mr. Sanderson chimed in, disregarding the mention of his heritage. "I simply need to speak to Miss Carrington in confidence."

His words dissolved the image of Grant from my mind, and I gestured toward the old leather sofa in front of the fire.

"I'd be happy to hear you, Mr. Sanderson." I took my seat, not waiting for Miss Zephaniah to stop hovering or for Mr. Sanderson to help me sit. I took a deep breath, choked on the wood smoke, and coughed. Mr. Sanderson came to my side. I could smell the underlying notes of rye that always seemed to swirl around him.

"If you'll excuse me," Miss Zephaniah said, finally ambling back to her quarters.

"Are you all right?" he asked, once she'd departed.

"Yes, of course. I just—"

"I heard about what happened with Richardson. I'm sorry that she mentioned him. It must have come as a shock . . . his betrayal, I mean."

"I suppose, though I really should have expected it."

"Were you surprised at Buchannan? I certainly wasn't, though most of the brothers are behaving as though he's transformed into Judas Iscariot, as though he hasn't any right to love you if Richardson does. And, of course, they're mad as hornets over the fact that he told you about Richardson's bribe, but—"

"How dare they," I spat before he could finish. "Most of the brothers wander round this campus like they are integrity incarnate, yet they're going to isolate Will because he did what was right? Because they're afraid to disagree with the almighty, Grant Richardson?"

I could feel my heart beating fast, color rising to my cheeks. Not only did everyone know now that Will had defended me, they knew he loved me. I hated that I'd let Grant in, that I had any sort of feeling toward him. It was my fault that the man I loved was alone, that he was being ostracized by his brothers. I'd been too weak to expunge Grant from my heart the moment I found out that he'd betrayed me, and Will had paid the price for my fragility. That fact upset me the most— that I wasn't by his side, that I couldn't somehow come to his defense.

"It's all right," Mr. Sanderson said, patting my knee. "He's not completely without peers. He's got Stephens . . . and me, though I'm not sure that my alignment with him is doing either of us any favors."

I slouched against the couch.

"Richardson always acts as though he's hanging something over my head," he continued, rolling his eyes. "Which is why I needed to talk to one of you."

"Do you think he's found out who you are, Mr. Sanderson? About the rye?" I whispered.

He laughed.

"James, please, and no. You know from Katherine that I rarely place a finger in my father's dealings. She's made sure of that." James looked around and then leaned in to me as though an Iota would manifest from thin air. "I've just come to tell you a bit of information I found out during last night's chapter meeting—about pledge procedure."

"Oh! Do tell," I said.

He lowered his voice. "We're to pledge for exactly one month. In that time, we're tasked with proving our allegiance to the brotherhood . . . whatever that means, though I figure in my case, I've got to do something extraordinary to win the favor of our esteemed president."

I was relieved that we were finally learning something we didn't know about the Iotas. It had been such a long time since our first meeting at Mr. Everett's house, and James hadn't brought us new information once. I'd begun to think that he'd started to harbor loyalty toward his new fraternity, as much as Mary and Katherine had insisted otherwise.

"Mary says I should sit back and do nothing, that my presence should be allegiance enough, but I doubt that," James said, turning his pearl gray felt derby hat in his hands. "Each time Richardson sees me, he feels compelled to recite a few lines from the Gettysburg Address as though he's reminding me which side won and that if I don't start cozying up to him now, I'll be on the losing side again. Since I have your ear, Miss Carrington, I'd recommend leaving the proving allegiance part out of your fraternity. It lends to mayhem and lunacy."

"Please call me Beth. How so?" I asked. Loyalty to a fraternity was one of the most essential tenets, I felt.

"Most of the pledges have either taken to stealing important relics from campus, or are contributing funds toward a gold bust of Richardson to be set up on the front walk upon his graduation," James said, his tone heavy.

A laugh burst from my lips.

"You're not serious," I said. "They're really considering a gold bust?"

James nodded and chuckled under his breath.

"See what I mean? Most of them have lost their minds in an attempt to outdo the others." He smoothed his thin moustache. "I don't feel compelled to do any of that. I've arranged for a shipment of rye.

I'll pretend that I merely placed an order from a random distillery, of course, but that'll do, I think. Ensuring that everyone's glass is full for at least the next year is allegiance at its finest, don't you agree? It's much more important than a statue of Richardson. It'll only end up a new shitting stool for the birds anyway. Excuse my language."

"No one told me you were here." Mary's voice cut through ours. I glanced up in time to watch her barely skirt a tufted armchair, scowling at it as though it had gotten in her way on purpose, and jerking her plain black conductor's skirt away from the wooden legs.

"I asked Miss Zephaniah to ring you, but she said you weren't here," he said, reaching out to her. She clutched his hand with one of hers. The other held a letter and her baton, and she shoved both under her arm.

"I wasn't," Mary said, drawing away from James. She paced toward the fire, and stood in front of it, staring. The logs had been reduced to thin gray limbs of ash by this point, embers flittering across them like summer fireflies. "I was in town conducting a small chorale at St. Paul's Episcopal. Mr. Wade and Mr. Russell were otherwise occupied, so they had no choice but to settle for the female," she said, her words muffled. "And after the concert, I posted a letter to Mother. I received a rather *lovely* note from her this morning and thought she deserved an immediate reply."

Clearly the letter was not pleasant. I thought to ask her what it had said, but didn't dare. Not in front of James. I knew she'd been meaning to tell Judith about him for some time, and I wondered if she had. Though I doubted Mary would risk writing about the Sandersons' business dealings in a letter, it was no secret that Judith would disapprove when Mary eventually told her—she was a prohibitionist, after all. Lily, and even Katherine, had suggested that Mary keep the Sanderson dealings a secret, but Mary refused. She said that she wanted her mother to know everything about the man she might someday love and that she abhorred lying to her, even if it meant she'd unsettle her relationship with Judith. Her resolve reminded me of Grant's.

Mary withdrew the letter and read it. Her face clouded as though she were reading it for the first time. James went to her, taking her hand, but her focus didn't waver.

"I'd only come to tell one of you about a bit of information anyway," he said. "I hoped it would be you, dearest, but—"

"What did she say, Mary?" I cut James off and went to my friend's side, figuring that if the letter had something to do with her courtship she'd choose not to answer me.

She leaned away from James's embrace and tossed the letter into the hearth.

"Nothing really, I suppose," she whispered. "It's just . . . Mother said something peculiar and it upset me. I told her about Mr. Richardson's ridiculous bribe—I hope you don't mind."

"Of course not," I said sincerely. Grant's misstep was something he'd have to own up to and I didn't care if the world knew what he'd done.

"I expected her to be outraged, but she went on and on about how we should take the opportunity to show him that he's incorrect about female motivation. That it's our duty, and if he's truly sorry, we should forgive him and begin to show him why he's wrong." The edges of the letter caught fire and curled. "She said that prejudice is bred by two things, hatred and upbringing, and as he's already been taught to view women as subservient, he will trust his beliefs are right until someone shows him he's mistaken."

"I agreed with her before," I said. "I hoped he would at least come to accept our views, but I've already tried and now—"

"I know," Mary said. "Perhaps she's simply grappling with something similar. I don't know for sure, but I think she finds herself entranced by men who don't share her views from time to time. When I was a child, she'd soften a bit on occasion, reminding me to be gentle and tolerant of the ignorant, but never to this extent. She's tried to validate her acquaintance with certain men on the point that changing them one at a time will further the cause, but once she sees they'll not budge, she casts them aside. I have no doubt she'd seek blood if this happened to her."

James snorted. "Richardson won't change," he said. "I believe that some have the capacity, but he's not one of them. A person must be a free thinker to embrace other ideas, and I've yet to meet a man as sure of himself."

"He's certainly sure of his views, but he's not as arrogant as he seems," I said, shocked to hear the words coming from my own mouth.

"After everything he's put you through, you'll defend him?" Mary asked. "His actions were the epitome of arrogance."

"No. I'm not defending him," I said. "What he did to me was terribly wrong. But I also know that beneath the confidence, he's broken. His family was less than picture-perfect . . ." I stopped there. I couldn't share his secrets, as much as I knew providence gave me the right to do so.

Mary laughed.

"That's a pathetic excuse. My father died before I could have any real memory of him. I only had my mother." Her eyes pierced mine in such a manner that I couldn't look away. It felt like she was holding a dagger to my throat, forcing me to heed her words and act accordingly. "Regardless of the fact that I've never truly had a father, I'm not campaigning against men and their right to live as decent human beings."

"I know, Mary, and I'm sorry. I—"

James whirled her around to face him before I could finish.

"You're an incredible woman," I heard him whisper. "And I know you're upset. But your mother's life's work is campaigning for changed beliefs. Perhaps she's only speaking from that place."

Thankful for the diversion, I stood and walked toward the stairs to my room without initiating discussion of Miss Rilk or the information I'd gathered from James. Regardless of what Mary had said, Grant was still a human. I wouldn't endorse his actions and I couldn't forget what he'd done, but I also couldn't ignore the dejected man behind the poised façade.

* * *

"Remind me why Katherine wants to bid on Victoria Simkins?" Lily huffed as she entered, and slammed the door behind her. The rosettes along the crown of her white and cerise hat were coated in a sheen of melting snowflakes.

I closed my anatomy textbook.

"She's the only architecture major, not to mention that she's whip smart," I said.

Lily unpinned her hat and placed it on the stand on our dresser.

"That's right," she concluded. "Well, she's also infuriatingly by-the-book . . . except for her secret Greek lessons, I suppose. It took me nearly an hour to talk her into coming with me tonight."

We'd each been assigned a pledge, with Mary taking two, tasked with convincing them to accompany us to an event of our choosing, while really planning on taking them to Mr. Everett's estate and asking them to join Beta Xi Beta. Miss Rilk had been relatively simple to persuade. I'd gone to her room and asked to take her for a soda at the counter in Green Oaks that evening. I'd left the reasoning fairly vague, but she'd automatically assumed that I wanted to talk to her about Grant, seeing as how she was the only other woman I knew connected to a full-fledged Iota Gamma.

"Do you think she'll agree to pledge?" I asked.

Lily leaned over the porcelain washbin, clutched a handful of her hair and squeezed the water from it.

"I'll be shocked if she does. She asked me at least three times if I'd asked Miss Zephaniah for permission to leave campus and another four if I was sure it was all right for us to go to Mr. Everett's home," she said, and rolled her eyes. "I told her that I knew his daughters, that I'd be happy to take her to study the colonial architecture, and that Miss Zephaniah had given her blessing."

"Did you really tell Miss Zephaniah where you were going?"

"Heavens no. She thinks I've asked Miss Simkins to accompany me to meet my former orphanage director for a late tea."

"Couldn't you have come up with something else? I doubt you'd even invite me to something as personal as that."

"Of course I would, but I doubt I'll see Miss Jordan again as long as I live, and there's no risk of her revealing my life. No one from the orphanage ever writes, but they do send my tuition on time, and for that I'm appreciative," she said. "In any case, I told Zephaniah that it would be quite emotional and I'd need a friend with me."

Lily unbuttoned the back of her wool cerise-colored dress. The sopping bulk of it puddled at her feet and she immediately picked it up, mopping the moisture with the hand towel next to the washbin. When she'd finished, she stood in her corset and cotton chemise, looking blankly over my head at the window displaying nothing but night.

"Is something on your mind?" I asked.

"You could say so. Professor Helms's replacement, Professor Moore, made me take my test in the hallway."

"What? Why?" I'd heard of professors forcing their female students to complete examinations elsewhere, believing that a woman's presence would break the concentration of the males, but thus far, it hadn't happened to any of us.

"He said that women make distracting noises while thinking—tapping their feet, drumming their fingers—and that he thought it best if I was removed."

"That's the most ridiculous thing I've ever heard."

Lily shrugged.

"It isn't the worst I've encountered, of course, but it was degrading all the same. David Langley, the man I met at the bird party, argued him on it, but it didn't work."

"You fancy him, don't you?" I asked, noticing a faint smile on Lily's face.

"I do. Very much." She turned to her armoire as though she was embarrassed to admit her feelings, running her hands across the sleeves of dresses. "He came to speak to me after. He apologized for the ignorance of the professor and we had a long chat. He's the son of George Langley of Wisconsin—a quite successful dairy farmer, apparently, though he died before Mr. Langley was born. Years later, his mother met Chicago real estate tycoon, Mr. Albert Torrey, and he took him as his own."

"Torrey? Is he on the board?" I immediately recognized the name of the man who had stood up for me in front of President Wilson.

Lily nodded and turned around quite suddenly, clutching a velvet evergreen dress.

"I told Mr. Langley about Professor Helms." The words rushed out of her quickly.

"Why did you do that? You know how word spreads around here and—"

"I did it because I knew he'd understand," she said. "He was outraged. He wanted Professor Helms's throat, but I told him that we'd already taken care of him. Mr. Langley wants to court me regardless . . . at least that's what he says. I can hardly believe it, but if it's not the truth, I suppose word will be circulating around campus by the morning."

"I'll pray he's the gentleman you say he is," I said. "You deserve nothing less." I narrowly avoided scolding her, wishing she hadn't confessed to a man she barely knew.

"Oh, I nearly forgot," Lily said, and reached into the pocket of her soaking frock to withdraw a rumpled letter. The blue ink had soaked through the envelope, and I recognized the sweeping cursive. "I thought about throwing it away. He doesn't deserve to converse with you in my opinion, but I figured you had the right to do with it what you will."

I took the damp paper from her hand.

I ran my finger along the envelope seal, and carefully opened the letter.

Dearest Beth,

I realize that you don't want to hear from me. I'm not even sure that this letter will reach you, but I had to write it regardless— call it an attempt to settle my soul. I'm tortured by the misstep I made. It wasn't my place to try to manipulate fate, but please understand I was honest when I said that I only did it for the assurance that you'd be near me. I can't bear to think of you, but do each second, as though my mind enjoys the anguish. If it's true that you've found love elsewhere, I wish you happiness. For all of his follies, he's a man who loves deeply.

I closed my eyes as melancholy flooded through me. I looked back to the page. I could feel Lily's gaze on my face, no doubt trying to deduce what he'd written.

But, if you still feel for me, I beg you to reconsider. I meant what I said that night in the library. I'll spend the rest of my life making up for my actions. I thought about calling on you this evening. I wanted so badly to see your face, but didn't think it best. So for now, I'll say farewell my dear, and know that if you ever decide to forgive me, I'm yours.

My greatest affections,
Grant Richardson

I folded the letter and tucked it beneath my book on the nightstand.

"Thank you," I said, looking up at Lily. "It was right of you to give it to me."

18

THE FIRE BURNED at my back, but the rest of the room was cold. I tried to pull my gray velvet sleeves down over my palms, but the fabric wouldn't give, so I tugged my thin lace collar higher around my neck. At least it was a bit of cover from the chill. I rubbed the goosebumps from my arms, wishing for the warmth of a cloak. We'd decided to postpone wearing them until the end of the evening, until, in an act of sisterly solidarity, we'd put them on after helping our pledges into their ivory ones. It had been unintentional, the different color for the new sisters, but the only fabric Lily had been able to procure was the old winter tablecloths discarded from the dining hall. It would work for the time being—pledges were often set apart to begin with—but we'd have to find a way to craft matching cloaks upon initiation, wreath pins as well.

I cast a quick glance at the open door of the sitting room of Patrick Everett's estate. *Where was Katherine?*

"I demand to know why we're here," Sarah Van Meier declared as she narrowed her thin eyes and fluffed her copper-red hair piled atop her head.

None of us responded. I suppose we all figured it was best to try to buy time until Katherine would appear, though I was losing faith that she would. Mary said that she hadn't been in their room all day.

Miss Van Meier leaned forward, chin pointed up at me, waiting for my response. She was Katherine's pledge and had nearly been left out of the evening as a result of Katherine's absence, but at the last moment, Mary had talked her into attending the "opera" along with Collette Burns and Margaret Yance. I glanced at the five women sitting on the oriental rug in front of me. The others seemed almost frightened, with the exception of Miss Rilk, whose mouth had been contorted upward in a knowing grin since we'd arrived. Miss Simkins was visibly shivering with either cold or nerves—I guessed the latter—while Miss Burns ran her hand back and forth over the worn rug. Miss Yance was kneading her bottom lip so hard that I was shocked she hadn't drawn blood.

"I understand your concern," I said, "but if you could be patient with us for a few more—"

"Demand all you wish, Miss Van Meier, but it'll get you nowhere," Mary said, cutting me off. "The coaches aren't scheduled to arrive back until nine-thirty and seeing as we're not dependent on your father's copper money, we aren't beholden to you."

I glared at Mary, finding her response unlikely to foster a sisterly bond, but she only shrugged and ran a finger over the dark stones lining her high black neckline. She sat back against the settee adjacent to the girls.

"I'll walk back. I'll not be insulted," Miss Van Meier snapped at her, starting to rise from the rug. I put a hand on her shoulder as she stood, and coughed, inhaling a pungent cloud of rosewater perfume.

"Please stay. Mary is only speaking in jest. She has a rather odd sense of humor." *And an untethered mouth*, I thought.

"I do," Mary said. "I apologize, Miss Van Meier."

Mary kept looking out of the window beside me. She was worried about Katherine. I was too. She'd never miss a meeting, especially a meeting as monumental as this one, if she could help it.

"We're only waiting on one more." Lily's voice was soft, and she smiled at the women gathered on the floor. "I realize that you all want to know why you're in Patrick Everett's sitting room instead of doing whatever we promised you'd be doing, but please give us a few more moments. You won't regret your patience."

Sarah was still standing, doubtless thinking of whether or not she'd continue humoring us.

"Do sit back down, Miss Van Meier," Miss Rilk said, pulling at her gloved hand. "If my assumption is even close to correct, our being here is an honor and worth the wait."

"She's right," I said, as Miss Van Meier conceded and sunk to the floor. "That much I can tell you. You've all been noticed as exemplary women of your class. That's why you're here."

Somewhere in the house, the clattering notes of the Westminster chime sounded, echoing over us in a sinister out-of-tune manner that made me think of ghosts.

"It's eight o'clock, Beth." Mary said. Her voice was much gentler than it had been moments earlier. "I think that we should proceed. She'll understand."

"Very well." I forced a smile at the girls and tried to stop imagining Katherine's possible calamity. "Last month, I presented a proposal to the board to start a women's fraternity."

Miss Rilk beamed at me, while Miss Van Meier leaned into Miss Burns and whispered something.

"I see that you've already heard, Miss Rilk. Word travels easily through Whitsitt, doesn't it?"

She nodded, while Miss Yance and Miss Simkins stared at me blankly. "As you may know, the board turned it down because it was determined that we'd already organized," I continued.

"Thanks to Grant Richardson," Mary added. I eyed her and she lifted her hand in apology.

"Secret societies are forbidden," Miss Van Meier said evenly. "And didn't you get caught with illegal rye as well?"

"They were right," I continued, ignoring Mary and Miss Van Meier. "We had already begun." I walked around the back of the settee to stand behind Lily and Mary. "We are Beta Xi Beta, the first women's fraternity at Whitsitt. We formed late last year after finding that, regardless of our commendable contribution to our college, we are alienated from each other and often regarded with prejudice otherwise, as though we are second-class students, not equals."

I waited for the women to react, but they wore the same expressions they'd had on when they arrived. Perhaps we'd chosen the wrong women. They clearly didn't see their selection as an honor.

"We're sisters, perhaps not by blood, but we might as well be," I continued, hoping the latter part of my explanation would stoke their excitement, though Miss Van Meier's glare was still burning a hole in the side of my face. I decided to address her concern, though I didn't feel the need to share every detail. "And yes, Miss Van Meier is correct. We were in possession of rye, but we didn't consume it. It was left in our chapter room. We believe that our time at Whitsitt shouldn't be spent struggling to succeed alone. It's hard to be the only woman in a room full of men. It's difficult to make friends with our free time so limited. We need support. We need camaraderie. That's what Beta Xi Beta is—a sisterhood, a family who stand together, who stand for what is right. When we formed, the four of us decided on a motto, Aequabilitas Intellegentia."

"Equality and Intellect," Miss Burns said quietly.

"That's correct," I said, and knelt in front of the women. "When Patrick Everett helped found this college, he wanted men and women to have the same professional and educational opportunities, to be treated as equals. Unfortunately, as valiant as his attempts were, he wasn't successful. In the classroom, we're still viewed as distractions without the mental competency of our male counterparts, and in the dormitory we're completely overlooked since all the other girls know each other and are studying divinity."

Margaret Yance rose to her feet. Her nearly white blonde eyelashes blinked over widened lids.

"I-I can't do this," she said. "I heard that President Wilson nearly expelled you and I can't . . . I can't risk that."

"I'll be turning all of you in," Miss Van Meier's shrill voice rang out in front of me.

"Don't be ridiculous. Of course you won't," Miss Rilk said, rolling her eyes.

"I'm not," she said. "This is wrong. It's against the rules and—"

"Kindly stop talking, Miss Van Meier," Lily said, her voice bursting through the squabbling and silencing the room. The logs popped in the hearth. "Your participation is in no way required, but your confidence is. Unless, of course, you'd like your father to find out you've been getting a bit close to that older physician from Green Oaks."

Miss Van Meier's face blanched.

"How do you know about that?" she asked. "It's not what you think. He is simply interesting and I—"

Miss Rilk laughed out loud, interrupting Miss Van Meier's explanation. "I'm honored, and I'll join of course, but I can't help but wonder—do you have something on each of us? What about me?"

"Of course we do," I said. "Though, you were by far the most difficult. I heard your conversation with your father's former housekeeper earlier today."

"One has to do what she can to retain control of what she wants," she said, pursing her lips. "I'm glad Father won't be finding out."

She stared at me, as though she'd asked a question.

"Of course he won't," I said. "We only had to find something to protect ourselves, you know."

Without another word, Miss Van Meier made a beeline for the door. "I'll wait outside," she said.

Miss Yance alternated her gaze between me and the settee, as though one of us would force her to stay, before she followed Miss Van Meier.

"I think I should like to be a part of this," Miss Burns said. "Last week, I was made so uncomfortable in my constitutional law class that I walked out early. The professor said that women weren't intended to be protected under the Constitution, that even though the word 'persons' is used, the document was written from British precedents that suggest 'persons' only meant men." She sighed. "It wasn't that he was being cruel in teaching it—I suppose it's simple fact. After all, I may not even get to practice law after I graduate if the state doesn't see me fit."

"That's why this fraternity is so important," I said, very aware of Miss Simkins beside Miss Burns. She'd said nothing all night and was still shivering. "I know all about the Bradwell versus Illinois decision, and it's an abomination that the state has the power to deny women the right to practice. We must stand together to fight for change, to fight for each other. None of us can do it alone."

Miss Simkins looked down at her gloved hands, pinching the white embroidered wool across the top of her index finger.

"What are your thoughts, Miss Simkins?" Lily asked.

"I'd like to know what you've discovered about me." Her voice shook as she spoke—so did the golden brown hair neatly fixed in a high coiffure.

"Miss Simkins," Katherine said as she materialized in the doorway and I startled, tipping back on my haunches.

"Where did you come from? We've been looking all over," Mary said.

Katherine's hair hung to the right side of her head in a disheveled mass. She shot a hawk-eyed glare at Mary—apparently, her absence wasn't up for discussion with the larger group present—and knelt down next to me in front of the pledges.

"Lily was kind enough to bring you here tonight, but I chose you," Katherine said, wisely leaving out that we'd chosen all of the girls outside of the divinity school. "Do you know why?"

Miss Simkins shook her head. "Last semester, we had a discussion in the library. You were reading a book on Mediterranean architecture. I'd just gone abroad over the summer, to Italy, and asked you what you were studying. Do you remember?" As Katherine talked, I glanced at her skirt, noticing that tiny bits of hay were stuck to the blue silk. *Where had she been?*

Miss Simkins's mouth opened, but no sound came out.

"I'll take that as a no?" Katherine said.

"I do . . . I suppose. I told you that . . . that I planned to travel to Greece after graduation."

"That's correct. You also mentioned that you were planning to do it because traveling abroad was the only way that you'd be able to keep studying architecture with the hope of practicing some day. You said if you didn't go away after graduation that your parents would force you into marriage before you had the chance to finish your studies and establish your profession," Katherine went on. "You said that they allowed you to go to college so that you could find a husband."

Miss Simkins gasped. "I . . . I did? I told you that?"

"Yes," Katherine said. "It was rather late. We were both just talking to stay awake."

"We could help you, Miss Simkins. Even if your parents don't come around to the idea of their daughter pursuing architecture, you'd have us," I said.

"I . . . I don't know that I'm willing to risk my dreams for a fraternity," she said.

Miss Rilk blew air through her closed lips.

"Traveling halfway across the world to hide your ambitions from your parents is hardly a life."

Miss Simkins whirled on her.

"Doing whatever you're doing in hopes that your father will come to his senses is just as pathetic," she snapped.

"We formed this fraternity to support each other," I said, interrupting the argument while recalling the countless disagreements we'd overcome as sisters. "We may not always be of the same mind, but we're a family. Together, we can transform the fabric of this college. We can campaign for a better way for ourselves and those following us. I don't want to gamble my future either, but unless something changes, unless society starts to see us as equals, I won't have much of one when I graduate anyway. Very few are confident enough to take advice from a female physician. I can't even secure an apprenticeship."

Miss Simkins was staring at me, but her eyes looked blank, as though she couldn't really see me.

"What if I don't want to do this?" she said finally.

I shrugged.

"Then I suppose you'll go on alone."

"That is, unless you utter a peep about this fraternity, in which case we'll be forced to let President Wilson know about your secret Greek lessons," Mary said. She'd been altogether prickly throughout the meeting and I wished she'd show the girls a bit more of her compassion and loyalty. She was acting like Grant.

"How did you—"

"They clearly followed us," Miss Burns whispered.

Miss Rilk reached across her to grip Miss Simkins's hand.

"Don't you want to be a part of something larger than yourself? And help other women too?"

"Yes," Miss Simkins whispered. "Yes. I'll do it."

* * *

Katherine shut the door of the coach, whistled to the driver, and turned back to wait with us. Only one of the coaches had arrived on time, and we'd decided it was best to send our pledges—and deserters—back to Everett Hall before us. Everyone but Miss Rilk had seemed worried about the consequences of joining Beta Xi Beta, and we didn't want their nervousness augmented if Miss Zephaniah discovered they weren't back before the witching hour of ten o'clock.

Lily waved as the coach's wheels hobbled over the uneven drive and disappeared through the stone pillars.

"It's entirely surreal," she said, and turned to the rest of us, her face shadowed by the hood of her blue cloak. "We have three pledges now. Pledges. We're really doing this, aren't we?"

I grinned, basking in the silence of the early spring night interrupted only by the distant croaking of frogs. Mary wrapped her arm around me, and tucked her free one around Katherine's back. I tipped my hooded head into hers and closed my eyes, trying to capture the moment in my memory—the four of us huddled in the arch of the ancient circular drive, the smell of our fire on the crisp air. I didn't want to talk. Nothing I could say could capture the elation of the moment.

"Now that they're gone, perhaps it's time I tell you why I was late," Katherine said, her voice cutting through the quiet.

"Finally. I was hoping you'd say," Mary said.

"I couldn't. Not in front of the girls," she said. Something in her tone made me nervous. She broke away from Mary and glanced around, as though someone could be eavesdropping from the thicket of ancient oaks.

"Out with it. You're worrying me," Lily said.

"James's shipment to the Iota house was detained a few miles from the barn Daddy's renting in Green Oaks," Katherine said.

"What?" Mary breathed.

"Y'all know that he'd ordered seventy-five gallons for his pledging and—"

"We know that. What did—" I said, but Mary cut me off.

"Is he all right? Are you all right?" Her arm dropped from my back. Even in the darkness, I could tell that her face had paled.

Katherine nodded.

"So far." She pushed her hood back and sighed.

"Thank God," Mary said.

"So, everyone's okay? You're all right?" I asked, staring at Katherine, wondering if she'd finally woken up, if she'd finally realized that what she was doing could have serious consequences.

She tore a few pins from her hair and thrust her hands through the strands at her crown, trying to straighten her ruined coiffure.

"For now, but my driver came straight to find me after he delivered it to the Iotas. He was uneasy. He kept looking behind him as though he was sure he'd been followed. He said the agent had a strange way about him and kept making comments about how coming across this order could restore his life." Katherine paused and tilted her head back to the stars. "Big Jim's worked for us for ten years. He's come in contact with dozens of agents and hasn't ever reacted this way. It took me an hour to talk him into heading back to Daddy and he's not even carrying any rye home."

"What did the agent say?" Lily asked. She seemed genuinely concerned, but I could tell that she was likely thinking what we all did— that continuing to run an illegal rye business was asking for trouble.

"That's the peculiar thing," Katherine said. "He asked where it was headed, and when Big Jim said Whitsitt, the agent asked him where. Big Jim's smart enough to know you don't answer questions like that, so he said he didn't know. Then, the man got real close to him, almost like he was telling him a secret and demanded that he empty his pockets. The order slip was in his pocket, but Jim didn't mind handing it over—it's written as a mask letter just in case, same strategy the spies used in the war. In order to find the delivery details you'd have to know that the correct letter sequence is arranged in an S on the page—for Sanderson Rye." Katherine stopped and paced toward me.

"Apparently, the agent knew about the mask because he traced his finger along the letter and read it," she went on.

"How would he know to do that? How would he know which distillery Jim was from?" Mary asked.

Katherine shrugged.

"He said the agents know which distillers come through the area, though that's news to me. None of our letters have ever been deciphered like that before." Her gaze locked on mine, as though this conversation had some sort of significance to me alone.

"He told Big Jim that he knew everything about our operation anyway, letter or no. He said that even though bringing down our still would earn him a promotion, he wasn't interested in interfering because the letter had given him all he'd need to take back what he'd lost. I don't believe it, but . . ." Her fingers drifted across her cameo and she let out a breath that dissipated in a vaporous cloud. "Beth, I know you're keeping your distance, but somehow you have to . . . you have to tell him to be careful. He could be arrested . . . at any time if they find it. The agent seemed particularly interested in Grant Richardson's name written on the order slip."

19

I'D ARRIVED EARLY to class for once, and sat staring at the leather bound notebook in front of me and at the pencil I'd sharpened to precision next to it, wondering if I should move to the back of the classroom. I was just two rows back from Professor Cassidy's desk—a prime location for being called on—and knew that there was absolutely no way I'd be able to pay attention today.

I hadn't slept the night before, with Katherine's words of warning echoing in my brain. I knew I had to talk to Grant, but hadn't any idea how to convey the message. *What would I say without telling him of the Sanderson family business?* I'd started toward the Iota house at sunup, thinking I'd get it over with, but something had stopped me—namely, the thought that if I appeared to tell him to be careful without specificity, he'd think I was making excuses to see him, and I didn't want to lead him to believe that there was hope for us since there wasn't any.

I reached into my pocket. The new brown silk was stiff against my fingertips as my hand curled around his weathered note. I'd shoved it in my pocket after Lily had given it to me yesterday and had forgotten to remove it.

"Good morning, Beth," Will said, slinging himself into the seat next to mine. I was surprised to see him. Since our conversation in the barn the night of the ball, he'd been sneaking into class late, finding a spot on the other side of the room, but perhaps our talk yesterday had settled us back into normalcy.

He straightened his sage green jacket, settled his bowler over the crook of his knee, and sat back. I noticed that he'd shaved, and looked presentable for the second day in a row. He smiled. He was staring at the front of the classroom, at Professor Cassidy, but I knew that he could feel my gaze.

"What's gotten into you?" I whispered. He'd not only shaved and had his jacket pressed, but was early to class. For the first time in nearly ten hours, I felt myself settle, and knew it had everything to do with Will's presence, that it meant our relationship was being reset.

The bell tolled and at once, students filed in around us. Chairs screeched, followed by the muted thud of bags dropping to the wood floor.

"Whatever do you mean?" He scrubbed his hand across his cheek. "I'm still not used to it."

"Did you do this for me?" I asked. "The ironing, the shaving?"

His grin widened.

"Of course not. I'm so enamored by my big brother Richardson that I've decided to emulate him."

Will was handsome whether or not he was tidy, but when I thought of him it was there—the contrast of beauty and ruggedness, the abrasion of his face against mine. Grant had always been striking—the polish to Will's wild—but I didn't want a blanched copy of Grant.

"Good morning. Take your seats," Professor Cassidy said as he rose from behind his mahogany desk, gesturing to the students at the back of the room.

Unable to resist the spectacle of an elegant Will, I stole a glance at him in my periphery. Sunlight streamed in from a tall window beside us, lighting his face.

"Grow it back," I whispered.

"Today's lesson is on nervous disorders, but if you're following along in the syllabus, it's actually a lesson I intended for next week," Cassidy said before turning to the blackboard. "I was fortunate enough to visit a friend of mine over the weekend—a psychologist at Green Oaks insane asylum—and it inspired me."

I yawned, hoping the lecture would at least be interesting. The man had such a marked monotone that I had to work to stay awake after a night of restful sleep, let alone on a night where I'd had none.

"Are you sure?" Will said quietly. "I was trying to look nice for you, I—"

"You always do," I whispered, cutting him off. "I just prefer you the way you are." I lifted my hand to my mouth in time to cover another yawn, and Will snorted.

"You mean that you prefer me to appear as though I've been living out of doors, without access to razors or washroom services?"

I nodded, but didn't turn to him for fear that Professor Cassidy would call on me.

"Very well," Will said, "Though I'll warn you that my cheeks can feel rather barbed and I don't plan to stay away." Will's promise to kiss me made me blush, and I turned away before he could notice.

"Most of the patients at Green Oaks asylum are women, and the majority of them are suffering from hysteria," Professor Cassidy continued, and I glanced up to find him looking at me. "As most of you know, it's commonly believed that a quarter of all American women will suffer from some variation of the disorder, so you'll likely see it in many of your patients."

The professor began to walk up the aisle. My stomach began to swim—an effect of the panic that came with being singled out. I knew he was coming to make an example of me. He began to turn down our row, but Will leaned in front of him.

"Excuse me," Professor Cassidy said, but Will didn't budge.

"If you're planning to make Miss Carrington a specimen of some theory, don't. She's neither hysterical nor insane," he said in a low voice.

"This is my classroom, Mr. Buchannan," Professor Cassidy said. "Kindly get out of my way." Will didn't move, forcing the professor to remain where he was. I could feel the blood drain from my face. "Class, as you've likely read in your text, hysteria has many symptoms. One physician in the Sixties chronicled seventy-five pages of them, but the most common indicators are dizziness, irritability, muscle spasms, loss of sexual appetite, and insomnia. Most of the time, hysteria is treated by rest, hypnosis, or pelvic massage, but in some cases, a physician should recommend an asylum accompanied by surgical hysterectomy. When the afflicted organs are removed, the woman's emotional well-being will be corrected."

I couldn't breathe. Of course, I knew of hysteria—many of my mother's peers had been diagnosed with it at some point or another—but I'd had no idea that physicians had been directed to send women to asylums. Everyone I'd known with it had recovered normally.

"I observed many cases this weekend, several of whom were recovering from hysterectomy, and I can speak for its remarkable results," he said. "As a physician, you must be aware of the early signs. I've seen one of them in Miss Carrington here, just this morning. She was yawning rather frequently, and—"

"I sleep soundly almost every night," I said, stunned that I'd found my voice. "And the insinuation that I'm succumbing to hysteria is nearly as ridiculous as the college's hiring a man who hasn't any field experience in psychology save a weekend foray to an asylum."

A collective hush fell over the class. Fire rose to my cheeks, but I didn't apologize. He was a lifelong professor who knew nothing except what the psychology journals told him.

Professor Cassidy laughed.

"You're demonstrating my point more clearly than I could, my dear. A tendency to cause trouble is the most marked indicator that a woman's organs have succumbed to—"

"Come with me," Will said, and pulled me up, spilling the notebook and pencil from my lap. He pushed past Professor Cassidy and I followed him up the aisle.

"Don't be surprised to hear from President Wilson. The both of you," the professor called out.

"I'll look forward to it," Will said. He flung the door open and pulled me through it into the sanctuary of the empty hallway. The door slammed into place behind us, and we stood together, staring at the stones jutting out from the wall in front of us.

"I'm sorry," he said, facing me and reaching for my hand. "I shouldn't have said anything. Now we have President Wilson to deal with. I know that you're going to say that you had it handled, and you did, but I couldn't take it, Beth, I—"

I leaned into him, cutting his sentence short.

"Thank you for standing up for me."

I looked around, and finding no one in the hall, let my lips whisper over his cheek. I felt his body tense, and then his arm wrapped around my back. He sighed, and I smelled a hint of ginger. *He'd been nervous to see me.* I opened my eyes, finding his pinched shut, as though it pained him to be close to me. Something in my heart seemed to snap. I was hurting him. He wanted me, all of me, and I hadn't been able to give myself completely. I pulled away and stared down at the tips of my brown leather boots.

"Your mother would be so proud of you," he said suddenly. "For everything you're fighting for, for the woman you've become."

My eyes blurred. I blinked to stop the tears and her smile flashed in my mind—her mouth, wide like mine, indenting the swipe of a dimple in her left cheek. She'd always loved Will. Oftentimes, I'd come home to find him talking with her. He'd stay for hours, making her laugh—a bright spot in her days that were often dull.

"I love you," I said.

"You know that I love you too." He lifted a finger to my face, catching a tear that I hadn't realized had escaped. The simple touch stirred my soul, and in that moment, I knew, without a doubt, that I belonged with him.

"Walk me to the house?" he whispered.

As he said it, I remembered my promise to Katherine. I still had to talk to Grant. It was the last thing I wanted to do.

"I've got to speak with Grant today." The words came out quickly, and before I realized I'd said them, Will let me go and stepped back.

"Oh," he said, his eyes dark.

"You misunderstood. I meant that I *have* to speak with Grant." Will's eyebrows rose, clearly not understanding the difference. "I promised someone that I'd get a message to him."

Will laughed.

"There's no need to explain yourself," he said, starting to head down the hallway.

I followed, trying to make my case.

"I wanted you to know, so that if you saw me with him, you wouldn't think . . . you wouldn't think that I'm considering him."

"Why? You're not sworn to me, Beth."

"What do you mean?" I said. "I just told you that I loved you and—"

"If you're planning to speak with him today, you'll want to go to the house straightaway. He had some harebrained notion that we're going to initiate the pledges early—tonight, in fact—and it takes considerable effort to prepare," Will said, ignoring the rest of what I'd said.

James had mentioned that it would be a month until they'd be sworn into the brotherhood. It had only been a few weeks.

"Isn't it early for initiation?" I asked.

"It's not uncommon," Will said. "They're never told the real date. It's supposed to come as a surprise, but Richardson usually gives us more time to arrange everything."

He opened the door for me, and before we stepped out to the quad, I lunged in front of him, blocking his way. Will glanced down at me before lifting his eyes to the stained glass pane above my head. "What're you doing?"

I grabbed his hand and pried his fingers open. "When I said I loved you, I meant only you."

"There's no way you can be sure. It's only been a few weeks yet," he said softly. His fingers closed around mine. I took a deep breath, inhaling his sandalwood scent. I remembered the note in my pocket and knew at once why I hadn't felt compelled to respond to it: I didn't love Grant, not a bit. My heart was whole again, and it belonged to the man standing in front of me, the man who'd held my hand all along.

"It doesn't matter. I'm sure," I said.

"I'm sorry for the way I reacted when you told me you needed to speak with Richardson," he relented. "I'll wait the rest of my life, so long as I know that when you say you're mine, my name is the only one written on your heart."

"There's no one else," I said, squeezing his hand. "I'm yours."

20

If I'd known volunteering to spy on initiation would be an all-night commitment, I would have suggested shifts," I whispered to Mary, who'd been taking brief naps propped up on the edge of a limestone block. We'd been hiding for six hours on the side of the freshman men's dormitory, Wilson Hall, waiting for the Iota Gammas to come for James. It was now three o'clock in the morning and we had yet to see a soul pass through the arch separating campus from the dormitory down the hill. I was starting to think Will had been mistaken, though when I'd followed him back to the Iota house, all of the members had been scurrying around as though they were preparing for something—everyone except Grant, who'd been absent.

"Perhaps Grant's in trouble and they had to postpone. I couldn't find him today, you know." I'd asked around, but none of the brothers had had any idea of his whereabouts. I'd been content to postpone my warning him until the morning, but now I worried I hadn't been diligent enough, that I was too late. "Or do you think we could have missed them? I suppose they could have gone in the back door." I lifted to my tiptoes, trying to relieve the bridges of my feet that had begun throbbing. "Mary!" I poked her in the shoulder.

"I heard you," she muttered. "I didn't feel the need to answer, because nothing's amiss with Grant Richardson. If there was, we would have heard about it on campus. And, you know good and well that they have to come through the arch regardless. There's no way we'd fail to notice them."

"Unless they went down to Main Street and came up the back of Hideaway Hill," I said, choosing to accept Mary's logic about Grant. The Iota house was located on the southeast side of campus, separated from Wilson Hall by a patch of woods and a little river that ended in a pond at the base of the Five and Dime in downtown Whitsitt.

Mary shook her head, the hazy moon casting a golden sheen on her hair, which was gathered in a low bun beneath her black cap.

"Too much effort. Those men will take the path most traveled," she said, and glanced up at the three rows of windows above us, craning her neck back to find the one at the top. "James obviously isn't concerned that they haven't come for him yet."

James's room had been dark since he'd left us standing behind the hedge of boxwoods at five minutes to nine. He'd asked repeatedly if we'd rather he just tell us about it later, rather than hide behind shrubbery for hours on end to see for ourselves. But I knew that even with the best of intentions, he'd leave something out, and we wanted every detail. Plus, I was uneasy about Grant's absence given Katherine's apprehension about the rye delivery. There was no other option but to wait.

"Perhaps Grant changed his mind," I said through a yawn, hoping that that was the reason for the Iota Gammas' absence and not that Grant had been apprehended by the authorities. I yanked a pin from my hair. Sighing with relief, I scratched at the spot and then withdrew another. It was like playing dominoes—once one fell to the temptation of comfort, they all did.

"I surely hope not," Mary said, and scooted closer to the stone and closed her eyes, shifting her head along the limestone as though she could actually get comfortable. "You're on a short leash with Miss Zephaniah. It's a miracle that she permitted us an overnight pass at all, let alone at the last minute. I doubt she'd do it again."

It was one thing for Miss Zephaniah to grant evening permission and another altogether for her to agree to girls being absent overnight. Mary and I had pleaded with her, saying that Mary's mother had offered us second-row opera tickets in Chicago, and we'd somehow been convincing.

I laughed.

"Who says I'd want to do this again?"

"It's for the fraternity. Of course you would," she said. I shoved another pin into the pocket of my dress, thankful that at the very least, the early March night was somewhat balmy. I breathed in the old-estate scent of the boxwoods in front of us, reminded of the first time I'd ducked behind shrubbery. It had only been last fall, during my second week at Whitsitt. Lily and I had been coming back from lunch when my stepmother, Vera, emerged from the dormitory. I hadn't been expecting her, especially alone, and had listened with equal parts shock and expectation as she questioned Miss Zephaniah on the particulars of the tuition on the front stoop. She wasn't asking after me, or inquiring about my studies, but simply wanted to know how much it cost to send me, to house me. "We have a son to educate, you see." I could still hear her words at the end of Miss Zephaniah's explanation, and realized that she hadn't come to see me; she'd come to make sure father wasn't squandering their money on me, money that she wanted for Lucas.

"It's only one night. I'd give twenty if it'd mean the board would grant us permission," Mary said, rattling me from the memory.

I stared through the new lime green growth stretching nearly to our faces to the arch, as though if I concentrated hard enough, the Iotas would finally show up.

"Still. If we're forced to do this again, Katherine and Lily can do it," I said.

Mary snorted.

"Lily can barely keep her eyes open past nine o'clock, as you know, and Katherine is always sneaking off to meet her father's drivers. If they never come, we'll let James recount it. He's got a lawyer's mind; he'll not forget the details."

I didn't agree, but didn't bother arguing with her. I'd heard enough about initiation to know that it was complex, that the pledges might not be privy to everything. I leaned my head against the stone and shut my eyes.

"Both of us can't sleep," Mary said, jostling me. The chapel clock began to ring, bellowing the Westminster chime through the silent night, followed by four tolls.

"Come with me," I said. I'd had enough waiting. "We're going to the Iota house. If they haven't come yet, we'll see them leave, and if we've missed them, then at least we'll know."

I pushed through the hedge of boxwoods, but Mary remained seated, eyeing me as though I'd gone mad.

"And if we run into them crossing campus? Or if one of the faculty sees us?" Her brow rose, and her lips pressed together as though I'd just suggested we dance naked across the quad.

"We'll walk along the wall—in the shadows. If we see them coming, we'll hide. No one else will be traipsing across campus, trust me."

"Very well," she conceded. Sweeping a bit of brush from her black sleeves, she wrapped her skirt in front of her and followed me.

"Are you sure we shouldn't wait at James's dormitory?" Mary whispered, as we stalked under the arch.

"Why are you so nervous?" I asked. It was strange to see her uneasy.

Mary had the most gumption of all of us, except perhaps Katherine, though I classified the latter's dealings as something else entirely. Perhaps foolishness.

"I'm not," she said. "I don't want to miss them. That's all."

If initiation was actually taking place, no one would know it. The lack of wood smoke on the air told me that there wasn't a fire blazing at the Iota house—or anywhere else on campus for that matter—indicating that everyone had abandoned the tending to sleep. I cast a glance across the quad to the north, toward the small hill cloaking Everett Hall in a haze of white-gray fog, wishing for the warmth of my bed, but we couldn't go back.

We reached the Iota house and Mary groaned. It was dark, every window a blank canvas of black against white clapboard.

"Let's go home," I said. "We've wasted enough time." I started to turn back, but Mary paced past me around the side of the house.

"Beth," she whispered. She gestured to me and then pointed at the ground, where light spilled onto the lawn from a tiny window in the foundation. Mary squatted down next to it and spun away as quickly, pressing herself against the siding.

"Look."

I stooped down on the other side of the window and peered through. A row of silver-hooded figures knelt on the floor in front of a man dressed in gold. He donned a yellow headdress lined with orange and gold thread—a poor depiction of the Iota's lion. Two candles blazed from crude sconces on either side of the room, lighting the dirt floor.

The man began to walk and at once I knew it was Grant. The confident stride and broad shoulders could belong to no one else. He was talking, though I couldn't hear a word through the window. Suddenly, he pushed the hooded headdress back from his face, letting it fall in a heap at his nape. I gasped. He looked angry—so angry that it had swollen the veins in his neck, on his face. His hair was saturated with sweat, and he lifted a hand to his forehead, wiping at the beads of moisture. He turned again, pacing back in front of the pledges. Something was horribly wrong. *Where were the other brothers? Where was Will?*

"Can you hear what he's saying?" Mary whispered. I'd forgotten she was there.

"No. But he's furious about something." I scanned the hooded men, trying to discern which was James.

"He's the one on the far right," Mary said, gesturing to the man closest to me.

"How do you—"

"On your feet!" Grant's roar rocketed through the glass and I jumped, swiveling around to face the window. The row of men stumbled to their feet and Grant disappeared. I watched James shift his shoulders and toss his head back in an attempt to free himself from the hood, but he was unsuccessful.

"Their hands are tied," Mary whispered.

Grant reappeared, carrying two stone jugs emblazoned with the same wing emblem I'd seen on the bottles Katherine had stored in our chapter room, and set them down in front of the pledges.

"What's he doing with the rye?" I asked, half to myself.

"Why do you seem so alarmed?" Mary asked. She looked at me as though I'd lost my mind. "It's rye, Beth. It's meant to be consumed. And, it's a celebration."

"That's not it. Grant . . . he's fuming, Mary, and I didn't get to him today. I don't know—"

I stopped short as Grant walked down the line, flinging back the hood of each pledge. He whispered something as he did and they each immediately dropped to the ground, holding themselves up on their hands. He got to James last, but instead of flattening like the others, James rose. Grant untied his hands and pushed him forward.

Mary chuckled.

"He loathes every moment of this." She leaned back against the house, but I couldn't tear my eyes away as Grant pried the cork from one of the jugs and gestured to James. James lifted the jug to his lips, and Grant's hands came out of his pockets, fingers escaping his fist one by one as he counted. When he ran out of fingers, Grant abandoned James to pace in front of the other pledges.

"He's going to be piss drunk by the time Grant lets him stop," Mary said.

She wasn't ruffled, but I watched, horrified. Clearly the board's examination of Iota Gamma hadn't included a ritual such as this. It had been a minute and a half and it didn't look like Grant would allow James to stop drinking anytime soon. Suddenly, Grant spun away from the other pledges and yanked the jug from James's lips. Rye sloshed down the front of James's cloak, plastering the fabric to his chest.

"Get down!" Grant yelled. James shrugged and knelt down, holding himself up on his hands like the rest of the pledges. I watched the faces of the other men. Some were laughing, while sweat rolled down the faces of others, gathering in small puddles on the dirt floor.

Grant's lips began to move again, and I leaned closer to the window, hoping to catch his words.

"Iota Gamma is an organization based on brotherhood and loyalty."

I waited for him to tell another pledge to take his place at the rye jug, but he didn't. "Pledge Sanderson. Get up and have another drink." James's blond hair shifted as he lifted his gaze from the floor. He glared at Grant and said something I couldn't hear.

"He despises that man entirely," Mary said. "He'd strike him right now if it didn't mean he'd break his promise to Katherine. He's too loyal for his own good, I swear it."

"I said, I'm not thirsty!" James's voice shot through the window and I looked down in time to see Grant grasp the back of his cloak and pull him up.

"Drink it." I couldn't hear Grant, but could read his lips as he lifted the jug to James's mouth. I thought James was about to refuse, until he snatched it from Grant and tipped it to his lips.

"As I was saying," Grant yelled, his voice coming through the window clearly, "the men of Iota Gamma are loyal, thinking of their brothers' well-being before their own." All of the pledges' arms were shaking. "One of you has already compromised that bond. One of you has forced me to deal with a devil that I'd already defeated, a man who now has the capacity to ruin my legacy."

Grant's voice boomed as he paced in front of the pledges. James stopped drinking. He lowered the jug slowly.

"I haven't any idea why you're accusing me, but at least have the nerve to say my name," James shouted. He took a step back and hurled the jug against the wall. The stoneware shattered and bits ricocheted toward the pledges, who stumbled to their feet. As Grant lunged for James, his eyes were ablaze with a fury I'd never seen. James tried to get away, but couldn't on unsteady legs, and Grant caught the front of his cloak, yanking him toward his own chest. Mary stood, but I couldn't tear my eyes away from the window, waiting for Grant to punch him. Instead, he jerked James toward the door that led up from the cellar.

Mary and I plastered ourselves against the house. My heart was pounding. If he turned our way, we'd be found.

"Come on, man," James said. I heard the steady stride of Grant's feet followed by the soft rake of something dragging across the dirt path. Seconds later, I saw what it was. The moonlight fell on the two of them, illuminating Grant's pinched features and knuckles still clenched to the front of James's cloak, dragging him along. James jerked to the right in an attempt to free himself, but could only muster the weak wobble of a drunk man.

"Where are they going?" Mary whispered. "Is this ordinary? Perhaps he's taking him as his little brother?"

I didn't know what to say to her. I didn't want to alarm her, but even having no idea of the Iotas' initiation rituals, I knew something was wrong. They disappeared into the canopy of trees below the house and I skirted around Mary, following them.

By the time we made our way to the foot of the forest, they were gone. Reaching my hand out, I stopped Mary and listened. An owl hooted in the distance, followed by the low hum of a male voice coming from my left. I clutched Mary's hand and turned away from the path to the stable.

"The lake," I whispered. Beyond the basin of water at the bottom of the hill, there was nothing to my left except the woods.

"The lake? Why?"

I shook my head to silence her. I didn't know. I clutched my skirt, pitching it to my ankles. The silk was cool against my palm, but my hands were sweating.

"You're uneasy, Beth. What's wrong?" Mary said as her hand squeezed mine and she stopped me, green eyes luminous in the stream of moonlight coming through the trees.

"Grant's angry. If it's about the rye . . ."

"Do you think he'll hurt James?"

She started running before I had a chance to answer.

"Surely not, but . . ." My words were lost to her. She quickened our pace, eyes fixed on the darkness in front of us as she practically dragged me down the rest of the hill.

"No." I heard Grant's voice thunder over us and we froze behind a grove of evergreens. I took a breath to calm, inhaling pine and spring.

"There they are," Mary said.

We could see two silhouettes standing on the bank of the lake. James pushed against Grant's chest, but couldn't break free.

"I said, that's enough!" Grant shouted. "You'll admit what you've done this instant or you'll be finished. You'll not disgrace me, and you'll certainly not disgrace Iota Gamma."

I relaxed. Grant was only being harsh because was trying to make a point. All of the fury was surely feigned for effect. Mary's shoulders jerked as Grant pushed James into the shallow water at the bank. James shook his head and laughed. He walked back up the muddy beach, but Grant caught the edge of his coat, pulling him back into the water.

"I've learned enough about you recently to know you're a man who enjoys deals," James slurred. I knew he was speaking of me, of Grant's arrangement with President Wilson. As though his words had ignited a fire, Grant lunged forward, hands closing in a fist around the hood of James's cloak.

"You're wrong. Why would you do this to me?" Grant shouted. "What did I do to deserve this?"

James swayed unsteadily in the knee-deep water.

"You've clearly gone insane. I haven't done anything to you," James said. Grant rocked back and punched James in the stomach. James's guttural groan sliced through me, and I clutched my own stomach in reflex.

"I'm going to stop this," I said. I took a step forward, but Mary caught my arm.

"It's only a fight," she whispered. "James will never forgive me if I send my sister swooping in to save him . . . or if I save him myself."

"Is that so?" Grant asked. He leaned over James's slumped figure, Grant's curls hanging haphazardly across his face. James didn't say anything, but lifted his arm to Grant, undoubtedly hoping to ward off any more blows.

"You're a liar," Grant said. "You entered into this brotherhood under false pretenses, to make a fool of me. Iota Gamma is sacred. My legacy is sacred."

My heart stopped. I'd initially assumed that his anger had something to do with the rye. It hadn't crossed my mind that he could have found out about our plan.

"Did you tell someone?" Mary's voice came beside me, soft but firm.

"No," I whispered, "of course I wouldn't."

Her eyebrows rose.

"Not this time," I promised her.

"How long has he employed you? How long have you associated with vapid scum like him?" Grant was yelling now, the edges of his voice frayed with strain.

James straightened, and in one swift movement pulled the cloak from his body.

"Who . . . are you . . . talking about?" Clearly still recovering from the blow to his stomach, James's question was breathy. "I don't want any part of . . . of this despicable fraternity."

He pushed the rumpled cloak into Grant's hands and Grant balled it up and flung it into the lake.

"Don't act as though you haven't a clue. You'll tell me about your association with Anthony Helms."

My breath caught. *Professor Helms.* Suddenly everything Katherine had recounted about the revenue agent—his comment about regaining his life, his interest in Grant's name—made sense. *He must have been the one to stop Katherine's driver.*

"No. James wouldn't," Mary said. Her fingers went limp around mine.

"He didn't. Professor Helms . . . he must've been the one to stop Big Jim. He must've either taken a job as a revenue agent or been following Grant and the pledges, looking for a way to blackmail him for ruining his career," I said.

James swayed.

"The professor? I've never laid eyes on—"

Grant pushed him further into the water. At once, the glistening deep seemed to engulf him. The shoulders of his white linen shirt disappeared, and James's head bobbed just above the surface.

"I've stepped in a hole," James gargled. "I'm telling you, Richardson, I've never seen the man."

"Don't lie to me!" Grant lurched into the water himself.

"As I said before, Richardson," James said, panting. "You seem like a man who enjoys engaging a deal, so how about this? I'll race you to the other side and back." He stepped out of the hole and stood next to Grant, his chest heaving. "If I win, you'll believe me that I had no idea, and if you're caught you'll let the board believe the same. If I lose, I'll accept the blame for this, even though I didn't—"

"As you should," Grant said, his voice like ice. "And will. I've been a trained swimmer since I was a child." He removed his jacket, flinging it on the bank.

I stepped forward, thinking I'd stop them once again, but Mary grasped my arm.

"Let them work it out," she whispered.

"Training means nothing," James slurred. "I want this more. I will not have my name slandered. I'll be waiting for you at the bank, Richardson."

Grant had no chance to respond before James pushed into the lake. He lifted an arm and slapped it into the water, then another before Grant dove in. Grant seemed to glide, his strong stroke surpassing James's limp, choppy movements with ease. I couldn't understand why he'd ever challenge Grant while he was so intoxicated, but perhaps that was the reason he'd done it at all.

"You're wrong about all of this," James called out, suddenly pausing, his head dipping up.

"I'm not," Grant yelled back, stopping in the middle of the lake in turn. "I received a warning from the man delivering the rye yesterday, a man who asked after you."

"Of course he did. I ordered it," James's voice echoed.

Both men were treading water, neither swimming for victory. It was a strange occurrence when pride was on the line, though I was almost sure that Grant's position so far ahead of James was the only reason he'd paused.

"James isn't one to take it. Mr. Richardson should watch his words. James is going to mutilate him when he sobers up," Mary said.

"This morning I received an unwelcome visit from Professor Helms," Grant called, his words broken by breaths. "He stopped me on my way to campus. Must have been hiding somewhere. He said that he couldn't resist delivering the warning personally—that unless I have him reinstated as a professor, he'll have me arrested for distribution. Seventy-five gallons is more than enough to convince a court that I'm a distributor. He said that even if I get rid of the rye, he has an order slip with my name on it. Now, how would he get that?"

"Perhaps because I had it sent to you," James said, his voice was quieter now, his breathing heavier. "It was my pledge gift. I . . . I suppose I didn't think there'd be consequences."

I blinked through the trees, barely hearing James's explanation. If Professor Helms took Grant down, he could return to campus. He couldn't get away with what he'd done.

"Do you know what he's done to your sister's friend, Miss Johnston?" Grant asked. The sharp edge to his voice was gone, replaced by the hint of a sigh, as though he was exhausted. They were both just specks on the water yelling at each other. "Do you?" Grant yelled. "I'll see you on the bank, Sanderson."

I heard a faint grunt from James and then they both began swimming again.

I lifted my gaze to the crescent moon as though the way to prevent

Professor Helms coming back would be spelled out in the wispy middle-of-the-night clouds. Surely Grant could find a solution. Professor Helms couldn't keep coming after Lily, ruining her happiness.

Mary gasped. She was looking out at the water, and I glanced down to see Grant making his way back to us, but there was no sign of James.

"Where did he go? Beth, do you see him?" Her hand gripped my arm. Suddenly, Katherine's words to her brother rang in my head, and my world stilled. *You're a terrible swimmer when you're sober, let alone positively bashed.*

"He can't swim well. He can't swim well, remember?" My voice rang in my ears, high-pitched and hysterical.

Mary's face was blank. She'd been intoxicated that night at Mr. Everett's, the night we'd asked James for help. The next day, she'd hardly remembered meeting at all, let alone an unimportant comment from Katherine to James.

Before I could explain, Mary ran from the trees. Grant emerged from the lake and turned toward the sound in time to see her dive into the water. I watched her black silk skirt disappear into the midnight depth, knowing I should move, but was unable. Rooted to the spot, my chest wrung tight with tension.

"What're you doing here?" Grant's questions went unanswered as Mary propelled toward James, her arms as steady as a sternwheeler's paddle.

"Please, God. Please," I whispered, but James didn't appear on the surface of the water.

"I asked you a question," Grant yelled. The demand seemed to shake me, force me from shock, and I ran toward the bank.

"Grant!"

"Beth, what—" His forehead wrinkled in confusion, but I turned away, my gaze fixed on Mary's form.

"Save him . . . Mary's trying to save him. James . . . James is a terrible

swimmer." My voice shook and goosebumps prickled my skin. Everything seemed to go silent then with Grant's realization, and I heard a
splash beside me as Grant dove in after them. I watched him hasten
across the water after Mary, barely allowing myself the luxury of a blink.
What if James wasn't breathing? There'd been a diagram of the Silvester
method in *The American Journal of the Medical Sciences* last year. It had
been on the last page. I pinched my eyes shut, trying to conjure the image of it in my mind. The steps had been drawn in little squares. The
first was a woman lifted at the shoulders, head dropped back. *What was
the second?*

"Beth!" I heard my name shouted, a panic-stricken noise that shot
a tremor up my backbone. Grant had stopped. I could see the outline of his white shirt idling in the water. "Beth!" He screamed again.
"She's not here either." My knees buckled, threatening collapse. Without thinking, I ran into the water, barely feeling the chill of it or my
skirts coiling around my ankles. I couldn't swim. I'd never had lessons
because I'd never needed them. The closest I'd been to swimming was
wading calf-deep in Lake Michigan. But I couldn't let them drown.

"Stay there," Grant yelled. "Stay!" he said again. His shirt disappeared as he dove under. I stared at the spot where I'd last seen him,
my vision fraying at the edges. Everything—the trees, the sky, the water,
seemed to close in around me. *One, two, three, four, five.* I counted
how long Grant had been down, and then he broke the surface. Nothing. He disappeared again and my mind flashed back to the Silvester
method. I had to remember. *Lift, then what?* Cross. I took a breath,
trying to focus, inhaling a puff of the crisp air laden with decaying
algae. *Cross the wrists over the lower chest.*

"I've . . . I've got him," Grant said. Even from this distance, I could
tell that James had lost consciousness. His body was limp against
Grant's.

"Mary," I said. I took another step into the water, searching the darkness. *How long had she been under? A minute? Five?* There was no way to calculate how long I'd been waiting on the shore. Speckled dots clouded my eyes and my body chilled. I swayed in the ankle-deep water, knowing I couldn't save her. At best, I'd kill myself trying.

"Save him." Grant's words forced me from the brink of fainting. His breath was labored as he pulled James's body to the bank.

"Mary," I whispered, the only sound I could muster, but Grant had already disappeared back into the water.

I dropped to my knees in front of James.

His mouth was open as though he'd been frantically trying to draw a breath, lips blue with cold. I pressed my fingers to his neck, felt a whisper of a pulse, and jerked his shoulders up with all the strength I possessed. I yanked his wrists toward me and crossed them over his chest. *Press.* I rocked forward, bearing into him. His head tossed to the side and I closed my eyes, feeling the dampness from his saturated clothing seeping through my skirts.

"Please, God." *Stretch.* The remaining squares of the Silvester method materialized in my mind and I stretched his arms outward and up. "Breathe." I repeated the steps, pushing his wrists as hard as I could into his chest. He wasn't breathing. I did it again, pausing to wait for a gasp, but nothing came. He couldn't die. He couldn't be dead. I wrenched his arms away from his chest, stretching them out as far as I could. Staring at him, I envisioned his chest cavity opening and oxygen entering. I thrust his wrists into his chest again.

I heard a dull thud beside me and saw a swath of black out of the corner of my eye, tangled around pale limbs. When I forced James's arms open again, something gurgled in his throat. I swallowed, forcing myself to ignore the urge to abandon him for Mary. I shoved James's wrists into his chest another desperate time.

"Breathe, breathe," Grant said. His voice rattled through me and my attention jerked to Mary. I caught a glint of glass jewels as Grant untangled the end of her train from her arms and pulled her shoulders up from the muddy bank. Grant copied my movements, propelling her wrists into her chest as hard as he could. I stretched James's arms out for the sixth time and heaved them down again. Water trickled from his nostrils.

"Is she breathing?" I called, amazed at how calm I sounded.

"No," Grant grunted. A knot settled in my throat. James's body twitched toward me and he coughed.

"Grant, he's coming back. Let me see Mary." Grant moved out of my way and I heard him muttering something to James as I extended Mary's arms, hand gripped to the saturated black lace at her wrist. I thrust her wrists down, but her body rocked limply beneath me, and my skin prickled. *Grant hadn't known to check her pulse.* I lifted my fingers to her neck. Nothing. My palm pressed against her chest, while my fingers frantically moved over her temple.

"Where's your heartbeat? Where is it?" I stared into her face, praying her eyes would open. "Mary! Wake up, wake up, wake up."

I shook her, fingers clawing into her back, and at once, my mind flashed to my mother. The same blank face, the same limp body, the same hysterical sound of my voice. "No. No, no, no, no." Darkness rimmed my vision as cold drifted up from my hands, permeating my heart, stealing the last bit of my strength.

"Beth!" Will's shout echoed down Hideaway Hill before everything went black.

21

THERE WERE WHITE flowers everywhere—tied along the ends of the simple oak pews, entwined in the boxwood wreaths hanging from the windows, propped in crystal vases sitting atop the closed black coffin. The college had decorated the chapel as though a child had died. Mary would have hated it.

"Why did you have to go after him?" I whispered before a sob burst from my lips, echoing through the vacant church. I sniffed, trying to compose myself, but my chest was wrung tight with grief. My shoulders heaved, and I turned away from the early morning sunlight coming through the windows, shielding my swollen eyes. I knew why she'd done it. The answer settled in my heart as though she'd been there to remind me. She loved James. She'd saved him—and could have saved herself too if she'd been wearing a swimming suit. Instead, her skirts had killed her, snarling around her limbs like a net.

"I'm sorry," I said. The last moments of her life played over and over in my head, like a phonograph record skipping forward and back over the same notes. I felt the cool water seeping into my boots, heard Grant's frantic shouts. I'd stood on the bank as she died, doing nothing.

"It should have been me." It felt good to say it out loud. Mary had been so full of life, so sure of the difference that she knew she could make, that we all could. In contrast, all I'd done was fold under pressure the moment it had been applied. I'd been so quick to abandon the collective good for my own. She'd brought me back to the fraternity, reminding me that we were doing something greater. Without her prodding, I would have abandoned my sisters and the women that would come after us. I would have been alone. I exhaled, letting my shoulders sag. Involving Mary in the fraternity was the ultimate cause of her death. That was my doing. Without it, she'd still be here.

I ran my black-gloved hand along the back of the oak pew in front of me. In three hours this place would be teeming with mourners. People would pretend that they knew her, that they'd actually cared, but except for a handful of us, they'd be lying. That's how it always was when someone passed before their time. It was a tragedy, and humans flocked to misfortune like a moth to flame.

The bell gonged overhead. The notes of the Westminster chime bellowed through the chapel, ending in seven steady beats. I glanced at the grandfather clock at the base of the pulpit. It was set to four-fifteen. Four-fifteen in the morning, the approximate time of her death.

The last thing I recalled from that night was my skin prickling cold, Will's voice shouting my name, and the flash of black as I'd fainted. It all seemed like a blur now. Will had told me how he'd found us—that several of the pledges had escaped the basement and come into the house, alarmed at Grant's demeanor. The minute they'd mentioned that Grant had taken James outside, Will knew where. Grant had taken Will to the lake upon his initiation, too.

Will told me later that he'd tried to wake me when he'd reached me, but hadn't been able to. Having no idea where to go, he'd taken me to Everett Hall, somehow carrying me past Miss Zephaniah's room. I'd woken a few hours later in my bed next to Lily, sure I'd dreamt it all. The sun had just come up, filtering through our window in pink-yellow streams. A knock on our door had come shortly thereafter, and the moment I opened it, I knew it was real. Will was there, standing next to Miss Zephaniah. His face was gaunt, the knees of his suit saturated with silt from the bank.

No one had seen Grant since. I pinched my eyes shut, trying to force the image of him out of my mind, but couldn't. The vision of him pushing Mary's wrists into her chest, face gripped with panic, white shirt dripping streams of water into the mud, had haunted me for days. It had been rumored that he'd quit the college after the board had refused to have him arrested, after they'd refused to dissolve Iota Gamma. They'd tried their best to make her death seem like no one was at fault, like it had been a complete and utter accident, as though it hadn't been preceded by the imposition of an initiation ritual—the reason they'd banned Greek fraternities in the first place. They still wanted Grant's money, after all.

I pinched the edge of the white ribbon tied to the pew next to me. I was burning with anger, but felt nothing when I thought of him. Only horror and pain and guilt. For as much as I blamed him and wanted to hate him, he hadn't intended for anyone to die. I knew that. James had provoked him, challenged him to a competition, and he'd foolishly accepted, his pride getting in the way. Even in the fire of his fury, he wasn't a murderer.

"How long have you been here?" The heavy hinge of the chapel door clicked back into place, and Katherine rushed toward me, fingering the emerald stitching on the cuffs of her black mourning dress. Her eyes were red, a spiderweb of veins overtaking the white. I hadn't seen her for days. She'd been watching over James at Mercy Hospital in Chicago.

"I got here at four," I told her. Since Mary's death, I'd woken each morning at nearly four-fifteen to the mark anyway, as though my body felt compelled to remind me of the exact time she'd died. Sometimes I'd wake screaming, jolting Lily awake. This morning I'd been calm. I'd left the room as quietly as I could, hoping to let Lily sleep. I knew that Will had volunteered to watch over Mary's body from midnight until five, so I went to relieve him.

"I couldn't sleep," I said. I scooted down the pew and Katherine sat down next to me. She lifted her hand to her hair, adjusting the black filigree comb.

"She wouldn't have wanted this, you know," Katherine said quietly. Her eyes were fixed on the coffin. "She was the most alive person I've ever known. Imagine what she'd say to us if she were here."

"I've grown so tired of watching you grieve," I said, trying my best to imitate Mary's high-pitched tone and sharp enunciation.

"Do away with these flowers. I spent my life in symbolic mourning and don't plan to give it up now," Katherine said, lips turning up in a smile. "I can't come to grips with it. That she's gone."

Her voice suddenly lowered, as though if she spoke the words too loudly, it meant they were true. "We didn't even like each other at the start," she continued. "We barely spoke the first few weeks. I thought she was a bit odd with the black costumes and she undoubtedly thought I carried the torch for the Confederacy. Thank goodness that neither of us could tolerate silence. Eventually we talked to each other anyway."

I took a breath, inhaling the gummy, ancient scent of old pine planking and the light aroma from the flowers. It smelled like death.

"I know she wouldn't want it to be this way, but every time I think of her, all I can see is her limp body, her blank face," I said. "I can still feel the clammy damp of her skin under my hands and the way her head bobbed when I tried to bring her back. I didn't save her. How could I have ever thought I'd make a good physician?" I balled my fingers into fists. "I'm just thankful that James is alive, I—"

"That's a big load you're preparing to carry," Katherine said. She leaned over and kissed my cheek. "James is alive because of you, you know. You're still learning, Beth. That's why you're here. You did the best you could."

A tear fell, warm and quick. I wiped it away.

"And Mary knows that," she continued. I glanced at the casket, knowing Katherine was right. I wasn't a physician, not yet, and without my unassigned study of the medical journals I wouldn't have known the Silvester method. James would have died too.

"Is James going to be all right?"

"They believe so, yes. He'll likely be released next week. They're only monitoring his kidneys. But . . . he insists that all of this . . . that Mary's death was his fault alone. He knows he should've never challenged Grant. He keeps saying it over and over. I don't know if he'll ever overcome the grief . . . if I'll ever overcome the guilt." Katherine ran her hands back and forth along the pew as her eyes filled. "If I hadn't forced him to rush, he wouldn't have been in that lake. Mary wouldn't have been there either."

"All of us asked him to do it, Mary included. She would have given anything for our fraternity."

"Even her life?"

Katherine's question settled like a yoke across my shoulders.

"No," I said finally. "But how were we to know what . . . what Grant would do?" I asked. I could barely say his name aloud. "If he hadn't forced James to drink to intoxication, James would've been thinking clearly. He never would've suggested a swimming contest. I hope Grant understands what he's done."

"He does," Katherine said. I turned toward her, sure she'd misspoken. She looked down at her hands. "He came to see James yesterday. He looked horrible, gray, as though he'd perished too. He kept saying over and over that he wanted to die, that Mary's death was his doing, and then James would dispute him to take the blame himself. It was horrible."

"It *was* Grant's doing," I hissed. The chains of grief that had harnessed my fury suddenly snapped. I was stunned that he'd had the nerve to show his face at the hospital.

"No." Katherine's response countered my fury. *Was she defending him?* "It wasn't. I blame him in part for what's happened to James, for the pain my brother will endure knowing the woman he loved died trying to save him, for the fact that he nearly drowned, but Mr. Richardson didn't kill Mary . . . and neither did we."

It was easier to blame Grant. He'd been the reason we'd gone down to the lake, after all, but I burned with guilt all my own. If I hadn't insisted that we follow James, we wouldn't have been at the Iota house in the middle of the night—or at the lake. We would have eventually gone home to our beds to rest before another day of mundane classes, another day of instruction from professors who would do their best to make us feel as though we hadn't a place here. But James would have died.

"I suppose you're right," I said.

"I've had to remind James of that over and over. I told Mr. Richardson the same," she said. "But regardless of what I say, we'll all live with the guilt of it for the rest of our lives." Wind whistled through the window pane next to us, disrupting the steady ticking of the chapel clock. Katherine wrapped her arm around my shoulders.

"I've got to go meet my father at the dormitory. He's asked for my ledgers," she said, standing and digging her fingers into her high black chiffon neckline, drawing the fabric out from her neck. "He told me that I'm no longer to work for him. He heard me talking with James. He knows I forced him to rush and believes that I don't have enough integrity for the job."

I found integrity a strange requirement for bootlegging, but didn't question her. She'd lost her best friend, and the only thing she'd ever wanted for herself.

"I'm s—"

"I am too," she said. Edging out of the pew, she walked down the aisle toward the door. "Oh, Beth. When you see Lily, tell her that Mr. Richardson's seen to it that Professor Helms won't be coming back. He asked me to pass it along."

"How?"

"It seems that he offered Professor Helms enough money that he's agreed to keep quiet about the rye and stay away from Whitsitt. I'll see you in a bit." With that, she disappeared into the courtyard, leaving me alone with Mary.

* * *

Judith stood over her daughter's open coffin, her cathedral-length black crepe veil fanning out with each breath. The funeral had been over for nearly an hour, but Katherine, Lily, Will, and I had remained with Judith, none of us able to bear the thought that the moment we left, Mary's body would depart as well, and we'd never see her again.

"The only thing she really wanted was the fraternity," Judith said. "She was serious about her musical studies, her dream to be a conductor, but rarely wrote to me about them. It was always about the fraternity, about her sisters. I know it wasn't easy for her, growing up without siblings or a father. The three of you were as much her family as I was."

Lily began to sob again. The gasp that preempted it rang through the chapel. She'd been crying before the service had officially begun, with the first notes of "Shall We Gather at the River," and had barely stopped since. I glanced over my shoulder, finding her huddled at the end of the first pew. Her head was in her hands, black feathers in her mourning cap trembling as she wept. I knew Judith's sentiments rang true for Lily and me, too. We'd become each other's family, true sisters.

Will squeezed my hand. I swallowed hard and looked down at Mary. She was pale, her soul clearly absent, a blue-gray tinge lining the edges of her painted red lips.

"We'll find a way to make it happen . . . for her honor," Katherine said. The thought of continuing Beta Xi Beta after losing Mary shocked me. I hadn't thought of the fraternity in days and didn't know if I could even bear to say the pledge without her. The bullheaded determination to start it had been the reason we'd followed James to the lake in the first place.

"She would want that. I was so proud of what you all were doing." Judith reached into the coffin, cupping her daughter's cheek in her hand.

"If we'd waited by Wilson Hall like she'd wanted, if I hadn't been so hasty . . ." The words croaked from my lips and tears sprang to my eyes. "I'm so sorry. It's my fault." Judith stepped away from the coffin, flung her veil back, and snatched my shoulders. Her light green eyes, so much like Mary's, were snaked with red veins, lids so swollen that the almond shape had been reduced to slits, but I'd been sitting beside her for nearly two hours and she hadn't as much as sniffed.

"I'll not allow you to say that again," she said. "I've had quite enough of you blaming yourself."

I stared at her, trying to remember how many times I'd apologized since she'd arrived.

"You sound just like her . . . Mary," I said.

"I *am* her mother. Consider it a message from her to you," she declared, then dropped her hands from my shoulders to drift over the black velvet lining the coffin. "I suppose it's almost time to go." Taking her words as a signal, the two men from the funeral parlor advanced from their posts flanking the chancel door. I felt panicked as though I should stop them, but I knew I couldn't keep her or bring her back to us. I leaned forward to look at Mary one more time, trying to memorize the face I'd never see again except in the small miniature Judith had given us to share. Katherine sighed heavily, and I heard the soft hiccups of Lily's sobs. Will drew me away from the coffin, but I resisted, clutching the edge. He reached in front of me, palm resting on the back of my hand for a moment, before he gently pried my fingers from the wood.

"She's not here," he whispered, and placed my palm on my heart. "She's here. You'll never forget her."

The hinges creaked as the men began to lower the lid.

"Goodbye, my darling girl," Judith said.

My bottom lip began to tremble, and I started to turn my head toward the coffin, but Will's fingers found my chin and tilted me back to him.

"Remember her alive."

"He's right, you know," Judith said, pulling the veil back over her face. The edges of the coffin met with a quiet thud—a note of finality.

"Would you like us to ride to Chicago with you? It would . . . it would be our honor." Lily's voice broke as she said it.

"We would be happy to go with you," Will echoed, momentarily tearing his eyes from me. I stole a glance at the two men standing at Mary's head and foot, waiting to take her away. The thought of her body being lowered into the ground made my stomach turn.

"No, my dears," Judith said softly. "Mary would rather all of you get on to your classes. You know how disappointed she'd be if you didn't pass them."

"Are you certain?" Katherine asked.

Judith nodded and turned from her to squeeze my hand.

"I am," she said. "But Beth, I must ask you for a rather difficult favor."

I nodded, barely able to see her face through the black crepe.

"The carriage is here, ma'am," the man said. Judith tipped her head at him, and the other man grasped the gleaming copper bar at the coffin's foot. The men lifted it with ease, and I stepped aside to let them through. Katherine reached out and touched the coffin, fingers trailing down the black wood until it disappeared beneath her hand.

"I need you to take me to see Mr. Richardson."

"Why?" The question came out of my mouth before I'd realized I'd spoken.

"There are some things I need to discuss with him," she said. "As much as I'd like to blame him for my daughter's death, I cannot, and he needs to know that. I've already told Mr. Sanderson as much, too."

Over Judith's shoulder, I could see Katherine staring at me, urging me to comply.

"I . . . I don't know where he is," I said, speaking as much to Katherine as I was to Judith.

"I'm sorry to say that he withdrew from Whitsitt, ma'am. He's likely gone back to New York," Will said, saving me from explaining.

I glanced out of the open chapel doors. Two Clydesdales stood at the front of the carriage. One stamped and snorted impatiently.

"Is there a message I could pass along to him?" I continued. "I'd be more than happy to write a letter or visit him personally—"

"No," she said, flipping her hand. "It's of no matter. I know his father. I'll simply call on him next—"

"Please. Have me arrested and killed. For the love of God."

The voice was a knife that plunged into my gut and twisted as Grant appeared out of nowhere. He looked completely undone. He hadn't shaved and his face was ashen.

"I shall not," Judith said. None of us moved; none of us spoke. His presence had frozen us all.

"Please," he said, his tone a ragged sob. "If you won't . . . no one will . . . I . . ."

Judith strode toward him, meeting him where he stood in the chancel doorway.

"Absolutely not," she said. "I will not. That's the last thing my daughter would have wanted."

Grant covered his face, leaned down, and wept. A strange mix of compassion and sadness passed through me, and I took a step toward him, but Will held me back.

"Let her speak," he whispered. "He'll be all right."

"I was standing outside," Grant said as he sniffed and righted. "I knew I didn't deserve to be here after . . . after everything. But I wanted to pay my respects somehow. I didn't intend to interfere, but when I heard you say that you wanted to speak to me . . . you deserve to tell me to go to hell or send me there."

I looked at her, wondering if she'd change her mind and have him arrested after all. Losing someone makes emotions a fickle thing—one moment you're overcome with anguish, the next, rage.

"I'll do neither," Judith said as she lifted her veil and reached for Grant's hand. "There's something you should know," she said. "Mary was . . . she was your sister. Half-sister, I suppose."

Grant's face paled. I heard Katherine gasp, and my mouth went dry.

"That can't be," Will muttered.

"What?" Grant said, barely audible.

"It's true," Judith said. "Many years ago, right after your mother left for Virginia, I met your father at the train station in Chicago. I was on my way to a rally at a tavern in the Bridgeport area and he was on his way back home from a holiday and . . ." She cleared her throat. "All of that is of no matter. He didn't know about Mary and two months later I met my dear late husband. I haven't spoken to him in nearly nineteen years, but from time to time, I'd catch a mention of your family in the society pages. When I saw that you'd chosen to study here, I encouraged Mary to consider it too. I'd been acquainted, rather intimately, with Patrick Everett before his death. The college was already at the forefront of my mind, but when I found that you'd chosen Whitsitt, I wanted her to study here. I hoped that she'd run into you from time to time, that she'd get to know you. It was my greatest wish that perhaps the two of you would be friends, even if you'd never be siblings." Grant swallowed. His lips parted, as if he was about to say something, but he didn't. "Don't misunderstand me," she said. "I didn't want any part of your father's life. I still don't, but I suppose, beneath it all, I had hoped that either you or Mary would start to suspect. I'm her only family. I thought that if she knew she had a brother—"

"Why didn't you tell us? Tell him?" Grant cried. His eyes welled and the cords of his neck bulged.

"Surely you know I couldn't," Judith said. "The knowledge of her would have ruined your father. A bastard child by an infamous suffragist would have been—"

"I killed her. I killed my sister."

Grant let go of Judith's hand, but she held tight until he pried his fingers from her grasp and walked away. I took a step toward him. He couldn't be alone right now. Not after everything. Will disappeared from my side and went after Grant, stopping him in the doorway.

"Please. Listen to what she has to say," Will said. "For her and for yourself."

Grant stopped, fixing his eyes on a small stained glass window over Will's head.

"I want to die," he said finally, turning to Judith. "At the very least, have me locked away, I beg you."

"It wasn't your fault," Judith said, her voice solid and unwavering. "It wasn't anyone's fault. You didn't force her into the water, she chose to go. Mary's heart was her calamity. I knew it was like mine from the beginning—a heart made for sacrifice. She paid the ultimate price for the things she loved the most—her fraternity, her sisters, and . . . and

James. She wouldn't have wanted you to spend the rest of your life suffering, blaming yourself. She would have wanted you to continue her legacy, to do something great by her memory."

Grant shook his head.

"It doesn't matter what I do," he whispered. "It won't bring her back."

"Honor her life and it will," she said, resting a hand on his rumpled black vest. "If you do that, she'll be alive in every person you help, every life you touch."

My eyes burned, and I blinked back tears.

"How?" he asked. "Nothing I do could possibly be a consolation."

Judith smiled, her eyes just like Mary's.

"You can start by helping her sisters establish the fraternity she loved." She patted Grant on the back and pulled her veil back over her face.

"I've already asked the board to dissolve Iota Gamma, to reinstate the ban on all Greek organizations. This was a . . . a death by hazing, Miss Adams, and I cannot help but believe Whitsitt was right to—"

"I'm aware that you asked, but they were right to refuse," Judith said.

"They refused only because I was away when they decided, because I haven't yet forced my hand," Grant said. "They think I'm only feeling a bit guilty and that I'll come around and try to reinstate it again, but they're wrong. Mary's death was my fault, Iota Gamma's fault, and—"

"From what I've heard, James presented you with a contest," Judith said, interrupting. "It wasn't a part of your Iota Gamma ritual. Those men are your brothers. They need each other . . . just as these girls need Beta Xi Beta." She started up the aisle without another word, her ruffled train shuffling across the old oak floor, and then turned in the doorway, streams of pink and orange lighting the fading sky behind her shrouded figure. "There's one more thing. My daughter was the epitome of spirit and light. I expect that all of you will live out the rest of your days accordingly."

Judith was right. Her whole life, Mary had draped herself in the color of death. To most, it had only made her stand out as a woman martyred to an unpopular and unlikely cause, but to those of us that had truly known her, the morbid tone of her dress called out something entirely different—the contradictory joy of the woman wearing it.

The coachman called out to Judith and she lifted a gloved hand in answer. "Your lives will never return to the way they were before, but I trust that you will make this new reality a better one . . . for her."

22

SIX WEEKS LATER

"Good luck today, Miss Carrington," Miss Zephaniah said as she stopped me at the bottom of the stairs. Her wrinkled lips were pinched together as they always were, but edged up at the corners as though she were actually about to smile.

"Thank you," I said.

I glanced through the windows on either side of the front door, appreciating the way the yellow light streamed dappled through the old oaks. The sun had barely woken.

Miss Zephaniah reached out and touched my antique lace cuffs, an elegant finish to my royal blue silk sleeves.

"Quite lovely," she remarked.

"The material came from a tablecloth of Mary's grandmother's," I explained. The lace had been brilliant white at one time, but had browned to ivory with age. It was perfect for our dresses. "Suppose I'll see you at the ceremony in a bit?"

Miss Zephaniah nodded.

"Of course."

As I made my way through the foyer, the dormitory was still silent except for a few muffled voices coming from the gathering room— the divinity girls had been practicing their final sermons there almost every morning for a month. In a matter of two hours, the place would be swarming and loud, hectic with family arrivals in preparation for the graduation ceremony. I wondered if my father would come when I'd earned my diploma in two years, if he'd even know the degree it held by then. I took a breath, inhaling the familiar scent of old wood and rosewater, and stepped outside. It didn't matter if he came or not, I reminded myself, or if he brought Vera and Lucas just to put on to everyone else that he cared. The people that mattered would be here. I'd have my sisters by my side regardless.

"Good morning, Miss Carrington."

I jumped, hand jerking to my heart, to the lone ivory rose fastened to my bodice by a sterling silver wreath pin, a gift from Katherine. Lily's beau, Mr. Langley, stood at the base of the porch steps holding a bouquet of identical blooms. He looked handsome, blue-green eyes fitting in with the shoots of indigo irises in bloom behind him.

"Same to you, Mr. Langley," I said.

"Will Lily be along shortly?" He grinned at me, twin dimples appearing in his cheeks. He'd rarely left her side since Mary's death, meeting her at the arch each morning before breakfast and some- times staying with her until curfew. His presence had been a blessing to Lily. She'd spent many days with the Torreys, eventually confid- ing to me that she thought she might love them as much as her beau himself.

"Eventually," I said, "Though I wouldn't count on it anytime soon. Last I checked, she was still asleep."

Mr. Langley laughed, resting the bouquet on the thick railing.

"I should be used to it by now."

"If you aren't yet, you will sooner or later," I said, walking past him. "She quite enjoys her rest."

"Wait," he said, and I stopped and turned back to see him chewing on his bottom lip, thumb running along the base of the bouquet. "I should like to tell you something . . . if you'll promise your confidence."

"Of course."

"I . . . I'm going to propose. I know it's only been a few months, but I love her. I could contain my feelings, I could wait, I suppose, but nothing would change. She is my match, and I just . . . I just feel that waiting any longer would only be wasting time, time that we could be spending together." The words tumbled from his mouth, and he stood staring at me, awaiting my approval. "Miss Carrington, you're her sister, the closest family she has. Do you approve?"

I'd been so enamored by his outpouring of love for Lily that I hadn't realized I hadn't spoken.

"Of course. Congratulations," I whispered, barely able to stop myself from embracing him. "I'm so very delighted that the two of you found each other."

"Thank you. If she says yes," he said.

"You say that as though there's any question," I said with a smile. "I'm so happy for you both." I began to walk away, but he stopped me once again.

"There's one more thing," he said, and dug into the pocket of his beige afternoon suit and extracted a letter. "I hope you don't mind, but Lily told me about your difficulty securing an apprenticeship."

He stopped, no doubt waiting for signs of fury or embarrassment, but I only shrugged and took the letter. I still hadn't received an assignment and had quite resigned myself to the fact that I wouldn't have one. The return address was handwritten, from a Hospital for Women and Children in Chicago. I'd never heard of it.

"I mentioned you to my stepfather," he continued. "He remembered you from the board meeting and was furious that you'd been turned down by so many institutions on account of your gender. The letter is from a physician and surgeon, Mary Thompson. She started the hospital in 'Sixty-five to treat indigent women and children, but the structure burned down in the 'Seventy-one fire. My father assisted her in securing a new building a few years ago. The institution is practically swarming with patients and they need help."

I slid my finger under the seal, removed the letter, and read it.

Dear Miss Carrington,

My name is Doctor Mary Thompson. I'm a surgeon by trade, a graduate of the New England Female Medical College, and the founder of the Chicago Hospital for Women and Children. As Mr. Torrey may have been kind enough to relay on my behalf, we are significantly understaffed. Our wards fill to overflowing daily, but unfortunately, our ability to recruit skilled physicians to our cause has been crippled by other hospitals' recruitment efforts as well as the sort of patient we treat—impoverished women and children whose needs and care are so often ignored.

It's my understanding that you are one of the brightest pupils in your class. It has also come to my attention that you're seeking an apprenticeship. I would value your service should you find a hospital such as mine a satisfactory environment in which to learn.

Sincerely,
Doctor Mary Thompson

I looked at the letter again, hardly believing my fortune. My hands would be working after all; I'd be learning.

"Thank you so much for doing this for me. It means the world. How lovely you are—to our Lily, to me," I said.

"You're very welcome." He straightened his jacket and glanced over my head at the door.

"She'll be coming out soon enough," I said. "And please tell your father how grateful I am for his help and that I'll write to Dr. Thompson straightaway."

"Very good. Say hello to Buchannan for me," Mr. Langley called out as I made my way through the aisle of oaks and down the hill. He and Will had become friends since Mary's death. Together, they'd kept us fed and occupied in the dark days after the funeral, forcing us to keep up with our classes, reminding us that we couldn't wallow in despair.

I passed under the arch and walked the long way across the quad. Black-robed professors and faculty scurried back and forth from the chapel on the other side of campus to Old Main. I looked across the plain of flat green grass to the chapel's stone walls and towering steeple—at the cheery ribbons of fuchsia, lavender, and green swooping down from the door, and the vibrant bouquets of peonies, irises, and hollyhocks at the base of the steps. The Women of Whitsitt had done a remarkable job decorating the chapel. It was hard to imagine that it was the same grim place we'd said farewell to Mary.

I ran my hand along the boxwoods as I passed Old Main and walked under the arch toward the Iota house. Most of the brothers had already dressed for the day and were congregating on the porch in their tuxedos, smoking foul-smelling cigars. Absorbed in their conversation, no one took notice of me.

I snaked around the side of the house, watching Mr. Stephens lean back against one of the pillars, gray rose flopped sloppily against his black vest, cigar clutched in his teeth. The pungent scent of peat and earth drifted toward me in a cloud, and I coughed as I walked through it, relieved when the house blocked the wind. A horse whinnied in the distance—a breathy snort from the stable down Hideaway Hill—and I paused at the basement window. Closing my eyes, I saw Mary's face as clearly as if she'd just been in front of me—eyes fixed on James's robed figure, mouth turned up as though she couldn't wait to poke fun at him for his compliance with Grant's schemes.

"I will always remember you," I whispered.

I walked into the house, and paused in the drafty dimness. My fingers rested on the carved mahogany railing, eyes fixed on the lion mural. It was a bit improper to walk right in, but it was a much easier way to Will than through his brothers on the front porch. I doubted that anyone would be keen to abandon their cigars to fetch him for me anyway.

"It seems like years since you came in that first time." My gaze lifted from the silver rose to see Grant, who was sitting on the other side of the stairwell. He rose from a small wooden chair. "You could have come through the front door, you know."

"Why start now?" I asked. Grant smiled, a handsome complement to his black tuxedo adorned with silver threading—the graduation suit of an Iota Gamma.

"Beth, I . . . before I graduate, before I leave this place, I need to thank you. You changed me."

I shook my head.

"That's not true," I said. His forehead wrinkled in disagreement. "It's not. You always had it inside of you, the capability to do the right thing."

"Perhaps. But I didn't. Until you . . . and until . . ." He reached into his pocket, withdrew a gold locket and opened the hinge to a miniature of Mary nearly identical to Beta Xi Beta's shared portrait. In the few times I'd seen him since her death, I'd caught him looking at it, forcing the reminder of the sister he'd never really known.

"She would be proud of you," I whispered. "She doubted you'd come to our side, but always hoped you would."

"My redemption came at the cost of so many," he said, his voice faltering. "Father will be here today. He wants me to take him to Everett Hall and to the music college. To see where she lived and studied before we depart tomorrow."

Grant had just turned down a position working on his uncle's political campaign to accept a post running the New York operations of his father's company. He'd resisted the role at first, not keen to work alongside his mother, but had eventually conceded that his family's company was where he belonged.

He cleared his throat. "I know it was Miss Adams's wish to keep Mary's paternity a secret to the rest of the world, but would it have been hers?"

"Yes," I said immediately. It hadn't been the first time I'd thought of it since Judith had asked Grant to keep the secret of Mary's paternity between him and his father. She'd been right to ask. The news of a deceased bastard child of a well-known coal tycoon would be a scandal, one Judith wanted to avoid—mostly for herself as well as for the Richardsons. "As much as Mary loved a good rumor, I don't believe she'd want the cost of the world knowing hers."

"What cost?" Grant's eyes narrowed. "Our reputation? It would be nothing compared to a life . . . to the lives I've destroyed. Mary is gone and Sanderson will never be the same, I—"

"James leaving Whitsitt was his choice," I interrupted. "Katherine says he's doing well at Washington and Lee."

"He left because he couldn't bear the reminder that the woman he loves is dead," Grant said.

"Stop." I clutched his hand and let it go. "Remember all the good that you've done, all the lives that you've changed by fulfilling Mary's last wish."

The morning after her funeral, I'd gone with Grant to petition the board to officially establish Beta Xi Beta. With Grant's promise to finish his degree at Whitsitt and his money, they'd granted our request, even agreeing to help us secure a charter when we felt it was time to expand Beta Xi Beta to other campuses. I'd been amazed, standing there, at the ease of it all, at the way greed ruled over the otherwise antiquated ideals of Whitsitt's board members. Mr. Torrey had given a standing ovation when President Wilson finally gave his consent, a gesture that prompted the president to immediately retreat to his office.

"I should have helped when you asked the first time," he said. "In any case, I did nothing but throw my money at the board."

He leaned on the banister, closer to me. The scent of coconut and palm eclipsed the slight fragrance of cigar smoke, conjuring the memory of the time when I found his arms home, an echo of days that now confounded me in light of my love for Will.

"It doesn't matter how you did it," I said. "You made our dreams a reality. You changed the course of history for women studying here."

"Hardly," he snorted. "Don't give me credit when it should be given to you and your sisters. What will I do when I've gone back to New York and you're not there to talk me out of my guilt?"

I smiled.

"You and I both know that I haven't had to do that for some time. You're managing quite well on your own."

For nearly two weeks after Mary's funeral, whenever I was consolable enough to emerge from my studies or the dormitory, Will and I would hover around Grant, reminding him of Miss Adams's sentiments—a practice that had often been a balm to my own regret and immense heartache. Grant hadn't wanted to come out of his room; he'd refused to go to his courses. And then one day, he woke up and told Will that he hadn't been living for Mary and had decided to begin. Even he hadn't known the reason for his perspective suddenly changing, but we were all thankful that it had.

Grant looked down at my dress.

"It's a landmark day for the sisters of Beta Xi Beta," he said. He unpinned the gray rose at his lapel and fastened it next to my ivory one. "This is how it should be. Always. Just as you're sisters, consider Iota Gamma your brothers. We met on the matter last night. The others are in agreement. Well, most of them."

He grinned, and then his eyes met mine.

"I'll see you at the ceremony."

I watched him walk toward the foyer—the proud broad shoulders, the upturned chin, characteristics of a confident man—hoping that someday he'd feel the same inside.

"I haven't missed it, have I?" Will's voice was hoarse with sleep. I looked up and found him standing on the landing above me. He was still wearing his nightshirt, which he'd tucked sloppily into gray trousers. Of course he'd wait until the last possible moment to dress for the ceremony. He descended the steps to find me, and his hands instantly engulfed mine. "If I have, I—"

"You haven't," I said, grinning at his worried expression.

"Thank goodness," he said, pulling me closer to him. I knew I should resist—he wasn't even properly dressed—but the rest of the men were either on the porch or on the way to the ceremony, and I wanted to be close to him. The light scent of sandalwood engulfed the stench of dirty laundry and cigars as I sank into his chest, reveling in his body warm against mine. "I'd forever regret sleeping through Beta Xi Beta's inaugural graduation ceremony."

"I have some news," I whispered against his cheek. "I've been offered an apprenticeship."

"What?" He leaned away from me and smiled.

"I've just received a letter from a Doctor Thompson at the Hospital for Women and Children in Chicago. Mr. Torrey helped her obtain a new building after the fire in 'Seventy-one and knew they needed help. He contacted Doctor Thompson on my behalf."

"I'm so happy for you, but, I'm going to miss you terribly." Will had decided to serve as an apprentice to his grandfather's practice in Newark after turning down a few offers from smaller physicians in Chicago. "I suppose this means you'll have to tell your father about your studies?"

I startled at the thought. In the excitement, I hadn't considered the consequences, but of course I'd have to tell him. I'd be living with him after all, venturing out early and returning late.

"I . . . I suppose it does," I said, suddenly nervous. "He could turn me out, Will. He could stop funding my schooling. He could—"

"He could do a lot of things, Beth, but he won't."

"Surely you don't believe he isn't capable. He barely allowed me to go to Whitsitt in the first place. You know how he is. His reputation is supremely important to him, and fine families don't have physicians for daughters."

Perhaps I couldn't accept the apprenticeship after all. I couldn't risk my father's disapproval before I'd earned my diploma. After that, he could do nothing to hinder my ambitions.

"My parents know about your studies and find your aspirations altogether honorable."

"They do?"

"Do you think . . . do you think there's a chance my father already knows?"

Will shook his head.

"Probably not. At least they wouldn't have heard it from my parents. I told them to keep your progress close to the chest. But it'll be all right," he whispered as he circled an arm around my waist. "If your father threatens you or your future in any way, go to my house. My parents will keep you. They'll take you in and they'll see to it that your education continues, though I'm certain that the moment your father realizes his boss has offered to pay for it, he'll come to his senses."

He was right. My father both idolized Will's father and loathed the thought of charity.

"Are you sure your parents would do that for me? If he doesn't come around, I mean. My tuition would only be a loan of course, but—"

"Beth," he said, stopping me. "It wouldn't be a question. They love you . . . they know how much I love you. And they love us together. I'll write them about the matter today."

My mind raced, sure there was something else, something that would prevent me from accepting the apprenticeship regardless of the Buchannans' overwhelming generoslty. "Stop fretting, my dear. There's nothing to worry about and you're ruining your day."

"Please don't inhale too much ether this summer," I said suddenly, and he laughed. "I can't do without you and I'd like you to remember me when we come back in September."

"Anesthesia wouldn't have the power to take you from me. Even dead I'd never forget you."

He threaded a hand around the nape of my neck and kissed me. Though we'd made a habit of stealing kisses when we could, the mix of tenderness and ferocity still made me weak. I touched his face, palm resting on the sharp stubble. Brushing his hair back, I kissed his temple. His arms constricted around me and then his hands drifted slowly up my back. My body tingled at his touch.

"You, my love, are the most glorious sight I've ever seen," he whispered, and pulled my face to his. "And as much as I'd like to continue . . . this," he said, running his fingers over my arms, "it's not proper, nor is the stairwell suitable. Not to mention that I absolutely refuse to be responsible for the President of Beta Xi Beta appearing rumpled at the ceremony."

I laughed.

"So that's why your suits are always wrinkled?"

"No," he said. "I blame the armoire for my suits. It doesn't hang them for me."

"Buchannan! Where the hell are you? It's time." Grant's voice boomed from the front of the house.

Will rolled his eyes and grinned.

"I'll be there when I'm ready, Richardson," he yelled back. Since Mary's death, Grant and Will had both softened, and now tolerated each other nearly to the point of friends.

"I love you," I said. I started to turn away, but he pulled me back.

"Did Richardson give you that rose?" He tipped his chin at the gray rose fastened next to my ivory one.

I nodded.

"He said that he'd like Iota Gamma to act as a brother fraternity to Beta Xi Beta."

"And we will," he said, and lifted his hand to my face. "I'm rather thankful that I've got something for you. I wouldn't want to be out-done by another man. He may still love you, but I love you more."

Will reached into his pocket and withdrew a black velvet box.

"What . . . what is it?" I asked.

"I'm not asking you to wear my ring, if that's what you're wonder-ing," he said. "Not that I wouldn't marry you this moment if you'd say yes. But I think you want to wait?"

I nodded and took the box from his hand.

"I thought you could wear it today," he said.

I pushed the lid back to find a silver pendant etched with the Iota Gamma letters. Will turned it over, revealing Beta Xi Beta's on the other side. "I went to have a lavalier made, but it didn't seem right for you to wear my letters without your own."

I ran my fingers over the indention of our letters in the silver. Tears burned my eyes, but I blinked them away.

"It's lovely," I said. "Would you put it on for me?"

I turned so he could fasten it around my neck.

"You can wear it on either side to display your letters or mine." His lips pressed against my nape, and he let the clasp go. "I expect that you'll want to wear your letters most, but I want you to remember when you do, that there are letters behind it. Those letters have promised to support Beta Xi Beta, as I will always support you."

I sighed, fingering the new pendant.

"I suppose I should go up to change now before Richardson has my head," he said, then squeezed my hand and let it go before stepping around me to open a small closet door beneath the stairs. There was a lone jacket, just pressed, hanging on the rack. He grabbed it and started up the stairs to dress.

"You had your jacket ironed?"

"Of course," he said, hastening past me. "There are going to be quite a number of men in black tuxedos. I can't risk you finding another more handsome."

* * *

"Hold it just out from your chest," I said as I wiped a bead of sweat from my forehead and pulled Anne's arms down, dropping the wooden Xi to a position right in front of her.

The line snaking toward the chapel moved forward, and I glanced up in time to catch Will's wink at me as the black-jacketed Iota Gammas filed past the bouquets and through the ribbon-adorned doors.

Victoria craned her neck around me to look at Anne.

"Oh, like that," she said, and dropped the second of the two Betas into a similar position as the Unitarian Women's Chorale singing "It is

Well with My Soul" sounded over us. We'd decided that the pledges should carry the letters, leaving the three founders a position at the back. We hoped it would make a statement—the future ahead of the past, progress ahead of stagnancy.

Since Whitsitt's founding, each club and organization had been a part of the graduation ceremony, asked to proceed into the chapel behind the graduates as a tribute to the various facets of a student's life. This year, we'd been asked to join the celebration, the only other female group besides the Women of Whitsitt permitted to do so.

"Don't be ridiculous," Katherine said to Collette, who had whispered something in her ear. "You won't trip on the way down the aisle." Reaching over the Beta in Collette's hands, Katherine adjusted the ivory rose that had fallen lopsided against her royal blue bodice.

We were all wearing matching costumes and Lily, Katherine and I were wearing matching silver wreath pins—the mark of an initiated sister of Beta Xi Beta—compliments of Katherine's father, who had given her an exorbitant raise in wages when it became clear that James wasn't going to forfeit his legal aspirations after his hospitalization.

"It would behoove you to exhibit pride in our symbols. I won't see your rose leaning to the side again, will I, Miss Burns?" Katherine said. "I refuse to have my little sister looking shoddy."

We'd chosen the symbols at the first meeting as an official fraternity—blue for equality, ivory for intellect, and the rose as a tribute to the Iota Gammas' contribution to our start.

"We're the last group anyway, Collette," Lily said behind me. "No one would notice if you did stumble a bit."

I turned toward her. She'd extended her left hand, and was gazing down at the round solitaire.

"I'm so happy for you," I said.

"Everything is perfect. Well, almost. I miss Mary." She tucked a strand back into the plaited chignon at the top of her head. "I know that she's proud of you, Beth. So am I. I'm proud of us."

The chapel doors opened, and an old man in a black gown beckoned us forward. The united baritone of the Iota Gammas floated in the air, *"Fierce and brave, mighty and strong, we'll lead like lions into the throng. Tender and loyal, honest and right, we'll carry the silver rose into the light. A Fortiori, from the stronger we've come, to pass the Iota Gamma sword to our sons."* The last word wavered over us as we went up the steps. I ran my hands over a white-pillared hollyhock as I passed a bouquet, watching the back of Collette's head disappear into the chapel.

"We did it," Lily whispered. She clutched my hand and squeezed as I scaled the remaining steps. I heard the hum of wind rush through the pipe organ, followed by the flowing prelude to our song, a song Judith had found in a notebook beneath Mary's bed.

"Our sisterhood is but a spark, though small it won't grow dark," I sang as best I could through my emotion, thankful for Lily's strong alto behind me. The pews were overflowing and I could feel the burn of eyes on my face, but I kept my gaze fixed on Victoria's hair or the plain white cross in the chancel. *"God's hand stokes freedom, equality, and love, our inevitable fire predestined from above."*

"Look," Lily breathed, as the organ began an interlude of arpeggios. I glanced to my left and my breath caught. Grant and Will were standing, one behind the other, in their pews at the front of the chapel. *"Hands linked together, united we'll be . . ."* The old floor groaned as the rest of the Iota Gammas suddenly rose to join them. They started singing, the rich hum of their voices melding with ours. Goosebumps prickled my arms.

"How?" I whispered, wondering how they'd come across the words.

I met Will's gaze, not bothering to stop the tears trailing down my face. It had to have been him. Will grinned and shook his head, nodding toward Grant. Grant nodded at me.

"Thank you," I mouthed. *"Beta Xi Beta, our dear fraternity. Our song will ring true throughout time, of undying sisterhood, a transformative chime."*

23

I STARED AT THE white paint peeling around the edges of the clap-board house, clutching two top hats in my hands. Grant stood on a ladder holding a royal blue Beta. He was still in his tuxedo, but he'd unbuttoned his jacket. The heavy fabric fluttered as a warm spring breeze hedged the trees and drifted over us. He ran a hand through his dark hair, now damp with sweat, and reached across the pitched roof to retrieve a hammer from Will. Grant had insisted on helping us before his departure, sending his father off to dine with President Wilson while he waited.

"Can you believe it? That we have a house?" Lily asked. She shielded her eyes with her hand, watching Grant and Will fixing the Betas on either side of the already situated Xi. Judith had somehow convinced Patrick Everett's family to allow us to use the house. Their formal consent had arrived three days ago.

"No," I said. "I really can't." I pinched my eyes shut, sure that when I opened them, it would all disappear. The last few days had seemed like a dream.

"Do you suppose we've scared them off?" Katherine emerged from the house, her arm looped through three grapevine wreath door hangers adorned with ivory and blue ribbons bearing Anne's, Collette's, and Victoria's names. "I was hoping we'd be able to assign rooms today, but I suppose I'll simply have to hang these on whatever rooms I see fit."

"I'm certain we frightened them last night, but I doubt they've abandoned us. They all accepted their pins, remember?" I said.

We'd initiated the pledges last night, going into their rooms at two in the morning dressed in our cloaks, a single candle in my fist. "Are you prepared to pledge yourself to the cause of Beta Xi Beta?" we'd asked in hushed tones, startling each of them to the point that Anne laughed so hard she wet the bed, Victoria cursed, and Collette screamed.

After, they put on their yellow cloaks and we led them out of Everett Hall—with permission granted by Miss Zephaniah, who seemed altogether pleased at the notion of a women's fraternity since it had been approved by the board—and into the basement of Old Main. I'd been there, to the room where we'd begun, on two other occasions since Mary's death. It was where I felt her presence the most, and I knew that President Wilson hadn't had our name washed from the wall. Mary's perfect cursive was still there. It seemed only fitting to initiate the pledges in the dank, modest space where we'd hidden, where we'd dreamed the fraternity to life.

We'd sat on the floor in a circle, Katherine, Lily, and I taking turns telling the story of how we'd begun. When we'd finished, I'd passed two unlit candles to Katherine and Lily and they'd dipped their wicks to mine, a symbol of my idea catching. When the three small flames had been ignited, we'd sung the song Mary had taught us the day we swore to keep Lily's secret. Lily had started it, humming the opening note, and then we'd sung, passing the candles around the circle until the final note sounded. Then, one by one, our pledges blew them out, and we silenced, watching the smoke rise, giving last light to Mary's inscription on the wall. Katherine had affixed wreath pins against their hearts in the dark, and then, wordlessly, we'd departed, making our way back to the dormitory hand in hand, our numbers officially doubled.

"They're not here yet because they're occupied with Miss Zephaniah's spring cleaning. Remember?" Lily asked, bringing me back to the moment.

"Oh. That's right," I said.

"Grant asked me for the song lyrics a few days ago," Katherine said, disregarding Lily's explanation of our new sisters' absence. "I hope you didn't mind that I gave them to him. He wanted it to be surprise for you, for us."

Grant turned his head, as if he could feel us looking at him, but for once, his gaze didn't fall on me.

"It was a lovely surprise," I said. I could still hear the powerful chorale in my mind, and knew I'd never forget it as long as I lived.

"It was a very kind gesture," Lily said.

"Are the letters straight?" Will stared at the roof, eyes narrowed in scrutiny. His jacket lay in a heap on top of a boxwood and his shirt was untucked and wrinkled, the edges rimmed with wood dust and dirt from leaning against the house.

"Yes, are you certain you'd rather not hire a professional? I can have someone come around tomorrow," Grant said.

"You've both done a fantastic job. They look wonderful," I said.

"I'm going back to the dormitory to collect my things before Miss Zephaniah burns them," Katherine said. She was going to stay at the house for the summer. Though courses wouldn't resume until September, her business couldn't afford a break.

"I'll come with you," Lily said. "David said he's planning to have a coach come around about three to collect my trunks." She turned to me. "You're sure you won't mind us living in the carriage house? I'll feel terrible if anyone's family comes to visit and they're put out on account of—"

"Of course not," I said, cutting her off. She'd accepted a summer position as an apprentice to the librarian at the public library in Green Oaks, and planned on making the carriage house a home before she reported to the post next week and got married in two months' time. "I couldn't bear knowing you were going to abandon us."

"Very well," she said, looping her arm through Katherine's. "We'll be around shortly to see you off to Chicago."

I nodded and turned back to look at the letters, thinking I'd never tire of the sight. The metal ladder clanged as Grant lifted the base of it and disappeared around the side of the house.

I glanced through the front window, barely able to make out the pocket door to the study where we'd met that first night. How quickly everything had changed. How quickly Mary had gone. I took a breath, inhaling the sweet scent of honeysuckle blooming somewhere close by, and let it out with a sigh.

"Do you remember when you first told your father that you'd like to go away for college? Before he knew that my father would support it?" Will asked, materializing at my side.

"He was furious," I said, recalling the Christmas Eve dinner nearly five years ago.

"I've always remembered something your mother said to me while you were arguing with your father," Will said, brushing a strand of hair from my eyes. "She said that she hoped you'd go with me, that regardless of where she was or where you were, you'd always be with her. She told me that memories are really little bits of people's souls that live in the hearts of others. It was something your grandmother said."

"Will, I—"

"You were thinking about Mary just now," he said, as though he'd read my mind. "I thought you could use the reminder."

He squeezed my hand, and then let it go, walking away to meet Grant coming around the front.

At once, I found myself alone in the shadow of our house, in the glow of the Beta Xi Beta letters, and knew my mother was right. Mary hadn't gone. Her memories lived inside of us and always would—alive in the hope of our cause, and in the promise of the women we were born to become.

THE END

Author's Note

Oftentimes it's a stroke of serendipity when an idea for a novel is born, and this book began exactly this way. My critique partner and fellow novelist, Alison Bliss, emailed me a few years back saying that she'd just had a dream about me and a sorority and thought she'd tell me in case it meant anything or would spark inspiration. At the time, I thought it was a fun idea—I'd been an Alpha Xi Delta at Marshall University in Huntington, West Virginia, for a time—but I didn't write contemporary fiction and was deep into drafting *The Fifth Avenue Artists Society*. So, I wound up sort of forgetting about it. And then I finished *The Fifth Avenue Artists Society* and was emailing back and forth with Alison one day, bouncing around ideas for a new book as authors tend to do, when the topic of sororities came up again and she asked, "When did sororities begin?" I wanted to slap my forehead. Of course I should've thought of writing an origin story earlier. I'd heard about the start of Alpha Xi Delta, of course, and knew that most of the National Panhellenic sororities were founded in the mid to late nineteenth century by pioneers of their time, when—according to Christine Myers' *University Coeducation in the Victorian Era*—only one percent of the traditional college age group attended college. Though some of the members of these sororities, like the majority of women at the time, found fulfillment at home, some went on to be doctors and pastors and writers and staunch suffragists. At once I began imagining what it would have been like to walk in their shoes, and inspiration for this story came quickly.

Though Whitsitt College and Beta Xi Beta are fictional, they are grounded in truth. Many sororities were founded on coeducational Midwestern college campuses, so I thought it important to make Whitsitt similarly situated. Though common in the Midwest, coeducation was a somewhat controversial venture at a time when the sexes were generally believed to require different things both intellectually and emotionally. In Mary Caroline Crawford's 1904 book, *The College Girl of America and the Institutions which Make Her what She is,* Ms. Crawford explores some of the reasons for society's caution regarding coeducation, such as lessening man's instinctive respect for womanhood, making some women mannish, student distraction, an inferior social experience for women compared to colleges accepting only females, and the danger of inconsequent lovemaking.

Beta Xi Beta was formed from looking at nearly every sorority founding and melding them into one. For example, I used elements from Pi Beta Phi's meeting in secrecy to Kappa Kappa Gamma's founding on the need for companionship and support—similar sentiments are seen in most other sororities, as well—to the Sigma Nu's assisting with the establishment of Alpha Xi Delta. I also thought it important for accuracy's sake to term Beta Xi Beta correctly as a women's fraternity instead of a sorority, despite the fact that sorority is a much more common reference today. Most sororities were established as women's fraternities—the term sorority was coined by Dr. Frank Smalley, a professor and advisor of Gamma Phi Beta who thought the word fraternity inappropriate for a group of girls—and though a few Greek-letter societies were incorporated as sororities, the term fraternity is used to formally refer to National Panhellenic societies to this day. Like Beta Xi Beta, Beth, Mary, Lily, and Katherine are all fictional, but I chose their paths carefully, trying to make their motivations reflect various viewpoints of the time. I wanted this story to not only be a tale of a sorority's start, but also to speak to what it meant to be a woman at a coeducational college seeking a non-traditional degree at the time. For Beth in particular, I was inspired by the story of Elizabeth Blackwell, the first woman to receive a medical degree in the United States. Her education at Geneva Medical College in upstate New York was supposedly only permitted because when her acceptance was put up to a vote by the male student body, they jokingly voted yes. Even after her approval, she struggled to find clinical experience and many physicians wouldn't work alongside a woman. Though Dr. Blackwell's education occurred thirty-five years prior to the start of this novel, my research told me that her experiences would still ring true in Beth's time. Regardless of classroom treatment, some medical "truths" of the time were altogether incorrect, especially about the workings of the female body—including the few I mention in this novel—undoubtedly making it difficult for women to ever be seen as equals in the context of the classroom or in the field.

Even though my characters are fictional, only inspired by real people, it may surprise you—as it did me—that I have a much closer personal connection to this story than I knew while writing it. After I finished drafting the novel, I was sitting around doing family history research—my pastime between books—when I got an email from my distant cousin and ancestry buddy, Dana Lynch. The email was an exciting one. He'd unearthed some information about *The Fifth Avenue Artists Society*'s Franklin. One of the tidbits he found— though unfortunately I don't think we'll ever know what actually transpired between Frank and the rest of the family—is that he settled in Illinois by way of Arizona and married a woman there, Laura

Knowles. As I was scrolling through his email and looking through these pieces of our history, I saw sorority composites, two photographs of Laura Knowles in 1902. She was a Pi Beta Phi at Knox College in Galesburg, Illinois. I couldn't believe my eyes. I'd written a book I'd thought completely removed from my family history, and in an instant I realized that perhaps I'd been guided all along, that perhaps writing this story was more than coincidence. At once, this book meant more. It meant that for eight months I'd lived with the dreams and determinations of a relative I'd known nothing about, a woman tied to the greatest mystery of my family, an inspiration and wonder in her own right.

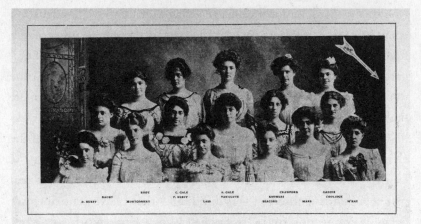

Acknowledgments

One cannot write a book like this without thinking of sisters—women who are with us always, women who shape our lives and make us better people. Though I don't have any sibling sisters, I have many that are just as close, and I'm supremely thankful.

First, I want to thank God for inspiration and for the gift of the bond between women, the unique magnetism that only occurs when you've met a sister for life.

To the incredible women in my family—to my mom, Lynn, to my "sister" and best friend, Maggie, to my sisters-in-law, Beth and Hannah, to my mother-in-law, Dianna, to my grandmothers, Sandra and Lee, to my aunts, Cindy, Sarah, and Lori, to my cousins, Samantha, Ellen, and Blair, thank you for the way you have always and will always stand beside me. And to the men who have inspired me, shaped me, and supported me—to my dad, Fred, to my brother, Jed, to my father-in-law, Johnny, to my brothers-in-law, Josh and Jeremy, to my grandfathers, Tom and Ed, to my uncles, Jim, John, and Bill, to my cousins, Jamie, Jeb, Keith, Ryan, Jeremy, and Davis. I love you!

To my dawgs, some of my earliest friends—to GraceMarie Thomas Bartle, Liz Thornberry Moore, Megan McCarthy, and Rachel Darling, thank you for the laughter, the memories, the comfort of always belonging.

To Courtney Chatfield-Joyce, Hollie Hogan, Sanghee Ku, and Joy Haser, thank you for the gift of forever friendship, instant understanding, and remembrances that will keep us cracking up always. I'm so thankful we get to hold each other's hands through every stage of life. You've all grown more beautiful with each step.

To Katie McLaughlin, Mary Brooks, Carolyn Wright, Alice Cuviello, Jessica Shanks, Amanda Shanks, Megan Fair, Ronni Bishop, Julie Cribb, thank you for being there, for being the picture of true friendship.

To my writing sorority—Sarah Henning, Renee Ahdieh, Cheyenne Campbell, Liz Penney, Alison Bliss, Sam Bohrman, Bethany Chase, Anna Rollins, Kim Wright, Marybeth Whalen, and Erika Marks—thank you for the time, the sharpening, the friendship. I love and appreciate you more than you know.

To the sisters of Alpha Xi Delta's Gamma Beta chapter, thank you for your example of what a sorority should be and for emphasizing the importance of remembering the remarkable women who started it all.

To the women who make my stories come to life, the women whose smarts and determination and dreams inspire—to my brilliant, lovely agent, Meredith Kaffel Simonoff, thank you for always believing in me and for your perfect insights into all of my works. And to my editor, the exceptionally talented Emily Griffin, thank you for your thoughtfulness, your perfect questions, and your support. I'm so very proud of what this book has become.

To the extraordinary minds at Harper—Mary Sasso, Amy Baker,

Abigail Novak, Paul Florez-Taylor, and Sarah Brody—thank you for your hard work, friendship, and time.

Lastly, to my little family—to my children, Alevia and John, you are the best gifts of my life. And to my husband, John, for your love, your humor, and your unwavering support. Thank you for making this journey everything I'd dreamed. I love you.

About the Author

Joy Callaway lives in Charlotte, North Carolina, with her family. She is the author of *The Fifth Avenue Artists Society*.

ALSO BY JOY CALLAWAY

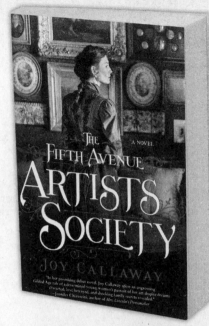

THE FIFTH AVENUE ARTISTS SOCIETY
A Novel

Available in Paperback, E-Book, and Digital Audio

*"A delightful, and at times touching, tale of Gilded Age society
and creative ambition with an inspiring heroine."* —*New York Daily News*

The Bronx, 1891. Virginia Loftin knows what she wants most: to become a celebrated novelist, and to marry Charlie, her first love.

When Charlie proposes instead to a woman from a wealthy family, Ginny is devastated; and though she works with newfound intensity, literary success eludes her—until she attends a salon hosted in her brother's writer friend John Hopper's Fifth Avenue mansion.

But when Charlie throws himself back into her path, Ginny is torn between two worlds that aren't quite as she'd imagined them, and begins to realize how high the stakes are for her family, her writing, and her chance at love.